THE EMPIRE OF YEARNING

A NOVEL

OAKLAND ROSS

Oakland Ross

HARPERCOLLINS PUBLISHERS LTD

The Empire of Yearning

Published by HarperCollins Publishers Ltd

First Edition

HarperCollins books may be purchased for educational, business, or sales promotional use through our Special Markets Department.

HarperCollins Publishers Ltd
2 Bloor Street East, 20th Floor
Toronto, Ontario, Canada
M4W 1A8

www.harpercollins.ca

Library and Archives Canada Cataloguing in Publication
information is available upon request

ISBN 978-0-00-225525-7

Printed and bound in Canada

9 8 7 6 5 4 3 2 1

For Cynthia Villegas Balta

CONTENTS

They are going to Mexico, which I cannot understand.
—Queen Victoria, writing about Maximilian and Charlotte in her diary

They hate us here. The foreigner in arms is always odious.
—Jean Pierre Isidore Alphonse Dubois de Saligny, the ambassador of Paris in Mexico at the time of the French invasion of 1863

PART ONE

The One-Armed Poet

CHAPTER 1

"THAT MUST HAVE HURT." A man's voice spoke up, a foreign voice, expressing itself in good but not native Spanish. "She must be very beautiful, this woman, to make you endure such suffering."

Diego Serrano gritted his teeth against the pang in his only hand, whose knuckles he had just rapped against the steel pillar of a street lamp. He had done so on purpose and for the same reason this intruder had divined. A woman. An exceptionally beautiful woman. Whenever he thought of Ángela Peralta, he felt an urge to cause himself injury, as a punishment for his idiotic cowardice. He had known her for half his life, and still he could do little more than stammer in her presence. Her brother, Baldemar, only made matters worse, with his jokes and obscenities and scorn.

Diego eased his smarting hand onto the ivory grip of the long-barrelled pistol that he carried in his belt, a Colt revolver. He turned, expecting to confront a grizzled, sallow-faced gunman bent on theft or worse. This was Veracruz, after all—a steaming port city, with all the perversions and dangers for which seaports are known. Instead, he found himself in the presence of a slender fellow of an almost eerily pale complexion. The man was elegantly if oddly dressed in a loose pink blouse with a red ascot, a pair of beige slacks, and brown patent leather shoes, now spattered with blots of grey mud, for it had rained heavily that afternoon. At his waist he wore a brightly embroidered sash that seemed to be of a Mayan design. He was smoking in the Teutonic fashion, his cigarette clamped between thumb and index finger.

"Oh dear," he said. "You don't remember me. I can see it from your face." He heaved a theatrical sigh. "It was always thus."

"Should I . . . remember you?"

"I certainly think so. At breakfast this morning—we were not more than two tables apart."

Diego frowned. Come to think of it, he did recall a couple at a nearby table that morning, a man and a woman, foreigners both. She had been blonde and very thin, with an ethereal beauty. He had noticed her but seemed to have overlooked her male companion. This was curious, as the fellow presented a memorable figure now.

"You were drunk at the time," the man said.

"¿Mande?"

"At breakfast. I smelled liquor on your breath. I detect liquor on your breath right now." The man drew upon his cigarette, paused for an instant, and exhaled. "I see that you are out for your customary evening stroll."

Diego said nothing, but his expression must have betrayed his annoyance.

The stranger shrugged and gave a pinched smile. "I am sorry. I fear it is a great fault of mine, always to know more than I should. Forgive me, please."

"That isn't necessary."

"I am so glad to hear it." He leaned closer, lowered his voice. "I wonder—what do you think of my Spanish?"

"It is . . . good."

"Really? Oh thank you. I value your words, coming as they do from one of this country's most illustrious poets and journalists."

The man extended his hand. He was handsome in his way. Straight brown hair fell over an ashen face bisected by a narrow, aristocratic nose and punctuated by precise features. Diego felt it necessary to avoid the man's gaze. The truth was, he no longer regarded himself as a poet. The Muse had deserted him.

"Allow me to introduce myself," the man said. "I am Felix zu Salm-Salm—in formal parlance, the Prince of Salm-Salm. But let us not be formal. Please, call me Felix."

Diego, who had lost most of his left arm years earlier in the Battle of Tacubaya, took the man's hand. The grip was weak, furtive. He said, "I take it you already know my name."

The fellow laughed. "Ah, well done. You have caught me out. You are Diego Serrano, as I have already ascertained." He motioned with his cigarette. "Shall we?"

Diego shrugged, and the two men ambled along the narrow, crumbling street, strewn with refuse and splattered with puddles of fetid water. When they reached the Malécon, they bore to the right and traced the seawall past a parade of royal palms, their trunks shifting in the slanting amber light, the fronds knocking gently in the breeze. It was dusk in Veracruz and the salt spray glinted all around, like particles of silver riding on the air. Everything seemed suddenly beautiful. It was as if the European had brought with him a change of atmosphere, a change of light.

They strolled along the sea's edge, and the man held forth about himself and his circumstances. It seemed that he really was a product of royalty. His father ruled a small German principality. Salm-Salm explained that he had been disinherited, owing to certain unfortunate reverses at the gambling table, reverses that he most certainly would have put right had only he been given the chance. Honour was his watchword. Unfortunately, his losses had redoubled, until eventually it had seemed prudent to depart Europe altogether. And so he had made his way to the

Americas, where he had roamed widely, learning customs and novelties as he went. He was cursed, he said, with an adhesive mind, acquiring knowledge without effort. He suffered from a similar tendency as regarded people.

"My wife, for example. For the life of me, I cannot seem to be rid of her. On the other hand, why should I? She is a most captivating creature, as you may have noticed."

Diego said he did recall her from that morning. "*La rubia*," he said. It was a rare quality in Mexico and could drive some men mad.

"*Precisamente.* Blonde hair. Lovely blonde hair. And blue eyes, of course. Agnes Leclerq is her name. She is from Montreal, in the Canadas, but it was in New York that I met her, in the damnedest circumstances. She was performing in a circus—an equestrian acrobat. Can you believe it? I wrote to my father to inform him of our nuptials, but I have not received a reply. I fear he may have suffered a coronary thrombosis, which would be most galling. I had been hoping for a generous wedding gift." He tossed away the remains of his cigarette. "Ah well."

After a brief silence, the man explained that he had made his way to New York by clandestine means, for he had previously fought on the Confederate side in the civil war that was even now afflicting the vast and sadly riven land that sprawled beyond the northern border.

"And now you are in Mexico," said Diego.

"Yes. And now I am in Mexico."

"May I inquire as to your purpose here?"

"You may. But you are a journalist. I imagine you are capable of ferreting out the truth."

Diego smiled. Of course. It was apparent why the man found himself in Veracruz—for the same reason he did so himself. "You have come to greet the Austrian."

"Just so. Good old Max. We are related, you know. Cousins, I think. Would you care for a smoke?"

Their cigarettes alight, the two men strolled the rest of the way back to the Plaza de Armas and entered their hotel, the Universal, a musty, decrepit structure that overlooked the city's small central square, where the moss-ridden hulk of the cathedral of Veracruz was just now being swallowed by a darkness so dense Diego could practically feel it, like a force contracting at his throat. The month was June, the year, 1864. Thirty days and twenty-nine nights he had languished in this dripping coastal heat, in this city redolent of open sewers and plagued by yellow fever, while he awaited the arrival of the Austrian. According to rumour, the man had already had himself crowned—he was the emperor, the emperor of Mexico—and Diego had come to plead with him in a matter of life and death.

CHAPTER 2

ALONE IN HIS ROOM, Diego lit a pair of candles, an awkward undertaking for a man in possession of just one complete arm and the remnants of another. But he was practised in such tasks. He removed his pistol and retrieved a half-empty bottle of *mezcal* from the wooden table by his bed. Using what remained of his left arm to clasp the bottle against his side, he removed the stopper and poured out a large dollop of the liquor into a chipped glass, greasy from use.

He closed his eyes and drank, letting the liquid burn a path down his throat. That helped. He turned and eased himself onto the bed, reclining on his back, the glass still clenched in his one hand.

What an odd character he had just met. God knew what exactly the man wanted from the Austrian—patronage or protection or simply an addition to his purse. For his part, Diego knew exactly what he meant to obtain. He had come to Veracruz in order to plead for the life of Baldemar Peralta, his old schoolmate from the Academia de San Juan de Letrán and his comrade during Mexico's long war between liberals and conservatives. Baldemar was incarcerated in the bowels of the Martinica

Prison in Mexico City, condemned to die for a crime he had hopelessly bungled. For one thing, the idiot had chosen a day of torrential rains to carry out his mission, and that factor alone—never mind his excessive weight—had been enough to ensure his failure. A fat man in a starving land is not a man who can easily hide. At the time of his arrest, Baldemar had been a fat man still. God only knew what he weighed now.

Based partly on what he'd been told and partly on what he could guess, Diego had a fair sense of the events that had unfolded on that afternoon of plummeting rain. He had imagined the episode many times.

Baldemar dismounts from his horse. He loops the reins around a post in the street outside the restaurant. La Hostería de Santo Domingo, it is called. He withdraws an antique English Dragoon pistol from his belt. No doubt he clutches the weapon in two hands, both of them trembling, for he has never launched an undertaking of this sort before. Dripping from the rain, he enters the restaurant and scans the room until he recognizes the conservative general, Leonardo Márquez, presiding at a dimly illuminated table. Baldemar weaves his way between the tables, his eyes fixed on the villain. No doubt there is some commotion among the diners, at least the more observant few, those who realize an act of violence is imminent. Baldemar ignores them. He thinks only of carrying out his purpose. If anyone in Mexico deserves to die, it is Márquez.

A large, grizzled man, his swarthy face criss-crossed by the scars of battle, the general is probably nearing the end of a long midday meal, likely smooching upon a cigar. Perhaps he is reaching at this moment for a bottle of mezcal. He snorts to himself happily. And why not be happy? Has he not returned to Mexico City in triumph after years in the mountains of Michoacán, where he almost beggared himself waging the savage rump of a nearly endless war? But he is back in the ascendance now—like all of Mexico's conservatives—and he is glorying in each and every consequent pleasure. He takes another puff of his cigar. Just now, some disturbance catches his eye. Or perhaps his hearing alerts him first—the creaking of chairs, the shifting of tables. He glances up, and for a moment or so he must be alarmed by what he sees—a pistol, just spitting distance away, pointed at his head. Anyone would feel a chill in the gut. The hammer slams down, and then what? A view of rose-bellied clouds drifting against the summit of a snow-glazed volcano, followed by . . . nothing. Darkness. A void.

But he is in luck. God, once again, has taken his side. The gun does not fire. This is no surprise, really. Even at the best of times, an English Dragoon pistol is an unreliable weapon—and is even worse when it rains. No doubt the powder in the firearm's flintlock is damp. In any case, the hammer falls, the flint sparks, but the powder fails to ignite. And so General Márquez lives to fight another day.

He would have been better pleased had his officers managed to collar the assailant then and there. By rights, they should have wrestled the waddling ferret to the tiled floor, enabling the Tiger of Tacubaya, as Márquez is known, to enjoy the perquisites of revenge on his own terms—not at once, but later, in private, and with the meticulous attention to detail that such occasions so richly deserve. But that is not what happens.

Instead, Baldemar bolts. He has brought with him just one pistol, which contains just one ball. When it fails to fire, his enterprise is doomed. And so he turns and runs. The general's officers scramble in pursuit, but Baldemar manages to get away. Fat as he is, he possesses surprising agility and speed. Besides, he well understands the course of his fate should he be taken alive. From what Diego understood of the tale, the last Márquez's men see of Baldemar that afternoon is the spectacle of a rotund individual hurling himself atop a large-boned bay with three white socks. Baldemar gathers the reins and gallops off through the rain along the calle Belisario Dominguez before careening right in the direction of the Zócalo. He must make a sight, with his legs kicking like a pair of broken wings in the driving rain and his ample haunches bouncing against the cantle of his high Mexican saddle.

Diego imagined it was Captain Cajiga, a sallow-faced Spaniard with sunken cheeks, who returned to General Márquez with the news that they have lost the felon, eliciting a tirade of obscenities. But Márquez is wasting his bile, because Baldemar's escape proves to be short-lived. For several hours he rides in circles in the pelting rain. In his eagerness to murder the Tiger of Tacubaya, he failed to map out his getaway. In the end, he attempts to flee the city by means of the Guadalupe gates.

Unfortunately, a pair of Zouaves—members of the North African force brought over by the French—has been alerted to watch for a stout, bespectacled malefactor mounted upon a bay horse with three white socks and armed with a poor excuse for a firearm.

"*Un moment, monsieur,*" one of them says.

They drag Baldemar from his horse, bind his thumbs behind his back with twine, and bundle him into a mule-drawn wagon. Sometime around midnight, Baldemar Peralta ends the worst day of his life sprawled on the filthy dirt floor of a dark cell in the Martinica Prison.

It was Baldemar's older sister, Ángela, who sought Diego out, bursting with the news. She hurried into his lodgings in Mexico City the next day, soon after she had learned the truth. Still groggy from drink, Diego was having breakfast at the time, and the last of his meal still littered the plate—a half-eaten roll, a smattering of egg scrambled with chilies. She collapsed into a chair across from him and begged him to do something, anything, to save her brother. Diego agreed at once, of course, although he had no further memory of what he'd said. As always in Ángela's presence, he could manage no more than a mishmash of incoherent syllables. Baldemar teased him about it every chance he got, and Ángela herself sometimes broke into laughter, unsure what to make of his pained stammering.

But she did not laugh now. She told him what he must do. He would have agreed anyway simply to oblige her, but he had no choice. At the Battle of Tacubaya only five years earlier, Baldemar Peralta had saved his life. Granted, he'd lost an arm that day, but he had survived. That is a debt that can never be fully repaid, a duty that weighs upon a man forever.

And so it was that Diego now found himself in Veracruz. He'd been here a month, waiting for the Austrian to arrive from Europe.

The candles were guttering, and he peered at his empty glass. He debated what to do next: prowl the steamy nighttime streets in search of companionship or find something to eat. He decided upon a meal. He got up, splashed his face with water from the porcelain bowl on the table by the window, and then made his unsteady way downstairs. The murky dining room was empty save for a barefoot servant boy, who brought him a clear soup, followed by red snapper smothered in a sauce of tomatoes and peppers. Either the fish was off or Diego was unwell. Before long his head was pounding, and his brow prickled with sweat. Something was wrong. He pushed back his chair and climbed to his feet as the blood ran from his head. He felt he might faint, and had to steady himself against the table. He wondered if he would survive this infernal place long enough to save Baldemar Peralta, even assuming he was still alive. There was no way of knowing, on either account, and so he trudged upstairs to his bed, praying that this distress end quickly and the Austrian come soon.

Chapter 3

Diego's eyes shot open and he sat bolt upright in the bed. What on earth was going on? Someone was pounding at the door of his room, calling his name. Groggy from sleep, he struggled to make sense of the uproar. "In the name of God," he shouted back, "what do you want?" His mind cleared a little, and he thought he recognized the voice. It was the hotel manager. Finally he could make out what the man was saying.

"¡El austríaco! ¡El austríaco!"

Diego called out his thanks. *Gracias.* Now go away. When the commotion ended at last, he dragged himself from the narrow, creaking bed. Three days had passed since his encounter with the Prince of Salm-Salm, and now at last the Austrian had come. He splashed some tepid water onto his face. His forehead pulsed, as if his brain had split into various mismatched pieces. He knew that he was not merely hungover. He was coming down with something—pray God, not the yellow fever. In his experience, a hangover worthy of the name could mask any number of infirmities or diseases, but not this wretchedness. He pulled on his boots with his one hand and clumped down the stairs into the musty and cavernous lobby, which enjoyed some relief from the coastal torpor owing to its lofty ceilings. He pushed his way through the front door and groaned out loud as he met the leaden heat full on.

"Ah, Serrano . . ."

It was the Prince of Salm-Salm. He was installed nearby, alone at a shabby wooden table in front of the hotel entrance. A young bootblack was attending to his shoes. The European raised a glass of what looked to be mezcal and grinned.

"Will you join me? My wife is asleep, and I hate to drink alone."

"Your Austrian has made landfall," Diego said. "I just heard. I think they will disembark soon."

"I know it. The SMS *Novara* is at anchor even now. Their Imperial Highnesses should be stepping ashore before very long. Rather inconsiderate on their part, I must say, to arrive in the full of the siesta. Please, sit down. I have a proposal."

There was something about his tone, some persuasive undercurrent. Diego set his hat upon the table and drew up a chair. The gap-toothed hotel manager shuffled out, took note of Diego's presence, and soon returned with an extra glass, as well as a bottle of mezcal. He poured out two drinks.

"Leave the bottle," said Salm-Salm. He raised his glass. "*¡Viva México!*"

It seemed an odd toast, with the country under French occupation, mired to the throat in debt, and an Austrian just arrived to rule the land as emperor. Still, Diego raised his glass and tipped it back. He closed his eyes briefly at the liquor's familiar sting. "A proposal, you said."

Salm-Salm folded his arms on the scarred tabletop. The bootblack quickly adjusted his position, as if attached to the prince by a combination of ropes and pulleys. "I have been thinking of what you told me the other night. I believe I may be able to help."

Two evenings earlier, after much drink, Diego had lowered his guard for a time and spoken to Salm-Salm about his purpose in Veracruz, a subject he had so far broached with no one except Ángela Peralta. He had not meant to unburden himself to the fellow, and yet that was exactly what he had done.

"Assist me?" he said. "How?"

"It is quite simple." Salm-Salm lifted his glass and smiled.

By now, the bootblack had completed his task but remained on the cobblestones, perched upon his knees, waiting for a coin. Salm-Salm did nothing, so Diego rooted in his pockets till he found a claco. He tossed it toward the boy, who snatched it from the air, fast as a frog snapping at a fly. He got up and trotted away.

Salm-Salm breathed in through his slender nose, as if testing the sweltering reek of the air. He said he was willing to advance Diego's case with the Austrian in person. "His Majesty is, after all, a relative of mine."

"A cousin, I think you said."

Salm-Salm puckered his brow for a moment, then brightened. "A second cousin, I believe. On my mother's side."

"You are close, then?"

"Oh, I should think so. Oh yes." Salm-Salm expanded on his proposal. He was willing to promote his Mexican friend's cause to the Austrian, encouraging the man to grant clemency in the case of Baldemar Peralta.

"That would be a great kindness." Diego drummed the tabletop with his fingers. "And you would expect, in return, precisely . . . what?"

"Nothing. Merely your good opinion."

"I see."

The prince leaned back in his chair, clasped both hands behind his head, and closed his eyes. "You know," he said, "what I best remember about Max is his taste for hikes. He was forever setting off on some great expedition."

"On foot?"

"Of course. How else?"

Diego shrugged. As it happened, walking was not a popular enterprise in Mexico, or at least not among those who could afford another means of conveyance. The use of one's legs as a method of locomotion? That was for the poor and the derelict. Europe, it seemed, took a different view. "I wonder what else I should know about your cousin."

Salm-Salm leaned in close. "That he is the very soul of discretion."

"In what sense?"

"Oh, for example, do not expect to encounter him at the principal entrance of any building. He does not like to be conspicuous, not Max. He is the very reverse of Mexico and its love affair with ostentation. Look to find him leaving by the most unrecognizable gate."

Diego frowned. "You think this information will be of use on some occasion?"

The prince shrugged. "You never know. Perhaps. In your case, I believe it will."

They both eyed their drinks.

"And what of my proposal?" said Salm-Salm.

"I would be greatly in your debt."

"Nonsense. Debts are for tradesmen."

"And gamblers."

"True. And gamblers." The European reached into the pockets of his trousers, as if in search of money, but he came up empty-handed. "Perhaps there *is* one thing you can do for me, if I help to save your friend's life."

Diego waited.

"Introduce me to Ángela Peralta. You know, your friend's sister."

"I know who she is."

"Of course you do. *The greatest singer Mexico has ever produced.*"

Diego waited, wondering what the man would say next.

"I have a proposal to make about her son."

"Son!" Diego laughed. "Your informants have misled you there. Ángela has no son."

"Indeed she does. It was all the talk in New York City not long ago. You may know of the father. Ángel de Iturbide."

"That's nonsense."

"I swear it's true."

"It is a lie and a slander. You would be wise to take it back."

The prince raised his eyebrows. He seemed about to speak but then reached for his drink instead. "All right then. I take it back."

"Good."

"Still, I would like to meet the woman. A small price to pay for the life of your friend."

Diego climbed to his feet. The exchange had unsettled him. He did not like to hear Ángela's name mentioned—or not by just anyone. His head was pounding again, and he felt as if mud were oozing through his vitals.

"Very well," he said. "I will give it some thought." Diego tossed the boy a pair of medios to cover the cost of the drinks. He took up his hat. "You're not coming to the harbour?"

"All in good time. First I want to look in on my wife. And about your petition—you may rest easy. I shall make your case for you, I promise." He glanced down at his empty glass. "Oh, and those coins of yours—you don't happen to have a couple more? I'll repay you, of course."

Diego gave the man half a dozen centavos, freshly minted.

Salm-Salm smiled. "Thank you. You're very kind. One last thing. The emperor and empress—you know they are without children?"

Diego knew nothing of the sort. He asked what difference it made.

"Oh, you never know," said the prince. "Something to bear in mind—in the months ahead."

Diego nodded, then took his leave of the man—such an odd fellow, always speaking in riddles. He set out for the harbour. His route took him along the perimeter of the Plaza de Armas in the direction of the seawall. It was patently a lie, what Salm-Salm had just said about Ángela, about her having a child. The idea was unimaginable. And Ángel de Iturbide the father? The most notorious rake ever to call himself a Mexican? That was even worse. The man's father was Agustín de Iturbide, a legendary opportunist who'd crowned himself emperor after the country gained independence more than forty years earlier. Agustín the First—and last. He'd ended his life before a firing squad. How dare Salm-Salm utter the name Iturbide in the same breath as Ángela Peralta?

Maybe it was these thoughts, or maybe it was something else, but Diego felt his legs buckle beneath him, and he nearly fell down. In a patch of shade, he stopped to rest and to recover his balance. Pray God this wasn't the yellow fever, but he suspected that it was. Still a little unsure of his footing, he continued on his way to the harbour, where the sudden stench nearly made him gag. But he forced himself to endure it. The Austrian had come, and Diego had a duty to discharge. He shuffled down toward the sagging docks that tumbled from the Malécon into the murk and brine. A squadron of vultures circled overhead, like dark skeletons floating on the air.

Diego looked out over the grey expanse of water and caught sight of a slender boat, a sort of skiff, that was tracing a course across the harbour's oily surface. The craft was a pretty affair, with a striped awning that obscured his view of its passengers. At first he thought the vessel was approaching the shore, but he soon realized his error. Propelled by a single boatman, armed with a long quant, the craft was actually bearing its passengers away.

Meanwhile, a half-dozen conventional landing boats were also knifing across the water in what seemed a general retreat. The flotilla carried a party of men clad in tropical uniforms, as well as a smattering of women in long white dresses that glinted in the sunshine, like bits of quartz. The boats were all making for a large warship that was anchored across the harbour, near the island of San Juan de Ulúa. A thin trail of smoke coiled skyward from its stack.

Diego squinted in the sunlight. So this was the *Novara*—a three-masted frigate, converted to steam, that dwarfed all the other ships in the bay. From what he understood, the warship had borne the Austrian and his retinue all the way from Europe. She had dropped anchor only a short while earlier as Veracruz dozed through its afternoon languor. With no breeze to stir them, a bevy of ensigns and banners drooped from the lines. Meanwhile, a gang of seamen crowded by the railings, waiting for the landing craft to return. It looked to Diego as if the travellers had intended to venture ashore but had decided to abort the mission before even setting foot to Mexican soil. And no wonder. There was no welcoming party, no bunting or garlands, no marching band, no evidence of ceremony at all. Besides, viewed from a few dozen *varas* offshore, Veracruz must have seemed to consist of little beyond rotting wharves, carrion birds, pariah dogs, and one-armed men.

¿Viva México?

The entire country was in ruins, and this city was no better off than the rest. Still, there was something about the scene that put Diego in mind of another arrival on these shores—Hernán Cortés and his army of brigands more than three hundred years before. In those far-off days, the natives of Mexico had thought the Europeans must be gods, conveyed across the sea aboard floating mountains, come to fulfill an ancient prophesy about the plumed serpent, Quetzalcóatl. The Aztecs failed to realize their mistake until it was too late, and here was the result—this backward and bankrupt land. He tried to envision his country as a foreigner might have done, a European who was seeing Mexico for the first time. It would not be a pleasant sight. True, just two years earlier, Mexico had won a stirring victory—el Cinco de Mayo—when her forces had turned back the French invaders at Puebla. That was a glorious victory but also a short-lived one, for the French had returned in greater numbers, and this time they had overcome all opposition. They were now installed in Mexico City, while Mexico's own government had fled to the north, its president and ministers reduced to the status of fugitives in their own land. What sort of country was this? Diego gazed out at the erstwhile landing party receding across the harbour. Before long, the retreating visitors began to clamber aboard their warship by means of gangways strung from the port broadside. The waiting seamen helped them onto the main deck, an operation executed with machine-like efficiency, so unlike the conduct of business in Mexico.

Diego turned and began to walk back in the direction of the Plaza de Armas. His head still throbbed, and he stumbled once or twice. It occurred to him that he had just lost his first and possibly best chance of making his way into the presence of the Austrian, in order to plead for the life of Baldemar Peralta. It was a life that absolutely deserved to be saved. All the idiot had done, or tried to do, was avenge the death of his uncle, a legendary statesman named Melchor Ocampo.

CHAPTER 4

AS HE SHAMBLED BACK to his hotel, Diego felt drugged by the afternoon heat. His head swam, and his limbs felt weak. He found his way to a broken wrought-iron bench and lowered himself onto the seat. He needed to rest, to settle his thoughts, to calm the throbbing in his head. He knew now that he was very ill. It was *el vómito* as likely as not. The yellow fever. The blood thudded in his temples, but his mind kept returning to thoughts of Baldemar. Even now, three years later, he remembered perfectly well all that had happened in that dark time when Melchor Ocampo was killed.

Baldemar and his sister were related by marriage to Ocampo, who was an uncle on their mother's side. Ocampo was also the leading architect of Mexico's sweeping liberal reforms, all effected during the early presidency of Benito Juárez, when Ocampo was already advanced in age. After reaching his seventh decade, the celebrated reformer withdrew from public service and retired with his wife and their four daughters to a hacienda in the highlands of Michoacán in central Mexico. There, he busied himself by writing on a variety of themes and by conducting a range of scientific investigations.

On the thirtieth day of May in the year 1861, Ocampo found himself alone at the *estancia* save for a handful of servants. His wife and daughters had journeyed to the town of Maravatío to attend a wedding celebration, travelling under armed guard. The most recent civil war had ended only five months earlier, a circumstance that meant little to those who continued to fight. Mexico was a treacherous country then, as it was now, and it would have been worth anyone's life to travel any distance at all without arms and the wherewithal to use them. Even given such protection, life was cheap and readily squandered. The armed guard that accompanied the Ocampo women to Maravatío meant that Ocampo himself was all but undefended.

On the day following the women's departure, a band of horsemen rode up to the main house. Ocampo strode out to receive them. As soon as he observed the men at close quarters, he must have known that trouble had come. It was easy to imagine what he saw—an assortment of roughriders, a hard-looking lot. From what Diego later ascertained, all of the men carried pistols in weathered leather holsters, and two had long arms affixed to their high Mexican saddles. Given the condition of their horses, whose legs must have been streaked with dirt, their flanks lathered with sweat, it seemed they had ridden a long way, over rugged country, and at speed.

The leader of the men introduced himself as Captain Saúl Cajiga, a Spaniard by birth to judge by his accent. He steadied his horse and tipped his large, round-brimmed hat. "To whom have I the pleasure of addressing myself?"

"My name is Melchor Ocampo, at your service."

"Formerly the minister of state?"

"Just so."

"We are well met then." Cajiga smiled and used his thumbnail to pick something from his teeth. He leaned to the side and spat on the ground, not far from Ocampo's feet. The other men with him—five in number—traded glances and sniggered.

"I am glad to hear it," said Ocampo, who could not have been glad at all. But he did not betray his alarm, deciding instead to make a show of hospitality. He glanced up at this Cajiga and observed that the day was hot, the sun nearly at its height. Might the men care for a drink? Why, only this morning he had ventured into the orchard and picked a quantity of *granaditas* that even now were being converted into a delicious libation. He had chirimoyas as well, not to mention limes, oranges, and sapotas. If his guests preferred, they might have mezcal.

"We have not come to drink," said Cajiga.

"No," said Ocampo. "I suppose not."

"We have come on an important mission, with orders of a most specific nature, whose terms we have committed to memory." The captain reached up and tapped his forehead twice with the tips of the fingers of his left hand. "We well remember what must now be done."

"You have the advantage of me, then," said Ocampo, "for I have never been able to remember the future."

"It is a useful skill. What a shame that now you will not have the opportunity to acquire it. You have left this project too late."

Cajiga nodded toward a barefoot manservant, one of Ocampo's Indian retainers, who had emerged from the house shortly after Ocampo and now stood cowering in its shadows. Policarpo was his name, and it was he who later related the gist of this conversation to Diego.

"You there," the Spaniard said. "Prepare a horse for your master. He is coming with us."

They departed in short order, Ocampo surrounded by Cajiga and his five companions.

In a matter of days, news of these events reached the offices of Benito Juárez, the president, who spoke at once with a new minister of state, Francisco Zarco. It so happened that Zarco was also publisher and editor of the liberal newspaper *El Siglo XIX*, to which Diego was a frequent contributor. As one of only two survivors of the Massacre of Tacubaya, he was deemed to be a man of grit and promise, and so it was his name that cropped up when Zarco required someone to seek out the kidnappers, determine their demands, and, if possible, negotiate with them.

Diego departed the capital the following day, in company with Baldemar, who had also survived the killings at Tacubaya and had long been his closest friend. *El gordo y el indio*, they had been called at school. The fat one and the Indian.

They set off through waving fields of blond grass, their horses scaling the pine-clad heights north of Mexico City. Later, the highland conifers gave way to groves of Mexican oak and mesquite scrub. The two men rode past maguey plantations and rolling cornfields, bordered by fences of organ pipe cactus.

Three days it took them to reach the hills of Michoacán, and they argued every step of the way. They called each other the worst names they could think of, and disagreed about everything imaginable, from the attractions or defects of women they both knew to the dismal state of Mexico. To Baldemar, the country's condition resulted entirely from the predations of conservatives—conservatives in alliance with the Holy Roman Church. But Diego wondered if liberals did not share their portion of the blame as well. He was a liberal. They both were. Both had fought on the liberal side. But, so far, the vaunted reforms instituted under Juárez had produced no improvement in the lives of the people. Yes, ecclesiastical property had been seized from the grip of the Church, but to what end? So that looters could sack the churches and convents, melting crucifixes down for the gold? Where was the advantage in that? But it had happened. And, yes, el Cinco de Mayo had been a glorious victory, but what difference had it made in the end? The French had returned in greater numbers, and this time there had been no stopping them.

But Baldemar had an answer for that, one that effectively cut off all discussion. After all, he had fought in the battle of el Cinco de Mayo, whereas Diego had not. One-armed as he was, Diego had stayed behind in Puebla to work in an improvised medical clinic and had suffered the French bombardment, same as everyone else, while Baldemar had ridden out to fight. That seemed to mean that nothing anyone else had to say on the subject warranted any attention at all.

"*Muy bien*," said Diego.

He pressed his heels into his horse's flanks, she broke into a loping stride, and the two men cantered across a broad plain stippled by scrub trees and saguaro cactus. It was nearing sunset, and clouds drifted in thin purple rafts above the low range of hills to the west.

They picked up the trail of Ocampo's kidnappers at the town of Maravatío. From there, they followed a trail of cooking fires and spoor. The men who had abducted Ocampo were either deeply inept or unimaginably brazen. A child could have tracked their route. It occurred to Diego that these men *wanted* to be followed. But why should that be so?

Two more days of riding brought them to the village of Huapango, where the local people said that, yes, a party of riders had shown up not two weeks earlier, with a prisoner in their power. General Leonardo Márquez had been waiting, along with his own party of riders. The two bands had merged and ridden off as one, making no secret of their destination. The villagers pointed the way to a hamlet named Tepeji del Río. There, the locals provided Diego and Baldemar with further guidance, and they took up the trail once again. Two hours later, they rounded a crest of rocks and rode into a forest clearing.

"*Ay Dios*," said Baldemar.

A man's bloated and shirtless body dangled upside down in the middle of the clearing, strung by the ankles from the branches of a Mexican oak tree. The dead man's head was suspended a good five feet from the ground, and his arms hung freely beneath him, the shoulders having dislodged themselves from their sockets by the force of their weight.

Baldemar kicked his heels, and his horse scooted forward. He drew a long-bladed knife from his belt and cut the rope, letting the cadaver fall. The two men dismounted and briefly observed what Márquez had done. The corpse was badly swollen and had started to decompose, but it did not seem that Ocampo had been mutilated in any way prior to his death. He had simply been strung up by his heels and left to dangle in the nighttime cold or burn in the late-day sun. It would have been a slow and miserable death.

Diego's eyes stung, and he blinked them repeatedly. "They couldn't have hanged him properly?" he said. "By the neck? Like civilized men? They couldn't have shot him in the head?"

"Guess not."

Baldemar looked away, out across the broad green valley that unfolded to the west. He said nothing. What could he say? For a long while, neither man uttered a word. They just glared off in different directions, both too angry to talk. They'd known the journey would end in something like this. Now that it had, they were in no way prepared. Diego closed his eyes, as if all of this could simply be willed out of existence—this path, this clearing, the corpse on the ground. But, when he opened his eyes again, nothing had changed.

"*Pinche cabrón.*" Baldemar turned away and spat, as though the taste of the obscene words was itself an affront.

Soon, they set about the task of binding the corpse in the blankets they had brought for their own comfort. Baldemar's horse was much the larger and sturdier of the two, and they draped the body behind his high-backed saddle and rode to Tepeji del Río. They stored the corpse of Melchor Ocampo in a disused shed of mud and wattles to protect it from the disrespect of dogs. The following morning, they set out to retrace their route. They wore kerchiefs over their mouths and nostrils, knotted behind their necks. The reek was vile beyond belief.

In due course, they reached the former minister's estate, where they delivered the body of Melchor Ocampo to his wife, doña Ana María Escobar de Ocampo, who was Baldemar's aunt. The nine days of mourning commenced.

Later, after Ocampo's body had been laid to rest, the government of Benito Juárez dispatched a succession of armies, each commanded by yet another in a seemingly endless series of inept generals, all charged with identical orders: to capture General Márquez alive, if possible, or else kill him in battle. One after another, the armies accepted the challenge but failed to meet it. Two of the generals gave their lives.

General Márquez remained in his mountain redoubt, biding his time and awaiting some change in his fortunes. In the meantime, Mexico was at peace at last—if you could call it that. What passed for peace in Mexico was really just a respite between wars.

CHAPTER 5

STILL WEAK AND UNSTEADY, Diego returned to the Hotel Universal near the *plaza de armas* of Veracruz. Immediately, the manager informed him that Salm-Salm and his wife had departed in a hurry. They'd taken all their baggage and ridden away in a hired cart bound for the harbour. The manager cleared his throat. It was his understanding, he said, that Señor Serrano would be settling the account on Salm-Salm's behalf.

"He told you this?"

"*Sí.*"

"And you believed him?"

The man gave Diego a sorrowful look. "The gentleman is a European," he said. He narrowed his gaze for a moment before raising his eyelids again and slightly rolling his eyes. He reached beneath the desk. "Here. He left you this."

He produced a grimy flax-paper envelope. Diego reached inside and withdrew a single leaf of paper. The letter bore no seal but was evidently from Salm-Salm, who conveyed his greetings and begged his new friend to indulge him by underwriting certain expenses he and his wife had incurred while in Veracruz. Owing to the unavoidable haste of their departure, it had been impossible for Salm-Salm to locate the funds on his own. But there was no cause for alarm—he could be trusted implicitly to settle the matter once they both found themselves in Mexico City. Meanwhile, he assured his esteemed acquaintance that he remained determined to promote Baldemar Peralta's cause with His Imperial Majesty.

Diego released a long, tired sigh. What choice did he have? He settled the prince's account. That done, he retired to his room and collapsed onto the bed, dog-tired and sore in every fibre, every bone.

The following morning, the imperial party—a group that numbered more than a hundred—finally made a proper landfall. A French military band and a small honour guard were mustered for the occasion, along with a smattering of curious city folk. Diego was not among them. He learned what had happened only later, from the manager of the hotel. Instead of hurrying out to confront the newcomers, he lay prone on his bed, barely able to move. His head felt as if hammers were pounding through his skull, and his entire body ached, alternating between burning heat and shivering cold.

Eventually, he managed to rouse himself, dress, and find his way to the railway station, where the Austrian had by now been conveyed, along with his wife and the members of their considerable entourage. The newcomers milled about the station's entrance, all finely dressed, gawking and jabbering, apparently in an immense hurry to board the train, the only such vehicle in Mexico. Crews of Mexican labourers struggled to attend to what seemed a colossal quantity of appurtenances, all of which—someone said—represented no more than the tenth part of the goods the Europeans had carried with them and that remained aboard the *Novara,* to be transported to Mexico City at some future date.

Hundreds of *veracruzanos* had ventured out to have a look at these exotic creatures, these European courtiers and this man who called himself emperor. They pushed and jostled against each other, straining for a better view. Diego soon caught a glimpse of the self-styled emperor—Maximiliano I—a tall, hatless figure, going prematurely bald. His broad dome shone in the sweltering sun, and he strode about by the station entrance, clad in a naval dress uniform. He pointed this way and that, issuing orders, as if giving a theatrical performance. He held himself utterly erect, almost as if his frame were suspended from the shoulders by a pair of invisible wires. He had a pale complexion, and a long, slender nose, but what most distinguished him was his beard, a great ruddy mass of whiskers combed into a long french fork.

Diego tried to make his way closer. He side-stepped, shoved, and struggled, hoping somehow to get close to the man, near enough to draw his attention and then to confront him head-on and make his case—amnesty for Baldemar Peralta! Over and over, he had rehearsed the words he would say. But the crush of onlookers grew steadily more suffocating, and he felt dizzier and fainter with each moment that went by. Just as he thought he might pass out, he sensed a flurry of movement on the part of the Europeans, followed by a ripple of renewed excitement among the crowd. Somehow, he willed himself to remain upright.

He watched as the Austrian disappeared into the station, along with a pale and severe-looking young woman whom Diego took to be his wife, the empress. Their entourage quickly followed. Soldiers took up positions behind the new arrivals to keep the rabble away. A quarter hour groaned past, and Diego could do nothing except stand where he was and helplessly watch as the locomotive released a piercing whistle. Soon, coils of smoke and vapour twisted against the blue sky laced with cumulus clouds, and a procession of wooden cars shuddered into motion. They chugged smartly away to the west, past a blind of royal palms.

Diego watched the train recede. It was strange that the Europeans had chosen to make their journey by these means. He knew perfectly well the tracks extended inland only a short distance, a matter of forty kilometres or so, not even as far as Paso del Macho. Further work had been suspended, owing to attacks by bandits and liberal partisans. As a result, this trek by rail would accomplish nothing at all, except to demonstrate that Mexico possessed a train. The Austrian's party would be obliged to disembark within a couple of hours, and Diego could easily imagine them grumbling in the leaden heat while they awaited the delivery of horses and carriages from Veracruz. Only then would they continue their journey to Mexico City. That was bad luck for them but an opportunity for him. He believed he could catch up with the Austrian at the railway's end.

He stumbled back to his hotel and collected a few belongings. A bottle of mezcal stood by the large ceramic bowl on the dresser. In two quick gulps, he drained what was left, shuddered, and let the liquor's warmth rise through his chest. Feeling somewhat restored, he staggered downstairs and into the lobby. He paid his own bill, and a groom was dispatched to fetch his horse.

He set off, riding westward along the lush coastal plain, but he had underestimated the effects of his illness. He felt dazed, light-headed, and slow. He found he could not properly sit his horse at more than an ambling gait, and even that was troublesome. It was clear to him now he had no hope of making up the distance that separated him from the Europeans. From what little he knew of the yellow fever, he expected to suffer like this for several more days at least. He forced himself to think of Baldemar, rotting away in the Martinica, and he tried to increase his pace, but it couldn't be done. More than once, he slid from the saddle and collapsed onto the ground, retching what little bile remained in him.

He had not yet reached Paso del Macho when darkness fell, but he knew he could ride no further. He made his bed on the hard ground of a forested hillside, with his saddle for a pillow and with his Colt revolver clutched at his side. He passed a fitful night, awakening the next day in a poor temper with a sore back, a worsened fever, and the distinct impression that something else was wrong. Even before he managed to open his eyes, he realized that his pistol was gone and that someone's shadow was blocking the dim morning sunlight.

He forced his eyes open. Not one but two men stood at his feet, both wearing large round-brimmed hats and each aiming at him with a handgun.

"Take off your clothes," said one of the men. He had a long scar running down the left side of his face, partly obscured by a dark moustache.

"What?" Diego slowly raised himself onto his one good arm. His pistol, he saw, was stuffed into the belt of the man who'd just spoken. He struggled to remain calm. If they were going to kill him, they'd have done it by now.

"Your clothes. Take them off. All of them."

Soon he was naked, a familiar condition for those who travelled between Mexico City and Veracruz, for the way was rife with thieves.

"Can I keep my boots?"

"A common request," said the man with the scar. He tilted his head and lowered his voice. "My name is Octavio. And yours?"

"Diego Serrano."

"I see. What is your purpose here?"

Diego's head still throbbed, and his heart still raced, but he managed a halfway steady voice. He thought he might as well tell the truth, and that was what he did.

The one named Octavio inclined his head again to listen, then nodded. "A friend in the Martinica?" he said. "Well, in that case, you are in luck. We won't kill you. We will spare your life in the expectation that you will also plead for the release of comrades of our own who now reside in that same place. They were taken a few weeks ago. Their names are Sánchez, Quiñones, and Rivera. Can you repeat the names?"

"Sánchez, Quiñones, and Rivera."

"Very well. In exchange, we shall spare your life and also leave you your horse."

"What about my clothes?"

"Sadly, that is beyond my authority." The man shrugged in commiseration. "You are liberal or conservative?"

Diego knew that bandits along this corridor liked to think of themselves as soldiers in the liberal cause. "Liberal," he said.

"Is it so? We are liberals too. Thanks to this happy coincidence, we shall also leave you your gun and your boots. Good luck."

The two men bundled Diego's clothes together, along with his saddle and almost all of his money. Out of habit, Diego kept a quantity of bills in one of his boots as a hedge against exactly this set of circumstances. The robbers mounted their horses. The one named Octavio led Diego's own horse a distance away, then wound the reins around a tree branch. He tossed the Colt pistol to the ground.

"Adiós," he said. *"Que le vaya bien."*

Both men soon vanished on their horses into a dense copse of trees.

Diego watched them go. Here he was, naked, alone, a long way from Mexico City, and too sick to greatly care. He stumbled over to his horse and picked up his gun, wondering where to put it.

Naked but for his boots, he swung himself up onto her back. He tucked his pistol into his right boot, wedging it there as securely as he could. He gathered the reins in his only hand and kicked his heels. *"Vamos."*

He began to ride west, but he got only as far as Paso del Macho before he collapsed near a wayside inn. He was vaguely aware of a pair of servants hurrying out to his aid. They darted from the building with two blankets, evidently accustomed to having their guests arrive without the luxury of a wardrobe.

After spending four days in bed, mostly delirious, Diego was finally well enough to continue his journey. Dressed in a second-hand suit of cheap cotton, he hauled himself up onto a broken-down saddle with a cracked tree that he had salvaged from the livery stable adjoining the inn. He set out for Mexico City, well aware that he had failed in every aspect of his plan. He had failed Baldemar, he had failed himself, and he had failed Ángela. It was her reaction he feared the most. He could barely speak in her presence at the best of times. What in God's name would he say now?

He dug his heels into his horse's flanks, and she broke into a canter, following a rutted trail that meandered to the west. Eventually, the ground grew more rugged and soon began its rise toward the highland interior. The sodden green plains of the eastern coast gave way to an abrupt and rocky ascent. The sky darkened with clouds, and the air turned damp. Diego and his horse scaled a narrow, serpentine trail that wound upward through sheer granite outcroppings, while a thin drizzle—the *chipi-chipi*—spattered down amid rolling waves of mist.

His horse scrambled up the precipitous incline, and soon the rain slackened, the light began to clear, and Diego ascended through a last rafter of clouds. He found himself on a broad undulating prairie that swept away to the west beneath an unblemished sky. The great volcano Pico de Orizaba towered above him. This was the high plain of Mexico, and he felt his spirits swell at the breadth of it and the grandeur.

He rested that night in Orizaba, the following night in Puebla, and then he rode the final leg of his homeward journey, entering Mexico City by the eastern gates. It was dark by the time he arrived, and a celebration was under way. Rockets cracked through the darkness and exploded in streaming bursts of light—in honour, it seemed, of the Austrian's arrival. He rode past the Metropolitan Cathedral and saw throngs gathered in the vast Zócalo. They were mostly members of the city's conservative elite, euphoric at having an emperor of their own, a monarch before whom they might kneel and genuflect. He doubted many ordinary folk would share their delight.

Presently, he crossed paths with a haggard man missing most of his teeth who was stumbling alone at the edge of the crowd. The man told him the new archbishop, Monseñor Pelagio Antonio de Labastida y Dávalos, had that evening celebrated a Te Deum in honour of the Austrian and his wife. As Diego well knew, Labastida had fled into European exile after the liberal victory of 1861, only three years earlier—just as many other conservatives had done. Now, like the other exiles, he had returned with the French occupation in order to assume power again.

A rocket exploded a few *varas* away, and his horse shied. Diego thanked the man, reaching down to hand him a couple of coins for his trouble. The man pocketed the money and turned away, but Diego remained where he was, at the edge of the Zócalo. It was likely that the Austrian and his wife and the rest of their party were even now installed in the National Palace, and he wondered whether the man might not appear on a balcony to greet the crowd below. But no doors swung open on the upper floor of the huge, austere building that housed Mexico's rulers, and no dignitaries appeared to address the gathering. Eventually, the crush of bodies began to thin as countless unconnected knots of people broke loose, drifting away through the darkness.

Diego guided his horse along the margins of the square. It was the sixteenth of June, in the year 1864. The national government of Benito Juárez had by this time been forced to retreat to Monterrey in the north, where its authority diminished with almost every day that passed. Juárez was an Indian, a pure-bred Zapotec, and Diego had wondered more than once whether it was entirely a coincidence that Mexico should descend to its present miserable state, bankrupt and under foreign occupation, just when an *indígena* held the presidency, something that had never happened before. Now this Austrian had come, to sign decrees, inspect hospitals, preside at balls, and no doubt issue pardons, all the while protected by a French army of thirty thousand and a stout guard of Austrian hussars. So much for Mexico's vaunted independence. As for Diego himself, all he had accomplished in his hopes of securing liberty for Baldemar Peralta was to reach a vague understanding with an impecunious and unreliable German prince. Quite a pair they made, Diego Serrano and Benito Juárez. Quite a pair of fools.

He clicked his tongue and nudged his horse's flanks with his heels. She broke into a jog, and he guided her in the direction of his lodgings near La Ciudadela. His meeting with Ángela could wait till the following morning. By then, with luck, he'd have worked out what to say.

CHAPTER 6

THE NEXT MORNING, Diego rode to the home of Ángela Peralta on the Street of the Sad Indian. He entered the walled premises through the main gate, dismounted, and turned his horse over to a stable hand. It seemed he was not the only visitor. Waiting in the stable yard was a wickerwork carriage, whose driver stood by the wooden shafts whispering to a pair of ponies and fiddling with their leather braces. He glanced up.

"Señor," he said.

Diego touched the brim of his hat, then turned toward the house. At that moment, the main door opened, and a manservant ushered another visitor into the yard—a priest dressed in dark vestments. He was thin, with pallid features that seemed oddly familiar. The two men eyed each other, and several moments passed before Diego realized the truth. It was the Prince of Salm-Salm. Diego was about to say something, but Salm-Salm pressed one hand to his lips, a bid for silence. In the other hand, he held a cigarette.

"There you are," he said in a low voice. "Just the man I wanted to see." He narrowed his eyes. "You look a bit *jaune*. Yellow fever?"

"I seem to be recovering," said Diego. "Why are you—?"

"Shh. Please." The prince took him by his arm and led him aside. "You are surprised by my robes, of course. Unfortunately, I can't explain just now. Later, I'm sure we'll have a chance to talk." He stepped back. "You do not look well."

"I've been better."

The prince eyed his cigarette. "Yellow fever—damned unpleasant, I'm told. Max was adamant about our getting to Mexico City on the double, for that very reason. His secretary seems to have come down with an awful dose, poor lad. Anyway, I decided it was better to leave Veracruz at once. Did you, by any means, ah . . . ?"

"Cover your account?"

Salm-Salm nodded, exhaling a small cloud of smoke.

"Yes, I did."

"I'm good for it, you know. The next time we meet."

"But why are you dressed as—?"

"Please, please. Discretion first, explanations later. All in good time." He glanced around, as if fearful of being overheard. "You have come to see Ángela, I take it."

"Yes. It was her brother, you see, who—"

"Of course. The one in prison."

"Yes. Did you speak to—?"

"His Majesty? Not yet. When an opportunity presents itself, I propose to strike. Have no fear. As for Ángela, you will find her somewhat harried—not quite at her ease, I don't think."

Diego hesitated, then frowned. "You know her well? I thought—"

"Know her? Not a bit. We've only just met."

"I see."

"Care for a cigarette?" The prince tossed his own away and, from somewhere amid the folds of his cassock, he produced a handsome silver case stamped with a monogram—*MIM.* He noticed Diego looking. "Maximilianus Imperator Mexici," he said. He lit Diego's cigarette and then his own, exhaling two thin streams of smoke through his nostrils.

"She is very fretful about her brother, to say nothing of her son."

"Son?"

"Yes. Her son."

"Ángela has no son. We spoke of this before." Diego felt his blood rising. He really could not stomach this slander. Who was this man? He advanced a step. "What are you talking about? And why are you dressed like that?"

"It's a long story—not one I'll bore you with now. As for Ángela, I defer to your no doubt wiser judgment."

Salm-Salm waved to his driver and hurried through the stable yard toward his borrowed carriage. Diego followed, and the prince rattled on.

"Max is in a fearful state, you know. They've put us up in the National Palace. What a miserable pile of rocks—infested with bedbugs and God knows what other vermin. The women are in torments. We've got to find another place of residence, and I've been charged with locating an alternative. It's a sort of test, I think. Max seems to be sizing me up for an important position at court." He hesitated. "You don't have any thoughts on the subject, do you?"

Diego did not.

"That's too bad. But think about it, will you? And come by the palace any chance you've got. Not the main entrance—you'd never get past the guards. Come to the side. I'll leave word." The prince gripped Diego's only hand in both his own, then climbed into the small cabin of his carriage and poked his head out the window. "And don't forget what I said about finding a better residence—something large and airy. Please. I beg you."

He reached up and rapped on the carriage ceiling. "Driver!"

The driver climbed into his seat, took up the reins, and gave them a slap. The ponies gathered the slack in their braces, and the little carriage lurched forward, tottering across the stable yard and out into the street.

Diego watched it go as he smoked the last of his cigarette. What a strange, slippery fellow. Perhaps Ángela would be able to shed some light on the matter. That would be a relief. He'd rather any topic of conversation that would save him from confronting her with the truth—that his journey to Veracruz had accomplished precisely nothing.

He turned back toward the house's entrance. An Indian maid greeted him at the door and guided him inside, into the large salon decorated in crimson paper and oriental tiles. A large grand pianoforte dominated the room, a great sheaf of sheet music spilling across its keyboard and onto the bench. Several wooden cases were piled on the floor near the instrument. Ángela had only recently returned from a lengthy stay in New York City and was still in the turmoil of unpacking. From an interior courtyard, Diego could hear the squawking of guacamayas.

Several minutes passed before Ángela hurried into the room, a maidservant scrambling after her, still struggling to secure the fasteners at the back of her embroidered beige blouse. Her shining black hair was gathered behind her head, and her eyes shone. She stopped in her tracks.

"Oh . . . it's you."

It was apparent from her expression that she had been expecting someone else, someone taller no doubt and possessed of two complete arms.

"Yes," he said.

He clutched his hat in his one hand. As always in Ángela's presence, he found it nearly impossible to think of what to say. By rights he should have been brimming with good news, news of her brother. She must have sensed something was wrong and waved him over to a nearby sofa. She settled herself upon a carved wooden settee, fidgeting with her hair.

"You look awful," she said. "You've been ill?"

He nodded. He was about to speak when a brief but impassioned howl erupted from some other part of the residence. He thought at first that the guacamayas had rediscovered their lungs. Then he heard a second outburst, and he knew it was not the parrots that were responsible for the sound. Somewhere in the house, there resided an infant.

Ángela flushed and put a hand to her cheek. Her scarlet fingernails flashed against the whiteness of her skin, blood on alabaster. "The maid . . . she has brought her child from home. The poor thing was ill this morning. Colicky. I am sorry for the trouble." She begged Diego's pardon and hurried from the room.

He settled back in his seat, swallowed, gazed out onto the courtyard. Could it be true what she'd just said? He waited, not knowing what to think. When Ángela returned, her hair seemed dishevelled, and he noticed a fresh patch of dampness on the shoulder of her blouse. Now that he thought about it, it seemed she had increased in weight. She resumed her place on the settee and put a hand to her forehead, as if trying to calm her nerves.

"About Baldemar . . ." she said.

"I'm sorry. I tried, but I just . . ." His voice trailed away. All he had was excuses. He had fallen ill. He had been robbed. Both setbacks had been real enough, but they seemed absurd and meaningless now. The plain truth was he had failed. "I'm sorry. I just—"

She waved him off. "No need to explain," she said. "Father Fischer told me most of it."

"Father Fischer?"

"Yes. He was just here. Surely you met him on his way out. He is close to the Austrian, it seems. He means to help us rescue Baldemar."

"He does?"

"Yes. He said so."

"He isn't a priest, you know."

"Of course he is."

Diego frowned. "I met him in Veracruz," he said, stumbling over the words. "He's a prince, a German prince. I've met his wife."

"His wife? Nonsense. He's a priest, come to serve the emperor . . . that is, I mean, the Austrian."

As liberals, both of them flatly opposed the French occupation and neither felt comfortable referring to the Austrian by the title he had chosen.

"I don't know," said Diego. He wanted to tell her to be careful of the man, but his nervousness in her presence prevented him from speaking. What was Salm-Salm up to?

Ángela was silent for moment, and then her eyes glinted, like mirrors catching the sun. "I have good news," she said. "I have it on excellent authority that Baldemar is alive."

Diego was astonished to hear it and should have said so. Instead, he asked, "Whose authority?"

She stared at the floor, then shrugged and looked up. Her voice was barely audible. What she said sounded like "Bazaine."

"I beg your pardon?"

"Bazaine." More loudly this time.

Maréchal Achille Bazaine? Commander of the French forces occupying Mexico—an officer of Napoleon? What business could Ángela be conducting with Bazaine? Diego tried to pose the question, but his voice failed him once more.

Ángela evidently understood. "He visits me," she said. "I mean. You know. Not often. On occasion. From time to time. To keep me informed."

Both of them were silent, uncomfortably so, until Ángela cleared her throat and spoke again.

"You know," she said. "Father Fischer told me that, in the past, this Austrian has observed the custom of hearing petitions. So I wonder whether we shouldn't try that route. We could go to the National Palace, seek him out, put our case to him directly. It could do no harm. It might succeed." She looked straight at him. "It has to."

Diego frowned, not because he disagreed but because he was angry with himself. Why had he not thought of this? Or why had Salm-Salm not mentioned it to him, rather than to Ángela? Why had he not come armed with solutions, rather than failure and doubts?

"The bloody palace . . ." Ángela shook her head. "Dear God, I hate it. I . . ." She groaned and put a hand to her brow. "What am I saying?"

"What?"

"Here we are, overrun by these bloody French. Baldemar, the fool, has got himself tossed into the Martinica, where they'll kill him if we don't do something, and here am I, thinking about the National Palace."

Diego knew she hated the place. She'd held forth on the subject innumerable times in the past, heaping scorn upon the building, which stood adjacent to the Metropolitan Cathedral in the city's central plaza, the Zócalo. It was difficult to be sure which she detested more—the palace, the cathedral, or the square itself. She hated all three, mainly for the vastness of their scale. She had said so before. One felt like an insect in their midst. No doubt this had been their builders' intent—to overwhelm, to intimidate, to make ordinary folk kowtow in the presence of viceroys and bishops.

Diego saw her point. The cathedral really was a blight—massive, grey, forbidding. He hated it too, but he wondered whether his views had merely been shaped by Ángela's. As for the National Palace, he could practically quote her words on the subject. That dark pile of rocks. It was too large, too severe in conception, too deprived of light. It was an insult to Mexico—just like everything else in that abominable plaza.

"They hate it, you know," he said.

"Whom do you mean? Hate what?"

"The National Palace," said Diego. "The Europeans. They say it's infested with vermin."

"I'm sure it is."

"They want to live somewhere else. The Prince of Salm-Salm told me so. Just now."

"The priest, you mean?"

Diego grimaced. He had no idea what the man was up to. "Anyway, he said they want to be quit of the place."

"And go where?"

"That's the problem. They have no other plans. Salm-Salm, the priest, whatever he is—he told me he's been instructed to find another residence. He said it's urgent. They're desperate, he said."

Ángela frowned and began to stroke her forehead. Suddenly, she brightened. "Diego," she said. "You're a genius. That's it."

Diego recoiled. A genius? He didn't know what she meant. What was she saying?

She shifted forward in her seat, reached out, placed the palm of her hand on his knee. The effect was immediate, like an electric shock. She outlined a plan—*his* plan, she called it. It was he, after all, who had sparked the idea, or so she said. When she was done, she kept her gaze on him, her eyes shining. What did he think?

He wasn't sure what to think. But he said he would try.

"That's all I can ask. Tomorrow?"

"Tomorrow, yes."

"Good."

She stood up, and it was clear that it was time for him to go. He reached for his hat and climbed to his feet. Still he had to gaze up at her, for she stood nearly half a head taller than he. The familiar curbs on his tongue had returned, as they always did, and he took his leave in his customary inarticulate fashion. Outside, a groom led his horse into the stable yard. He climbed onto the mounting post, threw his right leg over the saddle, and gathered the reins in his one hand.

He rode away, cursing himself for being the same addled fool he'd always been. As for the identity of the sobbing infant, he could contemplate no explanation other than the one Ángela herself had provided. What other explanation could there be?

CHAPTER 7

IT RAINED HEAVILY THAT NIGHT. The next morning, the streets in the central part of the city still ran with the dank overflow, and Diego was obliged to choose his way carefully as he proceeded on foot to the National Palace. He intended to make his case to the Austrian in person. But he was not alone.

An assembly of large, glass-windowed *carretelas* cluttered the side streets that adjoined the plaza—expensive carriages, the conveyances of the rich. It didn't take long for Diego to realize why. With their families in tow, the conservative grandees of the city had gathered near the great plaza for much the same reason he had ventured there himself. They hoped to meet the Austrian—and, like him, they had no better plan than to simply show up. But, while he meant to save the life of a friend, they craved a different reward. Diego could readily divine what it was. Over the years, most of them had accumulated sheaves of musty documents attesting to some ancient privilege or other, and each had begun to press his cause almost as soon as the French began their occupation of Mexico City—so far to little avail.

Now, with the arrival of the Austrian, it seemed they had new hope. Surely this archduke who had been crowned the emperor of Mexico would recognize their claims. He too belonged to nobility and so must surely understand their own rightful ambitions on this score, their wish to be designated the *duque* of this or the *conde* of that. God willing, they might even be invited to join the Austrian's court. Their wives might be appointed as ladies-in-waiting to his own wife, the empress. Just think of the distinction, the glory. Diego watched them as he made his way past. The men strode about in the rain-damp streets, smoked their cigars, grumbled among themselves. Meanwhile, their womenfolk remained aboard the carriages, all in full toilette, with flowers or jewels strewn through their hair, all eyeing one another jealously.

Diego pressed on, shaking his head at the folly of his compatriots. Did they not realize what an absurd picture they made? Did they imagine themselves to be European? Ángela had often lamented the provincial ways of Mexico's *haut monde*. The women were shallow and uncultured, she said. Why, their taste in clothing lagged a good two years behind the fashions of London or Paris. And the men! They were backward in every way. Dear God—these were the 1860s, not the Dark Ages. This was a time of ferment and reform in Europe, where new ideas were emerging about justice and equality, the dignity of all men. Yet here in Mexico, what passed for learned discourse in conservative circles was nothing but cant, jealousy, and greed. Are women human? Does the killing of a Jew constitute murder? Do Indians have souls?

Diego picked his way through the mud, the ruts, and the rivulets that riddled the street until at last he reached the huge plaza, where hundreds of other supplicants had gathered—Indians, in this case. They, too, must have heard of the Austrian's arrival, and so they had come to seek redress for their many grievances—debt peonage, the denial of holy sacraments, the wholesale seizure of their land. Diego was well aware of these offences.

The Indian men gathered in small groups, wearing loose buttonless blouses of cotton and striped breech cloths. They peered out from the shadows cast by their straw hats, their sombre faces a dull bronze. Some were barefoot, but most wore crude handmade sandals, fashioned of maguey fibre or rawhide. The Indian women kept apart, whispering in clusters, their hair in twin plaits intertwined with ribbons of cotton. Most of them had small children bound to their backs in great handwoven shawls.

Diego joined neither group—neither the conservative potentates nor the Indian supplicants. Instead, he took up a position by himself about halfway between the two assemblies. He was mestizo, after all. The conservatives would not have welcomed him into their midst, for they considered him an Indian—and he loathed conservatives anyway. The Indians would have accepted him, but their purpose in being here had little to do with his own.

Three times, he marched across the square and spoke to the French soldiers who guarded the main entrance of the palace. He asked to be admitted. He meant to speak to someone who could arrange an audience with the Austrian. Each time, he was gruffly turned away. After his third failed attempt, Diego withdrew to the shade of the Monte de Piedad across the plaza, where he stood on his own, looking back at the sprawling stone edifice. The National Palace. He supposed it would be renamed the Imperial Palace, with an emperor in residence. But, apart from the guards in front, he detected no sign that it was occupied by anyone at all.

There was nothing for him to do but wait—wait and think about the events that had brought him here. It seemed to him now that Baldemar must have been plotting his act of revenge for years, possibly ever since the day he'd discovered the dangling corpse of his uncle in that forest clearing in the hill country of Michoacán. Diego should have known his friend was capable of such an act, should have seen it in advance. But how? Baldemar's boastful talk had seemed to be nothing more than empty words. He recalled their times together, in the months and years that followed the death of Melchor Ocampo, searching for anything that might have warned him of Baldemar's stupid, reckless plan.

After their return from Michoacán, they had both gone back to their sporadic labours, writing anti-clerical screeds for *El Siglo XIX*. Baldemar wrote badly, if with passion, whereas Diego was just the reverse, and that, too, was a measure of the differences between them.

Neither ever received any payment for this work and so relied on other sources of income for his upkeep. In Diego's case, he accepted a monthly stipend from Eustacio Barron, his half-brother and a man of great privacy and even greater wealth. A poet, or one who calls himself a poet, has not the luxury of spurning his patrons. The best he can do is resent them, a practice to which Diego applied himself with spirit and invention.

At night, he and Baldemar frequented the capital's *pulquerías,* cantinas, and cockfight rings, its brothels and gambling dens, where they drank, lost money at cards, and whored. One night, they ducked into a wretched old cantina near the Plaza Santa Cecilia, where they called out for beers, and then more beers, and more after that. At some point that night, a couple of men fell into an argument that got louder and more heated, till one of them drew a pistol and, without hesitation, pulled the trigger. His companion frowned and tilted his head, as if about to pose a question. Then he collapsed to the beer-soaked floor, dead. The killer merely smiled. He glanced over at Diego and Baldemar and nodded his head. He replaced his hat, turned, and sauntered out of the bar. Later, the bartender and another man dragged the corpse away. Following a brief, respectful silence, the assembly of drinkers went right back to swearing and banging their glasses on the tables. It was almost as though nothing had happened.

Eventually, his eyes half open, his voice slurred from drink, Baldemar pounded his fist on the table. He'd been born on the Day of the fucking Dead—he swore—and was damned from the start, fated to lead a short life and meet a violent end.

"You're sure?" said Diego. He'd heard all this before.

"As sure as I am of anything. As sure as I am of the fucking past. But listen to this." Baldemar leaned closer. His face seemed to expand in the candlelight. What he said now he'd never said before. "I won't go alone. I'll take someone with me. I swear."

Diego reached for his glass, but he didn't get there. A hand gripped his collar, a hand much stronger than his own. At once, Baldemar's face pressed close to his. He felt the heat of Baldemar's skin, the flecks of his spittle. He smelled his sour breath.

"I mean it. I'll go. But I won't go alone." Baldemar sat back, still glaring at Diego, straight into his eyes.

Diego listened to those words again, this time in his mind, and what he heard was not the bravado of a drunken friend. Baldemar had been testing him. He heard it now. Why hadn't he heard it then? Now, nearly three years later, Baldemar was in the Martinica, in danger of his life, and it was up to Diego to rescue him. But that didn't seem likely, not today. He'd already waited several hours in this deadening sunlight, staring at the National Palace, that dreary heap of rocks, and so far he had nothing at all to show.

CHAPTER 8

DIEGO DECIDED IT WAS no use remaining in the plaza any longer. If someone of significance were going to emerge from the National Palace, then surely he would have done so by now. Off to his right, he sensed some movement, and he glanced that way. It was nothing, really, just a lone pony cart turning down a side street adjoining the palace.

A side street adjoining the palace . . .

What an idiot he was.

Only now did he remember something Salm-Salm had said, that it would be best to enter the building by a side entrance, rather than by the main gate. And here he'd been waiting for hours on end right across from the main gate. Diego rapped his knuckles against the wall behind him, hard enough that his fingers smarted. To think he'd accused Baldemar of being a fool.

He set off along the edge of the plaza and then turned down a side street that traced one side of the palace. He soon found himself gazing at an inconspicuous porte cochère tucked within a small courtyard, at a considerable remove from the Zócalo. He was about to draw closer when a sudden commotion made him stop. Just in front of him, a door opened. A pair of military guards appeared, followed by a tall, fair-haired individual with a french fork beard. Despite the warmth of the afternoon, the man wore a grey topcoat and a felt top hat, also grey. He was followed by a variety of companions. Diego stepped closer, and the man in the top hat looked up. He stood still, frowning for an instant. Then his face broadened into a smile.

"*Mon Dieu,*" he said. "*C'est le poète manchot.*"

Without hesitation, Diego replied in French, a language he had fully mastered during his years of study at the Academia de San Juan de Letrán. "*Vous me connaissez?*"

The man laughed. He continued in French. "*Je crois que 'Votre Majesté Impériale' est la forme correcte.* It is also customary in some jurisdictions to bow. At the very least—remove your hat." He laughed again, and it was difficult to tell whether he was genuinely annoyed or merely joking. "These Mexican republicans, Felix—do they have no manners?"

Diego removed his hat, although he could not bring himself to bow. He saw that the man's companions included Salm-Salm, dressed again in layman's clothes.

"I fear they do not, Your Majesty," said Salm-Salm. "They insist all men are equal."

"I subscribe to a similar doctrine," said the Austrian, for it was evidently he. He was smoking a cigarette and seemed at his ease. He included Diego in the conversation without ceremony or hesitation, as if he had stumbled upon a friend of long standing. He shrugged and made a theatrical flourish with his cigarette. "But we have need of forms and protocols just the same." He looked at Diego more intently. "Of course I know you. You are Diego Serrano—the one-armed poet and one of the survivors of the massacre at Tacubaya. Salm-Salm here has filled me in. I have been looking forward to meeting you."

He advanced a step and proffered his right hand, which Diego took in his own. He realized his heart was pounding. This was his chance. At last, it had come. He must not waste an instant.

"Your Highness . . ." he said. "I mean, Your Imperial Majesty . . ." The title seemed to form itself upon his tongue unbidden. He had never used such an honorific before, but the words were not as difficult to pronounce as he had imagined. He took a deep breath. "In this city, there is a young patriot who has been imprisoned unjustly. He is to be tried before a court martial, and I greatly fear he will be condemned to death. He—"

"Yes. Salm-Salm has spoken to me of this matter. Is this a formal petition?"

"He acted impetuously to right a grievous wrong—a personal injury—wishing only to ensure that justice be done in the case of a legendary villain, a murderer who thoroughly deserved such punishment. The incarcerated man is my friend, Baldemar Peralta. He is in the Martinica Prison facing trial on the charge of attempted assassination. He—"

"You wish to make a petition on his behalf, I take it. Is this a formal undertaking?"

"I don't know, Your Imperial Highness—"

"Majesty."

"Your Imperial Majesty. Sorry. I appeal to you as a man of generous spirit, as—"

"Because, if it is a formal petition, I am afraid this is not the time or the place. A schedule will be set out in due course for the hearing of such appeals. The hours will be published for all to see. I . . . yes . . . ?"

A large man laid his hand upon the Austrian's arm. "Your Majesty," he said, "the hour is late."

"Yes, yes, of course. You are right." The Austrian turned back to Diego. "I am afraid we have business to attend to just now." He tossed his cigarette away and smiled—a young man's smile. He hesitated. For a moment, his expression darkened into a frown. "I wonder . . ." he began. He gestured toward the hulking edifice of stone that reared behind him, the National Palace. "You don't happen to know of another palace in this city, do you? This place is bestial. Why, it's infested with parasites."

"Your Majesty . . ." The large man said again. "The hour . . ."

"Right you are, Charles. Coming." The Austrian shook his head.

"Anyway, it's out of the question that we should live here. The place is an abomination." He gave Diego a look that somehow combined charm, arrogance, and utter helplessness. "You must know of some more suitable address. You are Mexican, after all."

And it was as if God himself had suddenly appeared, to clear the heavens or part the sea. This was the moment Ángela had anticipated, and she had equipped Diego with a response.

"It so happens," he said, "that I know of an ideal location."

The man raised his eyebrows. "You do?"

"Yes. As for this building, I agree with you. It is a monstrosity—too severe, and sorely in need of light. Why, look." He waved the stump of his left arm in the direction of the Zócalo. "The entire plaza is far too big. Those who designed it lacked any sense of human scale." He tried to recall Ángela's exact words. "They wished only to intimidate, to sow fear among the common folk."

"Dear God," said the Austrian. "But this is my view exactly. Hold hard, Charles." He fumbled for another cigarette. "And you say you know of another building, something preferable?"

"Yes, Your Majesty." Diego knew he was not responsible for this proposal. Ángela was. "The place I speak of—it is not in the city proper."

The Austrian dismissed the question with a wave of his hand. "*No importa.*"

"It serves another purpose at present."

"Irrelevant. What is its name?"

"Chapultepec, Your Majesty—a word that means Grasshopper Hill. That is the name it goes by. Chapultepec Castle." He sounded the word out, syllable by syllable.

"Cha-pul-te-pec . . ." The man repeated the word aloud, as if testing its shape and heft upon his tongue. "Chapultepec Castle."

"Baldemar Peralta," Diego said.

"I'm sorry . . . ?"

"The name of my friend."

"Oh . . . ? Oh yes. Make a note of that as well, would you, Charles?

Chapultepec Castle. And Baldemar . . . ?" He glanced once again at Diego, his eyebrows raised.

"Peralta. Baldemar Peralta."

"Precisely. We shall speak again, I promise. Salm-Salm, why didn't you mention this place? I thought I gave you a commission."

The Austrian glanced back at Diego and touched the fingers of one hand to the brim of his top hat in a kind of salute. Then he and his companions set off on foot, strolling away from the Zócalo. Soon, they disappeared from view.

Diego watched until the imperial party had dwindled from sight. He felt strangely exhilarated—euphoric almost. Who knew if he had succeeded in persuading this unexpectedly affable man—and, if so, to do what? It didn't seem to matter. He felt restored. In his chest, he sensed an unfamiliar lightness. He'd met the emperor in the flesh. Just why that should please him, he did not know. He replaced his hat and set off in the direction of the Zócalo.

Two days later, a letter arrived at his lodgings near La Ciudadela. The document was embossed with the imperial coat of arms, bearing the motto *Equidad en justicia*. It was affixed with a ribbon and sealed with the letters *MIM* in scarlet wax. In the very first sentence, the Austrian announced that, in the names of Mexico and the Almighty God, he had decided to grant Diego's appeal. Baldemar Peralta would be freed.

Diego let out a whoop and hopped around the room, nearly tripping against the leg of a chair. He managed to regain his balance and immediately returned his attention to the Austrian's letter. He read the rest of what was written there—a command for the recipient to present himself at the emperor's temporary chambers in the National Palace three days hence.

What on earth was this? Diego poured a tumbler of brandy and carried it to a casement window. He perched upon the broad sill and read the letter through again. For Baldemar—freedom. For himself—an audience with the Austrian. He sipped his drink. Was this what lay in store for Mexico under imperial rule? Not the catastrophe he had imagined but instead something like an improvement? Granted, almost anything would be an advance on what had prevailed till now. Since gaining independence four decades earlier, Mexico had been ruled by a succession of vain and swaggering men who governed for their own amusement and enrichment. The country had been vastly diminished as a result, deprived of half its former territory, mired in poverty, and burdened by unpayable debts. Diego swallowed a mouthful of brandy and thought of Antonio López de Santa Anna, an infamous megalomaniac who had ruled as Mexico's president on eleven separate occasions, embroiling himself in one disaster after another. He had sold Arizona to the gringos in order to bankroll his army. Might not the Austrian do better? Was it possible he could do worse?

Diego didn't know. All he knew was that he had been commanded to present himself before this European archduke three days hence—and he intended to do so. He penned a reply and dispatched it by courier. That done, he sent word to the stable for his horse to be saddled. Soon, he was riding in the direction of Ángela's house and, this time, he had good news to tell.

CHAPTER 9

DIEGO'S HAT SLIPPED FROM his hand and tumbled to the floor. He slumped into a sofa in the main salon. He felt as if someone had just punched him in the chest. Hard. What was this? This was madness. Even as he tried to absorb Ángela's astonishing news, it occurred to him that he smelled cigar smoke in the room, which seemed strange. But Ángela's news was even stranger. Diego closed his eyes and shook his head. He opened his eyes again.

"He does *what*?" he said.

"He refuses to be pardoned."

It was the sort of thing you needed to hear at least twice before you believed it. Even then, it was a challenge.

Ángela balanced herself on the edge of the wooden settee. She told him she had only just received the news, a half hour ago, maybe less. It was Achille Bazaine who'd told her.

"Bazaine in person?"

"Well . . . yes."

"He came here?"

"He would have to, wouldn't he? To give me the news directly? He would have to come here. I mean, I haven't been out of this damned house in . . ." Ángela fell silent. She put her hands down on the settee, as if steadying herself. "I'm sorry," she said. "It isn't your fault. It's my idiotic brother. Again."

Diego took a deep breath. Bazaine commanded the French army in Mexico. Would he really have time to attend to a matter such as this in person? It seemed unlikely. It seemed . . . again Diego shook his head to free himself of unwelcome thoughts. Besides, the issue now was Baldemar.

"Did he say why?"

Ángela nodded. It seemed her brother had formed a bond of friendship with some fellow inmates in the Martinica Prison, a dozen or so, all of them confined to the same subterranean cell. Baldemar refused to accept his own release unless his new comrades were set free as well.

She raised both hands and held them before her, as though some kind of solution were written there. But, of course, it wasn't. "Goddamn him. The fool."

The fool? Maybe. Diego suspected that, beneath her distress, she was actually proud of her brother, the stubborn, headstrong hero. She was angry, frustrated, yes, but also proud. He remembered the names of those other men, the *compinches* of the two thieves who'd waylaid him on the road from Veracruz. Sánchez, Quiñones, Rivera. He wondered if they were among Baldemar's fellow inmates.

He realized that Ángela was still speaking. She was saying she had presented Bazaine with a possible solution—do as Baldemar demanded. Extend the offer of clemency to the others. What was wrong with that? But the Frenchman had only laughed. He'd made it plain that the prospect of freedom for just one liberal prisoner—even if it *was* her brother—represented an affront to every French soldier who had died in this war, not to mention every French combatant still living. He was glad this had happened, glad the offer had been refused. And, on that note, the Frenchman had picked up his cap and left the house.

"Charming," she said. She was silent for a time and did not look at him. Finally, she sighed. "*Bien. Así es.*"

"I'm sorry?"

"It's Baldemar. He won't change his mind. You know that. You know him as well as I do. He's too stubborn. But maybe . . ." Her voice trailed off.

Diego could imagine what she was thinking. Maybe Baldemar wouldn't change his mind—but the Austrian would. Was that it? If that was what she was hoping—that the new emperor would free all these men, Baldemar and the rest—then she was certain to be disappointed. He shook his head.

"I don't think so. I can't conceive of it. One man, yes. But not more, not as his first official act. They're probably all liberals anyway."

He sat back, wondering what to do or say next. The truth was, he had a duty—a solemn duty—to rescue Baldemar from death. What was he going to do now?

Just then, a howl erupted in another part of the house. It rose and fell, then rose and fell again. Diego turned to Ángela. He arched his eyebrows. What was that?

She sighed. "Diego . . ." she said. She eased forward and reached out with one hand, as if to place her palm against his knee, but something made her stop.

"Yes?"

"There is something I have to tell you. I should have told you before. I—"

The howl went up again.

Diego nodded, already knowing what she would say.

"My son," she said.

He felt hot, light-headed.

"My son," she repeated. "I have a son."

Diego tried to focus his thoughts. It was uncommonly warm in the room, and he was finding it difficult to breathe. Dear God. Could it be that Salm-Salm had been right all along? He found it intolerable that the fellow should know more about Ángela than he did himself.

He heard a loud, persistent drone emanating from somewhere in his head, making it difficult to comprehend what she was saying. He realized she was still speaking, but her voice seemed to come from a great distance. It seemed disembodied, distorted. He could make out the individual words but not their collective sense. He forced himself to concentrate. Ángela was saying that the child's father was Ángel de Iturbide. Diego knew him—rather, knew *of* him. His father had proclaimed himself emperor of Mexico and had ended his sorry life before a firing squad. The son, Ángel de Iturbide, the man Ángela was speaking of, had grown to be an individual of some property and wealth. Somehow, he and Ángela had met, and a child had been the eventual result. The boy had been conceived in Mexico but born in New York City, where Ángela had pursued the father in hopes of prevailing upon him to take responsibility for his actions. That was never likely—she understood it now—for the man was a notorious philanderer. It was in his blood.

"Diego—are you listening to me?"

"Yes." And he was listening. He was trying to. Goddamn this ceaseless drone. It was as if his head were on fire.

Ángela continued. Now she was explaining the reason for these visits from the man he knew as the Prince of Salm-Salm but whom she identified as Father Fischer, a Catholic priest. It seemed he had visited her repeatedly. What he wanted was both simple and terrible. He wanted her to give the boy up.

Diego said nothing, just looked at her, trying to take all of it in.

"He wants me to give up my son so that the Austrian and his wife can adopt him."

"Adopt him?"

"Yes."

"You mean, as an heir?"

"Exactly. They themselves are without child, and my son is descended from an emperor."

"An emperor?" He couldn't believe he was being so stupid, but simply repeating her words seemed to be all that he could manage. "They want you to give him up?"

"Yes. They—what do you think I am saying? Are you listening to me? Father Fischer said exactly that. Give him up."

"And will you?"

"*What?*" she practically shrieked. "Of course not. No, no, no." She buried her face in her hands and rocked back and forth on the settee, convulsed in tears. "No. Not ever. Never."

The child cried out again.

"*Ay Dios.*" Ángela sprang to her feet, tears still running from her eyes. She begged Diego's forgiveness—she had to go, to attend to Agustín.

So that was the child's name.

She left without another word. A maidservant saw Diego from the house. He retrieved his horse and rode off in the direction of the Gran Teatro Nacional. Something drew him there, some faint glimmer of an idea. A banner mounted on the theatre's facade announced that the forthcoming opera season would commence later in the month—a little more than two weeks away. Ángela—identified on the poster as La Peralta—would star in the opening production, playing the role of Violetta in *La Traviata,* by Giuseppe Verdi.

Diego reached out with his hand and slammed his knuckles, hard as he could, against one of the Romanesque pillars that stood at the theatre's entrance.

¡Santa Madre de Jesús!

The pain was impossible to describe.

Then he did it again.

His hand scorched, his vision flamed red, and his eyes welled with tears. He reined his horse around, his fingers burning as if they really were on fire. He had no choice but to keep using his hand—he only had the one. He shifted his heels, and his horse broke into a slow canter.

So much for Ángela. So much for love.

The next day at noon, his hand wrapped in bandages, Diego rode to the National Palace, meaning to confront Salm-Salm. He needed to know what the so-called prince was up to. Why was he tormenting Ángela? And why dress up as a priest?

When he reached the Zócalo, Diego slowed his horse to a trot and proceeded along the cobbled perimeter of the great plaza. He decided to enter by the porte cochère located well back from the main gates. Once there, he informed a guard that he had come to speak to the Prince of Salm-Salm. Minutes later, he was received by the prince in a gloomy antechamber with cracked plaster mouldings. The carpets were badly worn, and a dark gelatinous substance clung to the ceiling in one corner, dripping a viscous liquid onto the floor. Diego took a seat in a wobbly ladder-back chair. He sniffed suspiciously at the air.

"Black mould," said Salm-Salm. "I'm surprised the place is still standing."

Diego shrugged. No wonder the Europeans were desperate to leave.

"You have spoken to Ángela Peralta, I take it," said Salm-Salm.

Diego frowned. "Why do you say that?"

"To judge by the condition of your hand."

"Ah yes. Yes, I have."

"I fear you must be in some pain."

"A subjective notion."

"Not in my experience."

Diego took a deep breath and, without additional formalities, he recited all that he had learned from Ángela. He focused especially on Salm-Salm's desire that she renounce her son. "Is it true?"

The prince settled back into his creaking swivel chair. He set the heels of his shoes atop an ancient wooden desk, crossing his legs at the ankles. He exhaled a plume of cigarette smoke that coiled into the murky light. He smiled at Diego for what seemed an inordinately long time. Only then did he speak. It was, of course, well known, he said, that Maximilian and Charlotte were without offspring, despite seven years of marriage. Naturally, the empress craved a child, and for all the usual reasons, having nothing to do with establishing a line of succession and everything to do with what many a woman in the prime of her child-bearing years might reasonably feel.

Diego tried to remain quiet. What he really wanted was a shouting match, not a civilized conversation, but he understood that a shouting match would accomplish little, as gratifying as it might be. "They cannot produce a child on their own?" he said.

"Well, they haven't managed it yet, after seven years. Make of that what you will."

"What do you make of it?"

The prince gazed about the room, then looked back at Diego. He lowered his feet to the floor. He leaned closer, his complexion seeming paler than ever. Did the man not go out in the sun?

"Most people believe that Max is the party at fault," he said in what was almost a whisper. He explained that Maximilian had made a journey to Brazil several years earlier to visit his cousin, Dom Pedro II, who was emperor of that distant and mysterious land. It was rumoured that, while there, Max had conducted an amorous affair with a Brazilian woman of a certain station, a woman who frequented the court. He had thereby contracted an unidentified infirmity that had left him sterile, or so it was said.

"Tit for tat," said Salm-Salm. He sat back. "We gave you smallpox. You give us syphilis."

When Diego failed to react, he smiled.

"A joke."

Still Diego said nothing.

The prince briefly contemplated his cigarette. Whatever its cause, he said, the condition seemed to be of a permanent nature, and it imperilled the future of what Salm-Salm now grandly referred to as the Second Mexican Empire. The first Mexican empire had of course consisted of the brief reign of Agustín de Iturbide, grandfather of Ángela's son.

"Bastard son," said Diego. "The child is a bastard."

"Not at all." Salm-Salm rose to his feet and began to pace about the room. "Nothing of the sort. The couple are married. All perfectly legal. Who knows what Iturbide was thinking? A moment of weakness? An attack of remorse? Maybe he was drunk. But he and Ángela Peralta were married in New York City. I possess an affidavit sworn out by an attorney of the firm Tweed, Bascombe, attesting to this fact. It is all quite in order."

Diego waved dismissively, as if this were nothing to him now. "Where is Iturbide?"

"Oh, God knows." Salm-Salm gestured in the air with his cigarette. "Still out whoring with showgirls, I imagine, in New York or Madrid. The marriage with Ángela Peralta was a deceit from the beginning. Still, it's perfectly legal. The boy is the legitimate grandson of an emperor."

"A self-proclaimed emperor. Executed by a firing squad."

"Sad to say." Salm-Salm shook his head in a brief show of sympathy for the former ruler, then quickly smiled. "But the child possesses the necessary pedigree. That's the important thing."

"I wonder why you told me none of this before."

"Oh, but I did," said Salm-Salm. "In Veracruz—don't you remember? I told you that Ángela Peralta had borne a child."

"That much, yes. But none of all this. Imperial lineage. Affidavits. The rest." He paused. "Why not?"

"Surely it's obvious," said the prince. He let his cigarette fall to the floor, where he ground it out with the toe of his shoe. He looked up. "You didn't ask. You didn't want to know." He clasped his hands behind his back, rocked on his heels. "But now you do know—and I have a proposal to make."

Diego had expected something of the sort. "Yes?" he said.

It was simple, said the German. Ángela would surrender her son to the emperor and empress. In exchange, Maximilian would pardon Baldemar as well as his new-found *compañeros,* all inmates at the Martinica Prison. Salm-Salm made a gesture of washing his hands. "Finished and done."

"Her son for her brother?"

"Crassly put. But yes."

"I take it the Austrian—the emperor, I mean . . . he has agreed to this?"

Salm-Salm's expression darkened a fraction. "Not exactly."

"You mean he hasn't agreed to it?"

"Not yet. But he must. Without an heir, the empire lacks legitimacy and, without legitimacy, it is nothing."

"What of Bazaine?"

"What of him?"

"He was furious about the original pardon."

"I fail to see how that matters."

"Well, he's bound to be even more opposed to this arrangement."

"So he is," said Salm-Salm. "But Bazaine is not the ruler here."

"And you think you can persuade the emperor to accept this bargain—a pardon in exchange for an heir?"

"I do." Salm-Salm began to pace about the room again, alternately smoothing his hair and adjusting his frock coat. "In any event, there is no choice." He stopped. "That reminds me. You received an invitation from His Majesty, I believe—an audience? Two days from now?"

"Yes. That's right." The reason for the invitation remained a mystery, but Diego saw no reason not to acknowledge it.

"Well, it's cancelled. Postponed, anyway."

"It is? Why?"

"I spoke out against it." Salm-Salm shrugged. "Sorry, but it's true. No reflection on you. It really has to do with the emperor's secretary. Very ill. They say it's the yellow fever. Poor man. Anyhow, this is not a good time."

He returned to his desk and began to poke through the drawers. In short order, he produced a bottle, half full, of what turned out to be an exquisite French brandy. He also came up with two crystal goblets, both embossed with the monogram *MIM*.

"Maximilianus Imperator Mexici," he explained once again. He said the same monogram had been emblazoned on almost everything the Austrian owned, all of it newly purchased from the best suppliers in Europe. He uncorked the bottle and began to pour out two glasses, but something made him hesitate.

"Oh," he said. "Your hand. The bandages. I forgot."

"I'll manage." Diego was in need of a drink. He accepted a glass and lifted it gingerly. He studied the liquid, the way the oblique light filtered through it, the colour shifting from bronze to gold. He had already more or less forgotten about the Austrian's puzzling summons and, now, its abrupt cancellation. He was thinking instead of Salm-Salm's proposal—Ángela's son in exchange for Baldemar's freedom. It was impossible, of course. Only a monster would put any woman in such a position, much less Ángela Peralta. Force her to choose between a brother and a son? It was unthinkable—especially if there were any other way to save Baldemar, and it so happened there was. At least, he thought there might be. The rough shape of a plan had occurred to him the previous day as he rode past the Gran Teatro Nacional. The memory of that incident sharpened the pain still coursing through his hand. He took another swallow of brandy. The drink calmed him a little, and his idea seemed to harden in his mind, take on greater detail. Maybe, just maybe, a woman would do something out of gratitude that she would never do under duress.

"You haven't answered my question," said Salm-Salm.

"It isn't up to me."

"But you'll talk to our friend Ángela?"

Diego bridled. '*Our* friend'? What did that mean? But instead of protesting, he merely shrugged. "I'll try. I'll do what I can."

"I'm counting on you."

"Yes. Well . . ." Diego gazed around the room. He had another thought. "The emperor," he said. "Would it be your judgment that he is governed by the head or by the heart?"

"Why do you ask?"

In fact, Diego was thinking about this scheme that was taking shape in his mind—his plan for Baldemar's rescue. Much would depend on the Austrian. But he didn't say so. "I'm just curious," he said.

"How quaint." Salm-Salm flicked a trace of lint from the collar of his frock coat. He frowned. "'Just curious'? Really? Nothing more?"

"That's right."

"I see. Well, since you ask, I would say the answer is quite clear. By the heart. Max will always behave according to the dictates of the heart."

"You're quite sure?"

"Oh yes. It is a great weakness in him, a great weakness in anyone. But he is a younger brother, you see, and suffers a younger brother's frailties." Salm-Salm smiled and raised his glass. "Like you."

Chapter 10

For Diego's plan to succeed, he had no choice but to recruit Ángela, and so he was obliged to visit her again and make his case. He said nothing of her sham marriage or her infant son. He was unsure which of these two circumstances enraged him more, but he did his best to put them out of his mind. All that was in the past, or so he told himself. He handed his horse off to a stable hand and walked up to the main door. A maidservant ushered him into the main salon. Within several minutes, Ángela appeared.

"Your hand . . ." she said. "What happened to your hand?"

"A reaction to circumstances."

It was the response he had settled upon, sufficiently vague it could mean anything at all. Besides, he felt remote from Ángela now. Possibly, it was this distance that freed his tongue. Whatever the reason, he found he could speak with a greater assurance than he could remember ever having experienced in her presence before. He explained his plan to rescue Baldemar. She listened without speaking and, when he was done, she promptly agreed to play her part. She had no better proposals of her own, she said, and Diego's scheme might even work. It had to.

He looked at her, then at the floor, then at her again, managing somehow to hold her gaze. The pain in his hand still throbbed, and this seemed to balance the other distress he had suffered on her account. He felt clear in his mind. They had one goal: to rescue Baldemar. Before, other factors had always complicated his motives. Now nothing else mattered.

Still, it was a gamble. Everything depended on Ángela's performance, not during the opera but afterward. As the banner had announced, the production on the opening night at the newly renamed Gran Teatro Imperial was to be *La Traviata,* and Ángela would play the part of Violetta. But her real performance would come after the curtain had fallen—the performance that would determine Baldemar's fate. She assured Diego she would prepare herself fully. She would be as ready as it was possible to be. It was all anyone could do.

But much could still go wrong.

The opening night arrived at last, and Diego paced back and forth near the entrance to the theatre, impatient for the evening ahead to be over. If this venture failed, he had no idea what else could be done to save Baldemar. It would be hopeless.

By a quarter past seven, a procession of carriages began to totter up to the entrance. The women alighted from their coaches and paraded forth like walking ornaments, in gowns of silk, sparkling with diamonds. Ostrich plumes fluttered in their hair. The men kept ebony canes tucked beneath their arms and saluted each other with their cigars. French military officers squired the daughters of Mexican society. The archbishop,

Monseñor de Labastida y Dávalos, was a study in purple, radiant in his immense vestments and glittering jewels. He clutched a large amethyst cross and scattered vague benedictions as a half-dozen priests struggled to help him negotiate the stairs.

The cream of Mexico had flocked to the theatre and, miraculously, they had managed to arrive on time, a rare feat for Mexicans. But it was the opening night of the opera season, after all. More to the point, the emperor and empress were themselves to preside, providing everyone in attendance with an opportunity to strut and preen and, just maybe, to share a private word with His Majesty on some confidential matter or other. Besides, word had got out that no one would be permitted to enter the theatre after the emperor and empress had arrived, and so punctuality became the watchword, if only for tonight.

Diego spat discreetly onto the ground, a bitter taste in his mouth. He cursed himself, but he couldn't deny feeling a faint tremor of excitement. Who could explain it? An emperor, an empress—they were just mortal creatures, like anyone else. He knew this to be so. Yet what was he to make of these ripples of anticipation, this gooseflesh, this racing of the blood? He turned and strode into the theatre, along with the rest.

Built in the 1840s, the theatre had been newly rechristened in Their Majesties' honour, but it remained a troublesome affair, prone to drafts, chilly at night, and poorly lit. Patrons ascended to their boxes by means of dark, narrow stairways that posed a particular challenge for the archbishop and his acolytes.

Still, the audience members all managed to find their seats in good time. Those in private boxes made an ostentatious show of settling themselves, for they were on full display and knew it. The booths were open in front to within inches of the floor, so that the women might more easily show off the grandeur of their dresses, the perfection of their shoes. Meanwhile, in the orchestra pit, the players tuned their instruments in that strange but inevitable ritual of blissfully discordant sound.

At the stroke of eight, the emperor and empress ascended to their box, and a hubbub of excited whispers reverberated through the crowd.

Known now by the Spanish versions of their names, Maximiliano and Carlota took their seats, accompanied by a retinue of courtiers and guards. The other patrons craned their necks in order to obtain a better view, some leaning perilously from their balconies. For once, Diego thought, they were more eager to see than be seen.

He, of course, felt nothing but scorn for this entire spectacle, and yet he couldn't stop watching. Carlota wore a gown of emerald silk, with a diamond-studded tiara and a brooch of jewels in the form of water plants and dew drops. Her tall and angular husband was decked out in the dress uniform of a Mexican general, with an ermine robe draped over his shoulders. Both waved and smiled while exchanging inaudible pleasantries with their companions, a party of nobles that included both Salm-Salm and his ethereal wife.

Diego sat alone in his half-sibling's box. Neither Eustacio Barron nor his wife was in attendance. Barron was away somewhere, on some pressing international business or other. He had investments in a dozen countries or more.

Soon, a team of ushers filtered through the house extinguishing the candles by means of doubters mounted on long wooden poles. The orchestra began to play the overture. The drop curtain lifted, revealing a salon in the Paris apartment of one Violetta Valéry, who is entertaining a bustle of guests. Diego settled back in his seat, seeking to lose himself in the music and the story, trying not to think of what would come afterward. Let the evening lead where it might. It was too late to change course now.

The performance went passably well, apart from some confusion with props, not to mention a backdrop that failed to settle properly into place. But the cast were excellent, none more so than Ángela. Despite her troubles, and the nervousness she must have been feeling, she seemed to lose herself in the part of Violetta. Despite all that had lately passed between them, Diego could not help admiring her talent, the control and purity of her voice, the authenticity of her bearing on stage.

Even before the final curtain fell, the audience members had surged to their feet. "Bravo!" they cried. "La Peralta! La Peralta!" Many tossed flowers to the stage, and waves of applause rolled across the balconies and over the orchestra pit. The cast were summoned back no fewer than three times before the cheering finally subsided. Only then, after the briefest of pauses, did Ángela make an unscheduled foray back to the stage, alone, unbidden, and with a Mexican flag draped in her arms.

The patrons noticed immediately and stopped in order to see what this was about. Something unusual—that much they could guess. Something unexpected was afoot.

Ángela raised the fabric of Mexico's three-coloured banner, holding it aloft for several moments before letting the flag settle over her shoulders. She wrapped the material around her breast and took a step forward. Without accompaniment, she began to sing. But the lyrics and melody were not what Diego had expected, not what he and Ángela had rehearsed. They had agreed that she would perform a pair of verses and the chorus of Mexico's national anthem. Instead, he found himself listening to a sumptuous melody whose lyrics were unfamiliar to him.

If a dove alights at your window, treat it with kindness because it is me. Tell it the stories of your loves, my darling. Crown it with flowers because it is mine.

Diego wasn't sure he saw the connection between these words and Baldemar's plight, except that the song Ángela sang was so clearly an expression of love and not of war. It was also as poignant a melody as he had ever heard, an impression apparently shared by the rest of the audience, for everyone remained in perfect, rapt silence until the final note faded, and Ángela advanced a few more steps toward the edge of the stage. She peered out into the audience until her gaze fell upon the emperor in his box. She addressed him directly, her words meant for him alone. She spoke in what seemed an almost confidential tone, without embellishment or theatrics.

She said that she brought a message on behalf of the great majority of Mexicans—the poor, the landless, the forgotten. Like them, she said, she wanted peace instead of war, life instead of death. She implored the emperor to begin his reign with a gesture of reconciliation. There were many Mexicans who did not subscribe to the doctrine of war or the fetish for inequality and division that blotted their country's history. They yearned for a Mexico as it ought to be, a land of *Equidad en justicia*. Deliberately, it seemed, she used the very words the Austrian had chosen as his imperial creed. Then, slowly, she lowered herself to her knees and held her arms above her head, gripping the flag in both hands.

"Free my brother, Baldemar Peralta," she said. "Free him, and those imprisoned alongside him in the Martinica. Amnesty for all who love Mexico!"

Then, silence.

After several moments, Ángela climbed back to her feet. She took a single step forward, awaiting the Austrian's response. The emperor did nothing at first. But all eyes were on him, and it was clear he had to make some reply. He had to do something. He slowly rose from his seat. He seemed to tower above the box and above the audience, a lone silhouette in the half-lit house. He really did make a commanding presence, tall and erect, enfolded in his ermine robe, with his light-coloured hair, pale skin, and reddish beard. He looked every inch a monarch. Those watching might have thought that all this had been planned in advance, each word, each gesture. But Diego was sure the emperor had no more warning of Ángela's petition than anyone else.

Diego clenched his fist. Baldemar's freedom was so close, he could almost imagine reaching out with his one hand and being able to touch it. Maximiliano had only to speak and the pardon would be granted. A few simple words. Nothing more. A spasm of pain flared through his still-bandaged hand. He winced but made no sound, just held his breath. He mouthed an entreaty to the emperor. Say them. Say the words. Say yes. The strains of Ángela's voice seemed to echo through the half-darkened house.

But the Austrian was silent. He must have been affected by Ángela's appeal, for he lifted both his hands and held them out, palms forward, as if preparing to say something. Diego tightened his fist even more, shuddering at the pain. Speak, why don't you? Speak now.

And now, at last, the Austrian did speak. His voice trembled only a little as his words filled the darkness.

"I, don Maximiliano the First, by the grace of God and will of the people emperor of Mexico, do hereby grant this petition. Let there be peace in the Empire during my reign!"

Immediately, Diego felt a burden lift from his shoulders. So familiar had that weight become that he hadn't been aware of it, not for weeks. But he was aware of it now—aware, at least, of its sudden absence. He'd been bound by a solemn duty to rescue Baldemar, and at last it was done. The words were out. They could not be taken back.

As for the Austrian, he gazed around the theatre, seemingly perplexed. Seated nearby, Salm-Salm put his face in his hands. His own proposal—the surrender of Ángela's son in exchange for Baldemar Peralta's freedom—had been dealt a fatal blow, even if only he and Diego knew of it. For his part, the emperor seemed uncertain what to do. No doubt he had expected the theatre to erupt in cheers, but nothing of the sort occurred. In his heart, Diego half hoped the Austrian's announcement would be applauded by someone, but he understood that this could not happen, not here, not among these people—conservatives all. If the Austrian had been ruled by his head, he would never have issued this proclamation. But it was just as Salm-Salm had said. The man had acted from the heart, moved by the music and the drama of the moment as much as by the substance of Ángela's appeal.

As for the audience, they must have been stunned by the man's words—stunned and horrified. What was this? Their fine new emperor, defending godless liberals? At first, Diego detected only a low muttering, but this was soon followed by coughs and the clearing of throats. Chair legs scraped against wooden floorboards, accompanied by disgruntled whispers, murmurs of disagreement. All this he had expected. But, just then, a single male voice roared above the other sounds, its harsh drunken tones bursting through the gloomy light.

"*¡A la chingada!*" the voice cried—a Mexican oath, the strongest there is.

A brief silence followed, and then a single gunshot cracked through the theatre. Instinctively, Diego ducked but then almost immediately turned toward the stage, just in time to see Ángela collapsing to the boards. The flag slipped from her hands, and a blossom of crimson began to spread across her white silk blouse. Now the audience did erupt—in shrieks and obscenities, in hundreds of shouting voices and thousands of shouted words.

Diego fought his way toward the stage, but it was nearly impossible to pry open a path through the crush and panic of the crowd. Before long, the drop curtain hurtled down, blocking his view of Ángela's crumpled body. Fists flew and so did boots, but he kept struggling to find a way to the proscenium. Off to the right, he saw a squadron of hussars muscling their way into the crowd to clear a route out of the theatre for the imperial party. Taller than most of the Mexicans, and armed as well, the Austrian soldiers soon imposed their will. Maximiliano and his entourage hurried from the theatre as quickly as they could. Everyone else continued to jostle, push, and shove, frantic to get out. From somewhere inside the building, Diego could hear the raw bark of a man's laughter. He recognized the voice, the same laughing voice he'd heard the day of the massacre at Tacubaya—or had he only dreamed it?

He twisted his head and peered up at the orchestra seats, tracking the source of that dark, terrible laugh. Sure enough, it was General Leonardo Márquez, surrounded by his customary retinue of thugs. The Tiger of Tacubaya lounged in his seat, his boots resting on the seat backs in front of him, his military frock coat open in front, his collar askew. He was waving a pistol in the air, and he was laughing.

There was no doubt it was Márquez who had fired the shot. Dozens must have seen him. It was he who had shouted the oath and he who had shot Ángela. Now he was not even bothering to leave the theatre. Conservatives were in power now. He could do as he pleased.

Diego tried to ignore the man's laughter, but it haunted him—that same guttural sound he had heard five years earlier in Tacubaya, the day he'd lost his arm. Or maybe he only imagined that he could remember that piercing sound. As Baldemar never failed to remind him, he'd been dead drunk at the time.

He struggled through the crowd of theatregoers, desperate to reach the stage. But by the time he got there, all he found was a Mexican flag lying crumpled on the boards beside a large pool of blood. Ángela was gone.

Chapter 11

"The girl survived—am I right?" The Austrian eased back the folds of a discoloured lace drape and peered out at the Zócalo. "She suffered no permanent harm?"

"I don't know," said Diego. "I haven't seen her. I don't know where she is."

"Oh? I understood you knew her." He let the curtain fall back into place and turned to look at Diego. "Salm-Salm told me so."

"He may well have done. I—"

"Your Majesty."

Diego nodded. "Your Majesty."

This hardly seemed the time for a lesson in courtly protocol. Diego had received no news of Ángela in the past three days, not since she had collapsed on the stage at the opera. Since then, he had tried to find her by every means he could think of—find her and determine her condition. So far, he had failed. She'd been shot, and he was the one responsible. The scheme at the opera had been his idea. But it was she who'd taken the risks. Now here he was, responding to an invitation from the emperor to appear before him, and it seemed even the Austrian knew more about the attack and its aftermath than he did, little though that was. It didn't help that he was being subjected to a seemingly unnecessary lecture in the niceties of etiquette at court. He realized Maximiliano was still speaking.

"Do not think me picayune," said the emperor. He strode across the room and settled his tall, spare frame into a high-back chair at a large marble desk. He stroked his beard, keeping his eyes fixed upon his guest. "Empires have fallen for a lack of attention to custom and form. Without order, we are nothing."

"Yes, Your Majesty."

The emperor smiled. "At any rate, I am informed that the girl is out of danger. Salm-Salm told me so not an hour ago. I thought you knew."

Diego reached for his hat and got to his feet. "Where is she now . . . Your Majesty?"

"In a hospital of some kind. It seems no lasting damage was done. I'd talk to Salm-Salm if I were you. But that is not the reason I have invited you here. Please. Sit down."

Diego had received the invitation the previous afternoon, delivered to his lodgings with what he now deemed to be the usual pomp—a European carriage, a pair of liverymen, a messenger in a dark frock coat. He had assumed the proposed audience would have something do with Ángela and the events at the opera. He now realized his error, for these subjects seemed to be dealt with only in passing. Before long, it became clear that what Maximiliano really wished to speak of was Chapultepec Castle and his delight in finding so suitable a residence. It reminded him a little of Schönbrunn, he said, explaining that this was the palace where he'd been raised, in Vienna. He said he was deeply in his visitor's debt, for it was Diego who had proposed Chapultepec. He regarded the building as a testament to his visitor's sound aesthetic judgment and overall perspicacity.

"I have summoned you," Maximiliano said at length, "in order to make a proposal. You are aware, I imagine, that Poliakovitz has passed on."

"I beg your pardon?"

"Poliakovitz. My private secretary. He succumbed to the yellow fever. A terrible thing."

"I am sorry to hear it."

"A great shame. His family will grieve the loss deeply. I only wish there were more I could do to ease their burden, but . . ." He shook his head. "In any case, his remains are to be returned to Europe. Meanwhile, we must accommodate ourselves to new circumstances."

The Austrian shifted in his chair. He reached forward, plucked a cigarette from a humidor. A servant hurried over with a wooden phosphorous match. Maximiliano inhaled with evident pleasure and then released two plumes of bluish smoke through his nostrils.

"I have decided," he said, "to offer the position to you."

Diego realized that, in some inexplicable way, he had been expecting to hear these very words ever since Salm-Salm had first mentioned the emperor's European secretary and his fragile health. Even so, he found he couldn't speak. Expected or not, now that it was being made, the offer had the effect of dumbfounding him.

"I see I have rendered you . . . *verblüfft,*" said the Austrian. "How do you say it in Spanish?"

"I'm not sure."

"The French would say *sidéré.*"

"Ah, *pasmado,*" said Diego. "Yes, it's true."

He was speechless, or very nearly.

It was a dilemma. What should he say now? He did not hesitate long. "Baldemar Peralta," he said.

The Austrian cocked his head. "I beg your pardon?"

"My friend, in the Martinica. That night at the opera, you said you would pardon him. I wonder . . ."

"You wonder if I shall keep my word, even if my word was wrested from me in a most reprehensible fashion." The Austrian ground out his cigarette. "Yes, I shall. This Peralta fellow and all his *confrères*—they will go free, as promised. *On one condition.* I insist that—"

"You know that Maréchal Bazaine opposes the measure."

The emperor frowned, evidently unaccustomed to being interrupted in mid-sentence. "Of course he does."

"I'm serious. He is dead set against it."

"He told you so?"

"No . . . I mean, no, Your Majesty. I have heard it from others."

"Who would be well advised to hold their tongues. As for Bazaine, he is a military man and thinks in military terms. That is his profession. But I possess a wider brief."

"Won't this cause a rift?"

"Not for a moment. The man will carry out his duty no matter what. Personal happiness does not come into it. He is a field officer, whereas I am the emperor. They don't compare." He gave a low, gentle laugh. "Don't worry about Bazaine."

"What of Márquez, then?"

The Austrian shook his head. "Shameful business. The fellow has no remorse at all. Says he's glad he did it."

"He'll be tried, of course?"

"Yes, of course. Tried and acquitted. There's no other way. Bazaine and I have discussed this in detail. A conviction would play havoc with army morale. We can't afford it. We'll pack him off to Constantinople. It was Bazaine's idea, and a good one, too. He'll be my minister plenipotentiary to the Ottoman Empire. He can't cause much trouble there."

The Austrian waited a moment. "I believe I made you a proposal."

So he had. But the man had also mentioned a condition. He would release Baldemar and the others *on one condition*. Now Diego understood. By most lights, the idea was unthinkable—he, a liberal and a republican, acting as secretary to an emperor, and a foreigner to boot! He should retrieve his hat and leave this building at once.

Only he couldn't—for what then would become of Baldemar?

He sat back in his chair. So this was the condition the emperor was attaching to Baldemar's release, the price he himself would have to pay.

"Your Majesty," he said. Already, the honorific had become easier—not natural but not entirely alien, either. "I wonder if you have noticed that I am deprived of the use of my left arm?"

"The circumstance has called itself to my attention, yes. I presume you are not left-handed?"

"No. I somehow managed to avoid that curse."

"Then we need not worry ourselves further on the subject."

"Thank you, Your Majesty." Diego hadn't expected the absence of most of an arm to be sloughed off so easily. It unnerved him a little. He hesitated before raising another qualm. "I wonder," he said, "if Your Majesty has not also noticed the colour of my skin?"

"You mean that you are brown skinned? An Indian?"

Spoken without hesitation, as if these were niggling matters not worthy of consideration.

"Not Indian," Diego said. "Mestizo. Half Indian, half European."

"Very well. Mestizo then. I'm not sure I see your point."

"What I mean to say," said Diego, "is . . . I mean . . . would you not prefer someone who—"

"Is white? Is that what you mean?"

Diego nodded.

"What? One of these puffed-up creoles who call themselves Mexican? Dear God, they appall me, and I only just got here. No. Please. I beg of you. Spare me that."

What next ensued was a discussion of Diego's duties, should he accept the position. Mention was made of likely remuneration—an other-worldly sum. In the end, Diego begged leave to consider the matter. He would provide his answer in two days, three at most. He rose to his feet. "Your Majesty . . ."

Again the emperor arched his eyebrows. "Yes?"

"I have another question." Diego swallowed with some difficulty, his throat exceedingly dry. He said, "Why me?"

The man smiled. "Why you? Well, Chapultepec Castle, for one thing. Let's not pretend otherwise. It was a recommendation that showed great discernment. We expect to decamp for the palace in a matter of days. The women, especially, are in raptures. Besides, you are Mexican. You can explain things to me—customs, habits, principles, and beliefs. Moreover, you speak French, which is an immense help, given the state of my Spanish. Finally, your dress."

"My dress?" said Diego. "Oh—*charro.*"

"Eh?"

"Charro, Your Majesty. It's our name for this style of clothing."

The stamped boots. The tight-fitting pantaloons, sometimes with spangles along the seam. The voluminous white blouse. The bolero jacket, sometimes with gold piping on the lapels.

"Charro. I see. Well, I was struck by it at once, that first time I saw you. In Veracruz, I think. No one else was dressed this way."

"No," said Diego. "It is less common now than before, for obvious reasons."

"Obvious? Why 'obvious'?"

"It is the way liberals dress."

"Explain."

"Mexico's liberals have mostly fled to the north, you see. With Benito Juárez. Or many of them have."

Maximiliano tilted his head. "And so I take this to mean that you are a liberal too?"

"Yes, Your Majesty."

"A happy coincidence then." The man smiled, revealing the yellow stains on his teeth. "For I may be counted as a liberal myself."

CHAPTER 12

In former times, Diego and Baldemar Peralta would often spend their nights at the cockfighting pit at San Antonio de las Cuevas, roaring with the other misfits who crowded onto the sagging wooden stands. It was a notorious dive, infested with gamblers, loan sharks, prostitutes, and other reprobates. A two-inch bog of sawdust, urine, vomit, and spittle carpeted the rotting wooden floor. Hordes of shrieking patrons crowded the perimeter of the ring. They dangled over the railings, beating their fists in the air and crying for blood as the fighting cocks tore each other to pieces. This was his and Baldemar's agreed-upon meeting place.

Diego knew he would find Baldemar here eventually, and eventually he did. But at first he barely recognized his old friend, who materialized through a dense fog of cigar smoke and evaporating sweat. For one thing, Baldemar lacked his customary wire-rimmed spectacles. His hair was long and stringy, his jaw grizzled by a patchy beard. Corpulent most of his life, he was now shockingly thin. Meanwhile, some kind of rash inflamed his neck and what could be seen of his forearms. He made a pitiful sight, but Diego recognized him all the same, and his spirits lifted at once.

He hurried over, pushing his way through the crush of reeking flesh that crammed every corner of the dank and fetid place. He set his still-bruised hand on Baldemar's shoulder. The man started. He looked up but at first seemed to recognize nothing. He was practically blind without his spectacles.

"Calm yourself, *mano*," Diego said. "It's me."

Baldemar was convulsed by a fit of coughing. His insides rattled aloud, as though his ribs were bits of scrap metal that had broken loose from his chest. He spat up something and groaned before wiping his lips, shaking his head, and struggling to his feet. He had tears in his eyes, from pain or effort.

"Let's get out of here," he said.

They left right away. The place was too loud, too bloodthirsty, too *loco.* They found their way on foot to a pulquería they knew from years past. Memorias del Futuro, it was called. Soon, they were both slouching at a sway-backed wooden bar in the faint light of a half-dozen tallow candles, quaffing *pulque* from crude irregular glasses, shaped like bottle-bottoms and tinted green.

Diego entrusted some coins to a boy and dispatched him to a taquería nearby with instructions to bring back two servings of *tacos al pastor.* There would be more coins when the food was delivered. The meal arrived in minutes, heaped on a pair of tin plates. The two men tucked in at once, rolling the hot morsels of beef into the warm tortillas, along with chopped tomatoes, onions, and jalapeños. With grease dripping down his scraggly beard, Baldemar recounted his ordeal in the Martinica. When he reached the part about refusing the initial pardon, Diego shook his head.

"Idiot," he said.

Baldemar wiped his beard with the back of his hand. "You'd have done the same."

"I would?"

"Sure. Anyone would."

Diego wasn't so certain, and he suspected Baldemar knew it. He raised his glass of pulque and took a long, slow draft. "You've seen Ángela?"

"You think—?" Baldemar began to cough again. When the fit subsided, he gestured at his miserable frame, from bony shoulders to crumbling boots. "You think I could walk into a hospital looking like this?" He snorted and shook his head. "As a patient, maybe. Otherwise, I'd be wanting a gun. Márquez must have a dozen of his goons stationed around the place, on the lookout for me."

Diego nodded. It was true. He himself had been barred from entering the Hospital de Jesús Nazareno, where Ángela was said to be convalescing from her wound. The hospital was under guard by Mexican soldiers, and it seemed a power struggle was under way. Until three years earlier, it had been the Roman Catholic Church that administered Mexico's hospitals. But, with the liberal reform laws, the state had confiscated most Church properties. Now, with conservatives in the ascendance again, the Church was trying to regain its real estate and its former powers. The army, or some part of it, seemed to be taking the Church's side.

Diego rubbed his jaw, wondering whether to speak of Ángela's son. He finally decided, why not? But it turned out Baldemar knew the story already. He had no more idea of the boy's whereabouts than Diego did. Servants at the house on the Street of the Sad Indian had told Diego that a party of priests had rounded upon the residence the same night Ángela had been shot, and they had carried the child away. They insisted they were acting on Church authority and had waved documents in the air, official-looking papers with red ribbons and seals. Nobody seemed to have any idea where the boy was now.

"I'll bet Labastida knows," said Baldemar. The archbishop. "He's behind this, one way or another."

Diego nursed his drink. Probably Baldemar was right. But he himself didn't know what to make of it. As for Márquez's fate, he told Baldemar what little he knew.

"They're sending him where?"

"Constantinople."

"To do what?"

"Stay out of trouble. Stop shooting people at the opera. That would be a good start."

"He won't go."

"I'm serious. They're sending him."

"I don't believe it."

Diego tried to explain. After the shooting at the opera, Márquez had stood trial. A sort of trial. The entire proceeding was a fraud, of course. The only charge against him was causing a disturbance—a joke in itself—and he'd defended himself with the claim that his gun had discharged by accident, a tendency it had. The magistrate acquitted him on the spot.

"He won't go," said Baldemar. "Or he'll get as far as Veracruz, and then he'll come back. He hates liberals too much to leave. He can't pass up a fight. Besides, he still has to kill me." Baldemar made a face, an oddly boyish expression. "I mean, I tried to kill him."

Diego nursed his drink. It was true. He found it hard to imagine Márquez letting that episode go unavenged. The recollection reminded him of something that had been troubling him ever since Ángela had first told him her brother was in the Martinica, sentenced to die. The truth was, Baldemar had acted alone in his attempt on Márquez. Apart from drunken bravura—boasts that no one could take seriously—he had failed to tell Diego what he had planned, much less enlisted his aid. He put the question now. For God's sake, why not?

Baldemar stared into the darting light of the candle flame. "Because."

A smarter man would have left it there, but he was bound to be stupid. "That's no answer. I mean it. I want to know why."

For a time, Baldemar didn't say a word. Then he sat up straight. He said, "Because I didn't think you'd have the sauce for it. Since you ask."

Diego felt the hackles rise at the back of his neck. He wanted to say something harsh, something that would prove to Baldemar he was wrong. But he stopped himself. This was not an argument he could win. Both men remained where they were, leaning on the wooden bar, contemplating the darkness broken only by uneven patches of candlelight.

After what seemed a reasonable period of silence, Diego announced that the Austrian had offered him a position as his private secretary.

"You're joking."

"I'm not. He likes the way I dress."

"He's a *maricón*?"

"No. He just likes charro. That's not maricón."

"Depends," said Baldemar. He took a swig from his glass, wiped his beard. "So. You're serious."

"I am."

"You a lifelong liberal . . ."

"He claims to be a liberal, too."

"The hell he does."

"Anyway, he offered me the post. His secretary died, of yellow fever. I haven't said whether I'm going to take it."

"But you are."

"I am?"

"Of course. What do you think?"

"In a way, I almost have to. After all, you saved my life once—and now the Austrian has saved yours. Where does that leave me?

"In the man's debt?"

"I guess."

"I don't. It leaves you very useful to our side. That's what it does."

"The liberal side?"

"What else?" Baldemar frowned. "You have to ask?"

"No. I just meant . . . I don't know."

He wanted to say something about the way the Austrian made him feel. In the man's presence, he could almost imagine having two good hands. He could almost envision himself being white of skin, or at least he felt no need to fret about his skin's darkness. It was the same way he'd sometimes felt with Baldemar and even with Ángela. He looked at the ceiling, locked in silence. It was hard to put these feelings into words. He wasn't sure he wanted to.

Baldemar looked up. "Just don't be a sap," he said.

"What do you mean?"

Baldemar sighed. "You know the way you get. All sappy. You see the other side of everything. God, do you see the other side of everything. This time, don't."

"You mean, with the emperor?"

"There you go. He's not an emperor. He's just a fucking maricón with a sorry excuse for a crown. Don't see things his way. That's all I'm trying to tell you. Just don't."

Diego felt his blood running hot. It was the same way he always felt when Baldemar took aim at him. Inevitably, Baldemar won. He was bigger, stronger—or so he'd always been. Right now, Diego could have put his old friend on the floor with one blow from his only hand, already clenched into a fist. He let the muscles relax. He wasn't going to hit anyone. Baldemar was wrong, that was all. But men had been wrong before.

"Fine," he said. "Whatever you say."

The two went back to inspecting the candle glow and the gloom. A small man with a wispy grey moustache replenished their glasses of pulque, scooping the liquid from a shallow tub with the half shell of a calabash.

Diego cleared his throat. "So, what are you going to do?"

Baldemar said he didn't know, but Diego didn't believe him. Surely he'd had plenty of time in the Martinica to plot out what he'd do if and when he got out of the place. One thing was sure, it was bound to involve guns. Diego pulled his Colt repeating pistol from his belt.

"Take it," he said.

"Hijo de puta."

"Go on. Take it. You said you were in want of a gun."

"And you won't be?"

Diego shook his head. "I'll be all right."

Baldemar pondered that for a time. Finally, he said, "A loan. When this is over, you'll get your pistol back." He closed his hand on the revolver and tucked the barrel into his belt. "What happened to your hand?"

"Which one?"

"Ha. That one there. I know all about the other."

"A reaction to circumstances."

Baldemar nodded. It seemed to be all the explanation he needed.

Diego paid the account, and the two men walked out into the cool night. They embraced stiffly and parted company. Emaciated and bedraggled, Baldemar limped off into the darkness. Diego watched him go, watched him dwindle into the shadows and then vanish altogether, the way a memory does. He waited a while, then shrugged and turned and walked the other way.

PART TWO

The Pretty Indian

Chapter 13

"Dear God, what does the man expect of me?" Maximiliano shuddered in exasperation. "These are not the Dark Ages."

It was not yet six o'clock in the morning, and Diego had just read aloud a letter from the newly installed archbishop of Mexico City. Monseñor Labastida was insisting upon an audience with His Majesty. There was little doubt what the man wanted—everything the Church had once possessed and only recently lost.

"Why does he keep hectoring me?" Maximiliano worried at his beard, a sure sign of agitation. "There's nothing to discuss. The separation of church and state is an established principle. Freedom of religion is not a radical idea. Besides, the man's a reptile."

Diego laughed. "I always imagine him as an amphibian myself. A toad."

Now they both laughed.

A month had passed since Diego's acceptance of the Austrian's offer of employment at the imperial court. Nothing could have prepared him for the result. He had expected to be banished to some dark cell located far from the emperor's quarters, where he would transcribe documents, receive dictation, and carry out other mundane duties.

Instead, he was almost always at the Austrian's side. His counsel was sought on nearly every matter of state that came to the emperor's attention. This was far beyond anything he could have imagined. Already, he had outstripped even the Prince of Salm-Salm in the emperor's confidence and was surpassed in influence only by a few of the man's venerable Austrian *confrères*. Any of the Mexican ministers at court—a constellation of conniving and genuflecting men—would have sacrificed his firstborn to gain the degree of impact and intimacy that Diego seemed to enjoy as if by right. They all seethed with jealousy and made no effort to disguise the fact. Salm-Salm pretended to take the new arrangement in stride, but it was clear he was furious at being displaced by anyone at all, much less a brown-skinned youth with a roman nose and just one arm.

Nor was that all. Contrary to his own expectations—indeed, contrary to every conviction he possessed—Diego found himself basking in the emperor's presence. He found he enjoyed the man's company immensely. Their personalities seemed effortlessly compatible. They laughed at similar coincidences, enjoyed the same sorts of jokes, and even saw eye to eye on matters political. It was a strange and remarkable thing, this bond they had formed. Or maybe that was wrong. Maybe it all made sense. Maybe it was just as Salm-Salm had observed: they were both younger brothers, after all.

In some ways, the finest hours of the day were the earliest hours. Sharp at four o'clock each weekday morning, both men were out of bed and ready to start work. Granted, at the outset, this required some accommodation on Diego's part. He had to curb his drinking, for one thing—something he managed with far less difficulty than he would have thought. He also had to get to bed much earlier than was his custom. But he prevailed upon himself to adjust.

Each weekday morning, in the deepest hours of the *madrugada*, he made his way to the emperor's private quarters, where they laboured together, reading correspondence, drafting replies, and exhaustively discussing the most pressing matters of the day, while Grill, the emperor's Austrian valet, plied them both with cups of hot chocolate and the sugary Viennese biscuits that Maximiliano adored. No one interrupted them during these long daily sojourns, which extended until seven o'clock in the morning, and undoubtedly it was these marathon sessions that most aroused the ire of those who competed for the emperor's favour.

Diego loved these early hours. Yes, Maximiliano was a foreigner. Yes, he was a monarch imposed upon Mexico by an occupying power to lead a conservative regime. But the man truly seemed a liberal at heart, and he reviled the stalwarts of the old guard—men such as Labastida and Márquez—as thoroughly as Diego did. His goal, he said, was to unite this divided land, to forge a common cause between conservatives and liberals, and to bring peace through order. As much as he detested conservatives, Diego found that he was coming around to the same way of thinking. The emperor's enthusiasm had rubbed off on him. Either Mexicans would embrace each other or the country would tear itself apart.

"Even so," said the emperor, who was still on the subject of the archbishop and his demand for an audience, "it might be wise to mollify the man. It's just that I'd rather not do it myself. I don't think I can bear the cologne—or the gas."

The archbishop was notorious for his flatulence.

Maximiliano stroked his beard, a sign that he was thinking. At length he spoke. "What if we ask Charlotte to take this on? She's always looking for more to do."

"Labastida cannot abide the presence of women," said Diego.

"All the better," said the emperor. "This way, perhaps he'll leave us alone."

"Perhaps."

Maximiliano fell silent again. He shook his head, reached for a Viennese biscuit, and bit it in half. "We shall see," he said. "For the nonce, I propose to take the matter under advisement."

Under advisement. It was one of the man's pet expressions and generally meant that the subject in question would be deferred until it could be deferred no longer. Maybe, in this instance, it was for the best.

Maximiliano swallowed the rest of his biscuit, then slapped his hands together. "So," he said, "what's next on the agenda?"

"A letter from the Italian ambassador, Your Majesty. He wishes to present his credentials, signed by King Victor Emmanuel."

"Splendid news. You'll set it up then, Serrano?"

"Yes."

The emperor looked at him askance. "'Yes'?"

"I mean, yes, Your Majesty."

Maximiliano laughed and shook his head. "Bloody republican . . ."

They both laughed.

It sometimes seemed to Diego that Maximiliano embodied all that Mexico lacked. He was a creature of precise habits, a man who was forever revising and adding to lists—lists of personal resolutions, lists of rules for proper conduct. He insisted that the finer details of any enterprise were the key to its success. No strategy could succeed that was based on defective tactics. And so he tinkered constantly. Rarely a week went by that he did not sack at least one of his ministers, appointing another in his place. He insisted on being kept abreast of even the most minute matters of state. He worked frantically.

On this morning, as on others, the two men eventually accumulated such a quantity of documents and letters that the papers spilled over the desk and across an adjoining work table, leaving many more leaves to be arranged on the carpet.

The emperor frowned and set his cup and saucer down in a small clearing on his desk. He said, "About the opera singer . . ."

"Ángela Peralta."

"Yes. I wonder, what is her present state?"

To the best of Diego's knowledge, Ángela was still being held under guard at the Hospital de Jesús Nazareno. Her life was no longer in danger, or so he had been informed by Salm-Salm. Diego had not yet been permitted to visit Ángela himself.

"I see." The emperor straightened a stack of papers. "Look in on her, would you? And report back to me."

"It might be difficult. The place is under guard round the clock. I have tried I don't know how many times, but they would not allow me near the entrance. It seems they won't allow anyone."

"They allow Salm-Salm."

It was true—Salm-Salm disguised as Father Fischer. Diego wondered whether Labastida and other members of the Church hierarchy knew the prince's real identity. He wondered whether he knew it himself.

"You are aware," said the emperor, "that the woman has a son? An infant?"

Diego grimaced and said that, yes, he understood this to be so.

"Look into that as well, would you? The child's whereabouts. I'm sure that Salm-Salm knows, but he insists that he does not."

Shortly before seven o'clock, Maximiliano's valet reappeared to attend to his master's toilette, while Diego and the emperor worked through the last of the morning's correspondence.

Later, the two men set off on a hack through the nearby countryside. Normally, they enjoyed the company of several others—various officials of the court or even the empress. Sometimes Salm-Salm would join them. On this occasion, however, they rode alone, followed at some distance by a pair of grooms and a palace guard composed of half a dozen hussars. Together, they explored the forests and sprawling grasslands of Chapultepec and then rode along the Avenida de la Viga out to the canals of Xochimilco, where Indian women paddled their dugout canoes smothered in flowers, in sweet peas, double poppies, blue bottles, gillyflowers, and roses. Diego prided himself on knowing the names of things, a remnant of his former life as a poet.

As was usual on such outings, the emperor eschewed all talk of statecraft and grand affairs, contenting himself instead with banter about the weather, or observations about their physical surroundings, or gossip about members of the imperial court. There was a time for serious discussion, said Maximiliano, and a time to speak of simpler matters. As always, he sought to govern himself with rules and order. To Diego, this kind of discipline was unknown. He had never experienced anything of the sort. No doubt the emperor's approach was the product of his European heritage and the high station to which he'd been born. After only a month in the man's presence, Diego had revised his own thoughts on many subjects, sometimes dramatically. He now believed it possible that the forty-odd years of Mexican independence had been a mistake, not in conception but in the breech. The country had endured four decades of torment, death, and folly. Might they not have been avoided if only Mexicans had sought out a high-born European from the outset, someone to act as monarch, to embody the nation's ideals and resolve its contradictions? He didn't know the answer. But he did pose the question.

Either way, the emperor had come late, but at least he had come. In his presence, Diego almost forgot that he was a mestizo with just one arm.

"Come," said the emperor. He dug the heels of his stamped boots into the flanks of his favourite mount, the docile Anteburro. "We have work to do."

His horse broke into a canter, and Diego hurried to catch up. The sun was already high, and the morning chill had vanished. Both dressed in charro, the two men galloped toward Chapultepec. It was only a little past eight o'clock in the morning, and the day had barely begun.

Chapter 14

"I want to talk about Juárez," said the emperor.

He and Diego were seated in a polished black carriage that rocked along the rutted trail leading from Chapultepec Castle toward Mexico City. Among his many other projects, Maximiliano planned to build a grand thoroughfare along the route, an opulent boulevard that would rival even the Champs Élysées in Paris.

"Juárez? Yes, Your Majesty. What about him?"

"I'm just thinking how remarkable it is—a pure-bred Indian, elected president in a country where Indians are treated worse than beasts of the field. It really is a remarkable thing . . . as you yourself must know—I mean, as well as anyone."

"But I am mestizo, Your Majesty. Not Indian. These are different things."

"But your mother was Indian?"

"Yes."

It was clear the emperor made little distinction. Either a man was white or he was not. This was a common perception among Europeans and white-skinned Mexicans alike. Normally, Diego abhorred this view. He resented being lumped in with people who had no European blood whatsoever—but he understood that Maximiliano intended no insult.

He returned his attention to the emperor, who was outlining yet again his formula for bringing peace to Mexico. First, he must establish a dialogue with Benito Juárez, who still claimed the Mexican presidency from his redoubt in the north. If he and Juárez could talk to each other face to face, the emperor said, he was sure that good sense would prevail and they would come to an understanding. Think how many lives might be saved if he and his Mexican counterpart could form an alliance. He, Maximilian, would rule as the sovereign, with Juárez as his prime minister, and the people would make common cause behind them. Mexico would be united—united and independent. He asked Diego for his opinion.

Diego weighed his words carefully before replying. He said that, according to the most recent news, the liberal rump under Juárez had been forced to decamp from its provisional capital at San Luis Potosí and had withdrawn even further to the north, to Monterrey. It would be possible theoretically to send a messenger to cover that distance, but the man would be obliged to traverse rough and perilous lands. As likely as not, he would be robbed and murdered during his journey. If he somehow managed to reach the liberal outpost, he stood an excellent chance of being identified as a conservative and therefore assassinated.

"I see," said the emperor. He pursed his lips and frowned, then looked up. He said he wished to make the effort all the same. There was no choice, not if he meant to end the war.

Diego nodded. "Very well, Your Majesty. I will draft the necessary documents."

And the carriage bore them into the city.

That afternoon, the two men conducted an inspection tour of the capital, a mission the emperor undertook once a week or so. Maximiliano considered the streets to be in a pitiable condition, and he liked to travel at random, with no fixed route, in search of deficiencies that demanded replacement or repair. As they proceeded from one street to the next, he dictated a catalogue of needed improvements.

The emperor was particularly concerned with improving the circulation of traffic. He meant to realign dozens of roadways and to beautify them in the process. He wished the newly plotted streets to be shaded by *fresno* trees. Steel tracks would be installed along the middle lanes, where tramcars would travel, at first drawn by mules—*faute de mieux*—but eventually powered by steam engines imported from England. He desired that the aqueducts be thoroughly dredged. Where they were crumbling, they must be rebuilt. He was determined as well that a proper system of refuse collection be instituted. He particularly meant to end the disgusting Mexican practice of tipping waste water and night soil directly into the street.

Now the emperor looked out the carriage window at the passing scenery—the usual Mexico City bedlam. "I grow tired of this chaos," he said, his voice suddenly reedy and sad.

"I'm not surprised. We all do."

"As emperor, I find it especially wearying. I have seen more than enough of what is wrong with this country. Surely there is something that is right."

Diego said nothing.

"Serrano?"

"I'm thinking."

He did not need to think for long. It so happened that this was the fourteenth day of August—the day of the Assumption of the Virgin Mary. In Mexico, it was a rare day that wasn't holy for some reason, and Diego had an idea. It would involve an unexpected detour and some unanticipated travel. But, if His Majesty wished to see Mexico at its finest, then perhaps the inconvenience would prove justified. The emperor agreed at once.

At his orders, the imperial carriage and its guard of hussars lurched to a halt and reversed direction. They soon departed Mexico City to the south, lumbering along a not altogether unrecognizable excuse for a road that wound its way toward Coyoacán, an Indian village ten or so kilometres from the capital.

"And what shall we find in this place?" said Maximiliano.

"*Cohetes*, Your Majesty."

"I'm sorry?"

"Rockets."

And so it was. The day of the Assumption of the Virgin Mary was a well-known holiday in Coyoacán, and that meant rockets and fireworks and dancing and rockets and lights. And yet more rockets. The fiesta did not properly begin until darkness had fallen. By then, a combination of torches, stars, and a gibbous moon illuminated the night. When the people of Coyoacán learned that an emperor—*an emperor?*—was in their midst, they quickly accommodated themselves to this unexpected circumstance. They improvised a sort of throne, using a chair made of Mexican hardwood, and insisted that Maximiliano install himself there, across from the ancient parish church of San Juan Bautista.

Before long, Indian men and women approached Maximiliano, one by one, to bow and offer gifts of flowers and food. They knelt upon the cobbles, whispering to him in Nahuatl, their ancient tongue. They made the sign of the cross against their breasts, put tobacco before him, lit candles, splashed *aguardiente* onto the ground, drizzling the liquid from tarnished old bottles while reciting incantations in low, sibilant whispers.

The emperor motioned for Diego. "What are they saying?"

"I don't know, Your Majesty."

"You don't speak their language?"

"A few words. Nothing more."

"I thought you were Mexican," said Maximiliano. "Surely I was led to believe that you were."

"Yes, Your Majesty," said Diego. The truth was, he spoke only a little Nahuatl, even though it had been his mother's first language. To him, it had always seemed to be a low patois, an embarrassment. Now he wondered.

As for the rockets, Diego's prediction was borne out in spades. Before long, the projectiles darted into the purple sky, exploding in luminous shards that toppled back to earth. Next, some of the men fired into the crowd with *buscapiés*—literally, feet-seekers—missiles that swerved and veered in their flight, skittering along the cobbles. Everyone danced and leapt about—the men, the women, and the children too—all careening back and forth, and from side to side, laughing and shrieking, desperate to escape the rockets and yet delighting in the excitement.

Soon enough, a party of men coaxed Maximiliano from his makeshift throne and prevailed upon him to enter the thick of the crowd, where he, too, was enveloped by the explosions of sparks, smoke, and colour. He, too, clapped and cheered. He, too, scrambled out of the way to escape the *buscapiés*, laughing and waving his arms.

From the edge of the crowd, Diego watched the scene, focusing especially on Maximiliano. By rights, the emperor ought to have seemed absurd. Anyone else in his place would surely have made a ridiculous spectacle. And yet, somehow, he did not seem ridiculous at all. There was a strangely dignified aspect to his demeanour, the ease with which he gave himself over to the serious business of amusement. There was something almost childlike in his bearing, coupled with an undeniable quality of nobility. To Diego, it seemed a rare combination—to partake of foolishness while keeping one's dignity intact. To him, the emperor seemed all the more impressive for taking part in these games, and he was certainly good at it. He moved with surprising agility and often saved not only himself but also one or another young child, whom he plucked up by the collar, clearing the path for yet another sprinting rocket. Each time, he put back his head and laughed out loud, grateful to have survived the volley, or overwhelmed by the glory of the moment.

Diego watched as a tall figure stalked out from the church, his skin the colour of polished mahogany. He wore an elaborate headpiece made of woven saplings and affixed with a bevy of miniature firecrackers. Someone used a burning stick of wood to set the device alight, and the bizarre helmet soon began to sizzle, flare, whirl, and explode. The man danced through the crowd, clutching his flaming headdress with both hands as flames shot from his head. The children were both terrified and amazed, running away shrieking and then gingerly creeping back, only to dart away again. As soon as the first man exhausted his supply of fireworks, another hurried out from the church to replace him, his helmet also aflame. Soon, he was replaced by another. Then another. And another after that.

Eventually, someone climbed onto the church's high, slanting roof to light a multitude of fuses that had already been assembled there. Before long, a glistening wall of fireworks cascaded down the church's cracked and hoary facade, like a glimmering waterfall of light. Maximiliano grasped the hands of strangers—whoever happened to be at his side—and he watched with his eyes wide and his mouth agape, seemingly as transfixed as the others by this inexplicable pleasure, this iridescent river of fire splashing down from the eaves of the church.

Weeks later, the emperor would still be talking about that night, still exhilarated by what he had seen and felt. He would tell Diego more than once that he had experienced an unforgettable sensation, one he had never even imagined before. He struggled to describe it—*an awakening of the soul.* That was the phrase he used. It had struck him that night, he said, that a sovereign must not stand apart from his people, or not as a matter of course. There were times when he must go among them, to eat what they ate, sing their songs, know their sorrows, share their joys. He said he had never considered matters in this light before. "That evening in Coyoacán," he said, "I felt connected to the common folk in a way I had never known before. There is a bond between us, a force that unites us."

But these reflections came later. Now it seemed the fiesta in Coyoacán had reached its conclusion, and the emperor ordered his small party to return to Chapultepec. Exhausted by the evening's exertions, Maximiliano sprawled across the rear seat of the carriage. He said little but merely gazed out the window at the passing scenery, illuminated by the pewter light of the stars and the moon. He smiled all the while, and Diego wondered what was going through his mind. Perhaps he was taking the full measure of his new-found life, so far from his former home. To think that this was his empire, that these were his people, that he was their lord.

After a time, the emperor roused himself and leaned forward. "All of the preparations are in place, I take it, for tomorrow's fiesta?" he said.

Maximilian was to preside the following evening at a banquet at Chapultepec in honour of General Márquez, who was soon to depart for the Near Orient.

"I believe so, Your Majesty." Diego did not plan to attend. He would rather cut off his remaining arm.

"Dear God," said the emperor. "This Márquez. We'll be well rid of him."

"I couldn't agree more, Your Majesty. The Tiger of Tacubaya, they call him."

"So I've heard. Do you know why?"

"Yes. In fact, I lost my arm there."

"Did you? You must tell me the story one day."

Diego agreed that one day he would, but not today. Not tonight. Tonight, he preferred to think of pleasanter things, of the moon dangling in a purple sky above the parish church of San Juan Bautista, of Maximiliano dancing amid a shower of fireworks in the plaza of Coyoacán, and of the soporific rocking motion of the carriage as it bore them both toward Chapultepec and home.

CHAPTER 15

DIEGO LED HIS HORSE from the stables at Chapultepec and out into the open court. He climbed onto a mounting post and swung himself into the saddle, gathered the reins, and rode out into the night, wanting only to put as much distance as possible between himself and General Márquez. He meant to spend the evening in Mexico City, near the Plaza Santa Cecilia, in search of company and amusement there, an antidote to hideous memories: Ángela collapsed upon a stage, blood soaking through her blouse; or images of that day, high in the blue mountains of Michoacán, when he and Baldemar came upon the inverted corpse of Melchor Ocampo. The waxing moon cast a gauzy light across the highland plain, and he rode at an easy lope along the trail toward Mexico City. A cool night wind thrummed through the fresnos, bearing a scent of wood smoke and roasted corn.

He had not travelled more than a league, a matter of twenty minutes or so, when he heard padded hoofbeats behind him. He was being followed—or, no, not followed. He was being overtaken. He dug his heels into his horse's flanks. Just then, a man's voice spoke through the darkness, not a shout but a kind of heightened whisper that seemed to carry unnaturally far.

"Diego Serrano?"

He braced his weight in the saddle and drew back upon the reins. No highwayman out here was likely to know his name. Besides, if there was to be a fight, better to stand and make a fist of it than to be shot in the back as he fled. He swung his horse around and halted, waiting as a lone rider approached through the moon-washed darkness. The stranger slowed his horse as he drew close. He wore a woollen *serape* against the chill and now briefly removed his sombrero in a strangely formal gesture of salutation. Diego glimpsed a long, sad face with a high forehead, a dark moustache, and a long scar that ran down the man's left cheek. He guessed him to be in his middle thirties—and then realized he knew this man. It was Octavio, the thief who had robbed him of his clothes and money during the journey back from Veracruz. Even in this dim light, he felt sure of it.

But if the intruder recognized Diego, he gave no sign. Probably he had robbed too many men to be able to keep track of them individually, even those possessed of only a single complete arm. Instead, he nodded back toward the darkness behind him and said he had ridden a great distance with an important mission and wished to speak to Diego Serrano and no other. He had been waiting for more than two days, on the assurance that such a person would emerge from Chapultepec eventually and would most likely be alone.

"¿Es usted, señor?"

Diego said that he was the man so named.

"If that is so, señor, then you will be able to answer a question I have been instructed to pose."

"Which is?"

Octavio cleared his throat and spoke from memory. "To whom belonged the knife that cut down the body of Melchor Ocampo, when that brave man was found dangling by his ankles, dead?"

Diego felt his spine relax. This man brought a message from Baldemar. He gazed around in relief. The darkness was punctured here and there by the flickering light of distant cooking fires, just visible through the shifting branches of oak and fresno trees. He turned back to the man in the serape.

"The knife that cut down the body of Ocampo," he said, "belonged to Baldemar Felipe Peralta."

"So I have been informed. I was also informed that no one but Diego Serrano would know this."

Diego smiled. He said, "Were you also informed that I would be missing the better part of an arm?"

"*Sí, señor.* I am sorry to find it so."

"I wonder, how many one-armed Mexicans are apt to pass this way on any given night, riding alone?"

Instead of replying, the rider fumbled beneath his serape. From the folds of his clothing, he produced a cheroot, which he offered to Diego.

"I have brought a message for you," he said. "Please, open it, señor."

"Open the cheroot?"

"Yes. It contains a message."

Diego looped the reins over the stump of his left arm and used his one good hand to peel back the leaves of tobacco until he found a scrap of rough paper concealed inside. It was too dark to make out whatever words were written on it.

"In my left pocket," he said, "there are several *fósforos.* Please. Take one. Light it."

The rider did as instructed. He sparked the tip of the match with his thumbnail and leaned closer. Diego squinted at the wrinkled slip of paper. He thought he recognized the awkward, childish script of his old friend and, in the narrow glow, he was able to read what it said: *When does the Tiger leave Mexico City and by what route?*

That was all. Diego touched the scrap of paper to the match's flame and let it burn till only a cinder was left.

"I know you," he said. "You and another—you stole my clothes near Paso del Macho."

"Es muy posible, señor."

"You don't remember?"

"What I remember, señor, depends."

It was certainly the same man. "Depends on what?"

"On why I am being asked."

"I just wondered—that's all. I thought you would remember stealing the clothing of a one-armed man."

"Sí, señor."

"You do remember."

"Sí."

"You mentioned some comrades of yours. Sánchez, Quiñones, and Rivera. They were in the Martinica with Baldemar Peralta?"

"Así fue."

"And they were sentenced to death?"

"Flogging first. Then death. They and a quantity of others."

"And now they are free?"

"Así es."

"Thanks to Baldemar."

"*Sí.* But we call him el Gordo."

"Because he is so thin."

"Sí."

"And now you are all together?"

"Así es."

Diego nodded. And now they would finish the job that el Gordo had bungled so badly on his own. He cleared his throat. "In three days," he said. "By Puebla and Orizaba."

The man repeated the words aloud.

Diego nodded, satisfied. "Your name is Octavio?" he said.

"Sometimes."

Diego smiled and asked the man to convey his greetings to el Gordo.

The man touched the fingers of his right hand to the brow of his sombrero. "*Gracias, señor. Que le vaya bien.*" He reined his horse around and set off at a bounding stride, soon vanishing into the darkness.

Diego considered resuming his ride to Mexico City. But it seemed he had lost his hankering for lights and amusement. He was more concerned with what he had just done. He reached into the breast pocket of his blouse, rooted out a *puro,* one of several there. With the reins still looped over the stump of his arm, he lit the cigar, took a long pull that filled his lungs. He released the smoke slowly, watched it twist and glint, faintly silver, in the moonlight. So this is how, in time of war, a one-armed turncoat becomes a spy. He served two masters now, and the realization made him wonder which of the two he would betray in the end.

He dug in his heels and set off at an easy gait back toward Chapultepec, the cigar still clenched between his teeth—a flicker of light and a four-legged shadow floating through the highland darkness.

Chapter 16

"You require permission," said the soldier, one of several Mexican troops posted near the entrance to the Hospital de Jesús Nazareno. "No one enters without permission."

"Whose permission?" said Diego.

"El gringo."

"But I have tried. He won't see me."

It was true. Only that morning, he had twice sought to gain entrance to the cathedral in order to confront Salm-Salm. Salm-Salm was said to have an office somewhere in the temple. Twice, Diego had been denied admission. Now he was trying to make a direct assault on the hospital—and he would do it, too, if only he could find his way past this one miserable excuse for a soldier.

The poor fellow didn't look like much, outfitted in a mismatched uniform whose threadbare tunic was missing several buttons. His boots seemed about to shrivel into various worthless shreds, and he carried a black powder musket with a damaged bayonet, slung from one shoulder by a length of twine. Diego doubted the weapon would shoot. He had half a mind to make a run for it—first push his way past and then keep on going till he reached the hospital, only a short sprint away. But more soldiers were loitering in front of the ancient building, and it was evident he stood no chance. He decided he would seek out the archbishop instead.

He reminded himself that he was acting solely out of a sense of duty—the emperor had asked him to make inquiries as to Ángela's health, to see how the woman was faring after her injury. He was also to assess her emotional condition, particularly as it involved her son. Diego knew what that meant.

"You mean, whether she would consent to his adoption?"

The emperor had nodded. "Just so."

Diego wondered why Maximiliano did not obtain this intelligence from Salm-Salm directly. After all, the prince was in the best position to know. But it seemed the emperor did not quite trust the German.

"He pretends to enjoy a degree of intimacy with me that I do not consider he has earned," Maximiliano had said. "I wish to proceed with caution."

For this reason, he was assigning Diego the task of sorting through the morass of personal and political complications involved in such a delicate enterprise—the adoption of an heir. He most particularly wished to avoid any action that might raise Charlotte's hopes, unless there was good reason to believe those hopes would be realized. She was desperate for a child.

Diego knew this to be true. Not long after taking up residence at Chapultepec, he had accompanied the emperor and empress on an early morning ride that had taken them further afield than planned. Bombelles was among the party, along with Doktor Basch, the emperor's physician, and the Count and Countess Kollonitz, both members of the imperial retinue and intimates of the emperor and empress. The usual hussar guard followed behind. Eventually, they had reached a private estate called La Hacienda de los Morales, where they were served an impromptu breakfast by a small army of servants. The owners were absent for a time.

The meal was followed by several rounds of pulque flavoured with a variety of succulent fruits, and the unfamiliar libation had pleased everyone, the women as much as the men. As they prepared to depart, the emperor and his companions all gave repeated thanks to the servants. It was then that a young girl approached, all alone. She was a small Indian child, no doubt a daughter of one of the servants, and could not have been more than six years old. She wore an embroidered blouse over a narrow cotton skirt. Her dark, liquid eyes were almost preternaturally large.

Holding a bouquet of scarlet roses, she first curtseyed and then knelt before the empress. She looked up, raised her arms, and proffered the bouquet. "*Son para usted.*"

For several moments, Carlota seemed on the verge of tears. Then the tears broke, and she wept openly before recovering her composure. She bent down to receive the flowers from the girl. The child then rose onto her small bare feet, pressed her palms together in an attitude of prayer, and slowly backed away, never removing her gaze from the empress's eyes. Carlota straightened up, still clutching the bouquet. For a time, she remained still, taking slow, deep breaths.

"My dear . . ." said the emperor, but his voiced trailed off as his wife burst into tears again, deep, wracking sobs that seemed to surge from the depths of her soul.

Later, during the return to Chapultepec, the empress guided her horse alongside Countess Kollonitz, and both of them kept a little separate from the others, their heads bowed together, conferring in whispers. The emperor smoked a succession of cigarettes and said little as the party made its uneasy way back to the castle at Chapultepec.

It was clear to Diego that both the emperor and his wife longed for an heir, albeit for different reasons. He would not have considered acting on Their Majesties' behalf on this matter, not as long as Baldemar remained a prisoner. But his old friend was again a free man, and Ángela could choose what she would do. He was fairly certain what that choice would be, but he saw no harm any longer in putting the question. The empress had been so forlorn, so wracked by sorrow. And so it was he now found himself outside the Hospital de Jesús Nazareno, feeling useless. He saw there was no hope of gaining access to Ángela by this route. So, instead, he returned to the Imperial Palace and drafted a message to the Most Reverend Pelagio Antonio de Labastida y Dávalos, archbishop of Mexico City. He dispatched it by messenger. It was written on the emperor's vellum stock and sealed in wax with the emperor's emblem. He had little doubt that a reply would be received in short order, for the archbishop would almost certainly conclude that the subject for discussion would be the detested reform laws.

This was duplicity, but it worked. Within two hours, he received a reply inviting him to meet the prelate at once. The old palace of the archbishopric on the calle de la Moneda was in disuse, having been seized under the anti-clerical reforms, along with so many other Church properties. Just like all the rest, it too had then been looted and trashed. The meeting would instead take place at the man's temporary offices not far from the Zócalo.

Diego set off on foot and before long was being ushered directly into the chambers of the archbishop. A novitiate who could not have been more than fourteen years of age announced him and then quickly withdrew. The large oaken doors closed with a definitive thud. Diego gazed around, then took a couple of paces forward. When he saw the archbishop, he halted, unsure what to do. Labastida remained seated at a broad wooden desk, glowering and silent.

Eventually, he looked up. He invited Diego to be seated, indicating the appropriate chair with a wave of a white silk handkerchief that reeked of lavender. He observed his visitor for a time, then frowned. "What in God's name has become of your arm?"

"A reaction to circumstances, Your Excellency."

"I beg your pardon?"

"A war wound."

"Amputated?"

"It was."

"Perhaps in Paradise you shall recover it. Perhaps that is your destiny."

"Perhaps."

"You must pray for such an outcome. The Heavenly Father will hear you. He will provide."

"Thank you."

"So. What have you come to see us about? These demonic laws, I take it. Reform laws, they call them. Deformed laws, I say."

Diego said he was not authorized to enter into discussions concerning relations between church and state. He had come for another purpose.

"Another purpose?"

"Yes. I should have explained myself more clearly. I—"

"Another *purpose*?" Much louder this time. "I don't understand. What other purpose could there possibly be?"

Diego explained that he had come in hopes of arranging a visit with Ángela Peralta at the Hospital de Jesús Nazareno, but the archbishop did not seem to be listening. Instead, he was shaking his large, ponderous head back and forth like a pendulum and running his handkerchief across his brow, over and over. When he finally spoke, it was almost possible to detect the capital letters formed by the tone of his voice.

He said he did not believe there was any subject worthy of discussion apart from the bestial injustice of the reform laws. He had expected the French to put matters right. But nothing had been done. He peered at Diego. His eyes were watery and red, and yet they seemed to burn with intensity. "So we have been obliged to strengthen our hand, as it were."

It was clear what he meant. He meant Ángela, and he meant her son.

"You propose a bargain, Your Excellency?" said Diego.

"That is a rather blunt term," said Labastida. He pressed his handkerchief to his lips.

"But not mistaken?"

"No. Not mistaken."

"The boy in exchange for the resumption of Church privileges."

"And property."

"I see."

"Forgive me for speaking so plainly. But clear accounts make friendships, as they say." The archbishop smiled. "I take it you will communicate my thoughts on the subject to His Imperial Majesty?"

"Yes," said Diego.

"And reiterate my request for an audience? A private audience?"

"If you wish."

"I do wish. Oh, and please convey my highest regards to the empress."

"Very well."

"Good." The archbishop rubbed his hands together. "Now, to other business." The prelate said a visit to Ángela Peralta could be arranged. He said Diego should first seek out a certain Father Fischer—

Diego broke in to say he had already tried to do so.

"Oh? Without success, I take it."

"Precisely."

"Ah well. Protocol." The archbishop reached for a quill pen, dipped it in a pot of ink, and scribbled on a sheet of vellum. He blotted the paper and handed it to Diego.

"Here. Take this note to Padre Fischer. He can arrange a visit for you, but he requires my authority, of course. Now he will have it. You will find him at the cathedral."

"Thank you." Diego pocketed the document. "Fischer—that sounds German, I think."

"American, they say. From Texas." The prelate smiled again, gazing somewhere to Diego's right. "Off you go, then. And I do trust you will convey the substance of our little talk to His Majesty."

Diego found the so-called Father Fischer at the Metropolitan Cathedral, just as Labastida had said. The note from His Excellency seemed to open all doors. In no time, Diego found himself in the presence of the man—Fischer or Salm-Salm—in a gloomy little cubicle just off the nave of the church.

"I don't understand this," said Diego. "Why are you dressed as a priest?"

"Because I am a priest."

"I think you are not."

"Are you sure?" Salm-Salm settled back into his chair and lit a cigarette with an air of insouciance that did not seem precisely clerical. "To possess just one identity—I find this such a classical notion, so outmoded. I prefer to be more romantic. Besides, I would hardly hold much influence with the Church if I were just a minor European noble without prospects of any kind. Much nicer to be a fellow man of the cloth."

"Who was Padre Fischer then? The real one."

"Oh, a chaplain—an American of German descent. He served with the Confederate forces until his untimely death. I was able to purchase his documents for a nominal fee and—*voilà*." He leaned one elbow on his desk and lowered his voice. "You see how candid I am? I shouldn't be telling you any of this. So, what brings you here?"

Diego produced the archbishop's letter.

Salm-Salm fumbled in his black vestments for a pair of eyeglasses.

"Of course," he said. "You wish to visit La Peralta. I should have known."

"I wonder," said Diego, "what exactly is your position here? With the Church, I mean."

"Oh, nothing specific. Among other things, I serve as confessor to our friend."

"Ángela, you mean."

"The very one." He scrutinized the document once again before clucking his tongue. "Well, I see no objection, now that you have followed proper channels."

The man scribbled a note of authorization and held it out to Diego with an exaggerated flourish. “There you go.”

Diego accepted the document feeling like an idiot—again. To think, as easy as that.

Chapter 17

Ángela looked older, thinner, and frailer. More than a month after the shooting, she was still bedridden, lying supine on a narrow wooden cot in a dark room with stone walls and a single narrow window dissected by a pair of bars that formed an iron cross. Disparate sounds drifted up from the street below, the cries of vendors, the clip-clop of horse hooves, the sudden yapping of dogs.

Meanwhile, Ángela rested on her back, staring at the ceiling. She said she was not permitted to leave.

"It's as if I were in a prison."

Bags drooped beneath her eyes, and her dark hair lay dishevelled on the pillow. Her hands were clasped over her abdomen, her fingers as wizened as sticks. She said it had been more than four weeks since she had seen her son. They refused to tell her where he was. They refused to tell her anything.

Diego took a seat in the only chair, a wobbly piece of furniture with torn webbing. "Who won't tell you?"

"The priests," she said. "None of them will tell me anything. There's one especially—"

"Padre Fischer?"

She nodded. "You've met him, I remember. Dear God. He wants me to give Agustín up for adoption. To become the son of the emperor . . . the Austrian . . . the . . ."

"I know."

"You *know*? *What do you know*?"

"What you're saying. Your son. Adoption. The emperor and his wife are without child, you see. They—"

"Whose concern is that? Not mine. Agustín is *my* son."

"Of course. Yes." He paused. "You knew they released Baldemar?"

"Yes. I saw him."

"You *saw* him? When?"

"Just for a moment. A week ago. Maybe more. I lose track of the days. He managed to sneak in, disguised as a priest of all things. He wanted to take me out of here, but I couldn't leave, not like this. I'm still too weak. And Baldemar—he looked dreadful. He's so thin. I barely recognized him." She paused, dampened her lips with her tongue. It was an effort for her to swallow. "Can you help me, Diego? Can you find my boy?"

Diego said he would try—and he meant it. He would. But first there was something he needed to know. "About your son," he said. "The arrangement that this priest, this Padre Fischer, proposes . . . I wonder, is there any chance . . . any possibility at all . . . I mean—"

"*What?*" She raised herself on one arm, her reedy voice suddenly resonant, strong, though she gasped at the pain this exertion cost her. "What are you saying? You cannot be serious. Diego, not you, of all people. Oh God." She began to weep.

"No, no." Diego extended his good arm, as if fending off some demon. "That's not what I meant. That's not what I meant at all."

It was a feeble denial, but it seemed to calm her a little. He had promised to raise the matter, and now it was done—thank God. He felt like a traitor, for a traitor he was. Meanwhile, Ángela collapsed back on the bed, too weak to support herself any longer. She began to cough, then closed her eyes.

"Just help me," she said in a hoarse whisper, she who possessed the most glorious voice in Mexico. "Just find my son."

"Yes," said Diego. "I will try."

"Not 'try.' Find him. Bring him to me. As soon as you can. Not here, but . . . somewhere."

She struggled to sit up. She turned and looked straight at him. From somewhere deep within, she seemed to summon a portion of her old strength.

"You know," she said, "we can't let them win, the conservatives. It was Márquez who shot me. I saw him. And now it's Labastida and his thugs who are holding me here and who are after my son. They'll do anything to get their way. You know that."

Diego said he did. "But the emperor favours alliances."

"*Alliances?*" She practically spat out the word. Again something of her old vigour welled up. "Alliances with whom? With conservatives? You can't form alliances with them. The Mexican conservative will never be satisfied until he possesses every jot and tittle of wealth and power in this land. God in heaven, you would think the Enlightenment had never occurred. I don't care that they're stupid. What I cannot stomach is the pride they take in their stupidity. Do you think I would surrender my son to serve the interests of these vipers? Dear God, Diego. Find him. Find my son."

She unleashed this diatribe in a steady, powerful voice that recalled the Ángela he knew. But the effort left her drained. Her voice trailed away, and she fell back onto her bed, too exhausted to speak another word.

Diego retrieved his hat, and he left her there.

Diego and the emperor were riding alongside the canals at Xochimilco. It was shortly past eight o'clock in the morning, another brilliant day, with only a slight chill left over from the highland night. Slackening the reins, Maximiliano rubbed his upper arms and torso to get the blood flowing. They were accompanied on this outing by Salm-Salm, who had hastened to join them at the last moment. It was essential, he said, to discuss the matter of Ángela Peralta and her son. The survival of the Second Mexican Empire depended upon it.

"An heir is imperative," he said as they rode through the early sunshine. The subject seemed to be an obsession with him. "It is foolhardy to think otherwise. There is no telling what could befall Your Majesty. Forgive me for saying so, but you could suffer grievous injury at any moment. An attack of food poisoning. A fall from your horse. A wayward bullet. God forbid that any such thing should happen, but it could. You lead a perilous life, and precautions must be taken. I believe you should hold talks on this subject with Labastida."

"What?" Maximilliano snorted. The archbishop wishes only to discuss the reform laws, to have them revoked. He would trade the boy to achieve this purpose, but I will not give in to his demands. This is the year 1864, for God's sake. It's the modern age. We must abide by modern notions. In this, I am in complete agreement with Juárez. The Church has no place meddling in the affairs of the state. In any case, I am in perfect health."

"Pray God you remain so," said Salm-Salm. "But the point is, you may not. Then what?"

"There's Charlotte," said the emperor. "She could govern, if it came to that."

"Of course, Your Majesty. But what of the long term?"

Maximiliano was silent. To Diego, it was clear what Salm-Salm was up to. He meant to use the dilemma of the emperor's childless state to manoeuvre himself back into the centre of the man's confidence.

"I agree this is an important matter," the emperor said. "But we must not act in haste."

Diego broke in. "Our first goal must be to free Ángela. She is the child's mother, after all. As long as Labastida holds her, he holds the upper hand. Besides, it is a breech of justice to detain an individual against his will."

"Well said." The emperor gave his horse an affectionate slap. "But what would you have me do? Order my hussars to storm the place?"

"Surely not," said Salm-Salm, who appeared to take the remark literally. "Such an assault would poison the well for good."

"And so will never take place," said Diego. "That is not the point. The point is, the Church should have no part in this. The Church is no longer entitled to exercise control over hospitals, much less use them as prisons. Those powers were abolished by the reform laws. Labastida has no jurisdiction in this."

The emperor halted his horse. For a time, he gazed out at the view. Presently, he nodded. "I'll consult Bazaine. If he agrees with Serrano here, then we shall order the singer's release. We shall see what cards Labastida holds then."

He clucked his tongue several times and reined his horse around, aiming back toward Chapultepec.

"Come," he said. "We have work to do."

That afternoon, Maximiliano summoned Bazaine to appear before him at the Imperial Palace. After a rote exchange of pleasantries, the Frenchman offered his opinion that the Church was in no way entitled to hold Ángela Peralta against her will, despite her incriminating family ties.

The emperor shifted in his seat and whispered to Diego. "He means her brother, I take it."

"Yes, Your Majesty."

Maximiliano frowned for a time and then looked up. He instructed the French marshal to arrange for the woman's release, by any means necessary. She should be placed under proper medical care but far from the authority of the Church.

Bazaine said it would be done. With his cap tucked beneath one arm, he bowed, saluted, and withdrew.

The next day, the Frenchman returned to the Imperial Palace, this time with news that the singer was no longer to be found at the hospital in question. He was unable to say where she was. Someone had spirited her away before his men had found time to act.

"Someone in the Church, you mean?" said the emperor.

Bazaine shrugged. He assumed as much, but he was quite sure Labastida would deny it. "Somehow they got word," he said. He hesitated. "I have other news."

"Speak," said the emperor. "Out with it. I haven't got all day." He was often short with Bazaine, wishing to make it clear that the sword served the crown, rather than the other way around. "What news?"

Bazaine said that General Márquez had not departed the country as expected. In fact, he had returned to Mexico City. He was here, now. It seemed that on their journey to Veracruz he and his *compadres* had come under attack by a large band of heavily armed men led by none other than Baldemar Peralta.

"I speak of the man Your Majesty pardoned only short weeks ago," said Bazaine. "The—"

"Yes, yes," said Maximiliano. He scribbled at the air with his cigarette. "I know who he is."

"And now Márquez refuses to leave Mexico."

"On what grounds?"

"This is a rough country, Your Majesty. They have their own codes, these Mexicans."

The emperor nodded. "Yes, yes. But how dare he refuse a direct order? He is under instructions to proceed to Constantinople. Far from here."

"Let me repeat," said Bazaine. "The perpetrator of this attack was

Baldemar Peralta." The Frenchman hesitated, ran his tongue across his upper teeth. "Baldemar Peralta—the very man Your Majesty pardoned that night at the Imperial Theatre, along with a dozen others."

"I am aware of it," said Maximiliano. "You don't have to keep telling me."

"Ah," said Bazaine. "But surely that is the point, Your Majesty. It seems that I do."

The room fell silent. Several guards and palace aides stopped what they were doing, stunned at this sudden impertinence. How would the emperor respond?

Maximiliano ground out his cigarette. He moved his lips from side to side, as if unsure whether to swallow something he'd just put in his mouth, something that didn't seem quite right.

"Well," he said at last. "I leave the matter in your hands then."

"The matter of General Márquez?"

"Yes. Exactly."

"And what of the singer?"

Maximiliano shrugged. "Find her," he said. "If you can."

"Yes, Your Majesty." The Frenchman gave the briefest imitation of a bow and withdrew.

The following morning, at the end of their customary ride, the emperor informed Diego that he planned to depart the capital in order pay a visit to Cuernavaca, a town located a day's journey to the southwest. On Salm-Salm's advice, he had lately purchased a house there, sight unseen, and was having the place restored.

At the palace stable, they handed their horses off to a team of grooms. Once again, Salm-Salm had joined them.

Cuernavaca? Diego knew the town. Once the favoured resort of Aztec nobles, it occupied a lower altitude than the capital and enjoyed a more equable climate. It seemed this prospect carried particular weight with the emperor, who disliked the nighttime coolness and early morning chill frequently experienced in Mexico City.

Maximiliano said he wished to see first-hand how work was proceeding. He also wanted to learn something of the town, where he hoped to spend substantial portions of his time in future. Salm-Salm was among those invited, of course, and Diego would be expected to make the trek as well. The mail would be delivered by special courier at least once a day, and the party would be absent from Mexico City for a week at most.

"Thank you, Your Majesty," said Salm-Salm. "You are too generous, too kind. And, ah, may I see you for a moment? In private?"

"Why, yes," said the emperor. "Of course. Walk with me to my chambers." He glanced at Diego. "*Hasta mañana*, then, Serrano."

"Yes, Your Majesty. Until tomorrow."

There was a new distance in the emperor's manner, which Diego attributed to Salm-Salm and his machinations. He wondered what calumnies the man was spreading, what gossip and lies. But, just now, Diego had other matters to consider and other places to be. They included the cockpit at San Antonio de las Cuevas. He had a suspicion that el Gordo might show himself there.

CHAPTER 18

THE COCKPIT WAS AS raucous as ever, as chaotic, as disreputable. Diego skulked about the place for nearly two hours, observing the bloodshed and mayhem, dodging the spittle and bile, but he did not set eyes upon Baldemar Peralta. Finally, he'd had enough. He drained the last of a watery beer and left.

Out on the street, in the cool darkness, a beggar accosted him, pleading for alms.

"*Por Dios,*" the man moaned, his hand outstretched. "*Por Dios, señor.*"

Diego was about to turn away and continue on foot to the livery stable where he'd entrusted his horse but something about the beggar's voice stopped him. He swung around.

Immediately, the wretch began to laugh. It was Baldemar, of course.

Before long, the two men slumped into their seats at Memorias del Futuro, and were soon quaffing pulque from large green-tinted jars. Baldemar still looked woebegone, his clothes hanging from him like washing on a line.

Diego recounted what he'd learned about Ángela, that she had been spirited out of the Hospital de Jesús Nazareno and taken to some unknown location.

"Labastida," said Baldemar. "But the good thing is, he'll want to keep her safe."

It was what Diego thought, too. With both the mother and her son under his power, the prelate was in a stronger position to dictate terms to the emperor, but his position would erode quickly if either Ángela or the child came to harm.

"You're going to try to find her?" said Diego.

"Got to."

"I'll help you."

Baldemar nodded, sipped from his glass of pulque. "Maybe."

"Maybe what?"

"Maybe you can help."

Diego massaged the stump of his left arm. He said, "I'll do whatever you want. Whatever I can."

"All right then."

Baldemar said there was a priest who could possibly be of assistance to them—a good man, a committed liberal. His name was Padre Buendía, and he was the rector in Taxco, a silver-mining town a couple of days' ride southeast of the capital.

"He makes it his business to know things," said Baldemar. "If we find Ángela—I mean, *when* we find her—Taxco will be a good place to send her, to keep her safe. Along with the boy. Buendía could help there, too."

Diego said he would be riding out to Cuernavaca in a couple of days, along with the emperor and an entourage of courtiers. Taxco wasn't so far away. He would try to find some excuse to make a side trip.

Baldemar clapped him on the back. "*Ándele, hombre,*" he said. "So you're a confederate of emperors now. How does that make you feel?"

"Strange," said Diego. "It makes me feel very strange."

He didn't say more, didn't mention his changing sentiments about politics or about Mexico and the chance of unity. Nor did he say anything about the succession of messengers—three of them so far—who had been dispatched to make contact with Juárez, to propose an alliance. There had been no response. As likely as not, the men had been murdered by thieves or assassinated by liberal partisans. He made no reference to his own position, how compromised he had become, beholden on all sides, caught between the emperor, Baldemar, and Salm-Salm, to say nothing of Ángela or her son. For now, he said only that he would keep his eyes and ears open. He would try to contact this Padre Buendía, and matters would proceed from there.

"Good for you." Again Baldemar clapped him on the back. "Let me know what you learn. And, remember, the Austrian is your enemy, as much as Labastida or Márquez or any of these picaroons. Don't ever forget it." He shook his head. "That's what's wrong with this country. That's what has always been Mexico's greatest defect."

"What?"

"The hope of a saviour. Some great man who will lead us from the wilderness. First, we endured all those Spanish viceroys, then Hidalgo, then Iturbide, then Santa Anna. Now this Austrian. The bloody country's like an amphibian, flopping back and forth between water and the land, never making up its mind. You have to make a choice—that's all. Will you be liberal or conservative? Will you live on water or on land? You can't do both."

Diego swallowed another draft of pulque. His friend was a changed man—not just thinner, but more sinewy, tougher, more determined. "And what about you?" he said. "What have you chosen? What are you going to do?"

"Kill conservatives. What else? Maybe you can help there, too."

"Maybe." Diego hesitated. "About Márquez . . ."

"The old snake. What about him?"

"I thought he would be dead by now, but they say he's still alive. They say he's here. In Mexico City."

Baldemar rubbed his jaw, with its grizzle of whiskers, its patches of flaking, reddened skin, residue of a prison rash that had yet to fully heal. "Is that what they say?"

"It is. They also say a bunch of bandits ambushed him on the way to Veracruz, but he managed to escape. Either that, or they let him go. Why would that be?"

"You want to know?"

"What do you think?"

Baldemar nodded. He swallowed the dregs of his jar and wiped his lips. He raised a hand to indicate another round. "We hanged him," he said. "Right after we captured him. We roped him from an almond tree, not far from Soledad de Doblado."

"By his ankles? Just like your uncle?"

"Right. By his ankles. Just like my uncle."

"What about his men?"

"We killed one of them in the ambush. The rest dropped their guns and gave up. We tied their thumbs together behind their backs. A bunch of worms. Not men. They didn't trouble us after that."

"And Márquez?"

"We left him overnight, swinging upside down. Let him see what it's like. Find out how much he enjoyed it. At first, he didn't say a word. I went to check on him in the morning, and he wasn't so tough then. He begged me to cut him down. He'd do anything. Anything I wanted."

"And?"

"I cut him down. That was it. I didn't want anything else."

"You spared his life."

Baldemar nodded.

"Why?"

"Couldn't let him die like that. Couldn't let anyone. Not even him."

"You could have shot him. You could have hanged him in the regular way."

"Could have."

Diego drummed his fingers on the rough wooden surface of the counter.

A slender man refilled their jars, and Baldemar took a mouthful, nodded pensively before he swallowed. He said he had done a good deal of thinking while mouldering away in the Martinica. "I came to some conclusions."

"Such as?"

"Such as there are better things to do to a man than kill him."

"You don't say."

"Worse things, too."

"You think?"

"I'm serious. Instead of killing a man, you can let him live."

Diego saw what he was getting at. He repeated a phrase. "Spare his life."

"That's right."

It was a law in Mexico—not a written-down law, but the other kind—that he who saves another man's life has a claim on his soul forever. If Baldemar had simply killed Márquez out near Soledad de Doblado, that would have been the end of it—vengeance sought and won. But this way, it would be different. This way, Márquez would go to his grave knowing he owed his life to none other than Baldemar Peralta, the man whose uncle he'd killed, whose sister he'd shot.

Diego shook his head. "The mind reels."

"It does."

"He'll have to kill you now. If he doesn't, he'll go mad."

"Probably."

"But he can't kill you, not after you saved his life."

"I guess not."

"Christ almighty. You've got him by the tail. This will drive him mad."

Baldemar nodded once, then nodded again, and then he smiled.

CHAPTER 19

CUERNAVACA STOOD UPON A lush plateau on the western face of the Sierra Madre. The emperor's new purchase was a mansion that had been constructed by a silver baron of the previous century, a man named Borda. It was famous for its verdant gardens and artificial lake. But the building had fallen into disrepair and was in need of major renovations. Maximiliano told Diego he had approved them all. The mansion, he said, was part of Mexico's patrimony.

A modest party would be making the journey to Cuernavaca. Their numbers included Doktor Basch and Professor Billimek—the emperor's naturalist—as well as the Countess Kollonitz and her husband, plus the Count von Bombelles and several other Austrian officers. Sauerthal, leader of the imperial orchestra, made the journey as well, with several string players. Salm-Salm and his wife rounded out the list. The travellers set off early on a Saturday morning, accompanied by a platoon of hussars and a patrol of Mexican lancers. The emperor's carriage was a sturdy vehicle, newly acquired, drawn by a team of six dun-coloured mules. An outrider cantered alongside, wearing a black uniform with silver spangles.

The route to Cuernavaca took the travellers high above the capital, through a mountain pass of lofty, sometimes vertiginous inclines, flanked by fields of blond grass and dense pine forests that seemed to hum in the sharp, persistent breeze. Eventually, they began their descent along a serpentine course that wound through scattered clusters of adobe huts interspersed by organ-pipe cactus fences. Now and again, they encountered mule teams shuffling along the narrow road. Diego watched as the *arrieros* waved in greeting and then used their wooden switches to swat at their beasts, forcing them to clear a way so that the emperor and his retinue might pass. The creatures tottered off to the roadside, bearing huge loads of firewood or dried cornstalks or rough wooden furniture, their burdens a good deal larger than the animals themselves.

The journey lasted most of the day, and dusk was approaching by the time the convoy of carriages tottered into the semitropical valley surrounding the town of Cuernavaca. Diego wrinkled his nose—a faint perfume of jasmine scented the air. The temperature was noticeably warmer than in Mexico City. It seemed to him that the flora was more profuse and extravagant, the palm trees stouter. The *palmeras* swayed above a feast of vegetation—jacaranda trees, cherries, *amates*, and *guayabos*.

Unfortunately, there was bad news. The sorry truth was that the mansion *de la Borda* was uninhabitable owing to the renovations under way. Ladders and flimsy scaffolding clung to the place. Large sections of tile flooring had been dug up, leaving perilous holes and ugly mounds of earth. Whole walls had been knocked down, and plaster dust covered everything. The travellers managed to survive the rigours of their first night, but Diego had a feeling their hearts would quail at the prospect of sleeping yet again in these suspect and uncomfortable quarters. No doubt the mansion would one day make a fine alternative to Chapultepec Castle—but not now, not yet.

It was in these unsettled circumstances that the emperor's party trooped down to breakfast on the morning that followed their arrival. They gathered on an al fresco terrace in the shade of a small orange grove, while a string trio played a succession of Viennese airs. For a moment, it all seemed tolerable, but only for a moment. They had only to think of the creaking stairs, the dust and detritus, the sagging floors and broken windows, and their spirits drooped again.

A young woman did her best to cheer them up. She gave her name as Beatríz Sedano and introduced herself as the daughter of the chief gardener at the mansion. Her complexion was as dark as polished mahogany, and she had large, arresting eyes and a small Romanesque nose, all framed by a shock of thick black hair of striking iridescence. She took charge of the breakfast and went about her duties with a degree of ease, assurance, and aplomb that was remarkable in someone so young. Diego could not stop watching her.

Toward the meal's end, Maximiliano climbed to his feet and declared he had an announcement to make. It was impossible that the party should remain at the House of Borda, he said. Some other shelter would have to be found. As a temporary solution, he proposed an outing on horseback, with the aim of exploring the countryside beyond the town. Meanwhile, more suitable accommodation would be arranged, although he did not know exactly where.

At once, the girl, Beatríz, did an about-face and raised a hand. As if she had long ago mastered the art of contradicting monarchs, she announced that she had a superior idea. If a journey on horseback were to be assayed, she said, why not consider a more ambitious project, one that would entail a journey of several days?

"Go on," said Maximiliano. "What do you have in mind?"

She put out her hands in a theatrical gesture. The party, she said, must on no account miss the opportunity to pay a visit to *las grutas luminosas.*

The name alone sparked an audible reaction from the gathering, a low hubbub of whispers and murmurs. The shining caves.

The girl explained that the structures in question were also known as the caves of Cacahuamilpa, strange geological formations located a two-day ride from Cuernavaca. About halfway along the route there was a fine hacienda called Cocoyotla, whose owner was accustomed to playing host to parties of travellers. He was able to provide comfortable lodging and acceptable nourishment. Not many adventurers passed that way any longer, owing to the troubles now plaguing the land, but it was her firm understanding that the hacienda might nonetheless still serve as a staging point for such a journey.

All this talk of caves perked the interest of the normally dour Professor Billimek. "I have heard of these formations," he declared. "They are said to be extraordinary."

"Haunted, I fear," said the girl. "They are possessed by evil spirits. It is only fair to warn you."

"Oh dear," said the empress. "Why, then, are we even discussing the subject? Evil spirits? No thank you."

"Pish-tosh," said Professor Billimek. "These are mere superstitions. Pay them no mind. This excursion could be a great adventure, and I'll warrant we shall find some excellent specimens along the route."

The scientist was referring to the region's flora and fauna and particularly its insects. Diego knew from experience that Billimek never ventured out of doors without his wooden carrying case, stuffed with bottles of various shapes and sizes, which he used to contain his biological discoveries.

"Well then," said Maximiliano. "I am almost persuaded. But how shall we find our way?"

"I shall accompany you," said the girl. For once, she seemed to blush, although it was difficult to be sure, so dark was her skin. "That is, of course, if you wish me to. I am familiar with the terrain, which is difficult and even somewhat hazardous in places. We shall ride along cliffs."

"Dear Lord," said the Countess Kollonitz, who was rather plump and a timid horsewoman. "What are we thinking? First evil spirits. And now cliffs. I would prefer to conduct my explorations in the garden here, with a book and a glass of wine."

"Come, Polly," said her husband. "It can't be as bad as all that. As the girl says, many travellers have made the trip and lived to tell the tale."

Diego observed these proceedings without making any comment of his own. He wondered where this was leading. As it turned out, no further objections were raised, and so the emperor declared the matter decided. He smiled at the gardener's daughter and reached for his silver cigarette case. "The caves of . . . what did you call them?"

"The caves of Cacahuamilpa," she said. "The shining caves of Cacahuamilpa."

Chapter 20

Beatríz Sedano reined her horse about as though she were a miniature cavalry officer, grinning at everyone. She was mounted upon a tall bay mare of impressive conformation and was riding bareback, astride her horse, rather than sidesaddle, as she wove among the other riders. She wore a cotton blouse embroidered with a floral pattern, and a long muslin skirt with several white petticoats, all bunched up about her waist. A pair of loose dark pantaloons reached down to her ankles. Her face was shaded by a large straw hat. But there was something distinctly odd about her. Diego had first noticed it at breakfast. When she shifted her gaze from side to side, the dark pupils of her eyes moved in unison with the rest of her head. The balls of her eyes were immobile. She could not seem to move her eyes without also twisting her neck. She must have noticed him staring.

"I am under a curse," she said, laughing. "It is an ancient blight handed down through the generations since time before memory. In every generation of my family, there has been someone like this. They say I must be a witch. Do you think it is true?"

Without waiting for an answer and with a fleeting glance at Diego's missing left arm—did she mean to suggest that he was cursed as well?—the girl slapped the ends of her reins against the right flank of her mare. At once, the horse broke into a stately canter, neck arched, haunches tucked under, tail raised in an ebony plume.

"Remember what I told you, Serrano." The emperor drew the elegant bulk of Anteburro alongside Diego's smaller chestnut gelding. A hussar had brought Maximiliano's favourite mount out to Cuernavaca the previous day on a lead. Now he tapped the leather satchel that was slung around his shoulder. "We are depending on you."

Maximiliano had decided it would be Diego's duty during the journey to identify local flora they would encounter on their way to the shining caves.

"I'll do my best," Diego said, then added, "Your Majesty."

"That's the spirit." The emperor adjusted the sleeves of his blouse. He glanced up. "You, Billimek. You must hold your tongue this morning. We are going to test Serrano's knowledge of natural lore. Agreed?"

The scientist merely grunted.

Maximiliano seemed to be in his element, his excitement fuelled by the prospect of the journey ahead. He stood in his stirrups and shifted around in his saddle to address his wife and the Countess Kollonitz. "Are we managing all right, ladies?"

They both nodded.

"Capital."

With that, the emperor gave the order, and the party set off.

Before long, they had left the town well behind and found themselves riding down a narrow *barranca* thickly flanked with trees and foliage of diverse varieties. Diego was sure he had seen all these plants many times before, but he realized he knew the names of only a very few. He felt as if he were riding through a strange and alien land—a green, irregular valley, partly obscured by a webbing of trees, vines, and many-coloured blossoms, almost all of them unknown to him. Bees droned nearby, and snatches of birdsong darted up from the lower woodlands.

The emperor confessed to being baffled by the surrounding vegetation. He prided himself on taking a keen interest in naturalism, he said, but he recognized almost nothing.

"Serrano. Let us put your expertise to the test." He pointed at a white bell-like flower that dangled from a low tree with spade-shaped leaves of a watery green. "What, for example, is that?"

"*Floripondio,*" Diego said, feigning a nonchalance he did not feel. "Quite common at this altitude."

"So I see." As his horse stepped past the tree, Maximiliano reached up and plucked one of the blossoms.

Another voice spoke up. "Do you know the name of this one, my friend?" It was Salm-Salm. He held up a flower freshly picked.

Diego inspected the blossom, white petals around a yellow stamen. "Come, come," said the prince.

Diego had no idea what it was.

"Oh, leave the fellow alone," said his wife. "Can't you see he doesn't know?"

"I'm only asking. An innocent question. I see no harm in that."

"*Yoloxochitl,*" said the girl. She halted her horse, occupying a space that separated Diego from the rest. "This one is called *yoloxochitl*. It means flower of the heart." She smiled at everyone in turn, shifting her head in small increments due to the unusual fixity of her eyes. "Not a very common plant."

"It seems not," said Salm-Salm. "Credit one to the distaff side, then." As he rode past, he reached out and slapped Diego on the back. "You have let our gender down, my friend."

The emperor reached up and removed one of the blossoms from its perch, briefly testing its scent. He held the flower out to the Indian girl. "It would look very well in your hair. Take it, please."

She looped her reins over one arm and proceeded to wind the stem among the strands of her hair, above her left ear.

The journey continued with the accompaniment of scattered bursts of birdsong and the occasional piercing whine of the cicada. Now and again, Beatríz called a halt in order to provide the name and, in many cases, the nutritional or curative properties of this or that plant, fruit, or flower. Here, she said, was the *izgujochitl,* with blossoms as small and delicate as miniature roses. And this was the *ocelojochitl,* the viper's head, an eerily lovely flower of flamboyant colours—purple, white, and pink. Here were cedrats and plantains. That was a Mexican oak tree.

"This one I know," said Diego. "It was from a tree such as this that they hanged Melchor Ocampo."

"Did what?" said the emperor.

"Hanged Melchor Ocampo."

"Who?"

"The foreign minister," said the empress. "Or at least he was. Dead now. Is that not so?"

"It is." Diego recounted the tale.

"Dear God," said the emperor. "What a beastly experience. I had no idea."

"Yes, you did." The empress's horse balked momentarily at the moss-covered trunk of a fallen tree. She recovered her balance and coaxed the animal forward. "You most certainly did. We read about it even before we came to Mexico. And this man whom you pardoned, along with several others, this Baldemar Peralta. It was he who tried to assassinate the author of that crime, our good friend General Márquez."

The emperor was silent. It seemed he was thinking, taking all this in.

Beatríz spoke up. "Melchor Ocampo," she said. "A great man of Mexico and a particular hero of mine. It is true that he was raised in Michoacán, but he came many times to Cuernavaca. My grandfather once spoke with him."

Diego turned to look at her, a bit taken aback by her knowledge of events. "He did? Spoke of what?"

"Cacti," said the girl. "They spoke about cacti. Of course, this took place before my birth. But I believe it to be true. My grandfather is particularly knowledgeable about the varieties of cacti that are to be found in this region and, as you may know, Ocampo was an expert on these plants, as on so many other subjects. He wrote a book on the theme, if I am not mistaken."

It was certainly possible. Diego would not have been surprised. What did surprise him was this girl. The daughter of an Indian gardener? "A book on cacti," he said. "I must look it up."

"Indeed, you must."

For a time, they rode on in silence, following a partly overgrown track through dark pools of shade interrupted by beams of light that shot down from the canopy overhead like transparent columns. Darting insects and motes of dust shimmered in the glowing pillars. Eventually, the path led to a steep ascent, which they scaled by a series of switchbacks. At the summit, they passed through a set of ancient tumbledown gates and soon found themselves in a large orchard that must have been abandoned long ago, for the trees were thickly overgrown. The riders continued through the orchard until they reached a large clearing, surrounded by trees so densely laden with fruit that their limbs nudged the wild grass below. The emperor decided this would be an ideal spot to enjoy their picnic lunch. Everyone dismounted, and the girl immediately took charge of the logistics. The meal was served by several of the *mozos* who had shadowed the expedition with a team of donkeys. In no time, the travellers were feasting on cold chicken, hard-boiled eggs, and a variety of cut meats, served with several kinds of cheese and slivers of tomato sprinkled with chopped green chilies. The servants poured Portuguese sherry from embossed metal flasks into crystal glasses. Later, the *mozos* picked ripe chirimoyas from the branches, cut them open, and spooned the flesh onto china plates, like a kind of pudding.

When the meal was at last consumed, most of the party sprawled on the long grass, basking in the sun. The empress and the Countess Kollonitz wandered off with a pair of lady servants. Maximiliano lounged with his back to the trunk of a sapota tree, smoking a cigarette. He congratulated Beatríz for finding such a splendid place.

"We have half filled my satchel with specimens already," he said. "Before the day is out, I expect my poor leather case to be overflowing. You will have to help us with the identification, you know. I don't suppose you can write?"

She seemed taken aback by the question. "Of course. And read the result as well."

"Educated too?" He raised his eyebrows. "I must say, you are the prettiest Indian I have seen in this country. *La india bonita*."

She smiled. "*A sus ordenes, Su Majestad*."

Diego lit a cheroot and closed his eyes.

The remainder of the journey to the hacienda at Cocoyotla proceeded through handsome green countryside. Shortly before dusk, the travellers rounded the summit of a broad hill forested in Mexican oak. The hacienda sprawled below, large stands of sugar cane interspersed with the bowed pillars of royal palms, all arrayed around a cluster of stone buildings—the main house, a large stable, several sheds, and a network of low structures that made up the *trapiche*, or sugar works.

"Well done," said the emperor, addressing the girl. "Come. The future awaits."

It turned out that the owner of the property, a Señor Nuñez Escamilla, was absent along with his family. At first, the *mayordomo* seemed reluctant to receive the travellers. It was only on learning that the party included the emperor and empress of Mexico that he relented, although it was unclear to Diego whether the man had previously possessed any inkling at all that such a thing as an emperor or empress existed in Mexico or what might be their roles.

The following morning, the *mayordomo* roused the visitors. Groggy, still yawning, they wandered about like ghosts, mostly contenting themselves with bread and tea for breakfast. Professor Billimek alone declared himself famished and insisted on having eggs in the Mexican style, *revuelto* with chili peppers and tomatoes.

It was still dark when they mounted their horses and set out, with only a crescent moon and a smattering of stars to light the way.

Chapter 21

The early portion of the journey led through sparsely forested flatlands and low hills, but the terrain gradually grew more rugged. The sun rose in a clear sky, and this was a blessing, as parts of the route proved to be as treacherous as the Indian girl had warned—long narrow ridges strung like tightropes from the crests of adjoining hills. The riders advanced along a tenuous path, the earth spinning crazily away, plummeting down nearly vertical cliffs, sometimes on both sides at once.

Beatríz rode first. Diego couldn't help but admire her coolness. Any misstep might lead to catastrophe, but she seemed oblivious to the danger. She bunched the reins in one hand and swung around to glance behind her, insisting there was no need to mind the narrowness of the path or the perilous descents, as any horse worth its oats could be trusted to put one hoof in front of the other without pitching over a precipice. She suggested it might be best to interfere as little as possible with the horses' own judgment.

They rode on in silence for a time, until the terrain grew less horrific. Then, without warning, Diego heard a loud groan of pain. He swung around in his saddle. It was Billimek. The man was nearly doubled over, practically toppling from his horse. At first, Diego thought he must be suffering a bout of vertigo, perhaps a delayed reaction to the unnerving terrain.

Everyone dismounted and waited as the emperor's physician took charge. Doktor Basch soon produced his diagnosis—an incipient case of dysentery, beyond the shadow of a doubt. The eggs that the scientist had consumed at breakfast were almost certainly to blame.

"I think we had better return to the hacienda," he said.

"What?" Carlota shivered in horror. "And ride back along those cliffs! Dear God, no."

"Perhaps a brief rest," said the emperor. "Perhaps Billimek will recover. It would be a shame to turn back now that we are so close."

"Your Majesty," said Basch, "I fear that it is quite impossible for the man to continue. He is too ill."

"I see." Maximiliano whacked his crop against one of his tall riding boots. "Well, in that case, I suppose we shall all have to turn back."

"I have another idea," said Beatríz. She turned to Diego. It was not a great challenge to reach the caves from here, she said. She could easily point the way. "Look. From that valley over there, you have only to bear up the stream bed." She pointed toward what appeared to be the meandering course of a seasonal riverbed, flanked by fresno trees. "It will take only an hour or so to reach the caves. When you see a grove of purple plum trees, you are there." She smiled at Diego. "You can lead the way. It isn't difficult."

Diego nodded. "All right."

"And you?" said the emperor. He meant the girl.

"I shall guide the doctor back to the hacienda. The doctor and the patient." The others, she said, could continue their journey to the caves. She would try to join them later.

A pair of *mozos* came plodding into view from behind, guiding a pair of donkeys laden with large clay pots of water. The girl said they should divvy up the liquid. Both groups should keep an ample supply close at hand.

Maximiliano promptly overruled her. He said a donkey with its heavy burden would simply slow everyone down. Diego had a feeling the emperor was simply irritated at being deprived of the young woman's company.

"Besides," said Maximiliano, "We have Serrano here to guide us. He will deliver us from harm."

Diego said nothing, suddenly uncertain whether he had understood Beatríz's directions correctly. He should clarify them, but he didn't want to seem slow-witted before the girl.

With a leg up from one of the hussars, the emperor remounted his horse and gathered the reins. He nodded at Diego. "Lead on."

First, Diego swung around in his saddle to watch as Beatríz rode off, mounted upon her tall bay mare. Knotted in a single braid, her dark hair bobbed behind her. She turned and smiled and waved and then vanished beyond the green boughs of a fresno tree. Birdsong drifted down from the higher branches, and Diego found he could breathe more easily at last. He settled back into the saddle and caught the emperor's gaze. He, too, had been watching the girl as she rode away.

"*¡A las grutas!*" cried Maximiliano. He spurred his horse so that the animal reared back and then leapt ahead, like a charger into battle. "To the caves!"

"Are you sure this is the right way?" said Salm-Salm. "We do not seem to be going up. We seem to be going down. Are you sure you are not mistaken?"

"Quite sure," said Diego, although he too was feeling some doubts.

The girl had definitely said to proceed *up* the stream bed. By this, he had assumed her to mean they should trace the course of the bed toward the east. She was an Indian, after all. When a Mexican Indian says *up,* he means east, because the sun comes up in the east. Now, however, he wondered whether she hadn't instead intended to refer to the route that water would take when flowing through this channel. He and the others seemed to be travelling downstream, along a sandy, waterless trail that wound through a narrow forest. The sun was oppressive, stoking a dry, relentless heat that was heavy, ponderous, soporific. Not a leaf stirred. The only sound was the occasional whine of the cicada, rising slowly in the distance until it stung the ears, before gradually fading away.

Diego gritted his teeth. "This route will take us to the caves."

"It had better." Salm-Salm removed his straw hat and ran his shirt sleeve across his brow. "You are aware, I suppose, that the welfare of the emperor and empress of Mexico rests in your hands."

"Felix . . ." Salm-Salm's wife reached over and placed a hand on her husband's shoulder. "Please."

It was clear to Diego that Salm-Salm's words were really intended for the emperor. It was equally apparent that he himself was in the wrong. He should have insisted upon keeping at least one of the donkeys and its cargo. As the only Mexican in the group, he alone understood the punishing effect of the heat at midday. Now their only supply of water was on its way back to the hacienda at Cocoyotla.

The emperor stood up in his stirrups again and gazed ahead, like a general assessing the fortunes of battle. He turned to Diego. "A grove of trees, did she say? Some kind of fruit trees?"

"Yes, Your Majesty. Plum trees."

"Your Majesty," said Salm-Salm, "I fear your secretary is leading us astray. I say we should turn back. I cannot put the matter too strongly. Our lives hang in the balance."

The emperor called for Bombelles. The count considered the matter for several moments before leaning toward Maximiliano. "Your Majesty," he said, "I vote we carry on as we are."

"You do?"

"Yes. It is a well-known tenet in the lore of soldiering that, when in doubt, one should proceed downstream. It is in the nature of human settlements that they are built near water. By riding downstream, we are sure to come across a town eventually."

Disgruntled and weary, the travellers fell into line and coaxed their horses forward. They plodded through the dull languor, the dead brown leaves crackling underfoot. An hour passed, mostly in silence, until at last Diego caught sight of a grove of small fruit trees not far from the sandy bank, near a bend in the stream bed.

"Plums!" he cried out.

It was as if the party had stumbled upon the Promised Land. Here were plums to eat—plump, luscious fruit, something to ease their awful dryness and craving. Diego and the others all urged their horses up through a barricade of large boulders and onto the stream bed's banks and then straight into the copse of plum trees, where they at once began gorging themselves upon the fruit. Soon rivulets of violet syrup ran down every chin, staining their clothes, but no one cared.

The emperor was the first to remember their purpose in having ridden all this way. "I expect it will be cooler inside the caves," he said. His eyes lit up. "We might even find water."

Quickly, they dismounted, looping their reins around the branches of trees. They left the horses under the care of two of the hussar guards. Several large pine torches were unpacked and lit. The caves themselves were easy to find. The main entrance was as large as a church gate and stood only twenty *varas* or so from the stream bed, partway up a severe, densely forested hillside. The emperor insisted upon leading the way. A pair of tall *amate* trees flanked the cave mouth. Maximiliano hesitated, then squared his shoulders, took a step forward, and was suddenly swallowed by darkness. One moment, he was the emperor of Mexico, his ruddy hair and beard illuminated by the midday sun. The next moment, he was gone.

Chapter 22

It was Bombelles who acted first. He tightened his grip on one of the pine torches, barged ahead, and disappeared. The remaining travellers briefly held back but then seemed to reach the same unspoken decision. One after another, they ventured into the cave, passing instantly from the glare of day into the cavernous night. Diego was third in line. The remaining hussar guards brought up the rear, both bearing torches that provided a fitful illumination that danced against the craggy walls. The light was sufficient to let everyone grope his way forward—and downward. They descended along the uneven floor of the tunnel, unable to see more than a *vara* or so ahead. Before long, the passage veered off to the left, narrowed abruptly, and then just as quickly widened into a sort of underground salon. Here, they encountered the emperor and Bombelles, both of them standing against a damp slab of rock, each holding a torch, waiting for the others to catch up.

Maximiliano raised his free arm in a gesture of welcome. "*Mi casa es su casa.*"

His words echoed through the chamber and beyond. It occurred to Diego what a fascinating mixture of boldness and reserve was contained in the man's temperament. He could debate with himself for half an hour over an innocuous piece of correspondence, yet here he had charged into the subterranean darkness without a scruple of any kind.

"Halloo! Halloo!" the Countess Kollonitz called out in a high-pitched voice. The word repeated itself over and over in a hollow echo that seemed to recede further and further into the earth. The only other sound was the regular ping of water falling upon water.

"Come," said Maximiliano. "Let us tour the rest of our new abode."

After tilting to the left, the tunnel led downward and grew steadily narrower, so that they all were obliged to duck their heads to avoid brushing against the ceiling. Soon the tunnel widened again and then opened into a large cavern, where they could easily stand upright. The light from the torches seemed to flare around and above, glancing against several massive stalactites that projected downward from a high stone ceiling. A broad pool of water filled most of the chamber, its deep expanse seeming to glow in the reflected light of the torches, an eerie spectacle of luminous and variegated blue. The effect was uncanny—as if the water were somehow being irradiated from below, as if some mysterious source of light beamed upward through the pool. Aquamarine at its edges, the water darkened to a mass of liquid cobalt at the centre. So this was the reason for the name—*las grutas luminosas*. The shining caves.

Diego felt as though he were trespassing somehow. Water dripped from the ceiling of the great sunken hall and spattered against the surface of the blue pool, just as it must have done for centuries. His throat was dry, and he struggled to swallow, uneasy amid the ghostly surroundings. He felt an urge to escape.

For his part, the emperor seemed calm, almost delighted. He said he wished to enjoy a swim. He handed off his torch to one of the hussars and balanced himself by a large damp rock. He began to yank off his boots and stockings. He rose to his feet and then lurched forward, stumbling barefoot into the pool.

"Eureka!" he shouted, and the word repeated itself over and over before gradually fading. He threw himself forward onto his chest and plunged beneath the shimmering surface, gliding through the light like a dense blue shadow. Something caused Diego to follow the man's example. He, too, wanted the sensation of water. He tore off his boots and stockings and darted toward the pool, splashing through the shallows before diving headlong into the strangely radiant lagoon.

The water was shockingly cold, and when he breached the surface his skin seemed to ripple uncontrollably. But soon enough he grew accustomed to the temperature of the water, bitter as it was, and basked instead in the pleasure of being immersed in this shining blue element.

"Ah, don Diego. Is that you?"

It was the emperor, swimming easily on his side.

Without a word, as if by some silent agreement, he and Maximiliano began to stroke in the direction of the opposite bank, dimly visible as a series of shadows in the aquamarine light. Before long, Diego's hand nudged up against the hardness of rock, and he managed with some difficulty to haul himself up on to a low ledge. The emperor did the same. For a time, they remained where they were, hunched side by side in their dripping clothes, gazing out at the strange blue evanescence of the pool, at the dancing shapes cast by the torchlight upon the ceiling of the cave, and at the dangling blades of the stalactites.

"Serrano, you've acquitted yourself admirably. Well done."

Diego put back his shoulders and smiled to himself. It was no unpleasant feeling to have bested Salm-Salm, and it was rendered all the more gratifying by the emperor's words.

At his side, the emperor had begun to shiver. "Dear God, I do feel a chill. Don't you?" His teeth chattered as he spoke.

Diego began to shiver, too. The prospect of immersing himself again in the painfully cold water suddenly seemed like a kind of torture. He reached back with his right arm to steady himself and felt his hand brush against a rock, or something like a rock. He thought somehow of a small unripe calabash and immediately knew what it was he was touching. He closed his hand around the thing and drew it out into the faint blue light.

He was holding a skull, a human skull. It leered at him with an expression that should have been fixed but seemed strangely changeable, as if it were laughing through the havoc of shadows and light. He felt a weight behind him, a burden he had not sensed before. He did not need to turn. He did not need to look. But he was unable to resist. He did turn—and there they were, jumbled behind his back, a great hummock of bones piled atop a broad stone ledge. There must have been hundreds. Maybe thousands. What crime had been committed here? Some massive execution? He held the skull up in the dim light.

"God in heaven!" cried the emperor. He, too, turned and looked before plunging back into the pool and ploughing away through the ice-cold and shattering water. He gasped and spluttered, his arms flailing at his sides. Diego flung the thing away and threw himself into the lagoon. He swam toward the emperor. Before long, both men were clambering through the shallows and up onto the bank where the others waited.

Maximiliano said nothing but only rooted about for his boots and stockings. He staggered away barefoot, and Diego followed, clutching his own stockings and boots to his chest. The two of them blundered ahead through the darkness. Diego was vaguely aware of the other members of the party trailing somewhere behind, their voices dashing against the walls of successive caverns and tunnels. The climb seemed to take far longer than the descent, but at last he rounded a final turn, the light seemed to explode, and he stumbled out into the bright midday sunshine.

The heat seemed to pulse from every surface, from the dirt, the stones, the branches of trees, the brittle leaves crackling on the ground. Maximiliano stumbled off alone, bearing in the direction of the grove of plum trees. He was still barefoot, his boots and hosiery cradled in his arms.

Diego's mind raced. He wondered what chain of events had ended in that underground chamber, leaving that immensity of bones. He pulled on the first of his boots and was cursing under his breath as he struggled with the second when the torrid air seemed to split apart, pierced by a man's high-pitched scream.

CHAPTER 23

IT WAS THE EMPEROR. He'd been stung by a scorpion—Diego was sure of it. He hurried over to help, convinced that it was his fault. He should have warned the emperor to be careful, to inspect his footwear, just as he had done—it was practically an instinct among Mexicans. Without a doubt, the arachnid had crept into the emperor's boot while they both were swimming in the underground lagoon. Why hadn't he given a warning? Maximiliano lay prostrate on the parched grass, conscious but disoriented, while Diego and the others knelt around him. His eyes were open, but he seemed dazed and uncomprehending. He did not respond to their voices.

"Is he breathing?" said Salm-Salm.

"Breathing, yes," Diego said. "Damned scorpions. They're everywhere."

He began scouring the parched earth and shrivelled ground cover for some sign of the creature. He advanced on his knees, his eyes fixed on the earth in front of him. He kept thinking he'd spotted the beast, only to realize that what he saw was just a stick or a shadow of some sort. The damned things were well camouflaged. Still, he kept looking. He knew it was important to identify the scorpion in question, if he could. He kept at it until at last he saw the beast. There it was—its tail curled over its back, its limbs twitching in the faint breeze. Diego darted over, scooped up the scorpion with his hand, and smacked it against a rock. There. Done. He slipped the corpse into the pocket of his blouse.

If he expected congratulations, he got none. In fact, no one seemed to have noticed. Bombelles and several of the hussars had lifted the emperor up and were carrying him toward the horses, evidently meaning to help him onto his mount. Someone had knotted a makeshift tourniquet around his upper leg. With some effort, they heaved the man aloft, and he flopped into the saddle like a raggedy doll. He was still conscious, it seemed, but confused and weak. He hung his head and moaned.

"Hush," said the empress, who stood by her husband's horse. "Take deep breaths. Try to relax. You'll be fine. I promise."

Her words seemed to have a calming effect. At least, the emperor managed to take up the reins and to keep his balance. Still, his shoulders drooped, his head lolled forward, and his gaze seemed glassy and unfocused. It occurred to Diego that the venom must have worked uncommonly fast.

Carlota took command. She turned to address the party. "All right then. Everybody hurry. We must be quick."

Once all were mounted and ready, she turned to Diego. "Well?"

"I found the scorpion."

"You can identify it?"

"No, Your Majesty."

Her jaw muscles tautened. "Very well," she said. "Let's be off."

They set out along the stream bed, retracing their path in the direction of Cocoyotla. Ashen-faced and silent, the emperor slouched over the pommel of his saddle, clutching the reins with both hands.

"We must ride no faster than this," said Salm-Salm. He explained that excessive movement would only hasten the spread of the poison through the emperor's leg and to the rest of his body. He turned to Diego. "You could have prevented this. Why didn't you warn him? The man is without an heir!" He narrowed his eyes. "I mean to hold you responsible, whatever happens."

The party continued along the stream bed for another quarter-hour or so, until Diego sensed a disturbance just ahead. He saw the girl, Beatríz. Astride her bay mare, she rounded a bend in the riverbed, riding toward them at a brisk jog. A jaunty straw hat framed her oval face, and she wore a broad smile. In spite of the urgency of the situation, Diego briefly imagined her as a sort of princess, an Indian princess surveying her private domain. On a long hemp-woven shank, she led one of the donkeys. A pair of twin clay pots of water bobbed against its flanks, one on each side. She drew her horse to a halt.

"You needed water," she said. She explained that she had guided the others through the more difficult terrain on their return journey and had then left them to make the rest of the trek on their own. She frowned and fell silent as she realized something was wrong. "His Majesty?"

"A scorpion." Diego eased his horse forward and extracted the creature's remains from his breast pocket. "Here. Look."

Beatríz drew closer to inspect the small and misshapen corpse.

"Is it very poisonous?" said the empress.

The girl hesitated. She said she was of the opinion the scorpion belonged to the variety known as *alacrán tartarus*—the scorpion of Tarturus—sometimes known as the underground scorpion. She looked over at the emperor, who seemed barely conscious, his arms dangling at his sides, barely holding onto the reins.

"Very poisonous?" she said. "It *can* be."

She dismounted and instructed the hussars to lower the emperor from his horse. At her direction, the soldiers bore the ailing man toward the bank, where they laid him down upon a muddle of dried leaves, gnarled tree roots, and loamy soil. Maximiliano seemed wholly delirious now. His head sagged to the side, and his breath came in shallow gasps.

"Dear God, no," said Salm-Salm. He got down on his knees.

The girl crouched above the emperor and inspected his bare foot. She soon found the site of the sting, located in the hollow between his left heel and ankle. Without hesitation or ceremony, she pressed her lips to the wound and sucked out what fluid she could, discreetly spat it away, then wiped her lips on the sleeve of her blouse. She announced that the venom had probably already dispersed too widely into the emperor's bloodstream for it to be withdrawn effectively. She thought it would be best if they all proceeded as quickly as possible, not to Cocoyotla but to a town located in the opposite direction. Taxco was its name. The parish priest there, Padre Buendía, was well known to her. Moreover, she was also acquainted with another gentleman there who was singularly adept at treating ailments of diverse descriptions, including those resulting from encounters with vipers and arachnids of all descriptions.

"He is a doctor?" said the empress.

"Of a sort."

Carlota frowned.

"*Un curandero,*" said the girl. A healer.

"*A healer?*" said Salm-Salm. He turned toward Diego. "How could you let this happen?"

"Please," said the girl. "It would be best to go quickly."

No one had a better plan, and so they reversed direction and set out for Taxco. Everyone seemed apprehensive, but Salm-Salm was especially fretful. Periodically, he conferred in whispers with his wife, but Diego found it impossible to make out what was being said. He recalled his last conversation with Baldemar, who had exhorted him to seek out this very priest in this very town. He glanced over at the girl, who caught and held his gaze with those eerily static eyes of hers.

It seemed she meant to convey something—something about the emperor and the scorpion. But what? He was about to ask when she placed a finger against her lips.

He held his tongue, and the party continued on its way toward Taxco. All he knew was that the shadows were growing longer, the heat had at last begun to fade, and the emperor of Mexico had been rendered all but unconscious by a scorpion sting that he, Diego Serrano, should have anticipated and warned against.

It was twilight by the time the riders reached the town, a modest settlement of adobe houses clinging to the slopes of a large hill rising above a broad green plain. Barefoot Indian women padded through the shadows of dusk, tracing a series of rutted earthen lanes with infants clasped to their backs by handwoven shawls or with large cargos of firewood or other necessaries balanced atop their heads. Beatríz led the way to a small presbytery by the local church, an ornate baroque structure called the Templo de Santa Prisca. They were met by the priest, who strode out into the murky light with arms outstretched, greeting Beatríz warmly. A large, bald-pated fellow with twin fringes of greying hair, the priest wore a voluminous black cassock that was gathered at the waist by a hand-tooled leather belt, in which he carried a long-barrelled revolving pistol.

"Dangerous times, firm measures," he said, placing a hand upon the weapon. "Behold, Mexico—a land where even the clergy must bear arms."

So this was Padre Buendía.

"His Majesty is not well," said Beatríz. "He has been stung by a scorpion."

If Buendía was surprised to learn that his unexpected visitors included the emperor of the land, he managed not to show it.

"A scorpion?" he said. "Bring him inside at once."

Again the girl glanced at Diego, and again her expression seemed to express some secret they shared. But what was it? Diego had no idea. He watched as Bombelles and his men carried the emperor inside. Then he swung down from his saddle and hurried after them.

CHAPTER 24

THE HUSSARS BORE THE emperor into the presbytery and upstairs to a vacant room, where they set him down on a bed. Others crowded into the room, and Diego found a place for himself just inside the door. Someone handed him a tallow candle in a tin holder. He held it up, casting a narrow dome of light.

Padre Buendía dispatched a servant to fetch a certain don Plutarco. This, it turned out, was the curandero whom Beatríz had spoken of. Within a matter of minutes, the healer shuffled into the room, a thin, elderly fellow with a narrow, grizzled face and a deep bronze complexion. He wore a frayed old coat over a collarless cotton shirt, loose cotton pants, and rawhide sandals.

The Indian looked around at the gathering, nodding at each individual in turn, as if he had encountered this very set of circumstances before and was in no way surprised by what he saw. "Does anyone have the animal?" he said.

"I do." Diego took a step forward.

"Come," said the man, and he led Diego back out into the cramped hallway. "Let me see."

Beatríz joined them, and Diego handed her the candle. From his breast pocket, he slowly eased out the scorpion's crumpled remains, holding them up to the light.

"Tarturus?" she said in a whisper.

The old man nodded. "*Sí. Alacrán tarturus. No cabe duda.*"

Without a doubt.

"What is it?" said Diego.

Don Plutarco stroked his slender chin and, leaning close, spoke in a whisper. "It lives in caves," he said. "Its poison is weak."

"Not dangerous?"

"For an adult, no. Not very dangerous."

"But His Majesty—?"

"Shh." It was the girl.

"What are you scheming at out there? What are you plotting? Tell me." Salm-Salm called from where he stood at the foot of the bed.

The healer seemed to recognize trouble and told the prince that hot water was needed, the hotter, the better. "At once," he said. "Please. It is vital."

Salm-Salm heaved a sigh of impatience, but he did as instructed. He marched downstairs and soon could be heard calling for water.

Don Plutarco turned to Diego. He asked if the emperor's fragile state might not be complicated by some underlying condition. A mental upset, perhaps?

Diego briefly described the experience he had shared with Maximiliano that afternoon, the episode he not yet mentioned to any of the others—the pile of human bones heaped beyond the lagoon, deep in the shining caves. He spoke in a whisper.

The curandero nodded and gazed at the girl. She glanced up at Diego with a look that seemed to say she had suspected something of the kind all along, that she had known the poison was weak and had thought the emperor's distress must have some other cause.

"What is going on?" The empress called from the bedroom. "What does the man say? This is madness. I demand a proper physician."

Padre Buendía was at the stair landing. He assured the empress that he would send for a conventional doctor the instant it proved necessary, but he believed it might be as well to bear with don Plutarco for a time. He had never known the man to fail.

"I don't understand," said Carlota. She put a hand to her forehead and stared at the floor.

"In any case," said the priest, "there is no doctor within easy travelling distance. It would take a day at least, perhaps two, to summon a physician here."

Carlota gasped at this news. She took one of Maximiliano's hands in both of hers. "There, there. Be calm, my love. Be brave."

The emperor made a sound of acknowledgment, a low sort of moan.

Don Plutarco gazed back toward the room. "Poison or no poison," he said to Diego and the girl, "the cure is the same."

He began at once. He turned and shuffled into the bedroom, knelt beside the emperor, and murmured a series of incantations in his Indian tongue, Nahuatl, the ancient language of the central Mexican highlands.

Salm-Salm marched back up the stairs and settled himself in a low bench in a corner of the room by the window. "The water's on its way," he said to no one in particular. He fidgeted with his hands. Suddenly, he sprang to his feet and pushed the bench aside. He confronted Diego in the doorway, stabbing at him with a single outstretched finger.

"This is all your fault," he said, his voice strained with anger. "You have placed the empire in the gravest peril." He looked around at the small gathering. "Pray God he survives. Meanwhile, I must return to Mexico City without delay. The question of an heir must be resolved."

He said he meant to ride to the hacienda at Cocoyotla immediately. He would inform those at the hacienda of the misfortune that had befallen the emperor. "Otherwise, they will think we have been attacked by highwaymen, robbed and murdered."

Following a brief conference with his wife in the hallway, Salm-Salm gave a nod of farewell, turned, and bounded down the stairs, two at a time. The princess returned to the bedroom and perched on the bench just vacated by her husband. She seemed the embodiment of sang-froid.

"He'll stop at Cuernavaca and then continue straight on to Mexico City," she said.

The Count Kollonitz whistled. "That's a three-day ride."

"Then he will ride for three days," said the princess. "He's that stubborn. Besides, he's terrified the emperor will die."

Carlota turned and glared at the woman. "Max is not going to die."

"I know that. It would take more than a little scorpion sting to kill a Hapsburg. But try telling that to Felix."

"He certainly seemed upset," said Diego.

"It's just as I say. He's scared out of his mind that Max will perish without an heir. It's an obsession. It's all he thinks about."

"But why rush back to Mexico City?" said the count. "What can he do there?"

"Talk to the archbishop," the princess replied in her usual matter-of-fact tone. "They've become great friends, you know."

Diego would have liked to continue the conversation, but don Plutarco interrupted them.

"Bring me brandy," he said, addressing Diego. "And where is the water? We need boiling water, bolts of silk, and pine gum."

Apart from incantations in Nahuatl, the emperor's treatment seemed mainly to involve the frequent and copious administration of brandy. The curandero poured each draft from a crystal decanter that Diego had retrieved from the dining room.

Meanwhile, a pair of kitchen servants ferried boiling water into the bedroom in a succession of pots. They set the steaming containers on the bedroom floor and added resin of pine gum to the water before covering the vessels with bolts of silk. Soon, clouds of aromatic vapour swirled through the room, redolent of the high Mexican hills and of evergreen.

Don Plutarco asked everyone to leave so that he might be alone with the emperor for a time. Carlota resisted at first, but Padre Buendía assured her that all would be well, and so she trekked downstairs along with the others. The company huddled in the main salon, where they could hear muffled snatches of conversation from the bedroom upstairs. It was evident that don Plutarco and the emperor were involved in intense conversation, but it was impossible to determine what was being said.

Half an hour passed before the Indian healer appeared on the landing to say the treatment had been completed. Carlota hurried back upstairs, followed by a few of the others. The emperor was sufficiently revived that he was able to acknowledge each of them in turn, holding eye contact and nodding. He seemed both calm and self-possessed and was even able to speak, albeit in brief snatches. Whatever don Plutarco had done while the two men were alone, it had evidently worked.

The empress ran her hand across her husband's forehead and caressed his hair, but Maximiliano no longer responded, and for good reason. It seemed he had fallen asleep. Don Plutarco said there was no longer any danger and His Majesty would pass the night in peace.

The following morning, the emperor was well enough to take a turn in the garden. He asked Diego to join him, and the two strolled among the mulberry shrubs and citrus trees. Maximiliano apologized for the events of the previous day.

"There is no need," said Diego. "Your Majesty—"

"I always worry when you remember to call me that."

Maximiliano said there was something he wished to say. He eased closer to Diego, lowering his voice, and Diego sensed a warmth in his chest, at once strange and familiar, the return of a welcome but long-absent feeling—it seemed they were confederates again. The emperor explained in a whisper that he had long suffered a horror of bones, and he thought he understood why. His older brother, Franz Josef, now ruler of the Austrian Empire, had tormented him when they both were young, telling him all sorts of lurid stories involving corpses, disfigured faces, and mutilated limbs. Limbs and bones. Those experiences had marked him deeply and must have played some role in his behaviour the previous day.

"I know the scorpion bite was harmless," he said. "Or at least I know it now. It was all those terrible bones. They made me think of my brother's stories." He shuddered. "I'm sorry for the way I behaved. You must be disappointed."

Diego began to deny it, but the emperor waved him off.

"You may think me a weakling, but I assure you I am not."

Diego looked down at the grass. He had been considered a weakling himself once and, now that he had just one arm, he was a weakling. A weakling, squared.

Maximiliano said he was greatly in the debt of the Indian man who had ministered to him the evening before. "He told me things. He made me understand what was going on. The bones. My brother. The scorpion. They are all of a piece. Do you understand what I am saying?"

Diego said he thought he did. In a way, the emperor was merely confirming what Diego already knew. Every man has his weaknesses, and there is no shame in it, or not necessarily. What is important is to face up to weakness and not back down. It seemed the emperor was doing that. Diego smiled.

"You can forgive me?" said Maximiliano.

"Yes, of course. There's no—"

"Friends?" His Majesty offered his hand.

"Friends," said Diego.

They shook hands and then embraced, a Mexican *abrazo*.

The travellers spent that day and the ensuing night in Taxco. By the second morning of their stay, the emperor was almost fully restored, and the entire party set out early for the return journey to the hacienda at Cocoyotla.

As for Beatríz, she said she was mystified about the boneyard Diego and Maximiliano had found at the edge of the subterranean lagoon. She'd had no knowledge of its existence, and Diego had no trouble believing her. She wanted to convey her apologies to the emperor, but he suggested it was unlikely that Maximiliano needed reminding.

"Very well," she said. "I have faith in your judgment."

Before leaving Taxco, Diego spoke privately with Padre Buendía. The priest said he had no information about Ángela Peralta or her whereabouts, or those of her son, but he thought he might be able to acquire some intelligence on both counts. There was within the Church a network of priests who subscribed to liberal principles and were unhappy with the present hierarchy. He would make inquiries and report to Diego in the strictest confidence.

They shook hands, and Diego strode out into the stable yard, where his horse was waiting along with the rest of the party. The priest gave him a leg up and handed him the reins. Almost at once, the emperor guided his horse alongside Diego's.

"Ride with me, Serrano," he said. "Let us speak of happy things."

"Yes, Your Majesty." Diego's heart seemed to swell.

"Let us be off, then," said Bombelles. The Austrian officer reined his horse around and began the long journey home. The others all followed.

PART THREE

The Fat Man with Glasses

CHAPTER 25

IT WAS LATE AT NIGHT. After stabling his horse near the Plaza Santa Cecilia, Diego ambled along the rain-dark street, picking his way through the mud and dung, trying to avoid the beggars and hawkers. Suddenly, a wiry trollop hailed him with a cackle, followed by a disgusting proposition.

He waved her away. "*¡Váyase!*"

Normally, such a hag would have taken him at his word, but this woman proved more persistent.

"Go away," he repeated.

She replied that, as a *manco*—a man with just one arm—he might have need of her assistance in order to gratify himself, as she put it. It was a service she would be only too happy to provide.

"I said no!"

Diego turned upon the woman and would have applied a well-aimed boot had the creature not begun to laugh in a throaty voice that soon betrayed its owner—Baldemar. The two men embraced. Even dressed as an old whore, Baldemar seemed in much improved condition, his frame at least somewhat filled out, his complexion far less sallow, no sign of the terrible rash he had suffered previously.

They quickly found their way to their usual haunt, a dark and creaking place hidden away from prying eyes. Over jars of pulque, Baldemar announced that he was a *gamberro* now—an outlaw, as such men were called by Mexico's conservatives, who refused to flatter their enemies by calling them soldiers. Baldemar and several dozen other men, including those who had been freed with him from the Martinica Prison, were honouring a pact they had made while under sentence of death. They were dwelling among the people. They were fighting the monarchists and the French. Their numbers had grown, and they continued to grow.

"It began with Márquez," Baldemar said. "When we handed him and his men over to the French in Veracruz, they gave us three hundred reals apiece. A thousand for Márquez. Not only that, but they agreed to open the prison at San Juan de Ulúa and set the inmates free. Nearly a hundred of them. We promised each man a carbine and a horse, and they all joined up with us. Well, most of them did. They call me el Gordo de las Gafas."

Thc fat man with glasses.

The name had gained currency even though Baldemar was anything but fat nowadays. But he did wear glasses, a pair of green-tinted lenses that gave him a mysterious air, at once studious and daring. Already, he and his fellow gamberros had fought several battles in the rugged, precipitous lands to the east. They had taken dozens of prisoners each time. And, each time, Baldemar had followed a remarkable course, his signal inspiration. He actually set his prisoners free, something almost unheard of in Mexico, where prisoners taken in combat normally stood an excellent prospect of torture followed by execution. Word of this practice had spread widely, giving him a decisive advantage in battle.

"It means our enemies don't fight so much," he said. "There's no need to battle to the death. What would be the point? They might as well give themselves up. They know we won't kill them. A lot of them turn coats and join our side. The rest go back to their wives."

To the people who dwelled in the hill country to the east and on the coastal flats, Baldemar had already become a hero, a legend. As he spoke of this newly won status he betrayed no trace of false modesty but no boastfulness, either. It wasn't a hollow claim but simple fact.

"I should have killed Márquez, though," he said. "I can see that now. I should have put him under while I had the chance."

"Why?"

"He's put together his own band of fighters. They're based in Tampico." Baldemar spat on the floor. "Murdering scum. People call them the Blue Butchers on account of their uniforms." Baldemar tipped back his drink, swallowed, wiped his lips. "He means to kill me."

"That surprises you?"

"No. It's just that he can't. I have a claim on his soul. Remember?"

Diego did remember. But he wasn't so sure any longer that Baldemar was right. Other men might abide by that ancient code of honour. But Márquez? He glanced up at the barman, and motioned for their glasses to be refilled. He changed the subject. "What about Ángela?"

"I hear you spoke to Padre Buendía. In Taxco."

"I did. How did you know?"

Baldemar shrugged. "These priests," he said. "Anyway, I'm sure he'll find her—or at least find out where she is. It shouldn't take long."

"Then what?"

"Then we spring her loose. Or I do. You won't be in Mexico when that happens."

"I won't?"

"No, you won't."

Diego gazed at his surroundings, the murky light of the pulquería, the wavering candles, the half-illuminated men hunched over their crude irregular glasses. He had no idea what Baldemar was getting at, but he had little doubt that something was about to change and that he would have little say in the matter. He owed Baldemar a debt he could never hope to repay. But, unlike the Tiger of Tacubaya, he would keep chipping away at it just the same. He knew it, and Baldemar knew it, too.

But still his friend said nothing further on this subject he'd just raised.

Finally, Diego banged his palm against the wooden counter. "If I'm not in Mexico," he said, "then where the hell will I be?"

Baldemar turned his jar around in a circle on the bar. Then he turned it around again. "In Washington," he said. "In Washington, District of Columbia."

Diego looked down at the milky surface of his drink. He lifted the jar to his lips, tipped it back, felt the liquid well in his throat. He swallowed. He hadn't expected this, and he had no idea what it meant. But there it was again. He wasn't a free man yet. He knew he had only to wait and sip his drink, and eventually Baldemar would get around to explaining what all this was about. Eventually, Baldemar did.

"Fine," Diego said when his friend was done explaining, although it wasn't fine at all. But he would do it because he had a duty to uphold. Besides, who knew where it all might lead? He was the servant of two masters and did not have the luxury of knowing anything for certain.

Out on the street, in the chill nighttime breeze, the two parted company and walked off in contrary directions yet again.

It was either a very good time or a very bad time to be leaving Mexico. Diego couldn't decide which.

Since his return to the capital, the emperor seemed to have recovered from his strange ordeal at the shining caves and had thrown himself back into his daily round of duties and recreations. He rose early, as always. He continued to work on his magnum opus, codifying the innumerable protocols and formalities that pertained to the imperial court. He rode through the countryside near Chapultepec. He signed decrees. He visited orphanages. He received petitioners. He presided at receptions and balls. He appointed and sacked ministers so frequently that Diego sometimes wondered whether his own job was safe. But, no matter how quickly he lost patience with others, the emperor seemed to have an abiding faith in his one-armed secretary.

In most ways, everything was just as it had been before. Still, something had changed. The trauma Maximiliano had suffered that day in the rugged lands beyond Cuernavaca had left its mark. He did not talk about the cache of bones he and Diego had discovered. For the most part, he did not refer to the scorpion sting or the ensuing drama, but it was clear the experience had affected him deeply. He seemed distracted at times. He made excuses and neglected some of his former duties, eager to escape the endless ceremonies and rituals of high office. He began to take an inordinate interest in what seemed to be marginal enterprises—pet projects of his own devising. He began to absent himself more often from the capital. Diego could only speculate about what had changed or why. But when he looked back on that foray to the shining caves, he sometimes wondered whether Maximiliano had discovered in that excess of bones some premonition of his own death.

If the emperor spoke of that day at all, it was to recall the curandero in Taxco, his soothing, sympathetic ways. Once or twice he even called for pots of boiling water and pine gum to be set up in his study, so that he might purify his lungs while dictating his correspondence. Mindful that don Plutarco was of native blood, Maximiliano developed a new interest in Mexico's indigenous people. He officially declared himself "Protector of the Indians" and formally outlawed the practice of debt peonage. These measures produced no practical benefit as far as Diego could tell, but they did cause additional grumbling among the Mexicans at court and further alienated the emperor from the Church.

As for Salm-Salm, he had restored himself to the emperor's favour. True, his frenzied journey back to Mexico City had proved unsuccessful. He had meant to wrest control of Ángela and her son from Labastida and to formalize the boy's adoption by the emperor and empress. In that, he had failed. But Maximiliano was grateful for the attempt and appointed him grand master of the imperial household. Among other lucrative duties, the prince was now responsible for approving the petitions filed by Mexicans seeking formal recognition of their claims to nobility. He was delighted, for here was a highly remunerative post. Most of the petitioners were more than willing to pay handsomely for a favourable response.

Meanwhile, Mexico's internal war ground on in the hinterland, far from the occupied capital. The French were gaining ground, it seemed, and Juárez would soon have little option but to withdraw even further north. At this rate, he would soon find his back pressed against the border with Texas, where he would have no choice but to make a final stand. No reply had been received to the missives Maximiliano had dispatched. Maybe Juárez had received them or maybe he had not. In either case, the result was the same—exactly nothing.

By this time, it was well known that General Márquez had organized a private fighting force and that he and his men now marauded the coastal lands to the east, just as Baldemar had said. The Blue Butchers, as they were known, had their headquarters in Tampico on the torrid Gulf coast. From there, Márquez and his men terrorized the countryside. Their main goal, they claimed, was to protect the supply lines between Mexico City and the sea, but they mostly devoted themselves to savagery and mayhem.

CHAPTER 26

THE EMPEROR DREW TO a halt and frowned. "I confess there is a small risk of fire."

Diego gazed down at a huge expanse of double-layered taffeta that sprawled across the pavilion to the west of Chapultepec Castle. He said, "Is fire involved?"

Three days had passed since Diego's meeting with Baldemar. He had yet to make any preparations for his journey, the expedition to Washington, but he knew he could not put it off for long. Now it was late in the afternoon. In company with the emperor, he was strolling along the perimeter of a great swathe of stout grey fabric laid out upon a broad stone terrace. Fashioned at Maximiliano's behest, the material stretched more than sixteen metres in diameter and was lined throughout with heavy construction paper. The device was meant to fly.

Diego, however, wished to speak of a different matter. He explained that a letter had just arrived from the Mexico City archbishopric. It seemed the papal nuncio, a certain Monseñor Meglia, was to depart Rome soon, en route to Mexico. "I suspect he is by now on his way."

"Is he?" said Maximiliano. He glanced down at the reams of taffeta. "Well, of course, we are subject to the limits of available technology."

"That is so," said Diego, reflecting on the lack of an undersea telegraph cable linking Europe to the Americas. Then he realized Maximiliano was referring to the apparent imperfections of the aerial balloon unfurled at their feet—a Montgolfier balloon, he called it.

The emperor explained that there appeared to be no choice but to rely upon standard combustion as a means of propelling the device into the air. In Mexico, it was impossible to obtain a reliable supply of hydrogen gas. So, instead, the balloon would be filled with ordinary air heated by means of a wood fire contained in a suspended brazier. This was potentially hazardous, but one had to concede that hydrogen was also a volatile substance.

"I see," said Diego. He paused before continuing. Formerly, he told the emperor, he had opposed entering into discussions with Labastida about Ángela and her son, for the archbishop would inevitably turn the conversation to the reform laws—and to his demands for their repeal. Nothing could be gained in such a debate. But now, with the imminent arrival of a direct emissary from Rome, maybe it would be wise to learn what exactly the Church proposed.

"Yes, yes," said Maximiliano. He put his hand to his forehead, seemingly distracted. "I see your point. But perhaps we had better reflect on the subject for a while yet. I propose to take the matter under advisement." He withdrew his cigarette case from a pocket of his loose cotton shirt, removed a cigarette, tapped it against the case, and set it between his lips. Soon, he resumed his stroll around the perimeter of the balloon.

The next morning's mail included a lengthy communication from Napoleon in Paris. The emperor cringed. There was no one in the world he resented more deeply than Napoleon, unless it was his own older brother, Franz Josef, who had inherited their father's title and ruled the Austrian Empire. But, apart from his older sibling, it was Napoleon who most set his teeth on edge. Maximiliano put down his hot chocolate and settled into the padded leather chair at his desk, steeling himself. It was just past six o'clock in the morning.

"All right," he said. "Read it to me, please."

Diego did so. The emperor of France, Napoleon III, conveyed his most cordial respects to Maximilian and the empress of Mexico and wished them every—

"Yes, yes. But what does he *say*? What does he want?"

Diego scanned the contents of the letter. "Money," he said. "To be blunt."

"Dear God." The emperor rubbed his eyes. "Go on."

In short, Napoleon desired that Maximilian commence at once to reimburse France for the maintenance of the troops fighting in Mexico under the command of Maréchal Achille Bazaine. Furthermore, he wished to receive a schedule of repayment for the many long-standing debts that Mexico had incurred over the years and that were still owed to a host of French creditors. He requested that a precise timetable be submitted at once, setting out dates and other particulars. He made specific reference to the Jecker bonds, which Diego knew were a larcenous obligation incurred not by Juárez but by the conservative regime that predated him. This act of extortion was infamous in Mexico. Diego reminded the emperor of the details. The Swiss banking house of Jecker had paid out one million pesos but on the most usurious of terms. So far, the accrued interest amounted to more than fifteen million pesos, all still outstanding. It was well known that the Duke of Morny—Napoleon's bastard half-brother—had purchased a large interest in the contract. No doubt this circumstance played a role in Napoleon's demand.

"No doubt." Maximiliano sighed. "I call it an outrage."

Diego agreed. It seemed France had invaded Mexico for no other purpose than to collect bills, all hopelessly unpayable. By any reasonable definition, the country was bankrupt.

The emperor cupped his chin in his hands. "What else does he say?"

Diego found his place, then hesitated. This was awkward. The ensuing portion of the letter turned to matters of a more intimate nature. Diego was unsure how to proceed.

"Read on," said the emperor. He closed his eyes. "What does he say?"

Diego read on. Napoleon expressed his dismay at news he had lately received concerning expenses being incurred by the emperor for his personal comfort—the refurbishment of certain residences, for example, in particular a domicile being renovated at great expense in a place called Cuernavaca, not to mention the rumoured installation of an opulent and unnecessary new boulevard somewhere near the Mexican capital. He further complained of reports concerning the many banquets, balls, and other entertainments that were being held at the Imperial Palace in Mexico City. This profligacy seemed inappropriate in wartime and most especially in consideration of the territory's pressing obligations to Paris. He requested a prompt and specific reply.

"Dear God," said Maximiliano. He reached for his hot chocolate and drained the cup. "Where does he hear these tales? Does the man have a spy posted among us?"

"I don't know," said Diego, who in fact thought it extremely likely. He even had an idea who the agent of French imperialism might be, but he did not like to say so. These days, the Prince of Salm-Salm was once again in the emperor's good graces.

Maximiliano shook his head. "Pay up, pay up. It's all very well for Napoleon to say. But this country is at war. Outside the capital, chaos reigns."

Maximiliano was working himself into a rage. "How dare the man speak of money!" he said. "At such a time! We have other challenges to contend with—this plague of disunity, the question of succession, the conflict with the Church. Does the man not know that I rise at four o'clock in the morning? This castle was a shambles till I got my hands on it. And the House of Borda? In Cuernavaca? You saw the place. And the road? It's not a road. It's a monument. It will make Mexicans proud. Does he not realize any of this?"

For a time, Maximiliano remained ramrod straight in his chair, silent and distracted. Eventually, he let out a sigh. The letter deserved a response, but just now he was unsure what the response should be. "Let us leave the reply for another day."

"Very well, Your Majesty." Diego folded the letter and placed it in the document box.

The next epistle was yet another in the almost daily missives they received from the archbishop, who was yet again demanding an audience with His Majesty. Such a meeting was particularly urgent, the prelate insisted, in order to prepare for the imminent arrival of the papal nuncio, a prospect he had raised in his previous correspondence a day earlier.

The emperor moaned out loud. "I give up," he said. "I surrender. Very well then. Let there be a meeting with the archbishop. But you attend to it, Serrano. You talk to him."

His Majesty rose and wandered into his bedchamber. Diego tidied the papers that were now overflowing the desk. That done, he would compose a reply to the archbishop. But what on earth was he supposed to say?

Chapter 27

"You have read this, Your Excellency?" Diego produced a recent edition of *L'Ère nouvelle,* a gazette published in Mexico City in French. This issue contained news of the exploits of Baldemar Peralta, along with certain veiled but unflattering references to the Church. The article did not specifically mention Ángela Peralta or her son, but anyone conversant with events in Mexico City could draw the connection. He held the journal out to Labastida.

The prelate merely glanced at it before tossing the pages into the air. "Yes, yes," he said. "I have read the article you mean."

The leaves pulled loose from one another, fluttering away in the wake of the archbishop's carriage, an English-built landau with a remarkably advanced suspension system. Diego felt as if he were careening through the streets of the capital on the back of an immense cat. His stomach roiled at each elongated twist or turn.

It was a Sunday evening. As was customary at this time of the week, many of the capital's most distinguished residents were out on the promenade. They paraded back and forth in their carriages along the Paseo de Bucareli.

"Ah, look there." The archbishop's ruddy, moon-shaped face lit up. He raised his right arm to salute a carriage advancing from the opposite direction. "Why yes. It's the Marqués de Vivanco. Look, he's waving at us. How very fine. You know, his carriage is not worth half the value of this one, yet you can see for yourself how proudly he behaves. Do you know his wife, the *marquesa*?" He scrunched up his face, as if swallowing something rancid.

The marquis and his wife continued to wave gaily as the two carriages floated past one another. Like most of the other vehicles tottering back and forth, these two were open to the air. More than a few of the conveyances bore an elaborate and freshly painted coat of arms on their polished side panels. The newly minted peers of the realm flaunted their status to all, but mainly to each other.

The spectacle made Diego feel ill, but the archbishop was delighted. He waved to them all. The women were in full toilette, their elaborate coiffures bedecked with jewels and secured by mantillas of imported lace to protect the careful arrangement of their hair.

"I take it," said the archbishop, "that you wish to revisit the subject of the opera singer and her son."

Diego was about to reply, but Labastida held up a pink and fleshy hand.

"You will forgive me if I begin."

"Very well."

In his arch diction, Labastida declared that he had other matters to attend to that were far more urgent than the fate of any individual woman, with or without a son.

"I speak of the reform laws in particular," he said.

Before Diego could intervene, the prelate resumed his presentation. He said that any lasting agreement between the two sides—the palace and the Church—must await the arrival of Monseñor Meglia, the papal nuncio. In the meantime, he believed it was possible to anticipate the general outlines of an accord. All Church properties stolen by the previous liberal government must be returned. As for the cemeteries, they too must be restored to Church control, along with the registry of births and deaths and the performance of marriage services. All religious holidays were again to be officially observed. The schools were to be operated by the Church once again. Roman Catholicism must once more be declared the official and exclusive religion of the country. All heretical cults were to be banned.

"I see," said Diego. "But I am not here to discuss relations between Church and state."

"Nor am I," said Labastida. "That will be undertaken by Monseñor Meglia. All in good time."

"In the meantime, I would like to inquire as to the well-being of Ángela Peralta. And her son."

"I thought as much," said the archbishop. "Well, since you ask, I can confidently say that both are in excellent health physically and spiritually. The woman in particular is a shimmering model of piety. If only there were more like her."

"Where are they?"

"They are quite secure."

"But where?"

The archbishop said that, unfortunately, he was not at liberty to say.

"I see," said Diego. "You are not concerned that many Mexicans oppose you?"

"Rabble. Extremists. I discount them."

Labastida turned away, and a gust of wind nearly dislodged the purple skullcap pinned in place at the back of his head. He reached up to keep it from flying off, and immediately a smile lit his large, round face.

"Look there," he said. He raised his other hand in a magisterial wave. "It is Sánchez Navarro. How delightful to see him." In a low voice he added, "Poor man. I hear he has offered immense sums in bribes in order to earn a position for his wife at court, so far to no avail." He grimaced. "The woman's a peasant, you know—thoroughly ill-bred. Her father was in trade, I believe. Between you and me, I regard their marriage as an abomination. I have it on excellent authority that she was with child at the time of the nuptials. Scandalous."

He waved again and made a sign of the cross as the carriage swayed past, stirring up thin coils of dust along the rutted breadth of the Paseo de Bucareli. Slowly, dusk settled over Mexico City, and the stream of *carretelas* and conveyances gradually thinned until the only creatures remaining on the boulevard were the barefoot vendor women, the lepers, the beggars, and the pariah dogs snuffling through the gutters and the dark.

The next morning, Maximiliano announced that he meant to absent himself from Mexico City for a number of weeks in order to become better acquainted with other parts of his realm. He proposed a tour of the Bajío, the lofty, fertile valley that unfolded to the north of the capital. More or less peaceful, the region was said to contain a great deal of historical interest. The emperor tightened the sash of his dressing gown and plucked a biscuit from the silver plate on his desk. He said he expected to be away for the better part of a month.

"But the papal nuncio," said Diego. "He will certainly arrive during that time."

Maximiliano frowned, as if he had not thought of this difficulty till now. He bit the biscuit in half. "Hmm. That does pose a dilemma."

Diego decided it was time to announce his own plans. He, too, would be absent for no little while.

"Absent? Where?"

"Washington, District of Columbia."

"Whatever for?"

Diego had prepared an answer. To ascertain the fortunes of war in that immense territory, fortunes that would bear directly upon events in Mexico. If the southern states were to prove victorious—or at least if they were able to avoid outright defeat—then it was probable that Maximiliano and the Confederacy could make an alliance that would serve both sides. If, however, the north were to win, then it was difficult to think that Washington would look kindly upon a French military presence in Mexico.

"Your Majesty is undoubtedly aware of the Monroe Doctrine of 1823—"

"Declaring the Americas off limits to interference by European powers. Of course." Maximiliano brushed a smattering of sugar from his lips. "You know, I am inclined to agree with you. I will provide you with a letter of introduction, of course. And God speed."

"Thank you. And the papal nuncio?"

The emperor frowned. He reached for a document, seemingly at random, and briefly perused its contents. His face lit up. "I know." He glanced at Diego. "Why not leave the papal nuncio to Charlotte?"

"To the empress?"

"Yes." The emperor sat back and smiled. "Why, it's perfect. They won't possibly be expecting that. Inconceivable."

And Diego had to agree. Inconceivable was exactly what it was.

That night, Diego sprawled in his bed, unable to sleep, wondering what species of creature he had become. In a certain light, he was in the same predicament as General Márquez. Both of them were trapped in a contradiction that offered no way out. The Tiger of Tacubaya had a grudge against Baldemar that could be avenged only through murder, but he also owed Baldemar his life, which ought to have made murder unthinkable. Meanwhile, Diego was bound to both Baldemar and the emperor.

Baldemar had saved his life, but the emperor had saved Baldemar's. As a result, he was under an obligation to them both. So far, he'd managed to sustain this contradiction, but how much longer could it hold? Now he was to depart for Washington, supposedly as an emissary of the emperor but with no intention of acting on Maximiliano's behalf. One day, he was a monarchist, the next day, republican. It was as if the man named Diego Serrano did not really exist at all or as if he existed in multiple versions, like a chameleon—a chameleon that, in this case, had kicked off his bedcovers and kept rolling from side to side in his bed, trying to find a position that was halfway amenable to sleep. But, on this night at least, no such position seemed to exist, and so he kept tossing in his bed, worrying and fretting and doubting himself.

Whoever "himself" was.

CHAPTER 28

FIVE DAYS LATER, Diego departed the capital, bound for Veracruz. Despite the abysmal condition of the roads, the journey to the coast passed without incident. At Veracruz, he boarded a mail packet that ploughed away through the pale silver waters of the Gulf of Mexico, bound for Havana. From that Cuban city, he travelled north by steam vessel, foregoing the usual landings at Miami, Jacksonville, and Savannah, for those cities were located in states of the Confederacy and would provide no harbour for a Washington-bound ship. But the steam packet was able to make landfall at Wilmington. A Union army had lately wrested the city from the Confederacy, and Wilmington now swelled with northern soldiers, patrolling the rubble-strewn streets of a sullen and ravaged town.

Diego ventured ashore, where he found it an easy matter to engage several Unionists in conversation, in exchange for a bottle of good Cuban rum and some Cuban cigars. These were enjoyed at leisure in the dust-laden bar of a half-cratered hotel. Diego's English was inferior to his French, but he could convey an air of easygoing camaraderie when the occasion demanded. He learned that a large army of seasoned volunteers under General William Tecumseh Sherman was even now marching to the south and must soon capture Atlanta. Before long, he was told, Savannah would also fall to the Unionists. These worn-out men were resting at Wilmington before proceeding south themselves, and they painted Sherman's march to the sea as a project of terrible but necessary destruction. The Unionist general meant to ruin the economy of the south, laying waste to whatever he found along the way—farms, warehouses, factories, bridges. He would sap from his enemies not just their lives but also their will.

Diego reboarded the packet that evening. The following morning, the vessel steamed north, bound for Cape Hatteras, en route to Virginia Beach. There, he sent a cable to William H. Seward, the American secretary of state. He requested a meeting.

Diego understood that the government of Abraham Lincoln in Washington had so far followed a policy of strict neutrality regarding the conflict in Mexico, and it did not require exceptional intelligence to understand why. The Unionists undoubtedly feared a large French army stationed to the south and saw no reason to offend Napoleon III unnecessarily. This was where matters stood in the early months of 1865, but Diego wondered if the north's neutrality would long continue should Washington win its civil war. Such a victory, he was told, seemed likelier by the day.

"Look," said the vessel's captain, an avuncular and gregarious sailor from Santiago de Cuba. He spoke in the rapid-fire manner of his people and pointed off to the southwest, toward the mouth of the Appomattox River and the shores of Chesapeake Bay, forested in chestnut trees and elms. He said the supreme commander of the Unionist forces, General Ulysses S. Grant, was camped with his army not far upriver at a place called City Point. Grant was biding his time, waiting for Sherman to complete his march of devastation through the south. When the Confederate forces were surrounded, the Unionists would march on Richmond, the southern capital. The end would come quickly.

That night, the packet steamed north through Chesapeake Bay and

Pocomoke Sound, bound for Annapolis. Diego paced the deck, smoking the last of his Havana cigars.

Four weeks after departing Mexico City, he checked into a room at a small hotel on Pennsylvania Avenue in Washington, D.C. The following morning, he received confirmation that his request for a meeting with the secretary of state had been granted but could not be scheduled until ten days hence. These were cold, grey days in Washington. A drizzle pelted from the low tombstone sky, and Diego passed his time in long damp walks, interspersed with even longer interludes in the city's hotel lounges and bars, where he medicated his boredom with spirits while studying the American newspapers. As regarded Mexico, the journals in Washington were remarkably up-to-date, providing details of the conflict in his country that were unknown even to him, all reflecting miserably on the fortunes of the republican side. From a Washington paper called the *Daily Evening Star*, he learned that Benito Juárez had abandoned Monterrey and was in the process of installing himself at El Paso del Norte, a fly-blown speck of land on Mexico's border with Texas. From there, he would have no escape.

As a liberal, Diego regarded this as deeply discouraging news. As a member of the imperial court, he must take the opposite view. He lit an American cigarette, ordered another brandy, and vacillated between these two opinions, marvelling at the rapid progress of the news in this, the modern world.

The day for his meeting with Seward arrived at last. Diego found the American secretary of state to be a gruff individual, evidently intelligent but little given to divulging more information than necessary. The American briefly outlined the conventional Unionist view of Mexico—an outlook of strictest neutrality. This was undoubtedly the policy at present, but Diego believed it was likely to change once the war pitting the American states was concluded. In fact, given northern fortunes in that conflict, he suspected it must already be changing. He gave Seward every opportunity to say so, but the man stuck to the official line. Washington was neutral as regarded developments in Mexico.

Diego let the matter drop for the time being and waited in silence for the American to speak.

Seward ran a hand beneath his chin and cleared his throat and then, somewhat stagily, straightened his tie. "Whom exactly do you represent?" he said. "Hapsburg or Juárez? I can tell you have ties to them both. That can't have been easy to arrange."

"The politics of my country are a complicated affair."

"Contradictory, you mean."

"That too."

Seward said he was interested in any news his visitor might possess concerning recent events in Mexico. How went the war?

"Quite well for the French," said Diego. Without bothering to mention his source, he said the liberal president, Benito Juárez, had been obliged to retreat ever further north and must soon reach the border with Texas. Slowly and steadily, it seemed, the French were consolidating their military control of the country.

"And the emperor? Maximilian—how is he making out?"

Diego shifted his weight, easing forward. "For the moment, the emperor seems reasonably secure."

"I don't follow."

"It's easily explained. If your government were to alter its stance toward Mexico, the situation would become very different. Everything in my country would change in an instant."

"But I've already told you. Our policy is good as gold. We are not concerned with anything the Frogs might do, as long as they stay south of the Rio Grande. You can take that to the bank, my friend."

Diego frowned. If a man says something once, it is not out of the question for you to believe him. But if he says it twice, you must leave some room for doubt. And if he says it a third time, then you must seek another opinion, which was exactly what Diego decided to do. He remembered his conversation on Chesapeake Bay with the captain of the Cuban packet, who had told him that General Ulysses S. Grant was encamped with his army not far inland, in Virginia. Was this still the case?

Seward said it was.

"I am told this General Grant once fought against my country." Diego meant the American intervention in Mexico, when the United States captured roughly half of Mexico's territory. For a time, the gringos had even occupied Mexico City. He had heard somewhere that Grant later regretted his participation in that war. He told Seward he would like to meet this man if it were possible.

"Why wouldn't it be possible? We have nothing to hide. *Mi casa es su casa*. Isn't that what you people say? Leave it to me. I will arrange a letter of introduction."

The document was delivered to Diego's hotel that afternoon, and he set out the next morning in a hired coach that carried him south through the rolling farmland of Virginia to the confluence of the James River with the Appomattox. He found the Unionist commander at his headquarters, a tent pitched on the front lawn of a gabled and dormered house belonging to a certain Dr. Richard Epps. The building overlooked a view of shimmering aspens and silver waters, where the merging currents of the two rivers swirled and eddied in the winter sunlight.

It surprised him to see that Grant's accommodation was not much different from any of the countless other tents arrayed about the estate, housing many thousands of troops. This arrangement was very unlike the practice in Mexico, where generals surrounded themselves with luxuries and comforts, while their men went about in threadbare uniforms and makeshift sandals and slept under the stars. Diego observed that American military practice seemed to differ from Mexico's in another respect, too. In Mexico, armies were followed by columns of women on foot—the wives of soldiers, who did the cooking and cleaning and bore much of the cargo, and often shared in the fighting as well. As a result, a Mexican army was a slow-moving beast. But he saw no evidence of soldiers' wives at City Point, with the solitary exception of Grant's wife, who had a tent of her own that stood not far from her husband's, suggesting that American officers indulged themselves in some perquisites after all.

CHAPTER 29

GENERAL GRANT WAS DRINKING coffee at a trestle table set up on the lawn in front of Dr. Epps's house. He had evidently been alerted to the arrival of a Mexican emissary. When Diego appeared, the general was already on his feet. He invited his guest to join him for coffee, unless he preferred something stronger.

"Coffee would do well," said Diego.

Grant smiled amiably and got up. He was broad of face, with prominent, almost rock-like features, and he wore a full beard and moustache. He removed the pot from its place by the fire, filling two tin mugs. He returned to the table. "I have many fond memories of your land and your people," he said. Nonetheless, he wished he had never participated in the Mexican war, as unjust a contest as had ever been waged by one country against another. But it was done now, and its outcome would not be altered by any act of man.

"No," said Diego. "Unfortunately for us."

"Most unfortunately for you."

For a time, they continued to discuss the many injustices and sorry consequences of that long-ago war, until Grant shrugged and nodded toward Diego's mug. "Will you have more coffee?"

"No, thank you. But I believe you mentioned something stronger?"

"Then bourbon is the answer." Grant waved at an orderly, who promptly attended to the serving of drinks. The general raised his glass. "You would think this war would have blocked the supply of two commodities before all others—tobacco and bourbon. And yet it is not so." He raised his glass, settled into his chair, and took a first swallow. He glanced at Diego's left arm. "I take it you have known something of soldiering yourself."

Diego nodded and spoke without thinking. "But all that is in the past now."

"Is it? I have always found that the past has a disagreeable tendency to overstay its welcome. We would fight many fewer wars if it were not so."

"I stand corrected. What you say is true, in my country more than most. In Mexico, the past endures forever."

"So I have heard. But I do not think that you have come to speak of philosophy."

"No." Diego swallowed a mouthful of bourbon. "No, I have not. I have come to speak of the future."

"I thought as much." The American general thrust out his legs and crossed his arms behind his head. He told the orderly to leave the bottle of bourbon. It was in safe hands. "Very well," he said. "Speak to me of the future."

Diego spent the night in a tent set up for his use. When he left in the morning, he possessed a fair understanding of what might be expected from the United States once its terrible war was concluded. He understood as well that the conflict's end was closer than he had imagined, and its outcome was as plain as the lines upon the palm of his hand.

In their long conversation on the subject, Grant had left no doubt that the U.S. government would take an extremely dim view of the presence of French troops in Mexico. In time of war, he explained, a government does not like to antagonize another power unnecessarily, and so Washington had been reluctant to court the displeasure of Paris. But, once his country's own internal conflict was ended, he believed that President Lincoln would declare its firm support for Benito Juárez, the rightful president of the Mexican republic.

But no, he said—anticipating Diego's next question—this policy would not extend to authorizing the provision of arms or other military equipment to the republican side. He paused, and his expression changed, if only for an instant, into what might have been a smile.

"I refer to policy," he said. On the other hand, there is *practice.*"

"I believe I understand you," said Diego. "It is to discuss the practical aspects that I have come to your country."

"And sought me out," said Grant, "as a friend of Mexico."

"Yes. As a friend of Mexico."

It was now that the two men began to converse in serious terms. Diego learned, for example, that there was a most talented, resourceful, and innovative young man to be found in a Texas town called Franklin. His name was J.S. Bartlett, and he was the correspondent in that region for the *Boston Journal*, a reputable publication.

"'A reputable publication,'" said Diego. "In my country, many would call that a contradiction in terms."

"Yes, well . . ." said Grant. He laughed. "In *this* country, the press is invariably above reproach of any kind. But regarding Bartlett, I believe his sympathies correspond closely to those of President Lincoln, at least as regards Mexico. Moreover, he is employed as the United States customs agent in that region, which makes him a useful man to know. I would urge you, if you should ever find yourself in Franklin, Texas, to look the man up."

Grant continued speaking, and so Diego found himself becoming increasingly familiar with a variety of American weaponry called the Spencer carbine, a breech-loading rifle that had been introduced into service in 1863 and had proved itself in battle, especially when augmented by the Blakeslee quick-loading cartridge box. Some ninety-five thousand of these rifles had so far been purchased by the U.S. government for its troops, and it was more than likely that some portion of these firearms would become supernumerary once hostilities had ceased. It was difficult to say how many weapons would fall into this category but, in round numbers, one could certainly speak in terms of tens of thousands.

"I see," said Diego.

"You must speak with Mr. Bartlett," said Grant as the two men shook hands before parting. "If you are ever in the fine town of Franklin, Texas, Mr. Bartlett is certainly the man to see."

On his return to Washington, D.C., Diego conducted meetings with diverse individuals, all of whom had been recommended to him by Ulysses S. Grant. Later, he travelled by train to New York City, where he retained the services of a local portraitist, a man named Hoskins who was adept in the reproduction of images according to a process known as ambrotype. Hoskins accompanied him in a hired coach that transported them both to New Rochelle, a rather dismal suburb of the city, where Diego sought out a Mexican woman by the name of Margarita Maza de Juárez, a gracious matriarch who was living there with her three daughters and three sons. She was the wife of the Mexican president, and she had been dispatched to New York City some months earlier for her safety and that of her family. Baldemar Peralta had given him the woman's address during their last conversation. Diego's meeting with the woman lasted an hour or so. During its course, the man named Hoskins prepared two ambrotype images of the entire family, whose members included an infant son just a few months old. The portraitist said the image needed only to be mounted under glass upon a dark background—a bolt of black velvet, for example—to be complete.

Diego thanked him. He believed this modest acquisition, a likeness of Benito Juárez's exiled family, might stand him in good stead at some future time. Baldemar had assured him that it would. He left the second image with the woman.

Once these missions were completed, Diego returned to his hotel in Manhattan. At the services desk, he booked passage aboard a mail packet that was bound for Havana three days hence. That done, he rode the elevator to the sixth floor, watched the cage door slide open, and trudged alone to his room, where a bottle of contraband bourbon waited. With any luck, he would be back in Mexico City within a matter of weeks.

Chapter 30

"I may be the empress." Carlota adjusted the folds of her dress against the red brocade surface of her chair. "But I am not the general of an army."

She nodded at a servant, who hurried over to replenish her tea.

"You possess an army," said Diego.

"You think so?"

Diego counted them off—thirty thousand French troops, a like number of Mexicans, plus an assortment of Austrian and Belgian volunteers, and a quantity of African and diverse European mercenaries. Taken all together, they amounted to a considerable force.

Carlota nodded. "I'll grant you, the numbers are impressive. But the truth is, Bazaine commands almost all of these men."

"And he answers to Maximiliano."

She smiled. "I think it will become evident in time that Bazaine answers to himself—and to Napoleon. The crown in Mexico survives at the pleasure of Paris."

"You have spoken to your husband about this?"

"Oh yes." She reached up and fussed with several strands of hair that had come loose from her chignon. "But my husband . . . well . . ." Her voice trailed off.

Diego understood. Lately, His Majesty seemed more absorbed by projects of his own devising—the new boulevard or his Montgolfier balloon. He had occupied himself for several weeks on his grand tour of the Bajío and now had taken up residence in Cuernavaca, preferring its warm days and ample sunshine to the often cooler temperatures of Mexico City.

"My husband," said Carlota, "has a very high opinion of your judgment. What do you think we ought to do?"

"I'm not sure." Diego had returned to the Mexican capital only a day earlier. He had been summoned almost at once to Chapultepec Castle by the empress, who was exercising the authority of the Crown in her husband's absence. "Do you mean, as regards Napoleon?" He meant the Frenchman's demands for the repayment of Mexico's debts.

"No. Let us leave that for another day. I mean, what ought we to do in general, as those who govern this land? What ought we to do about relations between the palace and the Church?"

"Well, I don't see what can be done, other than await the arrival of the papal envoy and take the matter up with him." Monseñor Meglia had yet to reach Mexico, although it was said he would arrive almost any day.

"And adopt what sort of line?"

"A hard line. The hardest possible. These are not the Dark Ages. These are modern times. The Church must be separate from the state, and it must submit to the civil authority."

"In other words, the Church must do what the government says."

"In secular affairs, yes."

"Release Ángela Peralta, for example?"

"Of course."

"And her son?"

"Yes."

"And if the Church refuses?"

Diego shrugged helplessly. "That is the problem."

"We could threaten the use of force, I suppose." Carlota gave a wry smile. "But I wonder whether the troops of France would carry out our wishes. I would not like to issue a hollow threat." She sipped her tea. "But we shall see." She hesitated briefly. "Meanwhile," she said, "we shall have other threats to confound us, I am sure. Please, tell me of your travels."

Diego took a deep breath. He tried to release the tension in his chest. The truth was, he felt a little intimidated by the empress, who was a far more forthright and clear-eyed individual than her husband. Briefly, he told her what he had heard and seen during his travels, sharing what intelligence he could while omitting many details from his account. Of course, he made no mention of Spencer rifles or of the man named Bartlett.

Instead, he outlined what he had learned about the fortunes of war in the American states, making no effort to hide what was patently true. First, the Unionist forces were poised on the brink of victory. Second, such a victory would not serve the interests of Maximiliano or Carlota. He waited for the empress to respond.

"I see," she said.

"I am sorry the news is not better."

Once again, she fiddled with some loose filaments of her hair. She seemed both distracted and agitated. "I suppose that if we ourselves are aware of these developments, it is only natural to assume that Napoleon must be in possession of similar intelligence. Don't you think?"

Diego inclined his head. Yes.

She considered this, then straightened her shoulders. She fixed him with a strained and deliberate smile.

"Very well then," she said, her voice suddenly clipped and formal. It was as if she no longer recognized who he was. "Thank you for efforts on our behalf and for your report. I fear this is all the time I have for you this morning." She proffered her right hand, fingers extended. "Welcome back to Mexico. And good day."

She could be like that—all friendliness one moment and curt to the point of coldness the next. Diego made directly for the stables. He asked the grooms to saddle his mare.

One of the men glanced at his wardrobe. "*¿Inglés o charro, señor?*"

For a moment, the question caught him by surprise. Lately, he had taken to going about in a European style of dress—gabardine trousers and a cutaway frock coat. This was the sort of outfit he had worn while in Washington. It must have occurred to the grooms that he might prefer a different style of saddlery as well, the English style, rather than the more ostentatious Mexican finery.

"*Inglés?*" he said a little tentatively. He wasn't entirely sure. Then he nodded. "*Sí. Inglés.*"

The man shrugged in reply and set off to fulfill the commission, leaving Diego to wonder just who and what he had become: a one-armed Mexican in an Englishman's suit, at once an agent for the republicans and a servant of the imperialists. It seemed impossible that he should go on answering to both these masters, and yet what was to stop him? Who was to stop him? He was still debating these questions when the groom marched out into the courtyard, leading a small roan Arab rather than his horse, which would not have responded well to a European bit or bridle.

He was soon perched upon a thin, unsubstantial saddle, holding two pairs of slender reins attached to a Pelham bit. It was one of the few times he had ridden in this style, and it seemed strange and unpleasant. Besides—four reins in one hand. He felt like an idiot. He kicked his heels and clicked his tongue, and the animal somehow understood what was required and set off for Mexico City at a brisk trot, Diego trying to post to the awkward beat of the horse's stride. He had acquaintances to renew in the more disreputable parts of the capital, and he thought it possible that he might cross paths with Baldemar, too. The man seemed to know exactly when and where to appear, and it occurred to Diego that his old friend must have other spies in his service, men and women who told him all he needed to know—including news of the departure of a thin and swarthy Mexican dressed in an English suit, mounted upon a roan horse, and bound for the walled capital of Mexico.

He felt as if he were impersonating someone. He wondered who this individual might be—his true name, his genuine allegiances, his authentic identity. To whom was he loyal? Whom did he betray? Was he Indian or European? Mexican or something else? The answers should have been obvious, but they were not. Who was he? He posed the question in his mind, over and over again, and he failed to come up with the same answer twice.

Chapter 31

Diego spent the rest of that day and all that night in the walled city, but he found no trace of Baldemar Peralta. He made his way on foot through the hordes of eccentrics, derelicts, and crones that inhabited the city, eyeing each of them warily, as if this one or that one might suddenly break into laughter, remove a hairpiece or toss away a makeshift crutch, clap him on the back, and join him for jars of pulque at Memorias del Futuro. But no one did. If Baldemar was in Mexico City, he did not reveal himself to Diego.

The following afternoon, clad once again in gabardine trousers and a cutaway jacket, Diego guided his roan back to Chapultepec. He found the castle in a torpid state. It was the hour of the siesta, and most of the courtiers and servants were sound asleep. He was intent on following suit, but a palace factotum approached to say that *el señor* had a visitor—a woman who awaited him in an anteroom, one of numerous such chambers on the ground floor of the castle.

What Diego wanted was a bath, a change of clothes, and a long rest. He had barely slept the previous night and had consumed far too much raw *aguardiente*. He was tired, hungry, and sore. His head pounded. At the same time, he was curious to know who this visitor was, and so he followed the servant to the anteroom in question, where he found a young, dark-skinned woman in a white blouse and a long blue skirt, with a brightly woven Indian *falda* wrapped around her waist. He was in such a bleary, muddled state that for a moment he failed to recognize her—but only for a moment. Then he remembered. She was the daughter of the chief gardener at the emperor's house in Cuernavaca—*la india bonita*. He cast about for her name. Sedano? Beatríz Sedano? He had not set eyes upon her since their journey to the shining caves and on to Taxco. Months had passed by since then.

"Señor Serrano," she said.

"You haven't been here long, I hope."

"Only since last night."

"Last night? Here?"

"Where else?"

Diego took a seat opposite the woman. She seemed remarkably fresh given the circumstances. He imagined his own eyes must be bloodshot, his hair askew, his clothing rumpled and creased. Worse, he was wearing an English suit, which probably seemed ridiculous to her. He brushed his hair back with his one hand and tried to set his jacket to rights, smoothing one lapel and then the other. He sat up straight and sought to focus his gaze.

He said, "You came all this way alone?"

She smiled. "My father accompanied me. We rode."

"I see. And your father is . . . ?"

"In the stable. He prefers it there, closer to the horses."

"Ah." Diego inclined his head. "Well, I am sorry to disappoint you, but the emperor does not at present find himself at Chapultepec."

"I know."

Ah, of course. The emperor was in Cuernavaca, after all. She had just come from there. He frowned. "I don't understand. If the emperor is in Cuernavaca, why are you here?"

She coloured, and put a gloved hand to her lips. "I know of no one else I can trust. I . . ." Her voice trailed off. She seemed ill at ease.

It took a few moments, but then Diego understood. "Here." He got up, shut a pair of French doors, turned the latch, and returned to his seat. "Go on," he said.

She nodded and swallowed. "I have come to tell you," she said, hesitating before going on, "that I know the whereabouts of Ángela Peralta. She—"

"You what?"

She repeated what she had just said and then proceeded to explain. When she had finished telling her story, Beatríz folded her hands on her lap, cleared her throat, and looked at Diego.

She said, "We thought somebody should know, somebody in a position to do something. It isn't right."

Diego pondered what he had just heard. Ángela was no longer under the power of Labastida or the Church. She was under the authority of Maximiliano. In Cuernavaca. At a second house he had had constructed there. La Casa del Olvido—this was the name it had been given by some. The House of Forgetfulness. It was so called because it was said to contain only a single bedchamber, as if its owner had forgotten to construct a second.

It was Padre Buendía who had told Beatríz of the woman's whereabouts. He had got word through channels of his own, a network of liberal priests. Ángela was effectively a prisoner, and yet it was not difficult to gain access to the house. Beatríz had done so, on the pretext of running an errand. She had been granted entry and had fallen into conversation with Ángela. The singer was unwell. She barely ate and never went out, wasn't permitted to. Guards were stationed at intervals around the place. A captive in everything but name, Ángela had little to do but mope and fret all day, agonizing over what had become of her son. And, of course, she spent time, both during the day and during the night, with the emperor—and that particular aspect of her confinement was not, it seemed, entirely contrary to her will.

"You know this?" Diego said.

The girl nodded. "She confessed as much."

"To being his mistress?"

Beatríz lowered her head and nodded.

Diego tasted a thread of bile in his throat. He swallowed with difficulty and rubbed his forehead. He looked up. "What about the boy? Where is he?"

"No one knows," she said. "Ángela doesn't know. Neither does the emperor. She told me this herself. He torments her constantly on the subject."

"I can imagine. He wants the child as his heir."

She nodded, then tilted her head. "Perhaps the Prince of Salm-Salm knows about the boy, where he is."

"Salm-Salm? What's he got to do with this?"

She shrugged. "I can't explain it. It's very mysterious. He visits her, dressed as a priest."

"You've seen him?"

She nodded. "Once. He said his name was Father Fischer. I suppose he thought I wouldn't recognize him. But I did. What is he up to?"

"Whatever works to his benefit," said Diego. "That seems to be the sum of it."

The girl's voice dropped to a whisper. "What should we do?"

Diego had no idea. "What does Padre Buendía suggest?"

It turned out the priest had a proposal, and she quickly outlined its main elements. Diego listened without saying a word. It sounded sensible to him—in fact, the only course possible. When she was done explaining, Beatríz smiled briefly and then declared that Padre Buendía wanted someone else's authority for his actions. "Your authority," she said. "He said it was up to you."

"Tell him to go ahead," said Diego. He realized it was unusual for him to be so decisive, but he had been deeply disturbed by what she had told him—Ángela a prisoner, serving as the emperor's concubine, with Salm-Salm's complicity. "Tell Padre Buendía I agree."

"Very well," she said.

He stood up. "In the meantime, let me see about arranging some accommodation for you and your father."

"Thank you, don Diego," she said.

A week later, a letter arrived from Cuernavaca, sent by the emperor and addressed to Salm-Salm. Somehow, the missive found its way into Diego's mail. At once, he set off for the office occupied by the prince. The errand provided him with an excuse for a conversation with the man. Salm-Salm had recently returned from Cuernavaca, but they had barely spoken.

The prince waved Diego in.

"Dear Lord," he said. "What a relief to be away from that place. So remote. So provincial. I miss the city."

Diego held out the errant letter. "Here. I have brought you this."

Salm-Salm glanced at the wax seal and must have recognized the emperor's crest. But he merely nodded and tossed the document onto his desk.

Diego took a seat. "I want to speak to you about Ángela Peralta."

"Really?"

"And her son."

But Salm-Salm would not be drawn out on the subject. Had Ángela taken up residence at a house in Cuernavaca? Was she under guard there? Was the emperor in the habit of visiting the place at all hours? Salm-Salm declined to speak about any of these matters. Nor would he own up to having played any role in any of the events now unfolding in Cuernavaca.

"You know," said the prince, "you seem to have got hold of a fairy tale. It must be the poet in you. As for the woman's son, as far as I know, he remains under the care of the Church."

"On what grounds?"

"Something to do with the registration of his birth, I believe. Some irregularity there."

"But he was born in New York—as you well know."

"Ah," said Salm-Salm. "That might explain it."

It was clear to Diego that he had little to gain here. He rose to his feet. As he did so, Salm-Salm reached for the letter from the emperor and opened it. Almost immediately, his face fell.

"Dear God," he said. "She's gone." He looked up, apparently so shocked by the revelation that he was unaware he was speaking out loud.

"You mean Ángela?" said Diego. "Gone where?"

"I have no idea."

Diego turned to leave, smiling as he did so. He would have made a large wager that Ángela Peralta was safely installed in the presbytery by the parish church in the silver-mining town of Taxco.

Chapter 32

Within a week, the emperor returned to Mexico City and promptly sent word to Diego proposing that they resume their normal schedule the next morning at shortly after four o'clock. Precisely at that hour, the bell rang in Diego's apartment, as it always did when Maximiliano was at Chapultepec. He splashed water onto his face from the ceramic bowl on the dresser, smoothed back his hair, and stumbled out into the darkened, open-air corridor. A half moon peered down from the dark sky, and he shivered in the familiar early morning chill.

Even so, he still felt the heat rise at his collar when he thought of Ángela, of her treatment by the emperor. He stopped and gazed out at the shadowy view, took a deep breath, followed by another, trying to calm himself. Along the walkway below, the pineapple palms glimmered in the moonlight, as though fashioned of tarnished silver. The fronds shifted in the cool breeze. When he thought he was ready, he continued on his way to the emperor's study. At the door, he knocked and then entered.

Maximiliano was pacing the floor in his dressing gown, silhouetted by candlelight, sipping a cup of hot chocolate. He stopped, and his face lit up, as if Diego's arrival had taken him completely by surprise.

"Ah, Serrano. Good to see you."

He seemed unusually excited, his high spirits evident from the staccato tone of his voice. By now, Diego thought he could gauge the state of the emperor's mood with just a glance, and it seemed Maximiliano was bursting with news, with revelations he was eager to share. Diego half expected him to speak of Ángela, of the House of Forgetfulness, and of her mysterious disappearance. But if the emperor was distressed by recent events in Cuernavaca, he did not speak of them now.

Instead, he recounted the details of his journey through the Bajío, especially his visit to the town of Dolores, famous throughout Mexico as the birthplace of the country's struggle for freedom from Spanish rule. It was there more than four decades earlier that the renegade priest Miguel Hidalgo first uttered *el grito de la independencia*—the cry of independence. Maximiliano was evidently galvanized by the tale. He said he had walked in Hidalgo's footsteps. He had addressed a crowd from the same balcony where Hidalgo had appeared. He, too, had issued the cry of independence.

The emperor stopped his pacing and set down his cup of chocolate. He put back his head and shivered, as if reliving the sensations of that night.

"I've never known anything like it," he said. "It was like an explosion. I don't know how else to describe it."

There was, of course, much work to be done that did not bear on the Bajío or on the emperor's journey there, but he seemed to have trouble concentrating on anything else. He listened impatiently as Diego recounted his journey to Washington—a heavily censored version. When Diego was done, Maximiliano merely shrugged. He had been giving the matter much consideration, he said, and had concluded that it made little difference which side won the war now dividing the American states. He possessed a treaty—the Treaty of Miramar—that both he and Napoleon had signed. It provided firm guarantees of French support for the imperial cause in Mexico, without any reference whatsoever to events in other lands. What mattered was what happened in Mexico. And Mexico had a war of its own. That was the conflict that required his attention.

"Speaking of which," he said, "I don't suppose there has been any word as yet from Juárez?"

"No, Your Majesty."

"We must keep up our hopes." Maximiliano lit a cigarette. "Meanwhile, we have no choice but to fight on. I think it would be wise to summon Bazaine for an update on the state of battle. See to it, will you?"

"Yes, Your Majesty."

"Now." He clapped his hands. "Let us proceed to the mail."

Among the morning's correspondence was a letter that had arrived by diplomatic pouch from Franz Josef, Maximiliano's older brother. The emperor's manner changed at once. Diego could see the muscles tighten in his neck.

The emperor stubbed out his cigarette. "Read it," he said.

Diego did as he was told. After the usual pleasantries, Franz Josef reminded his younger brother of an agreement they had both reached in private—specifically, that "Maxi" formally renounced his place in the line of succession to the Austrian Crown in exchange for Franz Josef's approval of "this Mexican adventure," as he described it.

The emperor's expression darkened and he furrowed his brow, as if anticipating what would come next.

For reasons too complicated to explain, Franz Josef went on, he had lately found himself obliged to make this arrangement public—

"Make this arrangement *what*?" Suddenly the emperor buckled, splattering hot chocolate onto his robe and across the floor. He barely seemed to notice as he turned to Diego, livid. "*Public?*" he said. "An agreement that was reached in strict confidence? How dare he break my trust? My God, he goes too far."

With Grill's assistance, the emperor changed into a fresh dressing gown. He insisted that a reply be dispatched immediately, under diplomatic seal. It might still be possible to limit the harm caused by Franz Josef's reckless presumption.

Diego had paper, a quill, and a pot of ink at the ready. "But is it true?" he said.

"Is what true?"

"That you renounced your place in the line of succession?"

"No," said the emperor. "I mean, technically, yes. I had to. Franz Josef insisted upon it. A quid pro quo. In exchange, he supported my acceptance of the Mexican throne."

"And you agreed?"

"In a way. It was in private, and I had no choice. What kind of agreement is that? Franz is grasping at straws." He swore beneath his breath. "Ready your pen, Serrano. I mean to set that sheet of vellum on fire."

"But, forgive me, Your Majesty." Diego reached for a sheet of stationery. He knew he should let the matter drop. What difference did it make? But he was curious. Why was Maximiliano so tormented about losing the Austrian throne? Wasn't one empire sufficient? Wasn't he satisfied with Mexico? "Forgive me, Your Majesty," he said, "but do you want to be the emperor of Austria?"

"That possibility will never arise."

"Then what does it matter?"

"It . . . I . . . There is a principle here, a principle of confidence and trust. Take down my words."

And Diego complied, scribbling as the emperor fulminated. Later, he affixed Maximiliano's seal to the letter and had it placed in a secure diplomatic container. He dispatched the epistle to Veracruz by means of a special messenger under a guard of hussars. But what did it mean? Why did Maximiliano care whether he occupied a place in the Austrian line of succession? He was the emperor of Mexico. What more did he need?

That evening, Maximiliano encountered his wife for the first time since his return from Cuernavaca. They met formally in the Red Room, amid the scarlet paper, the oriental vases, the delicate wooden furniture. Carlota greeted her husband coolly. She cleared her throat. He cleared his. She smoothed the folds of her skirt and asked him about his travels. Had they gone well? He replied that they had. He felt he had learned much and looked forward to learning more.

"I am glad to hear it," she said. She declared that she was troubled by their present circumstances. These past several weeks, which she had spent in a position of responsibility at Chapultepec, had only deepened her concerns.

"Yes," said Maximiliano. He gazed indulgently at his wife.

"We face many grave threats," she said. "With the passage of time they grow only more dangerous. We rule a country we do not control. The treasury is bankrupt. We are beholden to Napoleon for our army. We have few allies within Mexico and even fewer outside. The Church opposes us, and now it seems the landowners do as well."

She said she had received angry reports from diverse sources concerning events that had taken place during the emperor's excursion in the Bajío. Was it true, for example, that he had given a speech in a town called Dolores, honouring the father of Mexico's independence?

"Hidalgo?" said the emperor. "You know, I believe I did. He is considered a great hero."

"Or a rabble-rouser and murderer. He massacred hundreds in Guanajuato."

"So say the conservatives."

"It was the conservatives who brought us here. We must build bridges."

"Bridges?" Maximiliano pounded his armrest with his fist. "*Bridges*? We have *built* bridges. Dear God, I have lost track of the balls, the banquets, and the galas at which our sole purpose has been the befriending of these bloody conservatives. We have bestowed titles of nobility upon practically every petitioner in the land. And what do we have to show?" With his cigarette, Maximiliano drew a large zero in the air. "All for nothing. They still oppose us. The Mexican conservative will never be satisfied until he again possesses every jot and tittle of wealth and power in Mexico. You might as well establish cordial relations with a den of bears. God in heaven, you would think the Enlightenment had never occurred. You would think Victor Hugo had never taken up a pen. Mention Charles Darwin, and the oafs stare back at you, blank as donkeys. I don't mind that they're stupid. What I can't stand is the pride they take in their stupidity. You know, my dear, I do not regard myself as the emperor of a few rich land owners who care for nothing in the world but their precious titles of nobility. I am the emperor of all Mexicans. This is the year 1865. This is the modern world."

Maximiliano fell silent. At first, Diego marvelled at the power and conviction of his words—not just their sound but their meaning, too. He wished he had said these very words himself. He then began to wonder if, just possibly, he had. Something wasn't quite right. It took him a few moments to recall what it was. In fact, he had heard this speech before, almost word for word. These were almost the exact sentiments Ángela had expressed to him that day, a year earlier, when he had visited her in the Hospital de Jesús Nazareno. He realized that Maximiliano was only repeating what Ángela must have said to him on some other occasion, the same thoughts she had expressed to Diego and no doubt to others.

The empress heard her husband out. When he was done, she nodded her head. "I agree, my dove. But we have to forge alliances, at least for the present, at least until we have consolidated our position. We must cooperate with many different interests."

"I hope you don't count Labastida and his bishops among them."

Carlota frowned. "As you know, an emissary is still on his way from Rome. Perhaps he will prove more amenable to reason than Labastida."

"A cactus would prove more amenable to reason than Labastida."

Carlota produced a thin smile. "That may be so. Nonetheless, if we must deal with cacti, then we must equip ourselves with gloves. We require alliances. The survival of the throne depends upon it."

"They are holding us to ransom, you know—the Church, Labastida, all of them. They've got that boy, the son of . . . you know. Peralta."

Diego winced. The man spoke as if Ángela were a complete stranger to him. He thought how easy it is to lie and remembered the countless lies he himself had told.

"Well," said Carlota. "We shall simply have to await the arrival of this Meglia." She eased forward toward her husband. "Max?" she said. "Are you listening to me?"

The emperor was peering at the ceiling. "I have heard from Franz Josef," he said.

"What news does he send?"

"Alarming news. He has publicly declared that I have renounced my right of succession to the Austrian throne."

"But I thought you had. Otherwise, you would not have received his permission to serve as emperor in Mexico."

Maximiliano fidgeted with an unlit cigarette. "It is one thing to reach an agreement in private, quite another for all the world to hear of it."

"Well, I don't see that it matters now what the world does. Do you *want* to be the emperor of Austria?"

"Of course not. It's the principle. Franz Josef has no right to betray a private arrangement arrived at in confidence."

"I see." Carlota let a few moments pass in silence. "What do you propose to do?"

"Oh, it's already done."

Maximiliano explained that he had composed a protest that very morning. Two months would pass before he could hope to receive a reply, but he was prepared to wait. The truth was that he and his brother were *both* emperors now, and Franz Josef could not abide the fact.

"As for me, I am feeling worn out." Maximiliano stood up. He bid Carlota a good night and nodded at Diego. "Tomorrow morning?" he said. "At the usual hour? We have much to do."

He turned and left the room.

Chapter 33

There was still no sign of Baldemar. Once or twice a week, Diego ventured into Mexico City hoping to stumble upon his old friend—or be ambushed by him—but he was always disappointed. Perhaps it was no surprise. By now, el Gordo de las Gafas had become a legend among the people of the east. He was a hero of the common folk, pitted against an arch villain—the Tiger of Tacubaya, the bloodiest murderer in the land. It was well known that Márquez was obsessed with the capture of Baldemar Peralta. Almost everyone seemed to know he owed his life to the Fat Man. Dozens of *corridos* had been composed to celebrate the episode, and now they were hummed by campfires and crooned in cantinas across the coastal flats that stretched from the central sierra to the torrid shores of the Mexican Gulf.

The songs even travelled to Mexico City, where Diego sometimes heard their lyrics on the Plaza Santa Cecilia, sung in furtive snatches, mostly late at night. From rumours and vignettes that came his way and from the lyrics of these *corridos*, he managed to piece together an impression of the new life that his former schoolmate had fashioned for himself as an outlaw and rebel.

Mexicans like a hero, and they especially admire a hero who pays close attention to his appearance. For that reason alone, Baldemar had earned their respect. He rode a tall bay gelding and went about in a black leather vest over a white blouse above a pair of beige breeches with silver spangles. He wore stamped leather boots with pointed toes and adorned with silver spurs. His long-barrelled Colt revolver, the one he'd got as a gift from Diego, he kept tucked beneath a wide belt. Beneath his black, round-brimmed sombrero, he wound a green bandanna that encircled his brow.

Baldemar was also distinguished by the steel-rimmed spectacles with green-tinted lenses that he kept perched upon the bridge of his sunburned nose. The eyeglasses gave him an incongruous scholarly cast that only added to the notoriety he had won through his reputation for courage, as well as his unheard-of habit of freeing his captives rather than killing them. There were other irregular fighters—gamberros—who roamed the Mexican countryside, launching hit-and-run attacks on the imperial forces, but none of them was as celebrated in myth or song as el Gordo de las Gafas.

Before long, a tangle of folk tales sprang up around him. Baldemar had failed to assassinate General Márquez that day in Mexico City only because a young Indian waitress had strayed into the line of fire, and he was forced to lower his weapon to avoid harming an innocent girl. Later, after being tortured and brutally abused in the Martinica Prison, el Gordo received a pardon from the emperor but refused to accept it until every other prisoner in the place also was freed. And so the doors of the Martinica were thrown open. On departing that jail, each of the former inmates received a grant of three hundred reals and a revolving pistol. Or so it was said.

It was also Baldemar Peralta who captured the Tiger of Tacubaya near Soledad de Doblado one day by assuming the shape of a jaguar and leaping from the branches of a mango tree. He fell upon his quarry and wrestled the man from his horse. Subsequently, and after reverting to human form, el Gordo dangled his prey from the limb of an almond tree, taunting the general until the man revealed the most closely held secrets of the state, including the routes of ingress to the imperial mint, a building that was filled to its cobwebbed ceilings with ingots of silver and gold, all the treasures of Mexico, systematically stolen from the common people and hoarded over hundreds of years. When the present war was over, every last Mexican would be rich, for el Gordo would share the plunder with all his countrymen, down to the lowliest Indian peasant. Thus, centuries of injustice would be redeemed.

These and other tales were told and retold, polished and embellished as they passed by word of mouth through the countryside. Steadily, the fame of el Gordo grew. Young men soon began flocking to his side, often with the blessings of their mothers and sisters. Gradually, he expanded his range of operations, until it seemed he was in a dozen places almost at once—one day in the rolling blue mountains of Michoacán, the next day in the ancient village of Ixmiquilpan, then in the green, orchid-festooned forests outside Xalapa. But he suffered one persistent limitation: the difficulty of acquiring sufficient munitions and powder—a constant source of torment and frustration.

Meanwhile, General Márquez steadily added to his own renown, although in a very different way. He conducted regular forays through the eastern lands, staging exercises that he liked to refer to as training sessions, designed to build confidence among the local populace. He strove to impress upon people that there were just two kinds of Mexicans in time of war: good ones and dead ones. Good Mexicans refused to have anything to do with godless liberal gamberros, did not feed them or provide them with intelligence or allow them safe passage across the land. Instead, as quickly as humanly possible, good Mexicans communicated everything they knew about the activities of godless liberal gamberros to the defenders of Mexico's honour and dignity, the contraguerrilla.

It was Holy Week, and Diego was striding across the Zócalo of Mexico City, through the clutter and commotion, the commerce and din—the vendors and *putas*, pariah dogs and mules, the shouting and braying, barking and laughter, church bells and screams. Not far from the Metropolitan Cathedral, a frail, morose Indian man was bound to a stout wooden post, doing enforced penance by playing the part of Judas Iscariot. All those who passed him, on horseback or on foot, availed themselves of the opportunity to hawk their phlegm and gob upon the miserable wretch. They called him names, denounced his sins, and spat at him again.

Diego tossed the remains of a cheroot onto the rutted street and observed the miserable creature. Mexico was its own worst enemy, it seemed. What need did the country have of French occupiers? All on their own, Mexicans were more than capable of savaging one another. Just then, from the corner of his eye, Diego saw a man running toward the sopping Judas. Something flashed in the sunlight—the blade of a hatchet. The blade sliced down, once, twice, three times, severing the bonds that held the fellow. With his free arm, the man with the hatchet raised the Indian up.

"*¡Vamos, hombre!*" he shouted. "*¡Corre!*"

Both dressed in rags, the two men darted toward the Monte de Piedad. Meanwhile, bystanders pointed at them and began to shout. More than a few gave chase, shrieking "Judas! Judas!" Diego broke into a run, determined to catch up with the two fleeing men, the Judas and his rescuer. In addition to his soiled and threadbare clothing, the man with the hatchet wore green-tinted glasses. It was Baldemar—Diego was sure of it.

Somehow, he managed to catch up with the pair, and the three of them kept running, weaving and doubling back through the side streets that skirted the Zócalo, until they reached the Plaza Santa Cecilia. Here, they stopped and rested, hands on their knees, chests heaving.

"*¿Estás loco?*" said Diego, still panting from the effort. "Are you out-of-your-mind crazy?"

"So it would seem," said Baldemar. "I can't help myself."

"Why are you dressed like that?"

"What? These rags? It's a disguise."

"Clever. The glasses go perfectly. And the hatchet?"

"I had to steal it."

"So it's true what they say. You're a common thief."

"And proud of it."

By now, the Indian man had straightened up. "Excuse me," he said to Baldemar. "You owe me three clacos."

"What? What for?"

"I was to be paid that much by the Church."

"Paid for what? For being spat on? You're joking."

The Indian shrugged. "Besides, it was a penance."

"What for?"

"I steal money for drink. I beat my wife. I neglect my children. You want more?"

"No. Never mind. Here. Never let it be said I cheated Judas Iscariot out of a few coins."

Baldemar gave him several clacos, which the man hurriedly stuffed somewhere in the damp folds of his rags.

"Are you el Gordo de las Gafas?" he said.

"Could be," said Baldemar. "Who are you?"

"A sinner. A humble servant of the Lord. Why are you dressed like that?"

"Just as I said. I'm in disguise." Baldemar tilted his head toward the man he'd just rescued. He lowered his voice. "Would you like to join me? I have an army in Xalapa. You could lead a different life."

"A different life? You mean, kill conservatives? Live off the land? Fight for the honour of my country?"

"Yes. All that—and no more spittle. Are you willing?"

"No."

"Why not?"

"I'd rather drink pulque and beat my wife."

Without another word, the man turned and trotted away on stubby bare feet. Diego and Baldemar watched him go.

Baldemar sighed. "You can rescue a man from servitude," he said. "But you cannot set him free."

"Come on," said Diego, "I'll buy you a drink."

Before long, they were huddled once again by the gouged wooden countertop at Memorias del Futuro. The first subject that came up between them was Ángela. Baldemar said that his sister was safe. Just as Diego had suspected, she was hiding out in Taxco in the presbytery occupied by Padre Buendía. Baldemar did not say how he knew this, and Diego chose not to pursue the matter. It was clear to him that his friend had his networks and his ways. Besides, everyone knew there were liberals in the clergy still, despite the staunchly conservative sentiments of the hierarchy.

"What about the boy?" he said.

"That will resolve itself. Eventually."

"How do you know?"

Baldemar tapped his forehead. "You watch. The French and the Church will come to blows. Labastida will let the boy go. He'll have no choice."

"And the child will be returned to his mother?"

"I hope so."

For a time, there was silence. They attended to their drinks.

Then Diego set down his glass. "And what about you? The war?"

"Better . . . and worse."

"Worse how?"

Baldemar shrugged. "Nothing a few rifles wouldn't solve."

They emptied their jars and ordered two more. Baldemar explained that Márquez had graduated to even greater acts of bloodshed and brutality on his rampages through the hamlets and villages near the eastern coast. "The truth is, he's losing the war—and this is his response."

"And what's yours?"

"Ah, that," said Baldemar. "That is what I came to talk about."

He put down his glass and spoke in a whisper. He set out what he had in mind. Those Spencer rifles, he said. They were needed. Now.

Diego nodded at intervals as his old friend explained what was required. The surprising thing was that he already knew. He had known this part all along, even before Baldemar began to speak.

Chapter 34

His Excellency Monseñor Pedro Francisco Meglia, nuncio of the Papal See, arrived in Mexico City on the last day of June in the year 1865, accompanied by a complement of Swiss guards, as well as a force of African Zouaves.

Soon after reaching Mexico City, Meglia communicated news of his presence to Her Majesty the Empress Carlota, who was carrying out the duties of the crown in her husband's absence. Maximiliano was again in Cuernavaca, availing himself of the sunshine and the warmer climate. Diego remained at Chapultepec, serving Carlota in the office of personal secretary, much as he had done with the emperor but with fewer demands on his time. Many who observed her said they were impressed by the empress's conduct, implying without saying so that she was a better monarch than her husband.

But this did not mean the empress was a match for the newly arrived papal nuncio. Carlota granted the man an audience at eleven o'clock in the morning, a week after his appearance in the city. It was rumoured the Italian had spent most of this period in solitude, working out chess problems on a miniature magnetized board he had brought with him from Rome.

Diego was among those who attended the meeting. The encounter took place in the Red Room at Chapultepec. Meglia made a cursory bow, issued a formal but barely audible greeting, proffered his letter of introduction, and then stood in silence, gazing about as if he had recently purchased the building and all its contents and was only now putting a number to their true worth. He projected an air of displeasure, as though concluding he had grossly overpaid.

Carlota cleared her throat and initiated polite conversation, but Meglia made only the most cursory of replies.

Had Monseñor enjoyed an agreeable crossing?

Reasonably so.

What were his principal impressions of Mexico thus far?

It was hot upon the coast, rather less so here in the interior.

What news did he bring of great events in Europe?

All was unfolding according to the will of the Almighty.

He offered these curt replies in a feeble monotone that emerged from a pair of lips that were as thin as wires and barely moved when he spoke. He had a sallow complexion, a long and narrow nose, and dark patches around his eyes, so that he somewhat resembled a plucked raccoon. His black hair was slicked back with a sweet-smelling pomade, and he wore voluminous purple robes. When addressed, he allowed several seconds of silence to precede his response. His manner suggested that he had never in his life been as monstrously bored as he was right now.

"You would like tea?" said the empress. "Or perhaps wine. It is nearly noon."

"A glass of milk," said the nuncio. After an additional pause, he added, "If you please."

Milk was provided, along with a selection of pastries. Carlota squeezed a wedge of lemon into her tea. She cleared her throat, apparently signalling that the time for small talk was done. She gazed at the nuncio and inquired how in his view the imperial government of Mexico and the

Roman Catholic Church could narrow the not inconsiderable gap that, lamentably, had opened between them.

"Well . . ." Meglia said. He reached into a leather valise to withdraw a document bearing the Vatican seal. "Allow me to explain . . ."

He placed a pair of reading spectacles upon the bridge of his nose and began to read from the sheaf of papers balanced on his lap. On and on he droned, always in his toneless, uninflected voice. It soon became apparent to Diego that the man had not travelled to Mexico to negotiate. He wondered whether Maximiliano's recent penchant for absenting himself from Mexico City might not have had less to do with the coolness of the weather in the capital than with the grim prospect of meeting Meglia in the flesh.

For her part, Carlota did her best, offering comments or objections in a tentative, diplomatic voice, but the man simply ignored her and carried on with his pontification, reading word for word from the documents he had brought with him. He concluded his performance by reciting a long and detailed list of apparently non-negotiable demands. He then withdrew into a sort of paralytic trance while Carlota embarked upon a response. It was clear to everyone that he was not listening.

Prior to the meeting, Carlota had informed Diego that she intended to strike an agreement of some kind with Meglia, much as it offended her principles to do so. The crown of Mexico—its very survival—depended upon firm and reliable alliances, arrangements that must include an accord between church and state. Matters could not be permitted to go on as they were, amid mutual suspicion and acrimony.

But she might just as well have said nothing at all. The prelate made no attempt to address her concerns. He simply declared, and subsequently repeated, that the document from which he had been reading would serve as a concordat between the Mexican Church and the imperial government—not the basis of a concordat, he said, but the final form of the treaty itself. Not a word might be changed. In short, the Vatican demanded the complete capitulation of the imperial government on every count, the repeal of every reform law, the restoration to the

Church of every power it had ever possessed, and more besides. Even as a basis for negotiation, it was untenable. But Meglia did not propose it as a basis for negotiation. This must be the final agreement.

Carlota attempted to shift the subject of their discussion. She mentioned the singer, Ángela Peralta, and her son. But Meglia wasn't interested. This matter lay outside his purview. He had no mandate to discuss it. Carlota protested that, as she understood the situation, both the woman and the boy were, or recently had been, incarcerated against their will by Labastida and his agents. They were being held to ransom, used as pawns in the Church's efforts to impose its demands upon the state. This was intolerable and must be condemned by all right-thinking people. Could Monseñor Meglia imagine such a travesty being committed in Rome?

The prelate inclined his head, as though to address a child. "But, Your Majesty," he said, "we do not find ourselves in Rome."

That night Carlota presided at a dinner that had been organized in the visiting dignitary's honour. But Meglia did not turn up or even convey his regrets, and the dinner went ahead without him. Bazaine was among those who attended, and on this occasion he was squiring his new Mexican paramour, a girl of just seventeen named Josefa de la Peña y Azcárate. She preened behind an oriental fan and made coquettish eyes at her suitor, who was her senior by a good four decades.

By long-standing custom, discussion of political affairs was prohibited during dinner, a fortunate practice in this instance, as nearly all of the guests would have sided vehemently with Meglia. Carlota would have found herself in a lonely minority, along with Bazaine, perhaps, and, of course, Diego.

Late in the evening, several of the guests wandered out onto the terrace, the ladies in their wraps, everyone intent upon enjoying the cool evening air, while admiring the silvery moonlit view out over the bosky plains that separated the palace from Mexico City. Diego ventured out on his own. The Mexican men smoked cigars and stood about, knees locked and bellies distended, complaining bitterly that they had been saddled, it seemed, with a pair of outright liberals in place of a proper emperor and empress. Who could have predicted such a thing? It was unconscionable. Emperors preaching reform!

Four days after his audience with Carlota, His Excellency Monseñor Pedro Francisco Meglia departed Mexico City. He was bound for Veracruz, and then for Rome. It was said that he did not cast a single backward glance from his carriage but departed the city with his head cast down, with his magnetized chess set close at hand and his attention focused upon a book that had been published the previous year in Paris—*Bibliographie anecdotique du jeu des échecs.*

For her part, the empress informed Diego that she had never met a more contemptible man. After Meglia, it would seem a pleasure to deal with Labastida.

Chapter 35

In the end, it was Bazaine who came up with a way to free Ángela's son. The French officer had lately been in noticeably better spirits, owing no doubt to his new romance. He seemed happy and at peace—a circumstance both rare and paradoxical. In such a state, he explained, there was nothing that appealed to him more than the prospect of a good, clean fight. And who better to lock horns with than Labastida? Bazaine loathed the man. It was time to trade words for blows.

He explained his thinking in unusually candid terms during a meeting with Maximiliano, who had returned to Mexico City from Cuernavaca not long after the papal nuncio's departure for Rome. On more than one occasion, said the Frenchman, Labastida had provoked him almost beyond endurance. Once, the archbishop had dared to bar a senior French officer from attending the celebration of Sunday Mass. It seemed the officer's wife had failed on some occasion to dress in perfect accordance with the archbishop's very particular ideas about feminine decorum. He had turned both the officer and the woman away. At the time, Bazaine had chosen to endure this insult to French honour, but he was bound to remember it.

On another occasion, Labastida had threatened to close the doors of the cathedral to the entire officer corps of the French army, vowing to excommunicate every one of its members, because it was they who enforced the reform laws as they related to Church properties and privileges in Mexico.

That time, the churchman had backed down, but only after a volatile exchange that Bazaine recalled even now with a mixture of pride and anger. He had informed the prelate that he possessed plenty of ordnance and would not scruple to make full use of it. If the cathedral was not opened at once to all his men, he would employ good French cannon to blast the doors from their hinges.

The emperor laughed. "This is the first time I've heard the tale," he said. "Marvellous."

"The events occurred before your arrival in Mexico, Your Majesty," said Bazaine. "Those were wild times."

"And harsh words. Did you mean them?"

"I did."

"You would have blown open the cathedral doors?"

"Without hesitation. Or regret."

"Oh, well done. Good for you."

The two men were meeting in an austere salon at Chapultepec, with Diego again delegated to taking notes.

"And did the tactic work?"

"It did. He backed down. The cathedral is Labastida's weak point, you see. He is besotted with the place."

The emperor folded both hands behind his head and rocked back in his chair. "So . . . you propose to try the same stunt again."

"Exactly."

"Give the boy up—or bang."

Bazaine nodded. "I intend to take down a bell tower at least."

"And what of the mother? The singer. You know . . ."

Bazaine gave a dismissive wave. The mother was not a part of his brief. He proposed only to liberate the boy.

"Serrano," said the emperor. "Where is the woman? Where do you think?"

Diego set down his pen. It was strange how lying could become almost automatic, a question of practice. "I don't know," he said.

"You've spoken to Labastida? You've spoken to Salm-Salm?"

"Yes, Your Majesty. I don't believe they know, either. It seems to be a great mystery."

Maximiliano turned back to Bazaine. "Well, I like your proposal immensely," he said. "But I wonder, why did we not come up with this stratagem before?"

"Timing," said Bazaine. He slowly stroked his jaw.

It was apparent to Diego that the Frenchman had something else on his mind.

Bazaine adjusted the sleeves of his military frock coat. "I understand Your Majesty is contemplating some changes to your council of ministers."

"I have some ideas."

"Good. So do I."

What Bazaine had, it turned out, was a problem—and the problem's name was General Leonardo Márquez. The Mexican officer had lately exceeded all conceivable limits on human savagery in his campaigns along the eastern coast. Even for Bazaine, it was too much. The pillaging and murders were counterproductive. You did not win a war by systematically bolstering the ranks of your enemies, and that was what Márquez was doing. However many Mexicans he killed, more took up arms against him. It was time to bring the man out of the field.

"And put him where exactly?" said Maximiliano.

"The very question I ask myself," said Bazaine. "My inclination is to put him somewhere I can watch him, and give him a title he would be likely to accept."

"For example?"

"Minister of war."

"What?" The emperor shook his head. "Not possible."

Bazaine narrowed his eyes and waited.

"You can't be serious," said Maximiliano. "That heathen? He hanged that man by his feet."

Bazaine fumbled in his pocket for his watch. He glanced at the time and briefly frowned before easing the piece back into his side pocket. "Your Majesty could go on for a good long while," he said, "listing the man's crimes one by one. Such reservations are completely justified. But I speak to a different purpose. Márquez is a liability in the field. We need to take measures to bring him in."

"It was you who put him out there, you know," said the emperor. "After he refused to go to Constantinople. That was your doing."

Bazaine sighed. "You are right, Your Majesty. It seemed like a sound decision at the time. But realities have changed, and we must change with them."

He reached for his cap on the table at his side, tucked it beneath his arm, and climbed to his feet. "With your permission, I will have a word with the archbishop, as we discussed. We are agreed upon that?"

"Oh yes. Thank you. By all means."

"And Márquez?"

"Ah," said the emperor. "I shall have to ponder on that."

"Not for very long, I hope? Lives may depend upon it."

"Not long, no."

Bazaine seemed disinclined to leave the subject. "I take it Your Majesty appreciates the connection between these two measures. I confront Labastida. Márquez becomes minister of war. They are linked in my mind."

"Yes, of course. I see quite clearly what you are getting at. I shall communicate my answer shortly."

"Very well, Your Majesty." Bazaine nodded and left the room.

As Diego watched him go, he thought he detected the glint of a smile on the man's face. And why not? The Tiger of Tacubaya would be named minister of war in the end. Maximiliano would accept the bargain. He would have no choice. But it was an outrage just the same. Diego could not believe that he would now serve the same government that employed the Tiger of Tacubaya as its minister of war. By rights, he ought to finish the job that Baldemar had begun and kill Márquez. Either that or leave Mexico entirely.

That was what he should do. Leave Mexico entirely. The truth was, he had Baldemar's authority to do so, to journey north by sea. That was what they had spoken of, in whispered voices, the last time they had met. They had discussed Spencer rifles and Baldemar's desperate need for weaponry and how Diego might help. He would have to head north yet again but this time by a different route and with a different destination. He had dreaded the prospect before, but now he saw it instead as a godsend. He could leave right away. Why not? There was nothing to stop him. Better that than remain here, serving a man who would appoint the Tiger of Tacubaya as minister of anything. The more he thought about the idea, the more convinced he felt that it was impossible to do anything except leave. Leave at once.

The emperor stood, reached out with both arms and stretched. He stifled a yawn. "Damned tired, all of a sudden," he said. "Well then, Serrano. Tomorrow at the usual hour? Serrano? Are you listening to me?"

Diego looked up. In fact, he had not been paying attention at all. "Yes, Your Majesty."

CHAPTER 36

DIEGO WOULD LEAVE MEXICO, but not just yet. First, he had to attend to one or two other matters. If only he could determine the whereabouts of Ángela's son, he might be able to reunite the child with its mother. That would hardly be the case if Bazaine were permitted to carry out his far more militant operation. It was a faint hope, but he felt honour-bound to try.

And so, two days after Bazaine's meeting with the emperor, Diego made his way to the archbishop's residence, not far from the Zócalo. He presented his card at the entrance and was soon ushered into the prelate's dining room. It was mid-morning, but Labastida was still at breakfast, a dish of crepes. He was alone except for the Prince of Salm-Salm, who was wearing clerical robes, in his role as Padre Fischer.

"*Ah, el poeta manco,*" said Salm-Salm. He raised a cup of coffee in a sort of salute. "I heard you were stopping by."

He had? From whom?

The archbishop remained focused on his meal.

"Come, sit down," said Salm-Salm. "Coffee?"

"Please." Diego took a seat by the long hardwood table. He rested his hat on the chair beside him. He wondered again what Salm-Salm was up to. Did he have some clear goal or did he merely love to connive? He turned to the prince. "What brings you here?"

"I like to keep up. Did you manage to meet Monseñor Meglia while he was in Mexico?"

"I did. Briefly."

Salm-Salm whistled. "*Huevos*," he said and made a rude gesture with both hands.

"*Please . . .*" said the archbishop. He pushed his plate away. "The man merely expressed the view of Rome, a view we share in every particular, I am happy to say."

Diego decided to plunge straight in. "I have come to discuss the boy."

"Ángela's son," said Salm-Salm. "We were just talking about the case."

"Nothing to talk about," said Labastida. "Not in that quarter. We have one subject to discuss. The reform laws. They must be repealed in their entirety."

"And only then will the boy be released?"

"I say nothing of the boy."

Salm-Salm edged forward, placed both arms on the table. "Personally, I would prefer to discuss Ángela," he said. "Do you know where she is?"

"No."

Salm-Salm narrowed his eyes. "You're sure? You're quite positive?"

"Yes—I mean no. I don't know where she is."

Salm-Salm narrowed his gaze still further, and Diego felt as if the man's eyes were boring a pair of holes right through him.

He shifted uneasily in his chair. "Is there more coffee?"

He wanted to turn the discussion back to Ángela's son. He was just about to speak when they were interrupted by a knock at the door. A minion of the church entered and announced the arrival of a messenger from Maréchal Bazaine.

"Show him in," said Labastida.

A young soldier strode briskly into the room and held up an envelope.

"Read it," said Labastida.

The soldier opened the missive and read the document aloud, speaking in a heavy French accent. It turned out that Bazaine stood at this very instant in the centre of the Zócalo, along with two batteries of sixteen-pound cannon. The pieces were primed to fire and were trained upon the twin bell towers of the archbishop's beloved cathedral. Unless the prelate acceded to his demands immediately, Bazaine meant to blow the building to rubble, starting at the top and working his way down.

This news was so shocking that a few moments were required for the full import to sink in. Once it did, the archbishop put a hand to his heart and slumped at his table, chest heaving, as the colour ran from his large round face.

"The gall," he said. "The unholy gall."

An able-bodied man might have been able to make the journey from the archbishop's residence to the city's central plaza in a matter of several minutes, but the archbishop was not an able-bodied man. Still, he set off on foot. Guided by his secretary and a coterie of priests, he lumbered up the cobbled street. Salm-Salm and Diego followed at a distance as the procession made its slow way up the cobbles toward the Metropolitan Cathedral, pausing often so that the prelate might catch his breath. Eventually, the party rounded upon the Zócalo.

Just as advertised, Bazaine stood near the centre of the square, several paces from a pair of cannons. When he saw the archbishop, the Frenchman removed his cap in a gesture of salutation.

"Good morning, gentlemen," he said in a voice that carried easily on the cool morning air. He announced that he had already ordered both his gun captains to arm their pieces. This, he explained, merely involved pushing half-pound paper sacks of powder into the cannon muzzles, followed by sixteen-pound balls of lead. It remained only for him to give the order to fire.

Bazaine paused and tilted his head. He conceded that the sixteen-pounders were ornery beasts, a challenge to aim accurately. Still, at this range and with this target, he doubted the difficulties would prove insurmountable. Besides, both batteries were well supplied with powder and shot. If necessary, they could pass the entire morning blasting away.

"My terms are simple," he said. "Release the son of Ángela Peralta into the protection of the French army at once. Or face the consequences."

The archbishop was still out of breath but had recovered some of his composure and pugnacity. He raised himself to his full height and held up a clenched fist.

"God damn you, sir," he said. "God damn you. I instruct you to remove your cannons instantly. You are committing a crime against the Church."

"Indeed?" said Bazaine. "Well, I have been accused of worse. As for the cannons, their presence or absence is entirely up to you. You have only to comply with my terms. Otherwise, your blessed cathedral will forego its bell towers, after which I shall give some thought as to the fate of its roof. You have considered my demands?"

"I have. They are an outrage."

Bazaine frowned. "This is your answer?"

"It is."

Evidently, the prelate had decided to call the French officer's bluff.

"He is making a mistake," Diego whispered.

Salm-Salm snickered. "I have no doubt of it. Delightful."

Bazaine consulted his timepiece and held up a hand to test the speed and direction of the wind. He replaced his watch in the side pocket of his military frock coat. "I urge you once again to accept my terms."

"You have heard my answer."

"I see." Bazaine turned to one of his gun captains. "*Monsieur le capitaine*," he said, speaking in a loud, theatrical voice. "How long are the fuses?"

"Three seconds, *mon maréchal*."

"Very good." The French marshal turned to the archbishop. "Three seconds, Monseñor. In my experience, they pass very quickly. You do not wish to reconsider?"

Labastida shook his head. No.

"Very well." Bazaine instructed his gun captain to proceed.

The artillery men took their positions behind the near piece. The captain accepted a proffered torch and touched the flame to the vent behind the breech of the sixteen-pounder. The fuse made a low, whooshing sound, followed three seconds later by a phenomenal blast and a billowing curtain of smoke. The cannon recoiled with an awful shriek, rocking back on its carriage like a rearing horse.

Diego turned at once toward the cathedral, expecting to see one of the steeples crumble. Instead—nothing. He heard a deep thudding impact somewhere beyond the cathedral. It seemed that the ball had overshot its mark. Had it landed upon a house?

"You are in luck," said Bazaine, addressing the archbishop. "You have been granted a reprieve. But I doubt that my men will miss a second time. Do you wish to alter your position?"

"Certainly not," said Labastida, who still seemed convinced that the Frenchman was merely testing his resolve. "I warn you that this entire episode will be reported to Rome, with the gravest consequences for you and your men. I do not doubt that you will all be excommunicated."

Bazaine thrust back his shoulders. "I warn you, Monseñor, that I grow weary of these threats."

"May your soul rot in hell."

"Where it will not lack for company." Bazaine ordered his second gun captain to proceed.

This time, there was no mistake. The morning air cracked as the ball raced headlong into the northernmost of the building's two massive, colonnaded steeples, each the size of a substantial church.

The impact was visible a few instants before it could be heard. Great shards of stone blew outward, and several columns seemed to crumple, tottering upon their bases before slanting sideways and breaking into huge pieces that tumbled into the square below, crashing upon the cobbles and scattering across the gardens and walkways. A great cast-iron bell, itself taller than a man, slowly began to slip from its sagging support beam. The beam cracked, broke loose, swung out over the square, and the entire works plummeted to the ground, where the great bell slammed into the stones with a colossal force, sundering into several sections.

The archbishop let out a cry followed by a long, anguished moan. He slumped to his knees. Several priests sought to manoeuvre him into his chair on wheels, which had been retrieved from his home.

Large knots of passersby had gathered in the huge plaza, and they gaped in silence. How many coups and civil wars had ravaged Mexico over the decades? Dozens or more—and many of them had been decided in this very square, with no shortage of death or destruction. But no one had ever imagined anything like this.

"Rearm the cannons," said Bazaine.

It wasn't necessary. The archbishop's aides were already rushing forward, arms outstretched. They pleaded with the French officer to stop, stop, for the love of God. Labastida slumped in his chair on wheels in a stupor. He gasped for breath, trembling and shaking as his attendants opened parasols to shade him from the sun and plied him with water.

Finally, the archbishop was well enough to speak. His voice was hoarse and feeble, his colour wan. Yes, he acceded to the Frenchman's demands. Yes, he would deliver the son of Ángela Peralta into the protection of the French army. Just please put an end to this merciless, demonic destruction. Spare the cathedral, for God's sake.

"Very well," said Bazaine. He adjusted his collar and straightened his cap. "As there is no shortage of witnesses, I shall take you at your word."

As a precaution, however, he ordered his men to leave the cannons in their positions and under guard. If necessary, they would be ready to fire again at a moment's notice.

Chapter 37

A letter arrived for Diego, written in a compact, precise hand and signed by Beatríz. She wrote that preparations were being made to receive a child at la Casa del Olvido, where Ángela Peralta had formerly stayed as the emperor's mistress. A governess had been engaged, and various appurtenances had been delivered, including a small bed, a variety of playthings, a pram, and other articles, all indicating beyond doubt that a young child was soon to take up residence.

Beatríz asked don Diego what he thought she should do. It was clear the boy belonged with his mother.

Diego put the letter down. He was sure the emperor had caused these arrangements to be made. He thought it likely that Salm-Salm was somehow involved as well. He composed a brief letter to Beatríz, suggesting that nothing be done for the moment. The boy would undoubtedly be kept safe. In the meantime, they should wait and see. There was really nothing else they could do. He did not think it would be as easy to pluck Ángela's son from the little house in Cuernavaca as it had been to rescue Ángela. Security measures were bound to be tighter now.

He was about to dispatch a reply by courier when it struck him that he might as well deliver the letter in person. He would pass through Cuernavaca on his way to the western sea coast in any case. The prospect of stopping there for a time immediately raised his spirits. That afternoon, he caught himself whistling aloud as he went about making preparations for his departure. In the evening, he informed the emperor of his intentions, without revealing their true purpose, and Maximiliano provided his blessing.

Diego departed early the next morning. His route took him over the high sierra to the west of the capital and then downward through waves of blond grass and humming pine forests. He carried in his baggage the ambrotype image he had obtained in New York City, wrapped in paper and cotton and carefully enclosed in a bolt of black velvet to safeguard it from harm.

It was late afternoon by the time he reached Cuernavaca, and he made his way directly to the House of Borda. He found Beatríz in the gardens, with a basket over her arm, clipping flowers. Her hair was done up in ribbons, and her dark skin seemed to shine in the dusky light.

"Don Diego . . ." she said in a voice that suggested she had in fact been expecting his arrival and had been wondering what was taking him so long.

He smiled. "I got your letter."

"And you came all this way in person to deliver your reply?"

"Yes . . . or, I mean, no. Or . . ." He shook his head. "Well, I am here."

"And most welcome, too."

She set the basket down on the grass and led him to a marble bench sheltered by a vine-encumbered trellis. The bench overlooked the artificial lake, where goldfish surfaced now and then, snapping at flies.

"We can talk here," the girl said.

"Talk?" he said. "About what?"

"I don't know." She glanced at what little remained of his left arm. "Why not about what happened to your arm?"

"It's a long story."

But he told it. He could sense that she really did want to hear it, and so he found himself talking about an episode that he had rarely recounted to anyone. Baldemar knew, of course, as did Ángela, but he had spoken to very few others. Six years had passed by since that day in April 1859 when liberals and conservatives squared off in the Battle of Tacubaya, named for the town located only a couple of leagues from Chapultepec. It was to be the first and last engagement in Diego's military career. At the time, he'd had no experience of war, but that was true as well of the other young liberals at his side. And yet they leapt into the fray just the same.

Diego carried his long-barrelled Colt revolving pistol. It was an effective weapon in the hands of someone adept with firearms but of limited use in the hands of someone like him. He and the others set out for Tacubaya on horseback but left their mounts in the care of a blacksmith who ran a livery stable at the edge of the town. They were close enough now to hear the din of combat, and Diego felt his heart racing. He shuddered and ducked instinctively at each roar, each blast, and his fear must have been obvious to his companions, but they did not seem to share it. They seemed excited rather than afraid—Baldemar most of all.

Something exploded nearby with a colossal din, and Diego ducked instinctively.

"You don't need to do that," Baldemar said. "We're out of range."

How on earth did he know? Diego's breathing came in shallow bursts. No matter how much he tried to calm himself, he was unable to. Every fibre in his body felt stretched to the limit, about to snap. They were advancing on foot now toward the source of the mayhem. They reached an intersection, mostly unprotected. They were so close to the fighting. One by one, Diego's companions darted across a rutted lane to take what shelter they could by a low stone wall. Here and there, the earth burst upward in miniature explosions as bullets bit into the ground. Diego was the last one to cross the road. Dear God, he did not want to do this. But he somehow willed himself forward. He gritted his teeth and ran, trying to keep down.

Something went wrong. Either he tripped over his own feet or some other force knocked him over. One way or the other, he was suddenly somersaulting through the air and wound up sprawled on the road, the crack of bullets and the rumpus of cannon fire all round. He tried to get up, but his left arm would not cooperate. He put most of his weight on his right, with his pistol clutched in that hand, but still he couldn't seem to manage it. He could not get up. It was Baldemar who hurried back and dragged him across the road to something like safety in the frail shelter of the stone wall.

Blood was pumping from his left arm, the limb badly mangled, a tangle of cloth, blood, and exposed bone—as if it had been hit by grapeshot from a cannon.

Or by a pistol. A pistol at very close quarters.

The others must have assumed it was a cannon blast that had caught him, but even then Diego realized it probably wasn't so. Either he had managed to shoot himself while in the act of falling down, or he had first shot himself and then fallen down.

Apart from Diego, only Baldemar understood what happened. He checked the chambers of Diego's Colt and, sure enough, one round was missing.

The firefight continued for an eternity, but eventually the battle shifted further to the east, and Baldemar announced to the others that he would take Diego with him. Together, they would look for help. He'd heard that a group of medical students from Mexico City had set up a front-line trauma clinic in the commandeered summer home of the archbishop, in Tacubaya. He and Diego would make their way there. The others should try to hook up somehow with the main liberal forces, and Baldemar would join them when he could.

The young men split into two groups, and Baldemar stayed with his friend. They staggered through the pocked and sun-dazed streets, amid the reverberation of gunfire and cannon blasts. Eventually, they managed to locate the archbishop's house. Diego joined dozens of other wounded men already receiving treatment of the most rudimentary kind. Torn strips of bedsheets were used in place of bandages. There was no anaesthesia, and so the injured fighters were made to drink great quantities of rotgut cane liquor, until they were rendered all but senseless. Teams of young students held them down by brute force so that surgery could proceed.

In Diego's case, it was apparent at once that the limb had to come off, most of it, anyway, a good bit above the elbow. Otherwise there was sure to be infection and gangrene. Six years later, he no longer had any clear recollection of what ensued. He'd been doused with drink and had probably blacked out. Nor did he remember much of what happened following the removal of his arm, when conservative forces led by General Leonardo Márquez stormed the makeshift clinic and set about murdering every last man in the place. Many who were already bleeding from grievous wounds were simply left to die.

For a second time that day, Baldemar saved Diego's life, and he did it by tipping his old friend onto the floor and then sprawling on top of him, motionless.

"Stay still," he must have whispered. Or something of the kind. "Play dead."

It was their only hope.

So much blood coursed over the floor, and from all directions, that it was impossible to distinguish the dead from the merely dying. Uninjured himself, Baldemar was drenched in blood. It was only later, long after he regained consciousness and had been conveyed back to Mexico City, that Diego learned of his friend's ruse and how it was that they had both survived the Massacre of Tacubaya, when everyone else was dead. In all, more than fifty were killed in that place on that day.

Following that act of slaughter, General Márquez won infamy as the Tiger of Tacubaya—and Diego ended his brief career as a soldier. Baldemar continued to fight, in a bitter war that the liberals finally won, or that the conservatives lost. Either way, Benito Juárez assumed the presidency, but not for long. Soon enough, the French invaded, and Maximiliano ascended to an improvised throne.

"*Et voilà . . .*" said Beatríz, gesturing toward the lake and the surrounding gardens.

Diego nodded. "*Et voilà.*"

Beatríz gazed out through the fading light. "I think you were very brave."

"By shooting myself? With my own gun?"

"By being there. By going across that road. By not running away."

Diego sniggered.

"Why do you laugh?"

"Because it isn't so. I wasn't brave, not in any way. The truth is, I was too scared to run away, too scared of what Baldemar and the others would think. I stayed out of fear, not courage. If I'd been brave, I would have got out of there, no matter what anyone thought. Baldemar was brave."

"Maybe he was afraid, too."

"Maybe. I don't think so." He told her about the killing of Melchor Ocampo and about Baldemar's failed attempt to assassinate General Márquez and all that had happened since, including the emperor's decision to pardon Baldemar—and his own dilemma, indebted to both Baldemar for having saved his life and Maximiliano for having saved Baldemar's.

"I thought all that was a myth," she said. "All those tales about what you owe to the man who saves your life. All that."

"Maybe it is. Maybe Mexico is a myth, too. It doesn't mean we don't have to get up in the morning or go to bed at night or deal with the time in between."

She pushed his left shoulder and laughed. "I didn't know you were such a philosopher."

"I'm not. Not anymore."

"*El poeta manco.* That's what the Prince of Salm-Salm calls you."

"Well, he's half right. The one-armed part."

She looked off toward the lake. "I think you are still a poet. You just have to convince yourself."

For a time, neither of them said anything. They remained silent and still, watching the dragonflies whisking above the surface of the lake, the pouting of the water where the goldfish snapped. Gradually, the light faded from the western sky, and the evening star blinked above the tamarind trees and the jacarandas.

He told her he was leaving in the morning, to travel north. He wouldn't be back for many weeks. She nodded but said nothing.

He said, "I don't know what to do about the boy."

For a time, she was silent. Then she said, "Neither do I."

"If the emperor finds out where Ángela is, I don't know what he'll do. He wants her son as his heir. He's determined to have him."

"Beware a weak man with a powerful conviction."

Diego glanced down at the space between them, where her left hand was couched upon the marble surface of the bench. He reached over and enclosed her hand in his own, and they both looked out at a last slender band of amber light as it drained beyond the treetops, beneath the weight of the darkening sky.

Diego left the following morning, and Beatríz came out to see him off. He kept turning back to look at her, and at first he could make her out each time, but soon the gates and trees and adobe walls blocked his view. He turned and sought to concentrate on the journey ahead, an unfamiliar heaviness in his heart.

His journey took him through Taxco, and there he sought out Padre Buendía. He spoke to Ángela as well—for the first time in many long months. She had recovered some of the weight she had lost, but still there were dark hollows beneath her eyes, which would suddenly glaze over without warning whenever she thought of her son. He remained in Taxco overnight and resumed his journey the following morning.

At Acapulco, he boarded a mail packet bound north for San Francisco. The vessel ploughed through the high Pacific swell, skirting the narrow, sunburned arm of the Baja and entering American waters off San Diego. Once ashore, he commissioned a dozen men to serve as his security, and he began a long, arduous trek across badlands and desert, aiming for a town on the American side of the Mexican frontier, a speck of little account that was known as Franklin, Texas.

Chapter 38

The journey took Diego through an arid landscape of parched stream beds, broad plains, mesquite scrub, and table mountains, and it finally brought him to what seemed to be a scattered and unremarkable town, overlooking the river known to Mexicans as the Río Bravo.

He soon found the sometime journalist J.S. Bartlett at work in his office at the United States customs house. The lanky American disentangled his long legs from beneath his desk. He strode toward Diego, hands outstretched. The two men exchanged introductions, and Diego explained that he wished to cross into Mexico in order to—

"Señor Serrano," said Bartlett, "I know exactly why you want to cross into Mexico. You want to speak to Presidente Juárez."

"That is so," said Diego. "I understand he is installed at El Paso del Norte." It was the small Mexican town just across the border from Franklin. "It seems you have been forewarned of my visit. You've spoken to General Grant?"

"Something along those lines. Let's just say we have been expecting you." The young man stood by a large window commanding a view of the slow, meandering river and, beyond it, Mexico. A dome of curly blond hair framed an oval face bisected by a pair of wire-framed spectacles. He wore a pale blue shirt with the sleeves rolled up. "Señor Juárez arrived some months ago," he said, "accompanied by his staff, some journalists, plus five hundred soldiers and half a dozen artillery pieces."

Diego fumbled for a cigarette. "You are precise."

"I am a journalist," the young man said. "Precision is my trade." He used the tail of his shirt to remove some smudge from the windowpane, then turned toward Diego. "But we are not averse to round numbers, either." He removed a cigarette from his breast pocket, lit Diego's and then his own. "For example," he said, speaking through a haze of smoke, "thirty thousand. Give or take."

Diego let out a low whistle. "That many? How will they cross the border?"

"Oh, they won't. Not officially. They'll be recorded as having been 'mislaid.'"

Diego smiled. "I want to arrange for some of these . . . these articles . . . to move further south. A town called Xalapa. Can that be done?"

"Oh probably. But it's not my department. You'll have to talk to Señor Juárez. A lucky thing he's so close."

The American returned to his desk and resumed his seat. He crossed his arms at his chest. "I imagine you know these are difficult times for Señor Juárez."

"For all Mexicans."

"I know, I know. But I'm referring to something specific. The man has just learned that his youngest son is dead. In New York."

It was the first Diego had heard of it. He remembered a boy, only a few months old at the time of his visit, nearly a year ago now. "I didn't know."

"How could you? I learned about it in a cable from my newspaper. I had the unfortunate duty of informing Señor Juárez myself. He'd never even set eyes on the boy."

Diego shook his head. "He must be suffering."

"He must. Besides, the war goes badly." Bartlett contemplated his cigarette for a moment before continuing. The liberals, he said, were in retreat on almost every front. Only the other day, they had been obliged to surrender the southern city of Oaxaca to the French.

This was news to Diego, but he understood at once how grave it was. The loss of Oaxaca was apt to hit Juárez especially hard, for he had been raised in that town and had been governor of the state. What was almost as bad was to hear the news delivered by an American, who seemed to possess far better intelligence about Mexico than Mexicans did themselves.

"My newspaper has a correspondent in Oaxaca," said Bartlett. He exhaled a cloud of smoke. "But I guess the military situation in your country will start to change now that the north has won the war."

The American meant the other war, the war in the United States. Until that moment, Diego had not known for certain that the conflict was over or that the Union side had prevailed. He'd known only that victory was imminent. So now it was done.

"But these . . . ah . . . these new articles—I'm sure they'll help." Bartlett meant the Spencer rifles. He rose and once again extended his hand. "Good luck," he said.

"Thank you," said Diego. "I intend to cross the border now. May I proceed?"

"Por supuesto, Señor Serrano. Vaya con Dios."

"Y usted también."

Diego strode out into the late afternoon sunshine. He told his companions—the men who had accompanied him from San Diego and who'd received half wages thus far—that he would return in a matter of days. They would wait for him on the northern side. He remounted his horse, gathered the reins, and in short order was venturing back into his own country. He forded the river, the water lapping at the heels of his boots. On the far side, his horse clambered up onto a rough beach of pebbles and gravel, and he was in Mexico again. Goats bleated on the slopes of dry, sun-bleached hills, dogs barked at intervals, and the road ahead seemed both narrow and badly in need of repair, the way stippled by low, scrubby trees and carpeted by patchy grass shorn to the ground by ungulates. He urged his horse into a trot and was soon riding into the town of El Paso del Norte, a forlorn collection of low adobe buildings, haphazardly assembled in the cool but brilliant sun. Rolls of sagebrush stumbled amid helixes of dust, and wiry, underfed pigs snuffled through the garbage for their supper. He drew the dry air in through his nostrils, sensing wood smoke and the pungent corn scent of tamales. For better or worse, this was Mexico again.

He rode on.

Before long, several armed sentries strode out from a low adobe hut at the entrance to the *plaza mayor*, not a complete uniform or a decent pair of boots in the lot.

"*Oiga, señor,*" said one. He raised his rifle. "*Deténgase.*"

Diego did as he was told. He declared that he had come to speak to His Excellency. He made no mention of the emperor, whose letter he had burned long ago, letting the ashes scatter across the blue Pacific. Instead, he carried a handwritten statement of introduction, scribbled and signed by Baldemar Peralta. He nursed a faint hope that the renown of el Gordo de las Gafas might have reached even this remote outpost. He handed the document to the elder of the guards. Unfortunately, neither this man nor any of his subordinates was able to read. Thus the letter was launched on a slow, uncertain way up the chain of command until eventually word came back—let the visitor through.

Diego found lodging that night at a dismal, slump-roofed excuse for a hotel, a building that seemed to be both very old and yet only half-finished. Diego slouched about the place, drinking raw *aguardiente* straight from the bottle and wondering at the strange contradictions of fate that had brought him here. He supposed Juárez must sometimes wonder the same thing. They were confederates in that respect, both of them far from home, he a mestizo, Juárez an Indian, both driven to the furthest edge of a country once again ruled by foreign, white-skinned men. Bazaine. Napoleon. Maximiliano.

He took another swallow of the cloudy liquor, and the kick of it caused his eyes to water. Before long, he found himself thinking of Beatríz. Another swig. Another swallow. More dampness about the eyes. The way she had watched him that morning, near the gate at the House of Borda, as he rode away. He hadn't known then if he would ever make it back, and he wondered now if he ever would. No other messenger had returned, not as far as he knew. For now, he could only wait while Juárez decided whether to grant him an audience. The contrast between her dark skin and her white teeth. The flowers she braided into her hair. Ah, he didn't know what he was thinking. He took another mouthful, and his eyes welled up again.

It was not until his third full day in the town that a messenger appeared at the hotel to announce that the president would be willing to receive him that same afternoon. Unwilling to wait that long, Diego pulled on his jacket, adjusted his blouse, and set out on foot at once, remembering to bring the ambrotype he had carried from New York to Mexico City and now here.

When he reached Juárez's provisional headquarters, a military orderly guided him to a second-floor office that overlooked the central plaza through rows of paint-flecked wooden jalousies, many of them broken or missing. The orderly indicated a chair and asked him to sit. He did so, surveying the room. The office contained a large wooden desk, its surface gouged and bare, as well as several straight-back wooden chairs of various styles. The light through the jalousies cast scattered images on the opposite wall that resembled rows of broken piano keys.

Diego held his document folder firmly in his lap and waited for the president to appear. It was true what he'd told Bartlett. He had indeed met Juárez on one previous occasion, years earlier, when the president had been making his way through a crowd in Mexico City. Juárez had singled Diego out from the crowd, no doubt on account of his missing arm, and had changed his direction at once. A host of soldiers cleared his path. The president was a small, dark-skinned man with a sombre demeanour, and he reached out with two hands to grip Diego's one.

"The war?" he said.

Diego nodded. "*Sí. La guerra.*" He did not elaborate.

But Juárez thanked him, anyway. "*Gracias por su sacrificio. Le agradezco yo y le agradece todo México.*"

Thank you for your sacrifice. I thank you. All Mexico thanks you.

It was odd to think of that encounter now, so many years later, and to realize that Beatríz and the president were the only ones who had ever put the matter to him in this light. For his own part, Diego thought of the loss of his arm mainly as a humiliating blunder, something he would rather not discuss or hear mentioned. But Beatríz had regarded his injury in a different way—and so had Juárez, all those years ago.

A soldier appeared at the doorway and announced that *el presidente* would see him. Before long, a small but erect individual entered the room—the president of Mexico. Diego leapt to his feet. Benito Juárez was much as Diego remembered from that one previous encounter—a compact man with burnished bronze skin and with a severe expression etched into the contours of his narrow, rectangular face. If he had known pain or pleasure during the course of his life, his features did not show it. The two men shook hands. Juárez took in Diego's missing arm—or the empty space it would have occupied.

"Ah yes," he said, as if he remembered exactly who this visitor was, and to Diego it truly seemed that he did.

The president lowered himself into a solid wooden chair and gazed across the chipped surface of his desk. He must have been sixty years old, but there was not a strand of grey in the sleek black hair that was parted on the left and combed tidily over his pate. His features remained fixed in an attitude of serious purpose. He said nothing at first but merely waited until the orderly entered with coffee for them both, served in mismatched cups and saucers.

Juárez took his coffee black. He sipped from the cup and replaced it in its saucer. He glanced up. "I am informed that you were recently in New York," he said.

"I was." Diego supposed that questions on this subject must by now have been posed to J.S. Bartlett. He also realized his movements in New York, as in Washington, must surely have been monitored. He was, at least in theory, an emissary from the court of Emperor Maximiliano. He said, "Some time has passed since then."

"I take it you visited my wife there?"

"Yes," he said.

"And my family."

"And your family. I am very sorry about your son. I only just learned of it."

The president sighed. "I have yet to hear directly from my wife concerning the boy's death. I have had no news at all. The mail is painfully slow." Juárez remained ramrod straight in his chair, his delicate hands folded on the desk in front of him. "A most difficult situation."

It took a few moments before Diego realized what was wanted—words, descriptions, recollections. These were what any man would want during a long, enforced separation from his wife and family, especially following the death of a child he had never seen. Juárez must be desperate for news.

Diego did his best. He recounted his visit to the crowded third-floor apartment in New Rochelle occupied by doña Margarita Maza de Juárez and her brood of youngsters.

Juárez was mesmerized. He remained immobile, transfixed. When Diego fell silent, the president said nothing, as if waiting for more words, more details, and Diego did his best to comply, until he ran out of things to describe. It was then he remembered the ambrotype. "I have brought you something," he said.

He had hoped this gesture would win him favour, but only now did he sense how inspired Baldemar's idea had been. He reached into his document folder and removed the black-and-white image he'd had made in New York. It was framed in wood, and still wrapped in the paper and cotton, and the bolt of black velvet. He reached across the desk to deliver the offering to Juárez, who carefully removed the velvet cover, the cotton, the paper, and finally exposed the frame. He said nothing but simply gazed upon the result, a starkly simple image of several wide-eyed youngsters gathered around a newborn child. Enfolded in his mother's arms, the infant occupied the centre of the picture, flanked by Juárez's three daughters, a son-in-law, and two other sons.

"It is known as an ambrotype," said Diego. Not knowing what else to do, he began to describe the means by which the image was created. A plate of transparent glass, treated with a clear binding agent known as collodion is first exposed to the light for a matter of a few seconds, then bleached, and finally mounted on a dark background. The result is both highly detailed and extremely accurate, yielding an image that is true to nature rather than reversed from left to right, as would have been the case with other photographic techniques in current use—daguerreotypes or ferrotypes.

"I see," said Juárez, who kept his eyes pinned on this single image of his family and of his now perished son, a child he had never set eyes upon until this moment. When he did glance up, Diego saw that his eyes glistened, the only clear sign of emotion the president had betrayed during their encounter. "Thank you," he said.

The discussion Diego wished to hold with the president might have proceeded in any case, but matters went smoothly now. Benito Juárez was a man embattled on all fronts, the lord of a single border town and not much else. But, with the war recently concluded in the American states, it could not be long before Washington turned its attention to events in Mexico. Much would change. Forty years earlier, an American president had declared the Americas off limits to European powers, and now France would find itself under overwhelming pressure to abandon Mexico. Meanwhile, weapons would begin to find their way across the border. Diego had received assurances to this effect from General Ulysses S. Grant, on the shores of the Appomattox River.

"The Americans are very generous," Diego said now. "They look to the future."

"The Americans look to their own interests," said Juárez. Every few moments, his gaze strayed toward the ambrotype, which stood in its frame a little to his right. "For the moment, it seems their interests coincide with our own. I do not expect this circumstance to last very long, but it is surely welcome."

He offered Diego a cigar from a humidor on his desk and took one himself. The orderly hurried over to light them.

Juárez eased his cigar from his lips, released a thin coil of smoke. "I take it," he said, "that you have something to ask of me."

Diego said that he did—a portion of Spencer rifles, perhaps five hundred or so. They would be delivered to Xalapa to strengthen the forces of Baldemar Peralta.

"El Gordo de las Gafas," said the president. "You know him?"

"Yes."

"In fact, you are here on his behalf?"

Diego nodded.

"And not on behalf of this Austrian?"

Diego shrugged. "I am in Maximiliano's debt. He once saved the life of Baldemar Peralta, who saved my own life some years ago." He glanced down at what remained of his left arm.

Juárez tapped the ash from his cigar into a small wooden tray. "A complicated situation for you. Divided loyalties."

"Not just loyalties. Obligations."

The president glanced again at the ambrotype, then inclined his head. "Your friend Peralta will have his rifles," he said. "You have my word. There will be no conditions attached. You have done me a great service today, greater than you can imagine."

For a time, neither man said a word.

"But I do have a request of you," said Juárez. "This is a separate matter. What I am about to say is not an order, but I ask it of you as your president."

Even before he spoke, Diego knew what the man would say. It was self-evident, really. When Juárez was done explaining, Diego did not hesitate before stating that he could not comply.

"Then you need not do so," said Juárez. "I understand and, as I said, it is not an order." He set down his cigar in the wooden tray and put his hands together, fingers intertwined, elbows perched upon his desk. "But circumstances may change," he said.

Diego nodded. It was difficult to imagine this to be so, but not impossible.

"As for the rifles," said Juárez, "you have my word."

"*Gracias,*" said Diego. "*Gracias, mi presidente.*"

The following morning, Diego commenced his return to Mexico City. His quota of bodyguards had been diminished by two, one the victim of a bar brawl, the other of a self-inflicted bullet wound. In the company of those who remained, he set out on the westward trek to San Diego. As for the task urged upon him by Benito Juárez, he could not even contemplate so treacherous an act.

Still, circumstances might change. It seemed almost unthinkable, but it was so. They might. He hoped they never would. At San Diego, he boarded a mail packet for the sea voyage south to Acapulco.

PART FOUR

The Weeping Woman

Chapter 39

Her Majesty sipped from a cup of chamomile tea and perused a copy of *Le Journal des débats,* a Paris newspaper that had arrived that morning. The copy was several weeks out of date, but it confirmed the worst. The war between the American states had ended with the north triumphant. Nearly all of the south lay in ruins.

"You realize what this means?" She crumpled the paper in her lap.

Diego said he did. It meant many things—that slavery would be abolished, for one, and that the south would fail in its dreams of secession, for another. But this was not what the empress meant. The victory of the Unionist forces in the conflict to the north had just one principal consequence for her and the emperor.

"Napoleon will withdraw his troops," she said. She reached for her cup, then apparently changed her mind and instead raised her free hand and worried at her brow. "Just you watch."

"And the emperor's treaty with Napoleon?"

Diego meant the Treaty of Miramar, under whose terms the French leader was supposed to maintain a large foreign legion force in Mexico until 1873 at least. The precise date had been deliberately left open.

Carlota made a face. "Treaties!" she said. "Why do men set such stock by them? They are honoured only as a convenience. When he invaded Mexico, Napoleon thought the Confederacy would prevail. The southern states would go their separate way and make common cause with our government here." She gestured toward the French newspaper. "But, as we know, the actual course of events has not proceeded along these lines. Besides, there is talk of a war between France and Prussia. I fear Napoleon will be wanting his thirty thousand men."

It seemed to Diego that the empress saw matters more clearly than her husband did.

"So," she said. "Tell me about your journey."

Diego provided a brief and not very accurate account of his meeting with Benito Juárez in El Paso del Norte.

"He said no, of course," said the empress.

"That's right," said Diego. "He said no."

"Of course he did." The empress gave a bitter laugh. "Idiotic idea."

In fact, Diego had never posed the question—would Juárez consider serving as Maximiliano's prime minister? He had never even thought of posing the question. How could he? It was ridiculous. He sipped his coffee. The emperor was again in Cuernavaca, but his return to the capital was expected any day, for he was to preside at a ball in honour of Maréchal Bazaine and his new paramour, who were engaged to be married.

"My father warned me," said the empress. "Before we left Europe, he said we would be most unwise to put our faith in Napoleon. I am very much afraid that he was right." Her manner darkened further. "Napoleon is a fool," she said. "Besides, he is French. They're all pigs. What have I been telling you?" She reached for the French newspaper again.

Diego looked at her askance, wondering what on earth to make of this outburst. The news had enraged her, of course. But still, Carlota's behaviour lately had taken a strange turn. She was given to sudden outbursts like this one. Usually so logical, she was now apt to make incoherent statements that seemed to bear no connection to anything. She seemed unbalanced at times.

Diego waited while she calmed herself. He wished to introduce a very different subject: the question of Ángela's son. Considering all the challenges that faced the imperial government, he said, wasn't it time to put aside the matter of an heir? Shouldn't the boy be reunited with his mother?

"*Mi muy estimado Señor Serrano* . . ." The empress seemed to rise in her chair, her voice arch and forbidding. "Have you heard nothing of what I have been saying? The question of succession is no longer a subject of *any* importance. The question of survival *is*. Your opera singer may do as she pleases, and so may her son. If Napoleon decides to go back on his word to my husband, we will all of us die in this country together. Mexico will be our grave."

"Yes, Your Majesty. But His Majesty seems to take a different view."

"His Majesty," said Carlota, "is not mine to control. I agree with you—he seems utterly set on possessing an heir. I don't know if it's Salm-Salm's influence or something else, but he refuses to be persuaded otherwise, not by you and certainly not by me. Yes, I desire a child of our own, if that is what you are implying. But all that seems beside the point now."

"Yes, Your Majesty."

The empress took up her newspaper again. A muscle pulsed beneath her left eye. Diego rose from the table, made a slight bow, turned, and left the room.

The ball for Maréchal Bazaine was a catastrophe. First, the Countess Kollonitz was severely annoyed that the fete coincided with her birthday. That was bad enough. What was worse was that the emperor seemed to be suffering unusual distress—physical distress. Recently returned from Cuernavaca, he began to drink heavily before dinner and did not stop. Diego thought he knew why. General Márquez was among those invited to attend the dinner—as the new minister of war, he could hardly be left out—and Maximiliano was plainly terrified of him.

Following dinner, the men and women parted company. The men made for the billiards room, all except Bazaine, who made his excuses and departed. Was he that eager to be alone with his paramour, or did he have a presentiment of what was about to take place at Chapultepec? By this time, the emperor was clearly intoxicated—his complexion florid, his manner overheated, his speech overloud. At times when under the influence of too much liquor, he was apt to be morose and silent. But now the drink seemed to be having the opposite effect, his uncustomary manic energy intensified by a quantity of fine Bordeaux and port.

"Billiards!" he said. He approached a mahogany side table to fetch a crystal decanter of port. He raised the flask and looked around the room. "Who is for billiards? I challenge anyone at all."

"I accept."

The speaker stepped forward—General Márquez. Freshly returned from the torrid eastern lowlands, the man was leonine, his shaggy grey mane having grown too long, his large facial features gone craggy with age. A deep scar—remnant of some ancient battle—gouged the right side of his face.

"Márquez? Is it you?" The emperor swayed slightly as he spoke. "I warn you, *mi general*, I shall give no quarter."

Márquez set his glass of port down. He was out of practice, he said, but he would play if His Majesty was willing.

"Willing?" said the emperor. "Of course I am willing." He advanced toward the rack of cues mounted on the wall. Partway there, he stumbled and almost upset his drink. He recovered his balance and snorted at his mistake. "Must be careful. The empress will be put out. Disorderly conduct, you know. I shall end up in the Martinica if I don't watch out."

He selected a cue, tested its weight, and called for play to commence.

He made the break shot and immediately seized control. Even in his inebriated condition, the emperor demonstrated superior skills. For his part, Márquez proved to be a fumbler, barely able to execute even the most straightforward shot. In more normal circumstances, Maximiliano might have taken pity on the man and reduced his own level to avoid humiliating his opponent. But he did not seem so inclined in his present condition. He strode around the teak billiards table holding his wooden cue. Before long, he removed his scarlet dinner jacket, his white silk blouse billowing out from the confines of his suspenders. His thin, reddish hair and ample beard seemed to glow in the candlelight.

"Ah, Márquez," he said. He surveyed the table. "I think I have the better of you again." He swiftly executed another shot, potting a ball with ease. On his next shot, he potted another.

As the match proceeded, Salm-Salm glided among the guests, speaking in a low, discreet voice, proposing a wager on the outcome. Diego expected the prince to bet in the emperor's favour, but he seemed to be doing the exact opposite, offering high odds that Márquez would win. Many of those assembled in the billiards room promptly accepted the gamble. It was the prince's money, after all. If he wished to squander it on a doomed bet, then so much the worse for him.

In other circumstances, Diego would have found it intolerable to occupy the same room as the Tiger of Tacubaya. He was able to do so now only because he had so recently returned from his meeting with Juárez in El Paso del Norte and knew of the arrangement that had been struck there for a quantity of Spencer rifles. This awareness seemed to counterbalance at least some of the repugnance he felt for the man who had murdered Melchor Ocampo and who had shot Ángela, to say nothing of the numberless other crimes he had committed.

Meanwhile, the game continued, with the emperor sinking one shot after another as Márquez stood by, expressionless, as if he were merely a spectator. He barely batted an eye, even as the emperor's drinking and his strangely agitated state began to tell. Gradually, the quality of Maximiliano's play diminished.

"Let me see," said His Majesty. He leaned from the waist and narrowed his eyes, seeking a clearer view of the table.

Even Diego could tell that Maximiliano's next play was a difficult shot, one that would have to be executed with a precise combination of spin and power, a matter of banking the cue ball against the felt so as to deflect the last red ball into a corner pocket. The emperor took an inordinate amount of time setting up the troublesome stroke. The men in the room kept perfectly quiet as Maximiliano drew back on his cue, lining up the stroke a last time. He released the shot.

For a moment, it seemed he had blundered, but the cue ball somehow nudged the red, which wobbled slightly yet somehow righted itself before dutifully tumbling from sight.

The emperor drained his glass of port and called for another. He put back his shoulders and smiled at Márquez. "There. What did I say? Now *that* was a shot. Remember that one, my friend. Remember it well." He accepted another glass of wine from a servant, took a large swallow, and put the glass aside. He hunched down, frowning at the table once more, assessing the positions of the remaining balls. He glanced up at the minister of war, who stood on the opposite side of the table, patiently watching the game unfold. "Two," said the emperor. "Two in the side pocket. What do you say, Márquez? Do you think I am up to the task? Eh? Do you think?"

"I'm sure I don't know, Your Majesty," said Márquez in a deep but uninflected voice. "You are in a better position to judge what you can and cannot do, while we in Mexico know only what we have seen."

The emperor straightened up, quaffed once more from his glass of port, set the glass down upon the edge of the billiards table. He turned to face Márquez. "What is this? Know only what you have seen?" He began to powder the tip of his cue. Had he just been insulted—or not? "I'm not certain I understand your meaning."

"Then let me be clear." With his billiards cue in one hand, Márquez stepped out of the shadows and into the full glare of the candlelight that bathed the table from the chandelier overhead. "Allow me to make a proposal, Your Majesty."

"What do you suggest?"

"Only this. If you fail to make this next shot—if you fail to clear the two ball from the table—why, then you must accept a challenge. You must say a truth or submit to a dare."

"Truth or dare?" said the emperor. "I am not sure that I—"

"Please, gentleman." It was Doktor Basch. The stout physician stepped forward and put up his hands. "I beg you, one contest at a time. Please. Your Majesty—"

"No, Basch. Allow me to consider this most diverting challenge." The emperor grinned at Márquez. "I accept on one condition—that the same obligation fall upon you. If I *do* make this shot, you must accept a similar challenge."

"Very well," said Márquez.

"Your Majesty," said Basch. "It is late. Would it not be better to complete the game without this additional complexity?"

"Nonsense, Basch. The wager is made." Maximiliano looked around the room. "Someone—more port. Can you not see my glass is empty? The emperor's glass is empty!"

A servant hurried into the room, bearing another bottle of fine port wine.

"Excellent," said His Majesty. He raised his fresh drink toward Márquez. "A most invigorating proposal. The evening grows more interesting by the minute."

"May it continue to do so, Your Majesty. Why should we not repeat this arrangement for each turn that remains in the game?"

"Gentlemen!" said Basch. "Really. I think this is going too far. It would be better, I think, simply to play out the match."

"Why, Basch," asked the emperor, "do you have so little confidence in my play?" He looked at Márquez. "I accept your challenge."

With his cue in his right hand, Maximiliano huddled over the green baize surface and appraised the task before him. He moved his jaw from side to side. Diego was no expert at billiards, but even he could see the man had left himself in a poor position. His previous two shots had owed more to luck than skill. This next turn was a perplexing shot, one that would require the emperor to somehow bend the cue ball around the orange before connecting with the two and coaxing it into the side pocket.

Maximiliano frowned at the table. He took an inordinate amount of time setting up his shot. Finally, he squared his weight and leaned down over the baize. As he drew the cue back with his right arm, he clicked his teeth and clenched his jaw. With a sudden impulse of his right elbow, he snapped the cue forward into the ball. Struck slightly off-centre, the white ball curved around the orange, but already it was off course. It barely touched the two before rolling helplessly away. The two ball drifted a little distance across the green baize and then came to rest, not appreciably nearer the side pocket than it had been before.

CHAPTER 40

"THAT," SAID MAXIMILIANO, "was not my intended shot."

"No," said Márquez. "You have missed completely." After a moment's hesitation, he added, "Your Majesty."

The emperor drained his glass, set it down once again on the edge of the billiards table, and lit a cigarette. Through a cloud of bluish smoke, he scrutinized the baize.

"So, which shall it be?" said Márquez. "Truth or dare?"

Once again, the room had fallen almost perfectly silent.

"Truth," said the emperor.

"Then truth it shall be," said Márquez. He took a step forward, placed both hands on the wooden edge of the billiards table, leaned into the swirls of smoke that drifted through the cone of sepia light cast by the candelabra. "Tell me, Your Majesty," he said, "is it not true that you have written to your brother in Vienna in an effort to reclaim your right of succession to the Austrian throne? Is it not—?"

"Gentlemen . . ." Basch lumbered forward.

The emperor raised his hand. He turned back to Márquez. "Yes," he said. "It is true."

"I see. Interesting, don't you think, considering that you are the emperor of Mexico? I take it you are not contemplating a change of crowns?"

"One question," said Basch. "One question, one truth. The emperor has replied in full. The game has concluded."

"No," said Maximiliano. "I am willing to answer." He addressed Márquez. "It is not true that I am contemplating a change of crowns. The issue you raise is a private matter, an affair between brothers, a question of principle, nothing more."

"There you have it," said Basch. "Question answered. That will be all."

Again the emperor put up his hand. "But may I ask how you came by this intelligence? I was under the impression that my correspondence was private and transmitted in code. How did you come to know of this matter?"

"It is the talk of Europe," said Márquez. "As surely you must have heard by now."

The emperor drew upon his cigarette but said nothing. After a time, he stepped back and gestured toward the table. "Very well. It is your turn, I believe."

Márquez stepped to the table and in one unbroken motion took up his position and made his shot, sending the cue ball racing into the two, which scurried into a corner pocket as if it had been lured there by a magnet.

"Well played," said the emperor. "You seem to have improved the quality of your game."

"Getting out the rust," said Márquez. With his cue held casually at his side, he drew upon his cigar. "In any case, I seem to have made my shot, which permits me another question."

"So it does."

"Tell me, Your Majesty, is it true that you have communicated on several occasions with that Indian swine Benito Juárez, with a view to inviting the scoundrel to serve as your prime minister? Is this so?"

"Please, gentlemen," said Basch. "Gentlemen. This has gone far enough."

Again the emperor waved his physician away. He turned back to General Márquez and informed the soldier that it was so. He would do what was necessary to end the war—but Juárez had turned him down.

"Is it not so, Serrano?" he said, scanning the assembly of men and fixing his gaze upon his secretary.

Diego wondered what to say. How had Márquez obtained this intelligence? From Salm-Salm? It didn't matter. What mattered was Diego's reply. If he answered truthfully, he would compromise himself. If he lied, he would only further embarrass the emperor. "It's a complicated question," he said. "It's—"

"I see," said the minister of war. He waved Diego off. "Well, I thank you for your candour. I think we may all draw the appropriate conclusions." Again he inhaled on his cigar and squinted at the table. "Now, let us see what else we can manage."

The officer made no further attempt to pretend that he was anything but an expert at the game. It was clear that his earlier ineptitude had been a ruse. Now the minister of war marched about the table with complete confidence. After each successful stroke, he addressed the emperor with another question.

Diego gazed about the room until his eyes lit upon the Prince of Salm-Salm, who seemed to be smiling to himself, no doubt in anticipation of his winnings. He must have known all along about the level of Márquez's game.

Before the night was out, the emperor had divulged—in round numbers—his salary and that of his wife, which together amounted to approximately a tenth part of the Mexican treasury's annual receipts, as Márquez observed. His Majesty was obliged to confess as well that he had constructed a second mansion for his use in Cuernavaca, a house that was furnished with only one bedchamber.

"Forgive me for being forward," said Márquez, "but is it not normal for a house in this country to contain a second apartment?"

"Really!" said Basch. "I really must protest. You go too far."

But Maximiliano failed to stand up to the man, even on a matter as personal as this. His gaze roamed about the gathering, no doubt on the lookout for Bazaine. Surely Bazaine would know how to proceed, would tell him what to do. Should he sack the minister of war right here and now? Pack him off to Constantinople once and for all? But Bazaine was gone, and the emperor seemed lost. The muscles of his neck bulged like cables. His eyes darted from side to side, and his complexion had lost its previous ruddiness. He was sombre and pale, his face damp with perspiration. Finally, he turned back to the table to address Márquez, and it was clear he had capitulated completely.

"What you say is true," he said. "Such a house has indeed been constructed."

"Enough. This is quite enough." Basch raised his hands. "I protest these remarks. They must cease at once. I cannot put it plainer."

Good for Basch. The portly, hirsute doctor was making the best fist possible of a very bad circumstance. But why was it only Basch who was mounting a defence on the emperor's behalf? Diego wondered if he should not be doing the same, but immediately he knew that he would not. He had no stake in this battle. Besides, all that Márquez said was true.

For his part, the emperor seemed stunned. He was wholly unaccustomed to this brand of abuse. Still, he had accepted the man's challenge. In a way, this was his own doing.

"Please, do not take me amiss, Your Majesty," said Márquez. "We are a crude people at times, we Mexicans. *Tropicales* is what we are. We lack your European refinement. Forgive me if I have given offence. It's just that His Majesty so poorly understands this country that he would collaborate with its vilest enemies while insulting its bravest sons. He spends his money on trifles while Mexican men are dying in battle. He would reduce the Church to a pile of rubble. He insults the ambassador of Rome. He—"

"The ambassador of Rome?" said the emperor. He squashed out his cigarette. "You are wrong there. I offered no insult to this Monseñor . . ." He cast about for the name.

"Meglia," said Diego.

"Yes. Meglia. I offered him no insult whatever. I did not meet the man."

"Ah yes. So I recall. That is so. It was your *wife*. The empress was left to attend to this important matter of state, and she refused every effort by the papal nuncio to forge a concordat between Mexico City and the Holy See. That is how our country is being ruled—by women and neglect." Márquez gazed down at the green baize, where two balls remained to be played. He shook his head and then glanced up at the emperor. "I see no shot," he said, a patent untruth. The cue ball was perfectly positioned, as even Diego could tell. The game was Márquez's to take if he chose. Instead, he placed his cue on the table. "I concede defeat. Good night, Your Majesty."

General Márquez turned and departed. At once, the room reverberated with men's voices, all barking away in tones of surprise and gloating. Only Salm-Salm was quiet. Márquez's decision to abandon the game at the final moment had caught him completely unawares, saddling him with a substantial loss.

"Leave it be," said Maréchal Bazaine. "This is my suggestion to Your Majesty. I see no better course."

"He was grossly impertinent."

"So I have heard."

"He should be hanged, shot, horse-whipped, and then brought before a military tribunal to answer for his crimes. The charge—gross insubordination."

"An unorthodox approach, Your Majesty. But I see your point. Once again, I recommend forbearance. He is a rough customer but a skilled soldier. You may come to value his services more highly than you do now."

"I may come to do no such thing. I recommend the maximum penalty under the law."

"Your Majesty, may I speak plainly?"

"Please do."

Maximiliano was in his office at the Imperial Palace in Mexico City the day following his altercation with Márquez. Diego was scribbling notes.

Bazaine eased his weight forward in his chair and lowered his voice. He said he disagreed in most respects with Mexico's conservative class, whose ranks most certainly included Márquez. They were an assembly of shallow, selfish men, with a severely blinkered view of the world, and yet he could understand some of their discontent. After much lobbying and politicking, they had brought an Austrian noble to their country, precisely to put an end to liberalism and godlessness. And what did this new monarch do? He filled three-quarters of his cabinet with men of known liberal sentiments and then sought to make a truce with the most villainous liberal of all, Benito Juárez.

Meanwhile, he spent what many regarded as an alarming portion of the national treasury on fancy uniforms, expensive balls, and personal indulgences, money that might have been added to the military budget. Even now, three years after they had first occupied Mexico, Bazaine said, his troops could properly claim to exercise control over something less than half the country's territory. Even the strategically vital route to Veracruz was insecure, swarming with bandits and rogues. Barely half a dozen large cities were firmly under French authority. Elsewhere, travel was a perilous business at best.

"My dear Bazaine," said the emperor, "that is all very well. But I—"

"Please, Your Majesty. Let me finish."

The emperor sat back, nodded. The air seemed to go out of him.

It was these bloody gamberros, said Bazaine. *Guerrilleros*, some called them. Hooligans was what they were. And the worst of the lot was Baldemar Peralta, the very man whom His Majesty had pardoned not long after his arrival, the same man who had humiliated Márquez beyond human endurance.

"Forgive me for saying so, Your Majesty, but it is perhaps not impossible to understand that Márquez might be disgruntled."

The emperor turned to his secretary. "Serrano—what do you say?"

Diego found it impossible to resist the urge to speak plainly. "I think," he said, "that Ángela Peralta's child should be returned to its mother."

The emperor put back his head. His jaw seemed to fall. He looked as if someone had just struck him in the chest. He put up his hands. "You treat me like a child, both of you. You behave as if you understood affairs of state better than I, a Hapsburg, formerly admiral of the Austrian armada and governor of Venetia and Lombardy. How dare you!" He turned to Bazaine. "You think I am a waffler—"

"Please, Your Majesty—"

"Don't interrupt me. Let me tell you both—on the question of succession I have not waffled by one degree. I have stood my ground. I will have an heir and, if my wife will not bear me one, then I shall make do with this boy."

"Very well," said Bazaine. "Very well, Your Majesty." He rose to leave. "And as for General Márquez?"

"I shall consider what you have said. I do not mean to act without considering all sides."

Bazaine nodded his head in lieu of a bow. He retrieved his hat and left the room.

Maximiliano was silent for a time and then returned his focus to Diego. His outburst of petulance was done, it seemed. He smiled and lit a cigarette. "We have not yet spoken of your journey," he said. "You met Juárez, I take it? Charlotte tells me it is so."

Diego said yes.

"In the flesh?"

"Yes."

The emperor settled back in his chair. "Extraordinary," he said. "Tell me—and spare no detail—what manner of man is he?"

Chapter 41

The emperor failed to make good on his threats against Márquez. Either he had decided to heed Bazaine's advice or he feared what the Tiger of Tacubaya, thoroughly enraged, might do. Besides, the fortunes of war had lately turned against the imperial forces, and Márquez's warrior instincts could no longer be easily spurned. In short, Maximiliano needed the man on his side, just as Bazaine had predicted.

Emboldened by the end of the war in the American states, and strengthened by new supplies of weaponry, the armies loyal to Juárez had begun to gain ground. Bazaine and Márquez were both adamant that more aggressive battlefield measures were necessary. In particular, Márquez demanded that his officers be authorized to summarily execute anyone suspected of membership in an armed group on the liberal side. Captured combatants would be dealt with in the same way. He seized every opportunity to promote his case, brow-beating the emperor to authorize the measures, not next week, not tomorrow, but now.

"*Chinga a su madre,*" the general swore one day. He roared out the words—a deeply offensive oath—loudly enough that anyone nearby could hear him, no doubt including His Majesty. The officer had just left another meeting with the emperor, a meeting that had evidently produced yet another indecisive result on the question of summary execution, and Márquez was leaving no doubt about his displeasure. Ever since the game of billiards at Chapultepec, he had abandoned any pretence of holding Maximiliano in anything but the roundest contempt.

This time, Diego happened to be advancing along the corridor and heard the officer's obscene outburst. He wondered how the emperor abided the man. Yet so he did, out of both necessity and fear. Lately, the atmosphere at the Imperial Palace had become deeply oppressive, rife with treachery and suspicion and doubt. Diego needed air. He hurried out onto the Zócalo, where a riddle of rickety scaffolding clung to the stone exterior of the Metropolitan Cathedral, and workmen bustled about, repairing the bell tower that had nearly been destroyed by the blast of Bazaine's sixteen-pounder.

"Serrano!"

A man's voice called out from behind, and Diego turned to see who it was. Salm-Salm. He waited for the man to catch up. The prince made as flamboyant a figure as ever, wearing a voluminous white blouse above a mauve cummerbund and a pair of wine-red trousers. He announced that he wished to propose a truce between himself and his old friend, *el poeta manco.*

"Are we in need of one?"

"Come now. We have been adversaries ever since that evening at the opera, when dear Ángela was shot."

Diego made no comment either way.

"I want to speak to you about the child," said Salm-Salm. "And the mother."

"Yes?"

"Look. It might not seem that the question of succession is the most pressing matter facing Max. But the affair should be settled just the same, in fairness to all. We should come to an agreement, don't you think?"

"I don't know."

Salm-Salm explained that Maximiliano and Labastida were at an impasse. Yes, Ángela's son had been handed over as agreed. No, the Church would not authorize his adoption by Maximiliano, or not without the mother's formal agreement.

"Which you do not have."

"Which we do not have. That brings us to the crux of my proposal. I know where the boy is currently residing, and I suspect that you know where the mother might be found."

"I see."

"I'm sure you do. And I don't believe you are alone. I believe that little witch in Cuernavaca knows, too. Twice, to my knowledge, she has communicated with you about something. Shortly after the first instance, Ángela disappeared from Max's, ah . . . from his second house in Cuernavaca. I call that an interesting coincidence."

"Where is the boy?" said Diego, although he knew perfectly well.

"Not so fast. I propose an exchange of information."

"But one of us might lie."

"Or both of us."

"An odd sort of truce. I'm not sure I'm interested."

"Don't be so hasty," said Salm-Salm. "I can make matters difficult for you. Don't think I can't. I know a great deal about you that you would not wish to have others know."

It was the first time Diego had heard the man issue so bald a threat.

"For example," said the prince, "I know whom you meet, all too frequently, at a filthy dive near the Plaza Santa Cecilia. I understand exactly why it was that you travelled to the north of Mexico. Yes, yes, to meet with Benito Juárez, but your real purpose had nothing to do with carrying out the emperor's commission. I make it my business to know things, you see. Now, what have you to say?"

Diego had nothing to say. So he and Baldemar had been under surveillance. He cast back in his mind to their encounters at Memorias del Futuro, wondering which bedraggled low-life had been spying on them.

Salm-Salm waited for a time, until he realized nothing more was going to be said. "Very well." He turned and strode back toward the Imperial Palace. Diego watched him go, trying to guess what the man might do. He might go to the emperor. He might not. On the whole, Diego thought he would delay. Knowledge might be power, but only if it is meted out slowly and by degrees.

Two nights later, Diego was patrolling the perimeter of the Plaza Santa Cecilia when a tall, bony slattern in dark spectacles and with long tangled tresses suddenly lurched into his way.

"*Mi amor,*" said the woman. She spoke in a strained and warbling voice and reached out to grab his only arm. "*Ven conmigo. Te daré todo.*"

Diego stopped dead. He knew at once who it was, but he let the charade continue a little longer, until they were both well clear of the square and he was certain they were not being followed. If Salm-Salm had his spies on the prowl, then they had missed their mark this time. Diego stopped by the portal of a tumbledown *vecindad,* a communal dwelling.

"Baldemar . . ." he said.

"*Mierda,*" said the gamberro. "What gave me away?"

"The voice. The glasses. That idiotic dress."

Instead of proceeding to their usual haunt, they made their way to an unfamiliar place, where they were less likely to be observed. Baldemar pulled off his wig.

"I take it you have news," said Diego.

Baldemar nodded. In a low voice, he told Diego that clandestine shipments of Spencer rifles had already begun to reach Xalapa. Those weapons, combined with Márquez's withdrawal from the field, had left the eastern sierra and the coastal flatlands largely under his control. Only the corridor from the capital to Veracruz remained in contest, and he proposed to impose his authority even there. It would not take long. He spoke confidently, even with a certain bravado. Maybe his recent string of successes had affected him. He seemed cockier than usual.

"We should be careful," said Diego. He eyed the dark interior of the pulquería—the wavering glow of candles, the darting shadows, the shifting silhouettes of men barely discernible in the murky candlelight.

Anyone could be watching and listening, even here, a place they'd never patronized before.

Baldemar looked around as well, then shrugged and took another drink. "I have my eyes open," he said. "We're all right now."

"You should be careful just the same. Not just here and not just now. But always."

"What do you mean?"

Diego explained that Márquez was seeking the emperor's consent for a freer hand in battle. The result would be summary execution for anyone suspected of acting on the republican side.

Baldemar adjusted his glasses. He chuckled. "The old goat's only trying to protect himself. He's been murdering innocents in cold blood for years. He doesn't need some formal decree to do that. He's just trying to make everything seem legal now because he knows he's going to lose."

"Anyway," said Diego, "it won't happen. His Majesty would never agree to this."

"His *Majesty*?"

"I mean, Maximiliano. The Austrian. I just can't—"

"You call him 'His Majesty'?"

"Everyone does. I have to. He's the emperor. I'm his secretary."

"Fine—but here? You're not his secretary here."

"Look. It was a mistake. I didn't mean it."

"I hope not. But I know how you get."

Diego gritted his teeth. He would let this insult pass, just as he'd done with all the others. "Anyway," he said, "the point is that the . . . the *Austrian* would never sign such a decree. It would be criminal, and he would refuse. But, either way, the war is going to become more dangerous and more bloody, not less. That's the point."

"Point taken."

"Just don't get caught," said Diego. "That's all."

"Don't worry. If I were going to be caught, it would have happened a long time ago."

"It did."

Both quaffed their drinks. Baldemar wiped his mouth with the back of his hand.

"Speak to me," he said, "about Ángela's son."

"That's what I've been meaning to tell you," Diego said in a whisper. "I know where he is."

"Where?"

"He's in Cuernavaca, at a house called la Casa del Olvido. The House of Forgetfulness."

Baldemar smiled. He tapped a finger against his head. "Memories of the future," he said. "I well remember what must now be done."

Diego could swear he'd heard those same words before. *I well remember what must now be done.* He strained to recall, but it was no use.

Baldemar was still speaking. "I want you to go to Cuernavaca," he was saying, "the next chance you get. I'll find you there."

Diego set his jar down on the cracked wooden counter and motioned for it to be filled. "All right," he said. "Fine. To Cuernavaca, then." He raised his replenished glass and looked straight at Baldemar. If he could have remembered the future—or divined it—he would have done so, and he would have known. But he lacked that particular gift, and knew it, and so he understood nothing at all.

CHAPTER 42

"HE LIKES TO WEAR SAILOR CLOTHES," Beatríz said. "He goes about with a little frown on his face and with his hands on his hips. He stops and scrutinizes every object or person he comes across, as if he were on an official tour of inspection. He asks questions about everything."

Diego and Beatríz were strolling through the zócalo of Cuernavaca, speaking in whispers. Diego had arrived the previous evening but had not yet spoken with the emperor, who was also in residence in the town.

Beatríz said she was now able to come and go at the House of Forgetfulness, where Ángela's son was effectively a prisoner. In some ways, it was a benign form of incarceration, she said, not to mention luxurious. Those charged with the boy's care—a governess and several other employees of the emperor—did not seem much concerned with secrecy, either. At first, they had taken far greater precautions, no doubt mindful of what had happened to the boy's mother, spirited away as she had been without leaving a hint of her whereabouts. It was not something that would bear repeating. But, with the passage of time, they had become more relaxed. The governess took Agustín out on walks openly, with only a single armed guard to watch over them. Deliveries of food, clothing, and other provisions were made without subterfuge of any kind. Beatríz found that she was able to visit as she pleased. It seemed to be taken for granted that Cuernavaca provided all the cover that was needed, a modest city hidden away in an intermontane basin a day's journey from the capital. Who would take an inordinate interest in anything that happened here?

"Does the boy ask about his mother?" said Diego.

"Strangely, no." Beatríz reached up and pushed back an errant lock of her hair. "He doesn't seem entirely clear on what a mother is. But he often says his father is the king."

"Does the emperor visit him?"

"No. Never."

They strolled about the plaza a little longer, content not to speak at all, just glad to be again in each other's company. Diego had already described his journey to the north, his meeting with the Mexican president. Eventually, they were obliged to part. Beatríz had errands to run, and Diego meant to return to the House of Borda by a roundabout route. He expected at any moment to be accosted by Baldemar, dressed in some outlandish disguise or other. By rights, such an encounter ought to have occurred already, and he wondered if something were wrong. Just in case, he stayed alert, carefully eyeing everyone he passed on the chance that one of them should turn out to be his old friend.

But Baldemar did not appear that morning, so Diego returned to the House of Borda, entering by the al fresco terrace. He flopped onto a wicker settee and rested his legs on a low table. He looked idly around. Before long, he heard Maximiliano's voice.

"A damned good morning's work . . ." the emperor was saying. He marched up onto the terrace, clad in sturdy leather boots, gabardine breeches, and a tweed jacket. He stopped and peered behind him at the brilliant morning light and iridescent foliage.

"*México, lindo y querido,*" he said. He sighed, turned, and then started. "Ah, Serrano. There you are. They told me you'd arrived. What brings you to fair Cuernavaca?"

Maximiliano crossed the terrace in the direction of a divan cater-corner to Diego's seat, scattering clumps of half-dried mud in his wake. He collapsed onto the sofa, leaned back, and stretched out his legs, in their earth-encrusted boots. Before Diego could reply, the emperor looked up.

"Ah, here they are," he said as Basch and Billimek trooped into view. He yawned and patted his pockets, searching for a cigarette. "Basch, how many species taken this day?"

"A half-dozen, Your Majesty."

"Well then, what did I say? A good morning's work all round." He lit a cigarette, rubbed his jaw, stifled another yawn. He glanced at Diego once more. "You look tired," he said.

Without waiting for a reply, Maximiliano kicked several more clumps of mud from his boots, climbed to his feet, and sauntered out into the garden, with its flowering vines, graceful wooden trellises, and topiary shrubs. Below him, the still waters of the artificial lake reflected the fine blue sky. The sunshine poured down, and the late-morning air was mild and sweet, redolent of flowers and wood smoke.

Doktor Basch shuffled over to Diego's side. "I warn you," he whispered, "His Majesty's mood has been changeable of late. One moment, exuberant. The next . . . pouf!" He shook his head.

The emperor swanned back onto the terrace, his boots clicking against the tiles. "What's that, Herr Doktor? Not gossiping about me again?" He laughed and drew upon his cigarette. "Hey," he said in what was almost a shout, "does no one hereabouts have something a civilized man might eat? Hey! Hey!"

A servant was duly instructed to secure something along the lines of coffee and pastries. Count von Bombelles appeared from somewhere within the house. He arched his back and stretched his arms out to the sides. He and the emperor, along with Basch and Billimek, settled themselves around a long table. At their behest, Diego strolled over to join them.

Soon more cigarettes were produced, as well as pots of coffee and baskets of croissants. The Prince of Salm-Salm emerged onto the terrace, yawning and running a hand through his dishevelled hair. It seemed that he had only just awakened. Another place was set at the table.

For a time, the mood was jovial. Maximiliano shared recollections with Basch and Billimek about their adventures that morning, yet another expedition in search of new specimens of botanical interest. The emperor insisted that he had made the greater part of their discoveries that morning. He lit another cigarette and announced that he would not decline a glass of Riesling, never mind the hour. The morning was too lovely to waste.

Riesling was served at once, and the emperor raised his glass.

"To Mexico," he said. "To Mexico and the sun." He raised his glass still higher and broke into laughter, the laughter of pure pleasure. "When the sun shines in Mexico," he declared, "you think it will shine forever."

He laughed again. He pressed the glass to his lips and drank. Before long, the flagon was empty. Another replaced it and was soon emptied, too. By now, the emperor had fallen quiet. He barely seemed to register what the others were saying. His head began to tilt to the side. Without warning, he pushed his chair from the table and stood up, gripping the chair back for balance.

"I will take my leave of the gentlemen," he announced. With that, he walked woozily from the terrace and disappeared into the cool shadows within the house.

Basch shook his head. "Up and down," he said. "Up and down."

"It's the laudanum you feed him," said Salm-Salm. "It would knock out a horse."

"Laudanum?" said Diego. He was unfamiliar with the term.

"A little opium, some alcohol," explained Basch. "To calm his nerves. The emperor possesses a nervous disposition, as you know. He has lately suffered from bouts of anxiety. The laudanum seems to help."

Before long, Bombelles excused himself from the table. One by one, the other men drifted off, until Diego found himself alone. He gazed out at the gardens, at the peacocks strutting across the shimmering grass and the topiary shrubs glinting, bright emerald, in the patchwork of light and shadow. He lit a cheroot and watched the smoke curl upward, glimmering in the sunlight. He wondered where Baldemar was. How would he reveal himself? What would happen then?

That afternoon, Maximiliano led an excursion to a local school, where he delivered a brief discourse to the assembled students. He then presented each of the teachers with a medal. Later, the emperor and his entourage returned to the House of Borda and took tea al fresco on the terrace.

The emperor announced that he meant to enjoy his siesta outdoors and invited the others to join him in the garden. Only Diego and Basch took up the offer. Soon, Maximiliano was reclining upon a gaily embroidered hammock that swayed in the shade of a large gazebo overlooking the lagoon. He smoked cigarette after cigarette and leafed through a French magazine devoted to the latest innovations in balloon aeronautics. He still intended to fly.

Diego read a novel. Basch huddled at a refectory table, methodically coaxing a succession of dead butterflies from glass jars and mounting them on pins. It seemed to be painstaking work, at least to judge by his periodic grunts and sighs. Somewhere in the distance, a dove sang mournfully.

Diego drifted off to sleep—until, without warning, a commotion erupted across the lawns. He lurched upright, and his book sprawled across the gazebo's tiled floor. He turned in his hammock and looked back toward the mansion, beyond the preening peacocks and the croquet hoops.

A guard of Zouaves trotted out onto the terrace in their scarlet kepis and short pantaloons. The Africans formed two rows and snapped to attention. A military officer strode out onto the polished tiles, clutching a peaked cap at his side. It was Bazaine.

The French marshal paused at the edge of the terrace, no doubt to take stock of his surroundings. His eyes blinked slowly and his cheeks inflated and deflated. He descended the several steps and advanced across the grass. Basch was holding up a small white butterfly, impaled on a pin. By now, Diego was on his feet.

Bazaine stopped at the edge of the gazebo and lowered himself to one knee in what seemed to be an unusually deep bow. In that position, he waited as the emperor struggled to his feet.

"Your Majesty." Bazaine stood upright. "I have news."

CHAPTER 43

"WELL, IT MUST BE important if you have come in person." The emperor slid his hands into the pockets of his cotton slacks and affected a casual pose, resting his weight against a wooden pillar. "So, then. What news do you bring?"

"Perhaps Your Majesty had best sit down."

"Oh?" Maximiliano padded across the gazebo in his patent-leather shoes. He retrieved a cigarette from a humidor set upon a low wooden table. He pressed the cigarette between his lips and blinked at the officer. "That has an ominous ring."

Maximiliano settled himself onto a long, low settee. He looked up at the Frenchman. "Please, Bazaine, and you, Serrano—please, *siéntense*. Sit down. Basch—join us." He glanced over at the Indian attendant who stood nearby, his expression perfectly blank. "Wine," said the emperor. "White wine."

Bazaine took a seat across from the emperor. He said nothing at first, merely waited as the wine was produced, decanted, poured. The tension seemed to be contagious, and it soon infected everyone—except

Bazaine. It was the emperor who broke the silence. He raised his fluted glass and declared a toast in honour yet again of the French officer, soon to be married.

"But," said Maximiliano, "I do not imagine it is matrimony that has brought you here."

"No, Your Majesty, I fear not."

"I must say, Bazaine, I'm confounded by your presence." The emperor reached forward and tapped a length of cigarette ash into a glass tray. He gave a nervous laugh. "I was under the impression you had a war to fight."

"That is so." The officer nodded. "It is for that very reason, Your Majesty, that I have come to Cuernavaca."

"Good Lord. Don't tell me we've won."

"No, Your Majesty. I—"

"A joke, Bazaine. I was joking."

"Ah."

"Go on. Say what you have come to say."

As the Frenchman delivered his news, Maximiliano remained completely still, with his cigarette held aloft. He preserved this attitude for the duration of Bazaine's presentation. The only change in his posture was a noticeable trembling of his right arm, an involuntary motion that gradually grew more pronounced as Bazaine continued to elucidate the new circumstances prevailing in Mexico.

When the Frenchman was done, Maximiliano remained quite still. "*Withdraw?*" he said. "Napoleon means to *withdraw* his troops?"

"Yes, Your Majesty."

"All of them?"

Bazaine blinked. He shifted in his seat. "I am merely transmitting a message, Your Majesty. It was the Baron de Saillard who brought the news from Paris. He is in Mexico City, preparing for his return. Based on the information he conveyed to me, Napoleon means to withdraw the entirety of his army from Mexico within a year. The baron was most precise."

The emperor seemed to be examining the clay tiles at his feet. After a time, he addressed Bazaine. His expression was briefly hopeful. "Within a year? All French troops to be withdrawn within a year? You know, that still leaves us—"

"Your Majesty, forgive me. Yes, the troops are to be withdrawn within a year. But their removal is to begin at once. It—"

"At once!"

"Yes, Your Majesty. My men are even now being recalled from the field, for assembly in the capital. From there, they will proceed to Veracruz."

"What? All this, before I was even informed?"

"I am sorry, Your Majesty. I take my orders from Paris, you see. I had no choice but to begin preparations."

Maximiliano reached for his glass. His face had gone starkly white, and a small blue vein throbbed at his right temple. The glass shook in his hand.

"But I have a treaty. The Treaty of Miramar. It is unequivocal on this point. French troops are to remain in Mexico until 1873 at least. That is seven years away."

Bazaine nodded and sipped his wine. "That, too, was my understanding, Your Majesty. But circumstances change. I confess that for some time I have been expecting to receive an order along these lines."

"On what grounds?"

"The situation in the United States of America. The situation in Europe. As Your Majesty is no doubt aware, the armies of Prussia have lately inflicted an unexpected military defeat upon Austria. By the way, my condolences to your older brother." Bazaine gave an arch smile. "I imagine Napoleon must be concerned about that as well. Might France be next? Besides, I am made to understand that public opinion in my country has lately turned against the presence of our troops in Mexico. It is said the imperial government here is profligate with its finances. So, you see, a great deal has changed." Bazaine set down his glass. "Perhaps Your Majesty might prefer to take the matter up with Napoleon himself."

"I already have. The treaty, I tell you. It was Napoleon who signed it. He signed the damned thing."

Neither Basch nor Diego uttered a word.

"I see," said Bazaine. He ran his tongue over his upper lip, and his features assumed a pensive cast, as if he were carefully considering what the emperor had just said. Then he shrugged. "Well, I'm sure Napoleon signs a great many things."

Chapter 44

On Bazaine's advice, Maximiliano summoned General Márquez to journey out to Cuernavaca. He meant to confer with him about the new prospects they both faced since Napoleon had gone back on his solemn word. When he arrived, the Tiger of Tacubaya was in a gruff, unruly mood, even for him. He was drunk from mid-morning until well past midnight, and the alcohol made him surly and mean.

He lumbered about the hallways and terraces, loudly proclaiming his contempt for all things Gallic. He cursed Napoleon most of all. He swore that Mexico didn't need the French *maricones.* Good riddance to them all. He'd brought Captain Cajiga with him, too. The dark-eyed Spaniard kept his silence, but his guarded manner seemed every bit as sinister as Márquez's ill-tempered bravado. The mood at the emperor's residence had turned gloomy even before these two men showed up, but now it became positively funereal. The servants shuffled about the place, almost soundless, as if afraid of giving offence for the crime of drawing breath.

And still there was no sign of Baldemar.

Diego wondered what had become of his friend. Had he suffered a change of heart? Had something gone wrong? Once a day or so, Beatríz ventured to the emperor's secondary residence in order to ensure that all was well with the child there. Each time, she reported back to Diego that everything was as it had been. There had been no unusual visitors. Nothing out of the ordinary had occurred. For his part, the emperor spent much of his time in bed. Nerves, said Doktor Basch. He was suffering from stress and anxiety. He corresponded with Carlota daily, and Diego, of course, was privy to their communication. She was tempted to hurry out to Cuernavaca to be with her husband but wondered whether it was wise to abandon the capital, especially in these treacherous times. As soon as Max was feeling better, he should return to Mexico City. She prayed it would be soon.

Márquez continued to stalk about the mansion and its grounds, his swarthy face a riddle of scarlet veins, his eyes watery, his breath foul. Late one evening, Cajiga returned to the mansion, leaving his horse saddled and ready in the courtyard. He hurried inside and held a whispered conference with Márquez, who suddenly declared he could not abide the House of Borda another instant. He called for his own mount to be got ready and barged out into the night in company with Cajiga.

It was not until the two men had been gone an hour or more that Diego came to his senses. What an idiot he was. Of course he knew where they'd gone. He raced out to the stables, called for a groom to saddle his horse, and soon he was scrambling through the darkened streets of Cuernavaca toward the House of Forgetfulness. He would find Beatríz there. He knew it, and he was certain Márquez had known it as well. He dug his heels into his horse's flanks. The road twisted to the right, and he drew the reins against her neck, guiding her through the turn and shifting his weight to the side. That instant, a shadow raced across the adobe wall bordering the street just ahead. His horse shied, and he was very nearly thrown from his seat. He heard a clatter of approaching hoofbeats and thought he saw another horse and rider fling themselves past him, galloping full out in the opposite direction.

He steadied his horse, and soon they were again careening through the twisting streets and the moonlit night. As for Márquez, he must have been having Beatríz watched. That was why the man had stormed off on this night of all nights. He'd known exactly where she'd gone.

When Diego reached la Casa del Olvido, he found the place in chaos. The governess was slumped in a chair, sobbing into a handkerchief, her eyes red, her hair askew, her dress torn. Chairs had been knocked over. Clumps of earth littered the tiles. From the governess, who was still nearly hysterical, Diego was able to gather that the boy was gone, Beatríz was gone, and the two drunken men—they were gone, too. And another individual—a man disguised for some reason as a female nurse—that person was gone as well.

"They left together? All of them?" Diego tried not to raise his voice.

"No," the governess said. "Not Beatríz."

The girl had managed to break away from the two drunken men and had ridden off on her own. The woman bowed her head and again began to sob uncontrollably. An Indian maidservant stood behind her, reaching out at intervals to console her mistress by resting a hand on her shoulder.

Diego thanked them both and hurried back out to his horse. He swung himself into the saddle and set off. He was certain that it had been Beatríz whom he had passed on the way, the cloaked rider who had nearly unseated him. It turned out that he was right. At the House of Borda, he found her in the small house she shared with her mother and father. She was huddled by a fire, sipping a mug of tea. She had ridden straight back, in expectation of finding him here. She took a deep breath to calm herself and began to recount what had happened.

Earlier that evening, she said, a mysterious individual had arrived at la Casa del Olvido, someone dressed in a nurse's robes—

"Wearing spectacles?" said Diego. "Green-tinted spectacles?"

She nodded. The woman—for the intruder had at first seemed to be a woman—announced that she had come on the emperor's orders to take the boy away for medical treatment. The governess had become agitated, insisting that she had been told nothing of this. An argument broke out, and God knew how it would have ended had it not been interrupted by the arrival of two men, General Márquez and Captain Cajiga, both of them drunk. On unsteady feet, they swaggered into the house—and the rest was bedlam.

Márquez had called out for Beatríz but instead had fallen upon the bespectacled nurse, whose ample black hair—a wig, it turned out—came loose in his hands.

What in the name of God was this?

The general stared at the dislodged tresses. He looked back at the so-called nurse, not yet comprehending. It was Captain Cajiga who seemed to size matters up. The Spaniard drew his revolving pistol from his gun belt and aimed it at the intruder.

"El Gordo de las Gafas," he said.

It was Baldemar, of course. He tried to escape, but Cajiga shot him once, in the leg, and down he went. The gunshot seemed to restore Márquez to his senses. In short order, he and Cajiga bound Baldemar's thumbs behind his back with a length of twine. Without explanation, they rousted the little boy, Agustín, from his bed. They carried the wailing youngster out into the night as the governess screamed and threw herself at them, beating on them helplessly with her clenched fists. They came back for Baldemar and took him off, too.

Everyone was screaming or shouting, said Beatríz. "I was screaming, too."

She said the two men would have taken her as well, but she somehow managed to break free, scramble onto her horse, and gallop away. She needed help and could think only of Diego. And so she raced back to the House of Borda, passing him along the way. In her hurry, she had failed to recognize him when they passed in the street.

She looked up at him now. "Where have they taken Agustín? Where do you think?"

"The local garrison, probably," he said.

"Will he be all right?"

"The boy? Yes, I think so. They won't harm him." Márquez would have nothing to gain by hurting the child. But what was he up to? The minister of war holding a three-year-old boy hostage?

Diego thanked Beatríz for all she'd done. He meant to find Maximiliano. Instead, he ran straight into Doktor Basch, who was emerging from the emperor's bedchamber. The physician declared that His Majesty had already retired for the night, distinctly unwell.

"But it's urgent," said Diego. "I must speak to him."

"It's no use," said Basch. "The poor man is heavily sedated."

That was that, then. What could Diego do now, alone? There was nothing to be done till morning. In his bedroom, Diego kicked off his boots and fell onto the bed, where he lay sleepless, cursing both Baldemar and himself. Why hadn't the idiot sought his help? Either the question was unanswerable or else the answer was obvious. Maybe in the end Baldemar had doubted whether he could rely on his old friend and had decided to go ahead on his own.

The idiot.

Diego closed his eyes, trying to will sleep to come. But it was no use, and he passed the night awake, despising himself.

The emperor failed to appear at breakfast.

"Indisposed," said Salm-Salm. He lit a cigarette, releasing a plume of smoke that he inhaled through his nostrils. "Coffee?"

"No, thanks. Not now. I have much to do." Diego intended to retrieve his horse. Emboldened by the light of day, he planned to ride straight for the garrison and make an attempt, however futile, to rescue Baldemar. What else could he do?

"Going off to find your friend?" said Salm-Salm. He stifled a yawn. "El Gordo de las Gafas?"

"What do you know about it?"

"Oh, nothing. Or everything." The prince raised his left hand above his head and snapped his fingers. "Bring coffee," he called out. He lowered his voice. "We have to talk, you know."

A servant appeared and filled both their cups. The coffee steamed in the cool morning air. The two men got up and walked side by side along the mown grass toward the artificial lake. Salm-Salm said he had already spoken to Márquez.

"Where? When?"

"This morning. Early. At the garrison. He is holding your friend."

"I know."

"I have, of course, taken the matter up with His Majesty."

"What? Already? I thought he was unwell."

"He was. He is. But he is the emperor. He must be kept informed."

"And?"

Salm-Salm stopped, gestured with his cup of coffee. "Here is the bargain. The emperor proposes to pardon your friend. Yet again."

"Just like that?"

"Not exactly. He'll want something in return."

Diego knew the answer without asking the question.

"By which I mean written authorization from Ángela Peralta permitting Their Majesties to adopt the child, her son, as their heir. The arrangement would be greatly to her advantage. She will receive the title of princess, ample visitation rights, and a sum of money—a large sum. The emperor is prepared to be generous."

"The emperor is practically bankrupt, from what I'm told."

"Exaggeration. His wife possesses ample reserves."

"I see." Even if it were so, would the empress devote a share of her riches to securing an heir? And would she do it now as the French armed forces withdrew? But why even ask? Diego could not imagine Ángela accepting money in return for renouncing her son. He said, "I'm sorry, but I think I should talk to His Majesty directly."

"Of course. But first let me clarify one thing. You do know where the woman is?"

Diego realized this was the only card he had to play. "Yes. I know where she is."

They found Maximiliano in his study, perched upon a dark leather settee. He was sipping hot chocolate, nibbling Viennese biscuits, and perusing his volume devoted to the subject of courtly protocol. He wore a dressing gown over a white blouse and an ascot tie of royal blue. He seemed unexpectedly alert, even buoyant. The laudanum and a good night's rest had evidently eased his nervous state.

"Ah, Diego," he said. He smiled before seeming to remember himself. He adopted a neutral expression and spoke with a grave tone. "I take it Salm-Salm has outlined the lay of the land?"

"Yes, Your Majesty."

"And you know the woman's location?"

"Yes."

"But you won't tell us."

"No."

Maximiliano shook his head, disappointed. "I'm sorry it should be so. I considered us allies. I thought we had a relationship of trust."

Diego said nothing.

The emperor shrugged. "Well, be that as it may, can you help us? Can you do what we require?"

"I can try."

"That may not be good enough." He frowned. "I have the document here. Salm-Salm?"

The prince withdrew an envelope from the pocket of his frock coat. He handed it to the emperor, who in turn offered it to Diego.

"Quickly as you can. The woman's signature."

"And in return?"

"I shall issue a pardon." He sighed. "Again."

"What of General Márquez? He has agreed to this?"

"Let me deal with Márquez."

That was difficult to imagine, but Diego saw no other course. He accepted the envelope. He said he would return within a very few days. He nodded his head, turned, and left the chamber.

"Quickly," Salm-Salm called after him. "If you please."

Chapter 45

The journey to Taxco lasted the better part of two days. Ángela received him in the main salon of the small presbytery. She was still thin, pale, given to fits of coughing, and beset by an abiding melancholy. She read the emperor's letter and promptly began to weep. What woman would not shed tears if confronted by the sort of dilemma she faced—either the loss of a son or the death of a brother? It was an impossible choice.

"Even if I make a decision," she said through her tears, "how can I be sure the emperor will keep his word?"

"You can't," said Diego, who had puzzled through these conundrums during his ride from Cuernavaca. "He could be lying. Or maybe Márquez is lying. Maybe Márquez will do whatever he wants, no matter what the emperor says."

"The idiot," said Ángela. "Why did he get himself into this? And why all by himself?" Again her shoulders began to heave.

Diego stood in the study. Ángela slumped at a small writing table, with the letter from Maximiliano unfolded in front of her. She knew its contents. She would be given the title of princess. She would be permitted to come and go at Chapultepec Castle as she pleased and to visit her son frequently. She would be assured a large annuity for the rest of her days. These were irrelevant details, of course. The real choice before her was both simple and unbearably complex: her son or her brother.

Diego watched her, helpless, as she grappled with the question. There was little he or anyone could do. She had to find a way through this by herself. She clutched her forehead, weeping softly.

In the end, the cold truth became clear. She said there was only one choice she could make, only one decision she would ever be able to live with. She returned the emperor's letter to Diego. Still crying, she asked to be excused.

At daybreak, Diego left Taxco and rode back to Cuernavaca. He felt as if the future were already withdrawing into the past, as if he could do nothing but watch its progress, like a man on the banks of a river as the waters flow away.

The emperor was in a changeable state. One day, he was determined to remain in Mexico come what may. The next day, he saw abdication as the only possible course. Then he changed his mind again. This was true in Cuernavaca, and it remained true on his return to Mexico City.

Bazaine counselled abdication. He presented himself before Maximiliano late one morning, several days after His Majesty's return to the capital. The emperor recruited Diego to take notes, in spite of the rift that had opened between them. He told the French officer that he intended to stay in Mexico and fight on against the republicans. He planned to repair his relations with the country's conservatives. What was more, he meant to command the imperial army himself.

"You mean, on your own?" Bazaine raised his eyebrows.

"I will take the advice of General Márquez, of course. But, yes, I shall command."

The emperor fished through his pockets. He produced his cigarette case and pried it open. Diego noticed his fingers were shaking.

"The truth is," he said, now with a cigarette quivering between his lips, "I have no direct experience of hostilities. But I was for various years commander of the Austrian navy."

Bazaine nodded, as if this made sense. "I take it you expect this war to be waged at sea?"

"Of course not."

"I see," said Bazaine. He paused. "And what does Your Majesty propose to use in lieu of troops?"

Maximiliano smiled. "You may not have heard, but I have been promised an army of more than twenty-nine thousand men. Márquez himself told me so."

"Indeed?" said Bazaine. "Well, I wish you luck with them. I would counsel Your Majesty, however, that they will on occasion desire to be paid. It is a great defect of the modern soldier, I fear."

"Fear not," said Maximiliano. "My confederates even now are raising a war chest of eleven million pesos."

"According to Márquez?"

"According to Márquez—yes. In addition to the rank-and-file troops and a sound budget, I will have almost two thousand officers, very nearly six thousand horses, and eleven batteries of artillery."

Bazaine smiled. "I assume that General Márquez also outlined how he plans to perform this miracle?"

The emperor did not respond at once. He peered at his cigarette, at its slow spiral of smoke, as though there might be something significant to take note of there. "Bazaine," he said, "may I speak openly?"

"Yes."

"I mean, in confidence."

"I hope Your Majesty has always felt free to confide in me."

The emperor slowly inhaled his cigarette, still gazing at Bazaine. His hands were shaking, and his complexion had turned pale. He leaned forward.

"How did all this happen? This reversal of my fortunes? I have thought about it at great length, and I confess I do not understand. How could everything have gone so hopelessly, so unspeakably, wrong?"

Bazaine closed his eyes and then opened them. He inched forward in his chair. "Your Majesty," he said, "I hope you will forgive me for speaking plainly, but your situation is, in fact, remarkably simple. May I ask you a question?"

"Of course."

"Very well. Here in Mexico, where is the locus of power to be found?"

Maximiliano answered at once. "The throne. In a monarchy, power radiates from the throne."

"No," said Bazaine. "That is not power. That is symbolism, the illusion of power. True power resides with him who has the most guns."

The emperor smiled. "Let me remind you that I have been promised an army of more than twenty-nine thousand. And a war chest of eleven million pesos."

"So you have. And perhaps you are right. Perhaps you will be provided these great gifts—although I doubt that you will ever set eyes upon anything of the sort. I think these are fictions. Mexicans, in my experience, enjoy the sound of words more than their meaning." He examined the liver spots on the backs of his hands. He looked up. "But even if you did receive these thousands of troops, these millions of pesos, what of it? They would afford you nothing."

"What on earth do you mean?"

"I mean that, in Mexico, the locus of power does not reside within this country's borders."

"Where then? I suppose you are going to say Paris. Well, don't bother."

"No, not Paris, although briefly it might have been so. That, however, has changed—and this explains Your Majesty's reversal of fortune. The real seat of power lies to the north, in the United States of America.

Once that country threw its weight against us, the game was over. Even if Your Majesty were able to count upon one hundred thousand troops—real troops, French troops, not some Mexican make-believe—the result would be the same. Your throne is lost. The Americans will take it away." Bazaine shifted still closer to Maximiliano, until their faces were little more than a few centimetres apart. "Your Majesty, forgive me. But I urge you to consider your situation carefully. There is no shame in leaving Mexico. Go back to Europe, where you belong. Where we all belong."

CHAPTER 46

THE IMPERIAL AUTHORITIES HANGED Baldemar Peralta in Mexico City on May 15, 1866. The execution was carried out summarily, without trial. In his guise as the priest named Father Fischer, Salm-Salm was permitted to view the body prior to its interment, and he reported to Diego later that it was not an agreeable sight. The man had obviously been made to endure great suffering before being put to the noose. By the time they killed him, he was probably already dead.

Diego didn't wait to hear any more. His mind could not contain the idea of Baldemar's death. He stormed out into the marble hallways of Chapultepec Castle, Salm-Salm trailing behind him. He meant to confront the emperor. Where in God's name was he? He wasn't in his study or in his bedchambers. He had not gone out for a morning hack. Diego finally found him where he had least expected—in the newly inaugurated nursery. It was a makeshift facility assembled on short notice to accommodate the little Agustín, all of three years old. Ángela had signed away her rights to the child in the expectation of saving her brother. Now her brother was dead, and she had lost her son. Diego had known it might end this way. But what else could Ángela or anyone else have done?

He stormed into the nursery and would have barged straight past the boy but something stopped him. Agustín was Baldemar's nephew, after all, and here he was, a round-faced child with a strangely grave demeanour. He tottered about in a sailor suit, hands poised on his hips, inspecting things. Wobbling in the middle of the nursery, the boy peered up at Diego.

"You have just one hand," the child said. "Where is your other hand? Is it hiding?"

The emperor watched. He was seated in a large chair with scrolled legs and a high back. There were dark patches under his eyes. "Ah, Serrano . . ." he said.

Diego glanced at the child again and then returned his gaze to the emperor. "They hanged Baldemar," he said, spitting out the words. "Last night, they hanged him. Did you authorize that?"

"Why are you angry?" said the boy.

"I can explain," said Maximiliano. "I—"

"Please, Your Majesty." This was Salm-Salm. "Not here, I think. The child."

"Let us go to my study." Maximiliano rose and led the way.

"Where are you going?" said the boy. "May I come too?"

He lurched after them, but the governess intervened, scooping Agustín into her arms and carrying him toward a large window overlooking the interior courtyard.

In his study, the emperor collapsed at his desk, let out a long sigh, and began to stroke his beard. He called out for coffee, then turned toward Diego. "Carlota won't so much as look at the boy," he said. "Ill-gotten gains—that's what she says."

"Your Majesty," said Diego. He struggled to control his voice, but it was impossible. He realized he was stammering. His shoulders trembled. He felt as if his head would burst. "Baldemar Peralta is dead. You promised he would live. This was our agreement. You lied to me. You—"

"It's all connected," said Salm-Salm. He lit a cigarette and blew out the match.

"I'm sorry?"

"Everything. It's all connected. You'll see."

"What are you talking about?"

"It's true what you say. His Majesty lied to you about your friend. Isn't that right, Max?"

The emperor stared at Salm-Salm, apparently not expecting such candour. Then he sighed again and nodded. "Yes, it's true. I had no choice."

"No choice?"

"There was never any hope of gaining a pardon for this fellow, your friend," said Salm-Salm. "D'you think for a moment that Márquez would hear of it? Besides, he had the emperor's permission to do as he wished."

Diego realized his fist was clenched. He wanted to hit someone. "What are you talking about?"

"The decree. Max signed the decree. It permits summary execution of anyone suspected of armed activity on behalf of the liberals. You might consider the implications for yourself. Call it free advice." Salm-Salm sat down, slid back in his seat. "I would think about it, if I were you."

"Felix told me about your journey to Texas—you know, to seek out Juárez," said the emperor. He stirred sugar into his coffee. "It had nothing to do with making peace. You were lying to me."

It seemed to Diego that they had all been lying to each other right from the start. He turned to the emperor. "You signed Márquez's decree? Why, for God's sake?"

"Why? Because Márquez insisted. It was his price for turning over the boy."

He didn't need to say more. Diego understood perfectly well. The emperor was afraid of Márquez. It had been true ever since that evening in the billiards room when the general had humiliated him in public. Perhaps it had been true even before that night.

"A necessary evil," said Salm-Salm. "These lies. All this subterfuge.

They're all a necessary evil. In a better world, it might be different. But this is the world we have. This is the way we live."

"Not Baldemar Peralta. Not now."

Salm-Salm grimaced and inclined his head, acknowledging what was patently true. Not Baldemar Peralta. Not now.

Diego waited, his breath still short, his heart still thudding in his chest. Then he turned and left the room. He made straight for the nursery, not entirely sure what he meant to do. He could not leave the boy there. But already several guards had been posted at the entrance. They would not let him pass. He made for his own chambers and packed what little he would need. In the stables, a groom saddled his horse and led her out into the courtyard. Diego swung up into the saddle and rode toward the gate. Once there, he halted and raised his only hand, ready to slam it against the wooden portal, hard as he could. But something made him stop. It wasn't worth it. He took up the reins again, kicked his heels, and cantered away from Chapultepec Castle, back to Mexico City and his lodgings near La Ciudadela. He expected never to look upon Maximiliano again. That debt was paid.

CHAPTER 47

"THE EMPRESS CALLED FOR YOU." The new porter stood in the doorway of Diego's lodgings. "She was here not half an hour ago."

It was still early in the day, and Diego had just returned from a morning outing to visit Ángela. She had recently returned to the capital, for there was no reason to remain in hiding any longer. She had lost everything. What Diego hoped was that Maximiliano would quash the adoption and return the child to its mother, but he had seen no sign of that. Now the empress? Why would she seek him out here? He glowered at the porter. "You're sure?"

"She left a message." The porter put back his shoulders and cleared his throat. "The empress extends her respects and wishes to inform don Diego Serrano that she will return at half past ten o'clock of the morning."

The man proffered a note left by the empress, along with a small bundle of other letters that had arrived in that morning's post.

Diego took the mail and gave the man a coin. He entered his lodgings and closed the door, then wandered over to his writing table. His mail contained a letter, badly weathered and soiled, that bore the letterhead of a U.S. newspaper, the *Boston Journal*. Diego tore it open, and out spilled a newspaper clipping and a handwritten note. It was from J.S. Bartlett, the customs agent and journalist in Franklin, Texas. Both the clipping and the letter contained news that the president of the United States, Abraham Lincoln, had been shot on the night of April the fourteenth during a theatrical performance. He died the following day. Bartlett expressed the view that this event, though of historic and tragic significance in his country, was unlikely to have much effect on events in Mexico. As before, the French would leave. The death of a president could not change that. Diego knew little of American presidents. Mainly, he marvelled at the speed with which the letter had travelled.

Diego reached for the next letter. He broke the wax seal and pulled the envelope open. He slid the missive out and saw that it was from Beatríz—fully three pages, bursting with ideas, impressions, and opinions. She wrote at length about the monarch butterflies that fluttered among the trees in the garden each morning. In the fall, they arrived. And in the spring, they departed. Where did they go? How long and how arduous was their journey? They seemed such fragile creatures. And yet was this not the way of life—that the most fragile among us were the ones most obliged to be strong? Halfway through reading the letter, Diego rose from his seat and wandered over to the casement window. He pushed the jalousies outward, letting the afternoon light flood the room.

He settled himself in his customary place of contemplation, the window's deep sill, a vantage point that provided a clear view of the street. He returned his attention to Beatríz's letter. She wrote that she had heard of Baldemar's death, and she wished to console her friend for his loss. She knew he must be grieving deeply and wanted him to know she would do whatever was in her power to ease his suffering. But she worried that there was little she could do. Sad to say, some sorrows had to be faced alone. Still, she longed to offer him what little comfort she could. At the same time, she wondered what had become of little Agustín— to whom she had become greatly attached—and urged Diego to send her news.

Finally, she declared that she had lately taken up the card game known as conquian and suggested he consider doing the same. She found it an excellent means of escape from worry and trouble. Maybe, one day, the two of them would play.

Diego read these lines and then reshuffled the leaves in order to read them again. Just then, he heard a commotion in the street—the empress's return. He didn't wait for her carriage to appear. Instead, he slid the letter into the side pocket of his jacket. He climbed to his feet, fetched his hat, and made his way outdoors, where sundry pedestrians were picking their way through the ruts and puddles that littered the avenue.

The empress's carriage—an elegant black coach-and-four bearing the imperial crest on its sides—swayed on the cobbles, and a quartet of horses pawed and shifted in their traces. One of the liveried coachmen sprang down to open the carriage door. The empress emerged, blinking in the morning sunshine, like a bejewelled butterfly, wings outspread. A small guard of hussars reined their horses into formation around the carriage.

One might have thought that Carlota's arrival would arouse some flurry of excitement on the street. But no one other than Diego seemed to take much interest in the spectacle at all.

"You there," she called out. She poked at the air with her parasol. "That's right. You."

A youngish man in a small bowler hat halted, turned, and looked at the empress with an almost bemused expression.

"Yes. You." Carlota stepped down onto the broken and uneven cobbles and advanced a pace or two. "Do you not recognize your monarch? Do you not know who I am?"

The man said nothing.

"Have you no tongue? Are you mute? Do you not understand plain Spanish when it is spoken to you? Are you human or beast? Speak, man. Answer me."

The man nodded. "Spanish—yes. I speak Spanish."

"Then reply to a question when it is put to you. Do you, or do you not, know who I am?"

"You are Mamá Carlota . . ." He hesitated. This disparaging term was in common usage now. "I mean, the Empress Carlota."

"So you do know." Carlota raised her parasol against the sun's rays and snapped it open. She set it upon her shoulder and stepped toward the man. "And are the gentlemen of this country in the habit of wearing their hats in the presence of empresses?"

The man reached up and briefly tipped his hat in Carlota's direction. "Begging your pardon," he said. He turned and sauntered away, leaving the empress speechless in his wake.

Diego watched him go. If the empress was offended, he didn't much care. Since Baldemar's death, it was as if the scales had fallen from his eyes. These Europeans—all of them—were an affront to Mexico. It didn't matter which side they took, or professed to take, whether conservative or liberal. They had no place here. Mexico must find its own way. Now when he looked in a mirror—saw the darkness of his skin—he was unashamed. He was proud. He was Mexican, no less than Benito Juárez or Beatríz Sedano or Baldemar Peralta.

Still, here was the empress, and he wondered what she could possibly want with him, after all that had happened. He stepped out of the shadows and into the morning light.

CHAPTER 48

"DAMNED IMPERTINENCE." The empress glared out the carriage window. "Damned bloody impertinence."

She and Diego were seated side by side, riding in the passenger compartment of her conveyance as it lurched along the rain-gouged street and the heaving cobbles. He said nothing. He simply waited while the woman recovered her composure. First she coughed into a silk handkerchief. Then she took several deep breaths. Finally, she said she was aghast at this news concerning the withdrawal of Napoleon's troops. One might have expected it, a bare-faced betrayal, but that was little preparation for the shock when it came.

Diego nodded but did not speak. It had been several weeks since the withdrawal had begun, and still it seemed Chapultepec Castle was in a turmoil. Some courtiers had already fled, others were on the brink of fleeing, while still others were biding their time, waiting to see which way their fortunes tended.

"Damn that man," she said. She meant Napoleon. "I knew he could not be trusted. I said as much to Max at the outset. My father did as well. But there was no choice. What else could we do? Nothing."

It wasn't true. There was much they could have done. They could have remained on the Dalmatian shores and never set foot anywhere in Mexico. The Europeans were not wanted here. But what was the point in belabouring this any longer? Surely their future was manifest now. They must leave. Diego listened as the empress railed on about the deceitfulness of men. The chaotic scenery of Mexico City rattled past them, the bright, incongruous showers of bougainvillea, the pools of fetid water, the carriages and donkey carts, the earnest vendors, the mournful *pordioseros,* as the beggars were called on account of their guttural chant. *Por Dios. Por Dios, señor . . .*

The imperial carriage looped back and forth through the streets, up one avenue, down another. Evidently, the empress had no particular destination in mind. She glared out the window for a time, then turned and looked at him.

"Max means to abdicate," she said.

This caught Diego by surprise. "I thought Márquez was raising an army. Twenty-nine thousand men, I think."

"Márquez is a liar and a murderer." She shook her head. "He won't stand by us, not in the end. We need Napoleon on our side. I am determined to achieve it."

Diego recalled a previous conversation with Carlota in which she had assessed her situation and that of her husband in the most realistic of terms. They would have to leave Mexico. Their reign was at an end. Somehow, her mind had changed.

"I shall go to Paris. I shall speak to Napoleon. Reason *shall* prevail. But, meanwhile, Max must remain here to keep our throne secure."

In a low voice, quivering with conviction, she told Diego that she could not bear the prospect of abdication. She would rather die. Yes, die. Diego listened to her words but also to the tremor in her voice. It was impossible to doubt what she said, even though he could not truly understand it. Her conviction was something outside his own experience, a need he could not fathom. A throne was a necessity to her, it seemed, like water or air to him. At the same time, he sensed a manic quality in her voice, and he wondered—not for the first time—if she were entirely sane. He had heard her outbursts before and had thought them evidence of a high-spirited personality, nothing more. Now this intensity of hers seemed less than stable, almost like madness.

She said, "You must help me."

"How?"

"By talking to Max. He'll listen to you."

"I don't think he will."

"Nonsense. He respects you. He finds you *sagacious*. He thinks you are possessed of some native Mexican wisdom. You were his first true Mexican friend, you know. He imagines the soil speaks through you." She gave a short, bitter laugh. "It might be madness, but he *will* listen to you."

Diego turned and stared out the window. "I owe him nothing."

"Perhaps not. But—"

"For a time, I did," he said. He was thinking of Baldemar, but that was done now. Baldemar was in his grave, and the debt was void. "For a time, I thought I owed your husband everything. I don't think so anymore. Besides, I am sure His Majesty can make up his own mind. I—"

"His Majesty," she broke in, "can do no such thing. I must face the truth. His Majesty is a weak and shallow man. He means well but only because he believes that by meaning well he will make others like him better. Beyond this, he has no fixed principles. He will always do as others wish."

Her words were harsh, but Diego appreciated their truth. It might be that the man possessed other, more admirable qualities—he *did* possess them and in abundance—but they did not matter now.

The empress continued. "I am convinced that I can have this decision revoked, this withdrawal of France's troops. It will not be easy, but I am sure that Napoleon will relent once the case is put to him directly. But first I must persuade Max to remain behind as emperor. For that, I require your help. I—"

"What about Agustín?"

"Agustín?"

"Ángela's son."

The empress's shoulders slumped, and she put up her hands in a gesture of helplessness. She shook her head. "I have tried. But Max is adamant on this question." She sighed. "But, very well, I shall try to persuade him. I *will* persuade him." She turned back to Diego, fixed her attention squarely upon him, summoning every last gram of her authority. "This, then, will be our bargain. I shall see to the child. You must see to Max. If you tell him to stay, it will be as if all Mexico had told him to do so. You have my word that he will receive you. He will listen to you. I implore you to help. I . . ."

Carlota's voice trailed off, and what happened next was almost beyond Diego's comprehension. The empress fumbled with the ties on the curtains, and the velvet fabric fell shut. A grey darkness filled the carriage. The empress pressed close against him. The scent of her cologne rose, drifted on the currents of her body's heat, swelled around him. Her décolletage suddenly released, and her bosom spilled against his chest. Her arms ventured around him, grasping, reaching. Her lips sought his. One of her hands probed below his waist, searched for him there.

For a moment, he felt himself surrendering to this bewildering seduction. He was in a dream, his blood suddenly racing despite himself. And then the sensation stopped. He owed this woman nothing, and he would owe her nothing. He pushed her away, reached up and pounded with his fist on the ceiling of the carriage. "*¡Pare, chofer! ¡Pare!*"

Nothing happened, and so he pounded on the ceiling again.

The coach tottered to a halt. Diego turned back to the empress, who was huddled in a corner of the carriage, her face barely discernible in the half-darkness.

"Your Majesty . . ." he began. But he could think of nothing further to say, and so he said nothing. He pushed open the carriage door and clambered out into the blinding midday light.

He found himself on the cobbles of some unknown street in some unfamiliar section of the city, and he watched as the black carriage creaked into motion and rattled away, kicking up waves of coppery dust. The conveyance was flanked by the half-dozen hussars on their tall European mounts, three to each side. They cantered away in unison, and he watched them go. A woman's hand emerged from the window of the carriage grasping a hat that then sailed through the vivid morning light. The hat spun on the currents of the air and gradually descended until it came to a rest beside a mound of litter. Diego waited until the carriage was gone and the dust had cleared, and then he walked over to his hat. He reached down and picked it up, slapped it against his pant leg, and set it on his head.

He realized now that he would indeed seek out the emperor a last time. If he had influence, as Carlota said, then he would use it—but not as she had proposed. He turned the opposite way the carriage had taken and began to walk in what he thought was the direction of his home.

Chapter 49

Diego approached the emperor, who was observing the view from Chapultepec Castle, as if rehearsing the role of a general in command of his troops. He had a leather case looped to his waist belt to contain a spyglass. Just now, however, he had the instrument out and was peering through it. He did not have the appearance of a man who was about to abandon the country and decamp for Europe.

That was why Diego had come, to use whatever influence he still possessed to persuade the emperor to leave for his own good and for Mexico's. Maximiliano was standing on the same balcony from which in former times he had liked to survey the construction of el Paseo de la Emperatriz, the great boulevard that would connect the castle to Mexico City. The work was still unfinished, and God knew whether it would ever be resumed. Maximiliano lowered his telescope and gazed unaided to the south, where the broad cobbled terrace was crammed with soldiers and tents. The castle's grounds had been converted into a garrison.

"Ah, Serrano," he said. He holstered the spyglass and greeted his guest in the Mexican fashion, with an *abrazo*—a cold and stiff embrace in this case.

A week had passed since Diego's encounter with the empress. He wasted little time on pleasantries. He told Maximiliano that it was not too late for him to abandon Mexico. The liberals under Juárez were certain to triumph. If His Majesty accepted his fate, the war would end sooner, with fewer lives lost and much suffering averted. Besides, if he remained and were to be taken prisoner, he would certainly be put to death.

"On what grounds?"

Diego squinted in the highland sun. It shocked him that the man, even now, so misunderstood the nature of war, the darkness of it. He tried to explain. In the eyes of liberals, the emperor's chief crime—apart from simply having come to this country—was the decree authorizing the summary dispatch of those who fought on the republican side. Already hundreds of men, perhaps thousands, had been put to death on the authority of this law. They included Baldemar Peralta. Among liberals, the edict was known as the Black Decree. It would not be forgiven, and Maximiliano would be held responsible.

"But that was all Márquez's doing. He drafted the thing. It was his idea. I had nothing to do with it."

"Your Majesty signed the document," said Diego. "Or have I misunderstood?"

The emperor rested both elbows on the chest-high stone balustrade. "It's all moot anyway, as I will not be taken prisoner. We shall fight, and we shall win. Look." He waved toward the rows of tents assembled on the terrace below, the bustle of men and horses. "My army grows by the day."

Diego shook his head. It was well known that three liberal armies were already advancing on the capital. The French had withdrawn, and the Americans were rearming Mexico's liberals—clandestinely, but with a real effect. If the emperor meant to fight, it would be better to leave the capital now, while there was still time. The city was badly situated and impossible to defend. He said so.

"Perhaps," said the emperor. "But I await the return of the French troops to our side. Most of them are still in Mexico, you know. They're camped out in Veracruz. Before long, their orders will change. The empress has already departed for France. She will explain the truth, and Napoleon will reverse himself. We have only to hold on till then."

"She has already left?"

"Yes. Three days ago. With luck, she has already put Veracruz in her wake."

"And the boy? Agustín? Surely now you will give him back to his mother?"

"Out of the question. The papers have all been signed. He shall be emperor one day. I've been more than fair. The woman is set for life."

Diego did not give up. Ángela would not accept as much as a claco in compensation, he said. She must have her child. But the emperor refused to listen. He turned to observe the activity below. It seemed something was bothering him and, after a while, he spoke.

"Old friend . . ." He removed his hat and reached up with his free hand to worry at his brow. "What you just said about the question of execution . . ."

"Yes?"

"Surely Juárez would never approve such a thing. He and I are of a single mind. We hold the same beliefs. It is absurd that we are even at war. He would never countenance my death."

Diego closed his eyes for several moments and then opened them again. He said, "Yes, Your Majesty. He would."

"He might send me back to Europe at worst."

Diego's throat felt dry. He swallowed with difficulty and debated what to say. "Your Majesty," he said, "please consider your situation carefully. I have said all that I can." He turned and took his leave of the emperor of Mexico.

The main force of the imperial army departed Mexico City several days later, on a cool February morning, and Diego watched the retreat. He had found room on the terrace of the Monte de Piedad, which stood across the vast plaza from the Imperial Palace. The emperor rode at the column's head alongside Márquez. The procession included a large wooden cart pulled by a single draft horse, and Diego thought he could identify its contents—large folds of taffeta, much roping, and a boxy wicker basket large enough to contain two or three men. It was the emperor's balloon.

Meanwhile, the imperial army stretched out behind its leaders, consisting of some nine thousand men, mainly infantry, but with a complement of cavalry and artillery. This small, ill-equipped corps fell far short of the force Márquez had promised to raise, and Diego wondered how long it could survive. It was known that the emperor's army was bound for Querétaro, to the north, where they would dig in and make a stand for as long as they could, hoping the French would rejoin them in time, once Napoleon had changed his mind.

The procession also included members of the emperor's private entourage. Diego could make out his valet and his chef, both mounted upon stout, shaggy ponies. Bombelles and a guard of hussars flanked their commander. Salm-Salm, easily identifiable by his wide-brimmed scarlet hat, rode not far behind. The loyal Doktor Basch slouched along atop a slowpoke bay horse with a sway back. Nearly all of the other European courtiers had remained behind, to potter about the hallways and the empty salons of Chapultepec Castle, though they too were on the brink of flight. Almost all the furniture and luxuries had been sold to raise money for the imperial army. The rest had been looted by their Mexican servants.

Diego lit a cigarette with his one good hand, rested his weight against the low wall that bordered the *azotea*, and watched the emperor and his army withdraw from Mexico City.

In a few minutes, the imperial forces had all but vanished from sight, receding toward the city's northern gates. A smattering of onlookers descended from the rooftops surrounding the Zócalo, and Diego joined them. The streets below soon bustled once again with beggars and pariah dogs, itinerant vendors, and sturdy Mexican coaches. It was as if the emperor and his army had never passed this way, as if these past few years had never happened, as if Maximiliano had never reigned at all.

CHAPTER 50

LIFE IS RARELY AS simple as anyone expects, and Diego's rupture with Maximiliano was no different. He had thought he would be glad to be quit of the man. He had thought it would be a relief to take one side and renounce the other, to throw in his lot with the forces that backed Juárez and furthered the cause of progress and reform. And he was right. It was a relief.

But it was also more complicated than that. He found that he missed Maximiliano—not the monarch or the sovereign or the politician, but the man himself. He missed their early mornings at Chapultepec, when it almost seemed they ruled the world, just two men in a candle-lit study considering petitions and proposals, offers and counter-offers that came from every part of Mexico and all corners of the globe. During those sessions, Maximiliano was for the most part the epitome of sobriety, and yet he would sometimes lower his guard and perform hilarious imitations of Carlota's father, the King of Belgium, or of his own older brother, the despised Franz Josef, or even of Labastida, the archbishop.

Diego missed their morning rides together out to the canals of Xochimilco, their breakfasts alone on a small private patio at Chapultepec, their carriage journeys into the city. He recalled that night in Coyoacán when Maximiliano had gone among the common folk and, like them, had raced back and forth amid the whoosh and collision of rockets. He remembered the sensations that had almost overwhelmed him that first time they'd met, on that long-ago afternoon by the porte cochère at the Imperial Palace. From the outset, Maximiliano had treated him not as an equal—far from that—but as a respected confederate, no less deserving of respect than any other man. It was impossible for him to think of Maximiliano without fondness, despite all that had occurred.

Diego could readily imagine the horrors that were unfolding now. The siege of Querétaro had begun soon after the emperor's arrival there. Almost at once, reports began to trickle back to the capital concerning the worsening conditions in that highland city. After decades of almost ceaseless war, Mexicans knew perfectly well what a siege entailed. It would not be long before the imperial army would run out of conventional sustenance, and so the long, dismal slide would begin. At first, men would slaughter their horses and sup upon their bones. When the horses were nearly gone, it would be time to butcher the mules. Still later, dogs would be put to the knife. Standards of hygiene would decline, slowly at first and then disastrously. The liberal armies that now surrounded the city would stop up the aqueducts with corpses. Maladies would flourish. Inevitably, the townspeople would suffer alongside the emperor's army. Children would lose their fingernails to malnutrition, their skin would peel away in large flakes, their hair would turn orange. Then they would go blind.

But Diego knew the war was being waged not by siege alone. The republican side had mounted artillery batteries on the city's outskirts and pounded the centre of Querétaro daily, from first light till dark. Regular skirmishes broke out between the two sides, with no decisive result. This standoff had dragged on for days at first and now for weeks. Diego knew the republicans could have unleashed an all-out assault upon the city, but that would be a perilous enterprise, costly in lives—and, worse, it might fail. By contrast, a siege was all but assured of eventual success, but it was a cruel and demonic enterprise, exacting a terrible price not only from the enemy but also from the innocent.

Diego knew of a third option. The republicans could decapitate the enemy by seizing its leaders, by taking Maximiliano and General Márquez prisoner or else by killing them in battle. But it seemed they were unsure of the exact whereabouts of Maximiliano or Márquez, or their officers. Lacking that intelligence, the republicans pressed on with their siege. Either the enemy would surrender or he would starve.

Diego could imagine the conditions by now prevailing in Querétaro—the disease, the hunger, the stench. Matters would only grow worse. Tens of thousands more would have to die before this war would end. It was Beatríz who finally persuaded him to act. On a morning early in May, she appeared at his lodgings near La Ciudadela. She had journeyed from Cuernavaca in order to tell him what he already knew but had been trying not to face. He did not want to be the one to take this measure, but he was left with no choice.

"Go to Querétaro," she said. "Find Maximiliano. He will listen to you."

Neither of them referred to the man as the emperor or His Majesty any longer. He was simply Maximiliano.

"I don't know if he will," said Diego. "I don't know if he'll listen to anyone."

"He'll listen to you. This time he'll have to. You'll make him."

"He didn't listen to me before he left Mexico City."

"His circumstances have changed," she said. "Everything has changed."

It was true. Everything had changed. But still Diego resisted. "He knows they'll kill him if he surrenders."

"They'll kill him if he doesn't—and take thousands more with him."

She was right, of course. He took a deep breath and made it clear he submitted. Yes.

"When will you leave?" she asked him.

"Today."

She seemed surprised, even though she must have known. "When will I see you?"

He produced a thin smile. "When this is over."

He left that evening. He pulled a woollen serape over his cotton jacket and set his wide-brimmed hat low over his forehead. An unseasonable chill clung to the highland air. He departed Mexico City by the northern gates.

The darkness stretched ahead. As he rode, he thought about Baldemar, but not only about Baldemar. He thought about Ángela, about Beatríz, about Benito Juárez. He wondered how he had ever imagined that Mexico's president was somehow responsible for what had gone wrong in the country. The opposite was true. Unlike so many others, Juárez had kept faith with his compatriots, firm in his belief that somehow Mexicans would prevail, the invaders would withdraw, and Mexican sovereignty would be preserved.

He urged his horse into an easy gallop, and they seemed to float through the highland darkness. By Diego's reckoning, they were about halfway between the capital and Querétaro, near the town of Tlaxcoapan, and had been travelling roughly ten hours straight. He decided he would ease his pace before long. He would slow to a jog or even a walk in order to let his horse recover her wind and her legs. But not just yet. He wanted to make as much progress as he could in the coolness of the night, and so he pressed on. It was then that his horse came down badly on something in the track—a rock or a hardened rut. Her stride broke, her hindquarters swung around, and she nearly went down. In a matter of seconds, she pranced in circles on three legs. A pale light crept across the broad grasslands to the east.

Diego flung himself from the saddle and dropped to the ground. Within moments, he saw what had happened. She'd injured her near hind leg, and his heart sank at the sight of it. Just beneath the fetlock, the pastern bulged like the sprung stave of a barrel. Her nostrils flared, her lips curled back, her eyes rolled up into her head. She was frantic with pain. He gripped the reins close to the bit and tried to calm her. "*Tran-*

quila, chica. Cálmate, mi amor." He knew it was bad, but he didn't want to face it.

"Shoot the bitch."

Diego swung around at the sound of a man's voice, and he saw a dark shape sauntering up out of the morning gloom. Despite the chill, the man was shirtless, and he carried a long carbine slung over his shoulder by a length of twine.

"One bullet just below the ear. There's nothing else you can do. That's a bowed tendon she's got. No cure for that. She's useless now. Got to shoot her."

"*Shoot* her?" Diego struggled to hold his horse still. The man was crazy. "No, no. She'll be all right. A little rest. She—"

"Sorry," said the man. "That horse doesn't want a little rest. It wants a long rest. That's a bowed tendon there."

By now, several other men had slouched up through the faint light of morning, past the rows of cactus that lined the dirt track running north to Querétaro. All were shirtless, and all carried rifles. Diego realized soon enough who they were—deserters from the army of Maximiliano. They'd thrown away their tunics, of course. That way, they'd be less likely to be recognized as soldiers. But they'd kept their weapons.

"Here," said one. He pulled a large Colt from the belt of his trousers. "Use this."

"We'll lie her down for you," said another of the men. "Easier that way."

As if they had practised this manoeuvre countless times before, the men gathered around the horse. One reached beneath her belly and yanked her offside foreleg away. Just like that, she went down, and they piled on top of her. She sprawled on the dirt, head flat against the earth, chest heaving, and it was almost as though she knew what was coming—knew and accepted it.

"Go ahead," said one of the men. "Do it. It's the kindest thing you could do. Poor thing's in misery."

Diego knew it was true. Sometimes the only kindness left is to kill those you love. He took the Colt revolver that had been offered him and hunched down beside her. "*Lo siento,*" he whispered. "*Lo siento, mi amor.*" He pressed the barrel against the brown fur beneath her left ear. He looked away, closed his eyes, and squeezed the trigger. The recoil drove the butt of the gun back into his chest. Her head jerked to the side, one leg kicked out involuntarily, and then his horse was still.

"Better kill her again," someone said. "Just to be sure."

He did that too. His hand was shaking, and he couldn't see a goddamned thing, but he managed to press the barrel of the pistol against her skull once more. He pulled the trigger again.

"There," said the owner of the pistol. "That's done." He took back his weapon, wiped it on his pants. "Not meaning to be a bother, señor, but that's two bullets I'm out."

Diego paid the man for the bullets. He said he wouldn't be needing the bridle or the saddle anymore. The men could help themselves to those, if they were of a mind to do so. He would be on his way. Quickly as he could, he shouldered his haversack and set out on foot for Querétaro.

CHAPTER 51

DIEGO WALKED ALL THAT day and most of the following night. As he proceeded northward, he encountered an almost constant stream of shirtless men trudging back south. It seemed the imperial army was collapsing. He counted hundreds of men. They paid him little mind, not much concerned with a one-armed, blood-encrusted fool who was going the wrong way on a bad road. Occasionally, one or another of the retreating men eyed him warily, shrugged, then returned to the more important business of leaving the war far behind.

Diego adjusted the weight of his haversack against his shoulders. In his mind, he heard that desperate keening, a stricken horse hobbling on three legs in the first light of dawn. His eyes smarted, and he clenched his jaw. He continued on his way toward Querétaro.

He must have trekked more than twenty hours straight when he first heard the reports of cannon fire—the liberal forces bombarding the city. Presently, he stumbled upon a large military encampment sprawling across several fields of blond grass. No one paid him any mind. Why would they? A man without a rifle shuffling along the perimeter of the camp? He approached a trio of half-dressed soldiers who were bathing by a large wooden barrel. They told him this encampment was the army of General Mariano Escobedo. Diego thanked them and soon found his way to the general's tent, where a young officer was making notes of some kind at a refectory table set out on the patchy grass. Diego introduced himself and declared he was looking for His Excellency Benito Juárez.

"You won't find him here," said the man, who had a rectangular face with a dark complexion beneath a wedge of dense black hair.

It turned out the president of the Republic had established his provisional capital in San Luis Potosí, a day's journey on horseback to the north.

"Maybe you'll find him there," said the orderly. "If you do, please convey my regards—and tell him I want to be paid."

Diego said he would try his best. He thanked the orderly and reshouldered his haversack. He departed the republican encampment and resumed his northward trek. Every few minutes, another blast shook the ground beneath his feet, followed by a whistling in the air and, later, a deep crash and the clatter of cracked stones and splitting wood. He barely reacted. Instead, he kept putting one foot in front of the other. He continued on his way, tracing a rutted track lined by thorn scrub and rows of organ pipe cactus on a trail that led north.

The temporary office of the president of Mexico consisted of a dark room, a row of wooden jalousies—almost completely shut—a large wooden desk, some cabinets, a few chairs, and a powdering of recent dust. Benito Juárez was at his desk. He adjusted the lapels of his jacket, and then reached with both hands to align the edges of a sheaf of papers. A faint mustiness clung to the air.

"No," he said.

"No?" Diego had expected exactly this response, but even so it was dismaying to hear. He had asked the president if he would consider issuing a pardon for Maximiliano.

"Not even if he surrenders?"

The president shook his head. "Not even if he surrenders."

"And abdicates?"

"No."

"And rescinds the Black Decree?"

"No. There are no circumstances in which I would consider such a step. None. The courts will decide the fate of your Austrian, assuming he is not killed in battle first."

"And if the courts sentence him to death?"

"Then he will die. I won't intervene."

Juárez folded his arms on his desk. He was little changed from the last time Diego had seen him—aloof and stern to the point of severity, at least on the surface. Occasionally, he fidgeted with his hands, the only visible sign that he was not entirely sanguine, not entirely in control.

"The Republic," he said, "is not something to be taken for the asking."

He explained that he was not thinking only of the Austrian. More than four decades had passed by since independence—a wasted time, a time of puffed-up grandees who strutted across the national stage, men with private armies, vainglorious ideas, and inflated titles, men for whom Mexico was merely a sort of offering, something to be seduced, enjoyed, and tossed aside.

"When these men look upon Mexico, what they see is not a nation of citizens but an instrument for expressing their own vanity, a dark sky in which to cast a brief star. But the star burns out, and the darkness remains."

Diego nodded. The wording was melodramatic, possibly rehearsed, but this was Mexico's reality. He thought of Iturbide, Santa Anna, and the other men who had held power over the land—men who believed they were gods. Was Maximiliano so different? He should never have come, but, having come, he should have abdicated and gone—long ago. Yet here he remained, and for what? To salvage his honour? To burnish a legend? Meanwhile, the war ground on, men died, and Mexico suffered. It was a harsh line that Juárez was taking, but it was just. Diego reached for his hat and rose from his chair.

"Wait," said Juárez. "Sit. Stay." He edged forward, and his low tone took on an unexpected warmth. "You did me a kindness once. Don't think I have forgotten."

Diego resumed his seat and set down his hat. "It was what anyone would do."

"I disagree. It was a deeply personal act. That picture made all the difference, you know. It gave me strength I did not realize I had."

Diego's heart thudded in his chest, but he merely inclined his head. "*Mi presidente.*"

"And now," said Juárez, "I have need of your services again. I take it you mean to seek out the Austrian—despite what I have said."

"Yes."

"You must be very careful, for it will be dangerous." He paused. "Besides, there is something I wish you to do."

"I know."

"When we last met, in El Paso del Norte, I made a similar request—and you said no."

"That is right," said Diego. "But circumstances have changed."

"So they have." Juárez hesitated. "I know about your friend—Baldemar Peralta. You are speaking of vengeance, then?"

"No."

"Good. Vengeance is a treacherous thing. But you will help us?"

Diego nodded. He had suspected all along that the conversation would come to this, but he had not known what he would say, or not until this moment. He remembered the keening he had heard on the road south of Querétaro, after his horse came down badly. There was just one thing he could have done, and so he had done it. A final cruelty, a final kindness—they amounted to the same thing. He understood it now.

"Fine," said Juárez. "I will prepare a *laissez-passer*. It will take you part of the way. For the rest, you are on your own."

The outskirts of Querétaro were clotted by large encampments of republican troops, dimly illuminated by scattered bonfires. It was night, and a half moon glowered through a screen of broken clouds. At first, no one paid Diego any mind. But eventually a pair of sentries emerged from a thicket of mesquite scrub and ordered him to identify himself.

From the folds of his serape, Diego withdrew the letter drafted and signed by Benito Juárez. It offered him safe passage through republican lines at the city of Querétaro.

The taller sentry took the letter, broke the seal, and unfolded the leaf of paper. He held it before him in the negligible light. He frowned at the letter. "What is this?"

"I have just come from San Luis Potosí, where I spoke to President Benito Juárez."

"Of course," said the young man. "We ourselves have just been in Rome, where we got pissed with the pope. Come with me."

The sentry pocketed the letter and led Diego away to be interrogated by his superiors. Security measures in the camp had evidently redoubled since he had last travelled this way. Now one interrogation followed another, and another followed that. The rounds of questioning resumed early the following morning, each session more energetic than the one that preceded it.

In the end, Diego was presented to General Mariano Escobedo, who apologized for the discomfort his guest had suffered owing to an excess of zeal on the part of his interrogators. In war, mistakes are made.

By this time, Diego was missing several teeth and could see only with great difficulty. His back throbbed with pain, and he heard a ringing in his ears.

Escobedo tapped the letter of safe passage. It was spread out before him on a folding table that stood beneath a canvas awning. "Your purpose in Querétaro, I take it, is to visit the Austrian?"

"That is so."

"Why?"

"To persuade him to surrender."

"You think he will agree?"

"No."

Escobedo reached up with both hands and smoothed his moustache. He smiled and tilted his head. "You seem to be caught in a contradiction."

"I know." Diego explained what he meant to do.

Escobedo lit a cigar, turning it around several times in the match's flame until it was burning evenly. "That would be very useful." He blew out a plume of smoke. "Oh, and you may wish to carry some dried beef with you. It could save your life." He hesitated. "Your arm—I take it that's an old injury?"

"Very old. Courtesy of General Márquez."

"He escaped, you know. He and a dozen men, give or take. They ran straight through our lines two nights ago. Made off to the south. We managed to bring down one or two, but the rest got away. They won't be back."

"No." Diego grimaced. This probably explained the tightened security in the republican encampment.

Escobedo tilted his head. "I'll send a physician around," he said.

With difficulty, Diego climbed to his feet and took his leave. Later, a doctor examined his injuries and did what little he could to blunt their impact. Before long, an orderly brought a quantity of dried beef wrapped in folds of oiled paper. Diego tucked the packet beneath the stump of his left arm. It was mid-morning, and a pair of sentries accompanied him on foot to the edge of the encampment and then followed him partway down an earthen slope scribbled with tree roots. Upon reaching some invisible line—probably the perceived limit of enemy rifle fire—they halted and let him continue alone.

He picked his way ahead, limping and sore. He was glad to be making this leg of the journey by day rather than by night, for this was a terrible place, reeking of evil. He counted fourteen corpses, all dangling from the branches of trees. He supposed that these were the bodies of men who had tried to escape from the city. They must have been captured by the imperial forces, and their bodies were being displayed as an example and a warning to others, a desperate attempt to hold a disintegrating army together. The corpses were bloated, and carrion birds had started on their flesh. Diego kept his gaze low. He increased his pace.

Moments later, a great shadow darted across his tracks—something passing overhead—and instinctively he spun around to look over his shoulder, then peered up at the sky. What in God's name was that? At first, the object seemed like nothing he had ever seen. But then the shape cohered into a recognizable image. It was the emperor's balloon. The contraption sailed overhead, carried on a steady breeze, quickly ascending. The wicker basket clung to the taffeta globe by a netting of ropes, and the entire contrivance soared away to the south at remarkable speed. The sight was both exhilarating and unnerving. It actually flew. Diego felt dizzy. He kept watching the spectacle until the balloon disappeared into the cloud-flocked sky.

He wondered whether anyone had been riding in the basket that dangled beneath the device. From his vantage point, it had been impossible to tell. Had Maximiliano escaped into the sky? He couldn't even begin to guess. Still shaky on his feet, his back sore, his eyesight diminished, he resumed his trek into Querétaro. Before long, he was challenged by several imperial sentries—haggard, hollow-looking men who stepped out from behind a crumbling adobe wall, aiming their carbines directly at him. Who knew if they possessed bullets? Diego held up the dried beef, and their hunger got the better of them. Gaunt as skeletons, they yanked the stuff from him and fell upon it, moaning like animals. Too busy eating to care about much else, they waved him through. He could pass into the city if he had a mind to, if he were as crazy as that. They obviously did not suspect him of posing any danger. A lone man on foot, battered, bruised, and equipped with only one arm? What danger was that?

At once, he set about trying to locate Maximiliano.

CHAPTER 52

"AH, SERRANO . . ." The Austrian rousted himself from his travel cot and struggled to his feet. "What a surprise. How did you find your way here?"

Diego recounted his journey, a confusing trek that had involved much doubling back and mistaken turns but that had eventually led him here, to this large room on the second floor of the Convent of the Cross, a disused building long ago looted of almost everything it had once contained.

"Dear God. You came through republican lines?"

"Yes. I managed to obtain a letter of safe passage. From Juárez."

"You spoke to him?"

"I did. Yes."

"May I see it? The letter? You have it with you?"

Diego produced the document. Despite his show of bonhomie, Maximiliano was clearly in a miserable state, ashen-faced and sickly. He slumped back onto his narrow cot gripping the letter from Juárez as though it were a holy relic. It was as close as he would ever come to meeting the man in the flesh. At the same time, of course, it was proof—if proof were needed—that Diego was on the other side. They were enemies now.

While Maximiliano pored over the letter, Diego examined his surroundings. Although nearly empty, the room was spacious, with high ceilings and ample light. A large window afforded a view of the chapel across a small interior courtyard ornamented with what might once have been orange trees but now were mere scrawls—a few scraggly branches attached to thin, barkless trunks. Maximiliano's long-time retainers, his cook and his valet, rested on the floor atop large burlap sacks stuffed with straw. Diego was surprised to find the Prince of Salm-Salm holed up here, too. He rested on another pair of sacks, his arms clasped around his knees. Every few seconds, he shifted a little and moaned.

"Dysentery," said Doktor Basch. "The poor fellow has an awful dose."

The physician occupied a lone chair set in a corner of the room near the window. Once rotund, he was barely recognizable now, little more than a rumpled suit and patches of pallid skin wrapped over an appliance of bones. They were all starving. That was obvious. In a weak voice, Basch observed that Diego seemed to have suffered some reversals of his own.

Diego thought of his broken nose, his two black eyes, his limp. "A misunderstanding," he said. "A reaction to circumstances."

Just then, another shell whistled through the air, and the doctor hunched his shoulders. A thunderous boom resounded from somewhere not so far away, followed at once by a crunch of wood, a cacophony of tumbling rocks. Briefly, the walls shook.

"I must say, one tires of this very quickly," said Basch.

"Well," said Maximiliano. He held up the letter of safe conduct signed by Juárez. "The man possesses a handsome script. I admire that."

He reached out with the missive and at once began to cough. Diego took the proffered letter, slipped it into the pocket of his jacket. He lowered himself onto a small wooden bench near Maximiliano. He didn't imagine the man would remain attentive for long, and there wasn't much time. He went to work at once. He said what he had come to say. It was time to surrender. This war had ground on far too long as it was. Victory was impossible. It was better to let the dead rest and to allow the living to put down their weapons, to resume their lives. Nothing could be gained by fighting on.

But Maximiliano refused. No, he would not surrender. He would not abdicate. He was the emperor of Mexico, and nothing could alter this truth except the intervention of the Lord. If it were God's will that he die, then so be it. But he would breathe his last breath as a monarch. He was a Hapsburg and had a lineage to uphold. He would fight to the end, for his own blood and for Mexico. That was his destiny.

Every several minutes another shell whistled overhead and crashed to earth with a deep rumpus, followed by the clatter of collapsing rock, the shriek of twisting wood, sometimes accompanied by the shouts of men, the cries of women, the wails of children.

"You will be staying here with us?" Maximiliano said. "Shall we make up another bed?"

"No. No, Your Majesty."

The emperor frowned but said nothing. He was evidently reflecting on what had just been implied. At length, he nodded. It seemed he now understood the significance of this conversation. He must have understood that Diego knew his exact whereabouts . . . and Diego would be leaving.

"Very well," he said. "So be it."

Diego looked around at the room once again. Something was missing. Before long, the realization surfaced. Agustín. Ángela's son. Where was he? A terrible thought gripped him—the child was dead. Pray God that it wasn't so, that he was alive and that Maximiliano would surrender him into Diego's care. He turned to the emperor. "Give me the child," he said.

"I can't." Maximiliano rubbed his forehead. "Boy's gone. This morning."

Diego furrowed his brow. "What?"

"This morning," said Maximiliano. Again he began to cough.

And Diego remembered. The balloon. He'd seen it as it rocketed above the alley of corpses. So, it had carried the boy. They'd packed the child off in the emperor's balloon. He hadn't known it then, but he had watched the child vanish into the cool blue air.

Maximiliano explained that the idea had come to him in a vision only the night before. They must salvage the child, the innocent boy. They must deliver him from evil.

"You sent him off in that device alone?"

The emperor nodded. Yes.

They stared at each other, and both then looked away, both contemplating what this meant—a three-year-old child hurtling through the clouds in a wicker basket. God knew how high the craft would rise or when it would descend—or where. It might as readily plummet to earth at a deadly speed as gently decline.

Maximiliano shook his head. "I'm very tired," he said. "I can't seem to stay awake."

He settled back upon his cot and placed his head on a pillow encased by a discoloured linen slip that was stitched with the letters *MIM*. He glanced at Diego. Their eyes locked. For a time, his gaze did not waver. It seemed he understood. Surely he understood. Perhaps he welcomed this fate.

Diego rose from his chair, nodded to the others, uttered a few parting words, turned and withdrew. Outside the emperor's chambers, in the amber light of the late afternoon, he stopped and leaned against a low wall of stone overlooking a small patio. He heard a shuffling of footsteps, a voice being cleared, and he turned to watch as Doktor Basch hobbled toward him. The physician put a pair of fingers to his lips and asked in a low voice if he and Diego might speak in private.

"Of course."

The two men trudged along a corridor of arched stone porticos, past the interior courtyard and another grove of tatty, denuded orange trees. In a laboured voice, Basch described conditions in the city, the lack of food and water, the predations of disease, the death rattles of children.

"I, too, have begged His Majesty to consider the possibility of surrender, but he will not hear of it, any more than he will entertain the thought of abdication."

"I don't understand," said Diego. "There was a time when I was sure he would renounce his crown."

"As was I." Basch stopped and supported himself against a pillar of stone. "But his wife persuaded him otherwise." He paused. "She is mad, you know. We received reports of it in the early days of the siege. She had a breakdown in Paris, caused an unholy scene, they say. It happened again in Rome. Hysteria. Paranoia. I take it she's been committed to an asylum."

"And Napoleon? Did the empress change his mind?"

Basch gave a sour smile. "No. Of course not."

"Maximiliano knows this?"

"He does now."

"But still he won't surrender?"

"He can't. His is an ancient family—five centuries of nobility. That weighs on a man. Besides, his older brother would never let him forget it. Europe would be torture for him now."

"He will die then."

Basch nodded. "Yes," he said. "Yes, he will." He swallowed with difficulty. "You are aware, I suppose, that Márquez has abandoned us? Three days ago, I think? He left with a dozen or so of his men. They fought their way out. They were supposed to round up reinforcements somewhere. But now I'm sure it was a lie."

"So. Your fate is sealed."

"I fear so."

Basch coughed, a deep, crepitating cough, and it was clear he was seriously unwell. He wiped his lips, flaking from dryness. He eyes were shot with burst capillaries, slender rivulets of blood. His skin was mottled, peeling. His bones sagged. He looked half-dead.

"You can help, you know," he whispered. "You can bring this story to an end. Please. Will you help?"

Diego surveyed his whereabouts and fixed them in his mind—Maximiliano occupied a suite of rooms on the second floor of the Convent of the Cross. The suite overlooked a narrow *plazuela*, a small grove of orange trees, now dead, and the ancient stone chapel, with its wooden entrance gates. He fixed the place in his mind. He felt he knew it exactly.

"Yes," he said. "Yes, I can."

Late that night, Diego slipped out of Querétaro. He encountered no difficulty with the imperial sentries, who might themselves have deserted by now. He clambered through a series of trenches and barricades and then picked his way through the wreckage and waste of the no man's land that divided the two sides. He forced himself to avoid looking at the swollen, festering corpses still dangling from the branches of the fresnos. He saw their shadows though, cast upon the barren ground and gently rotating in the moonlight. He scrambled up the precipitous ravine, desperate to be away from this terrible place. Beyond the battered city walls, he climbed to the republican line and presented his *laissez-passer*, along with a password he'd been issued that morning by General Escobedo. A pair of sentries marched him directly to the quarters occupied by their commander. It was late at night on the thirteenth day of May in the year 1867.

Chapter 53

"You are in possession of a horse, I take it?" said General Escobedo.

Diego said that he was not. He had been obliged to shoot his horse along the road from Mexico City.

"A great shame," Escobedo said. "Well, we shall fit you out with another. You will ride with us, of course? It would be a great help."

Diego had already described the location where Maximiliano might be found, along with what little was left of his once magnificent entourage. Wasn't that enough? But he understood it would be better to have a guide, someone who had made the journey already. Besides, he found that he deeply wished to be a part of this. He wanted to witness the emperor's capture in Querétaro, just as he had observed the man's arrival in Veracruz. Now, finally, the war would end. The siege would be lifted. The Black Decree would be revoked. No more men would be obliged to die as Baldemar had died, summarily, without trial.

"Yes," he said.

"Very well." Escobedo dispatched an orderly to see to the horses. They would ride in the *madrugada*, he said—in the darkness of the early morning.

By four o'clock, they were mounted—just two dozen men. This modest contingent was all that would be needed, said Escobedo. A larger group would follow at daybreak to secure the city once the main work was done. Escobedo reined his horse around and led the way, with Diego just behind. No one spoke. The moon had set, and the column advanced through the star-freckled darkness toward a treeless plateau and then filtered down a narrow *barranca*, the same ravine Diego had traced on foot early the previous day. They rode beneath the fresnos, whose cargo of dead men still strained from the branches, as if yearning even now to feel the earth against their feet. They entered the city proper through a gap in its walls, the horses choosing their steps warily through the heaps of rubble. The sentries had vanished.

Once within the city, Diego had expected to find the route without difficulty. But the darkness and its depths combined to unnerve him. Twice he misjudged the way, and the riders had to retrace their steps. Both times, he sensed Escobedo's impatience. At last, he peered through the shadows ahead and thought he could make out the shape of the convent walls and, above them, the convent's imposing bell tower with its tall wooden cross. The pressure eased in his chest, a signal of relief, but just as quickly the tension returned. Finally, the time had come. His heart pressed against his ribs.

He spoke in a whisper. "This way."

Behind him, the column of horses and riders swung to the right, and immediately an alarm went up. Someone cried out, "Who goes there?"

No one responded, and shots rang out at once.

The resistance was light—lighter than Diego had expected. Still, by the time Escobedo and his soldiers broke through the convent gates, all those within had been given considerable warning. Teams of republican soldiers fanned out on foot through the corridors and courtyards, but it seemed the emperor's party had fled on horseback. The only exception was Doktor Basch, who stumbled out into the stable yard all alone. He was still half-asleep, it seemed, and thoroughly confused. He did not realize he had been captured by liberals.

As for the rest of the emperor's party, they had made a break for it, escaping by a separate set of gates at the rear of the stable.

"Come on, then," shouted Escobedo.

He led the advance, and the others followed.

Diego kicked his heels into the flanks of the bay gelding he'd been loaned and cantered away with the rest. The horses careened through the debris-strewn streets and crossed beyond the city walls through another large gap, opened no doubt by an errant shell. Beyond a broad savannah, a large ridge of land rose in the western distance, visible in the thin light radiating from the east.

Someone shouted. "They've made for the Hill of Bells."

Fearful that the emperor's party would try to mount a last desperate stand from the summit, Escobedo ordered several of his best sharpshooters to veer out to the left and right, in search of a clear line.

"Then start firing," he ordered.

It wasn't long before the reports of their carbines rang through the cool air of morning. One of their bullets brought down the horse ridden by General Miramón, one of Maximiliano's senior officers. The general wound up sprawled beneath his mount, his leg apparently broken by the fall. On Escobedo's orders, several of the liberal riders reined back their horses to tend to the officer and take him prisoner.

The light rose, and flocks of sparrows sprang into the air, swooping crazily over the fields of cropped grass. The sun's oblique morning rays beat across the land, exploding through pools of low-lying mist as the liberal fighters galloped toward the Hill of Bells. Their horses' hooves thudded against the dew-slick ground. In the end, there was no battle. When the republicans reached the base of the hill, they found the emperor and a small party mounted on their horses, quietly awaiting their inevitable fate. Looking sallow and drawn, Salm-Salm slumped atop his horse at the emperor's side. Another general—Mejía by name—lifted his peak cap in a mournful salute as Escobedo and his men drew their horses to a halt. Diego held back a little, dreading this moment as much as he had anticipated it.

"Your sword," said Escobedo.

With some difficulty, Maximiliano separated his scabbard and its sword from the belt looped at his waist. He briefly held the scabbard high and only then surrendered it to the liberal officer.

"You have got the better of me on this day," he said. His eyes searched the remaining riders until his gaze came to rest upon Diego. He nodded. His lips moved, almost imperceptibly, forming the words *el poeta manco.*

"Your Majesty," Diego whispered in reply. It had been true once.

On the general's command, the party of riders turned and accompanied their captives back toward Querétaro and its coppery walls, glinting in the oblique rays of the rising sun. Desultory gunshots echoed from the town, but soon the reports abated, and the liberal squadron rode to the east, accompanied by scattered birdsong, toward what seemed like peace.

Chapter 54

In the days that followed, Diego joined a search party that ventured out from Querétaro in hopes of locating Ángela's son, along with whatever remained of the emperor's Montgolfier balloon. They found nothing. Still, word of the incident quickly spread as the tale found its way from one adobe hut to the next, from village to town and from town to village. After a month or so, Diego heard reports that the torn remnants of what must once have been a vast bolt of taffeta cloth had turned up, scattered across the overgrown slopes of the ancient Pyramid of the Sun at Teotihuacán, several hours' ride to the northeast of Mexico City. A large wicker basket was discovered there as well, battered but more or less intact. There was no mention of a child.

As soon as he could, Diego rode out to see for himself. He spoke to any number of *campesinos* who dwelled in that region. They had mostly heard stories of a magical boy in an airborne vessel, but the chronicle had got mixed up with the legend of Quetzalcóatl, the prodigal man-god of ancient mythology whose eventual return had been foretold long ago. Many of those whom Diego spoke to believed that it was the god himself or else the god's own son who had sailed over the horizon in a boat that rode upon the air. As a result, they said, Quetzalcóatl dwelled among the people now, alive but invisible. Were the *campesinos* imagining this? Had the boy survived the flight? Had he been injured or killed? Had someone happened upon the child and taken him in? Diego found no answer to any of these questions, not then, not ever.

Later, once again in the capital, he called upon Ángela at her home in the calle San Francisco. He told her what little he knew. He assured her that he would not abandon his efforts to find her son. She nodded as he spoke, but she could say nothing, so close to breaking into sobs.

Following their capture, Maximiliano and what little remained of his retinue were incarcerated in the Convent of the Cross in Querétaro. A chorus of foreign governments, dignitaries, and heads of state pleaded for clemency. The voices included Andrew Johnson, the new president of the United States of America, and Queen Victoria of England, as well as the government of Prussia and the great French writer Victor Hugo. They did not include Franz Josef, Maximiliano's older brother, who was overheard to have remarked, "I hope it doesn't occur to him to come here. That's all we need." The Princess of Salm-Salm managed to win the release of her husband through a combination of bribes and intrigue. It was rumoured she offered herself to General Escobedo in exchange for the prince's freedom. One way or another, Salm-Salm was released. He and his wife promptly departed Mexico, bound for France.

On the sixteenth day of June in the year 1867, the Council of War that had been convened to consider the charges against Ferdinand Maximilian von Hapsburg delivered its verdict. The Austrian was found guilty of thirteen charges, including the crime of acting against the integrity and independence of the Mexican republic. He was sentenced to death by firing squad, as were his two remaining generals, Miramón and Mejía. The execution was set for the nineteenth of June, three days hence.

Diego returned to Querétaro after the emperor's trial and immediately sought permission to visit the man. In acknowledgment of his services on behalf of the liberal cause, Escobedo approved the request, and

Diego soon found himself in the confines of the convent, where Maximiliano and his fellow prisoners occupied two desolate rooms on the second floor, one for the use of the deposed emperor and the other for his haggard entourage.

When Diego appeared, the Austrian was resting on his travelling cot. At once he clambered to his feet, his limbs unfolding like scissor blades.

"You look unwell," he said to Diego, although he himself looked vastly worse, worn and depleted, with dark shadows beneath his eyes, his thin hair dishevelled, his reddish beard flecked with grey. "Have you not been sleeping?"

Diego allowed that he had not.

"I see." Maximiliano nodded. "Another bond between us."

Diego grimaced. He was about to speak when Maximiliano cut him off.

"You did well," he said.

"I'm sorry?"

"I say, you did well. It was you, of course, who delivered me to my enemies. You informed them of my precise whereabouts. You did well."

Diego wondered whether Maximiliano was mocking him. But maybe not. Maybe he was truly relieved that the conflict had finally come to an end. Besides, it was like him to heap praise upon an act that most men would have considered an unforgivable piece of treachery. Diego swallowed with some effort. "I thought you would be pardoned at trial," he said. "I did not expect it to come to this."

Maximiliano laughed, and his laughter had a hard, brittle sound, despite his weakened state. "Come," he said. "We have been dishonest with each other a very long time. Let us not be dishonest now." He shook his head. "Let us think of happier times."

The two men embraced, and Maximiliano lowered himself onto his cot. He adjusted his weight. As he did so, he hummed a tune in a low, sad voice—"La Paloma." Before long, he was fast asleep. Diego retrieved his hat. He took his leave of the remaining prisoners, one by one, and then departed the convent.

The next morning, Maximiliano was roused early from his bed. His warders allowed him to make a final confession, or so Diego was later informed. After the prisoner had consumed a light breakfast, he was conducted in a black carriage to the foot of the Hill of Bells, followed by a second vehicle bearing his senior officers, Miramón and Mejía. Diego was among some two dozen observers who gathered to witness the event.

Overhead, a few slender clouds drifted through a pale blue sky, and the low sun cast an amber light. A company of guards led Maximiliano and his two Mexican generals to a grassy ledge partway up the Hill of Bells, where three stakes had been driven into the earth in preparation. Several saguaros loomed above the clearing, like thorny green sentinels. Diego watched as a pair of liberal soldiers led Maximiliano toward the stakes. The Austrian withdrew some coins from his pockets and turned them over to his guards. He glanced back at the members of the firing squad who were assembling, and it seemed he meant that the coins should be divided among them as well. Among his executioners.

The guards allowed Maximiliano to address the gathering, albeit briefly. The Austrian removed his hat and clasped it to his chest.

"I am going to die for a just cause, the independence and liberty of Mexico," he said in a thin voice that trembled only a little. "May my blood put an end to the misfortunes of this land. *¡Viva México!*"

He fell silent and closed his eyes for several moments before opening them again and seeming to smile. One of his guards took him by the shoulders and said something in a low voice. Maximiliano replaced his hat. He stumbled as several young Mexican servicemen stood him against one of the outside stakes, the one to the left of Miramón, who occupied the middle place. Maximiliano thrust his shoulders back and nodded at each of the two condemned men who were being manoeuvred into positions on his right. He shifted his gaze toward the east, toward the city of Querétaro and perhaps beyond, toward whatever could be imagined there. He held his head high, slightly tilted and with a quizzical expression, as if he were straining to hear something that came from far away. The soldiers in the firing squad raised their rifles, set the wooden stocks against their shoulders. They squinted down along the barrels, waiting for the order to fire.

Diego had seen enough. He reined his horse around and rode away from the Hill of Bells, back toward Querétaro. His mount quickened its pace and soon broke into a canter. Behind him, a fusillade of shots cracked against the still surface of the morning, followed by a second barrage, and a third. He counted seven in all. He did not turn around. He did not look back.

Still, his eyes began to smart, and soon his gaze was blurring. He recalled something Maximiliano had once said, in Cuernavaca, at the House of Borda. The emperor had been standing against a backdrop of jacaranda trees, poinsettia, and royal palms. In Diego's recollection, he was cradling a goblet of Riesling in one hand and a cigarette in the other, dressed in walking boots, knickerbockers, and a white cotton blouse. He was freshly returned from a morning of prospecting for botanical specimens in the tangled ravines nearby, on yet another glorious day.

"When the sun shines in Mexico," Maximiliano had declared, speaking to no one or maybe to himself alone, "you think it will shine forever."

And now Diego smiled. His eyes still stung and watered, and yet he smiled. Because it was true. You did. He dug his heels into his horse's flanks and rode at a gallop toward Querétaro. There he meant to collect his few possessions and then head south, bound for Cuernavaca, where Beatríz would be waiting. The wind whipped his hair, and the earth seemed to tumble beneath the quickening pace of his horse's hooves. By now, the sun had climbed well above the horizon. The early clouds had burned away, leaving a dome of marian blue that arched over the central highlands of Mexico.

The day ahead promised to be splendid.

AUTHOR'S NOTE

THE BROAD STROKES of this story are true, but most of the details are invented, and many are at odds with the historical record.

Maximiliano and Carlota were real, but most of their actions in these pages have been imagined.

Ángela Peralta—like many of the characters in this tale—is partly real, partly invented. She is also a conflation of more than one character, two in her case. A woman by her name did live in Mexico during the time this story is set and was a celebrated diva. But the historical Ángela Peralta did not bear a child by Agustín de Iturbide or suffer the particular torments described in these pages. Another woman did. Her name was Alice Green, an American, who was obliged to give up her offspring for adoption by Maximiliano and his wife. In the end, and contrary to the contents of this story, the boy was returned to his mother.

General Achille Bazaine was not the only Frenchman to have commanded Napoleon's troops in Mexico during the period described in this book. But he carried out that role during most of Maximiliano's rule.

Doktor Basch was not the only man to serve as Maximiliano's physician in Mexico.

General Leonardo Márquez truly existed and was responsible for the assassination of Melchor Ocampo. But he did not shoot Ángela Peralta—nor did anyone else—and, in fact, he accepted his commission to serve as Maximiliano's envoy to the Ottoman Empire. Later, he returned to Mexico and did indeed betray the emperor during the siege of Querétaro. It is said he fled to Havana and lived out his days as a pawnbroker there.

The Prince of Salm-Salm did exist, but he has been roundly misrepresented in these pages. The real Salm-Salm fought on the Union side in the American Civil War, not the Confederate side. His wife may have been from the Canadas or, just as likely, she could have been American: versions differ. The real Salm-Salm was among Maximiliano's most faithful adherents and did not impersonate a priest named Father Fischer, a man who did actually exist and who wielded considerable influence over Maximiliano.

Baldemar Peralta is an invention, but his career in arms closely parallels the experience of many liberal adventurers who struggled against the French occupation of Mexico.

Diego Serrano is also an invention and bears little resemblance to José Blasio, a Mexican who served Maximiliano in the role of personal secretary and who possessed two complete arms.

As for Beatríz Sedano, she or someone like her may well have existed. Maximiliano is said to have conducted an amorous affair with an Indian woman—known as *la india bonita*—in Cuernavaca. He constructed a house for her that became known as La Casa del Olvido, the House of Forgetfulness, because it lacked a second bedroom. But the Beatríz described in this book is a different proposition altogether and should not be confused with the historical figure.

The tale of the emperor's journey to the caves of Cacahuamilpa is an invention, although the Empress Carlota did make such a journey, albeit without her husband. For some elements of this episode, I am indebted to Frances Calderón de la Barca, a vivacious Scottish woman who was the wife of the Spanish ambassador to Mexico in the 1840s. Her book, *Life in Mexico,* is a constant and compelling delight. Everyone should read it and can easily do so. You can find it online for free.

Many events in this book are completely invented, including the Empress Carlota's attempted seduction of Diego in her carriage in Mexico City. That never happened.

Nor did Bazaine ever conduct a cannon attack on the Metropolitan Cathedral in Mexico City. It is true, however, that the Frenchman did at one point threaten to blow open the doors of the cathedral if the archbishop, Monseñor Labastida, did not allow French officers to attend the celebration of mass. Labastida relented.

The actual Labastida was not fat, as he is portrayed here, but he was a committed misogynist.

OAKLAND ROSS
TORONTO, 2012